"Who in the world am I? Ah, that's the great puzzle."

— LEWIS CARROLL

MAD WORLD

Bedlam Rising

BRANDON T BERNARD

MAD WORLD: Bedlam Rising

First Edition 2022

Any reference to historical events, real people, or real places are used fictitiously. Names, characters, images, and places are products of the author's imagination.

ISBN: 979-8-9851510-3-9

To Mom & Dad
for not always understanding,
but always encouraging my curiosity.

Mad World

·BEDLAM RISING·

BRANDON T. BERNARD

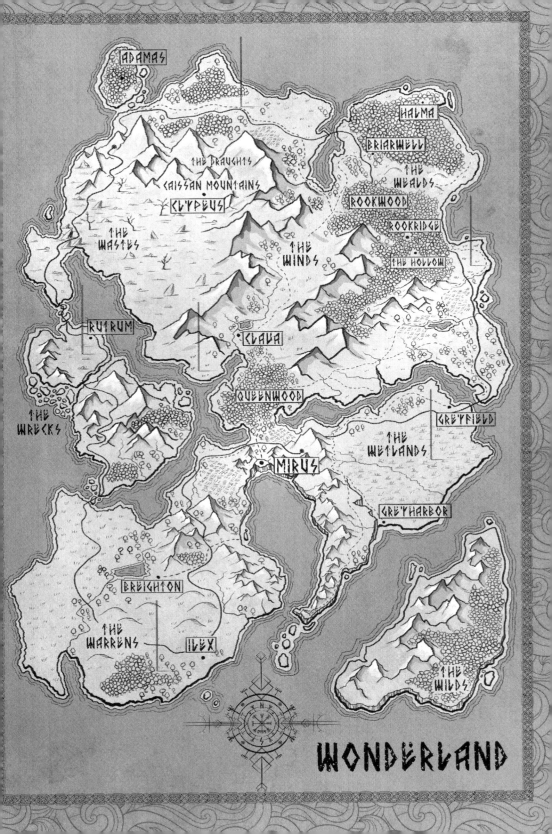

MIRUS

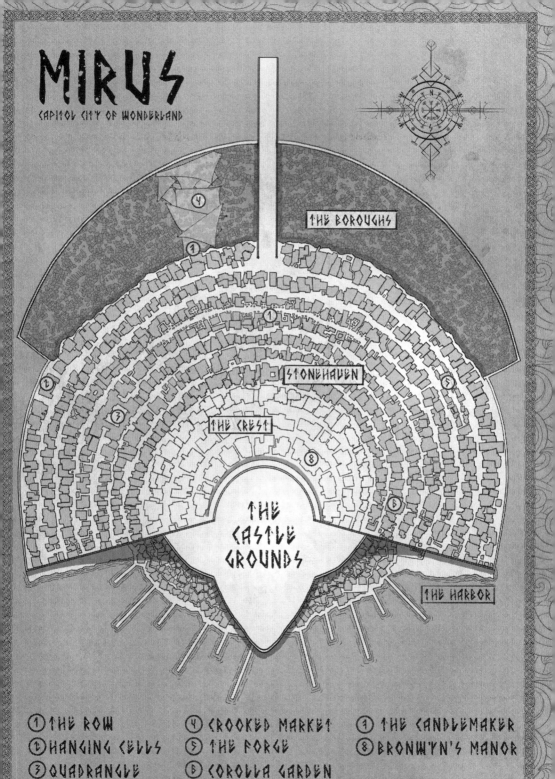

THE STORY THUS FAR...

While hunted by the Ace through the Rookwood, Cheshire, the Queen Slayer, stumbles upon a strange woman from another world—Mary Anne—and reluctantly saves her during his escape. His actions send her into the company of Jonathan Carter and Audrianna March, Cheshire's friends and lovers. In order to return her to her world, Jonathan and March, along with Dormy, plan to seek council from the Duchess in Mirus—Wonderland's capital city.

On their way, Cheshire joins them, the Ace attacks again, and they are separated from Mary Anne but are eventually reunited in the next village. It is there they find evidence of a mysterious cult who are after the strange woman, and face a band of hired mercenaries. They all survive the slaughter, but the Duchess, with the Red Knight and entourage in tow, unexpectedly arrives and takes Mary Anne into her care. Everyone journeys to Mirus in search of answers and safety.

Lysander and Uriah, twin brothers and last blood of the line of kings, bent never to see another woman sit upon the throne, follow them to the capital and stir dissension amongst the townspeople. All the while, cult members flood into Mirus with the intent of kidnapping Mary Anne and taking her blood.

Cheshire uses this unique opportunity to gain entrance to Mirus after a 1000-year exile. Inside the city, he searches for his mother but instead discovers the Gryphon—long lost general of Wonderland's armies—imprisoned in an oubliette and at the bottom of a bottle. He informs Cheshire he searches in vain. His mother died long ago.

Mary Anne learns she must become queen in order to leave Wonderland. Jonathan stays as her advisor—an unbreakable decision enforced by the Arcana flowing through the land. March stays to protect Jonathan. And a heart-shattered Cheshire sets his plan into motion. The city and all those who turned a blind eye to his mother will fall.

PART I

CROOKED MARKET

CHAPTER 1

CHESHIRE

The soldier regains consciousness. His groggy bloodshot eyes struggle to open—one then the other—until his pupils focus on the wavering darkness before him. He grits his teeth and squints, veins thick on his temples from the pressure of blood rushing to his head. He chokes on the dirty, bloody gag in his mouth as panic sets in and thrashes in his binds, but the coarse ropes only dig deeper into his wrists and ankles. Bound and suspended upside down, naked, from one of the Mirusian hanging cells, he cranes his neck backward to look down into the abyss where the pit full of centuries-old piss and shit festers in a thick quagmire far below. Its putrid warm air wafts up and gags him.

His eyes dart above his feet to the platform with the control levers to look for aid, his companions, any soldier still standing, but there are none. When he notices the black shadow hanging from the cell in front of him, he jerks his head back and locks eyes with the dark figure in the dim warm candlelight.

Cheshire hangs down also, without clothing, feet hooked through the square holes of the iron cell's grated floor, to welcome the soldier to his upside down world. The world he knows he controls. He holds a candle

9

right-side up in one hand—the thinnest trail of smoke snaking its way down past their feet—and plays with a handful of silver coins from the soldier's purse in the other, shifting them in his palm. Cheshire drops one coin after another until none remain, each spinning up past his head and into the darkness. The soldier's eyes follow them upward and watch as the small glints of light reflecting off the silver disappear into the pit above.

Even in the darkness, Cheshire senses the look of recognition in the soldier's eyes, stretched wide with horror. The soldier tries to scream but only mumbles through his rough gag.

"Queen Slayer," the soldier gargles, almost incoherent. The veins around his eyes and neck bulge like worms under a thin layer of soil.

"There really is no need to shout," Cheshire tells the struggling soldier. "Anyone who could hear you and come to your aid is already in attendance." Cheshire turns his head to the right to lead the soldier's gaze. Fourteen other soldiers, still dressed, bound in the same fashion, hang from the other nearby iron cells; twelve by their feet, two by their necks, dead. Each lured in one by one throughout the night.

Cheshire pushes against the soldier's forehead with a finger and starts him swaying back and forth. "You are the fortunate man to be closest to my measurements. Or unfortunate, depending on how you view the situation."

The soldier tries to reposition the gag in his mouth and whistle with his tongue to alert the hounds outside the jail, but he only manages a few feeble, garbled puffs of breath, saliva dripping up his face.

"No good either, I fear," Cheshire says. "They are streets away, gnawing on a choice cut of beef from a butcher in the Row. It seems hungry mongrels are not so loyal. Never cared for dogs."

Had Cheshire thought of this plan weeks ago, there would not have been a need to walk miles in the shit-filled tunnels beneath the jail. But on the other hand, had he not, then he would never have discovered the secret entrance built by Pat and Bill, which granted him access this second time. He never thanked them for their help. When he sees them again after today, Cheshire will need to apologize for what he is about to do.

Eight days prior.

Cheshire's eyes burn from exhaustion, hatred, and sorrow, drying any lingering tear he has to quell the fire within his heart. He sits, arms hugging his knees, slumped with his back against the cold gray walls of the unassuming castle hallway. There are no rich adornments hung upon the walls, no vibrant woven tapestries hang from on high, or polished candelabras to illuminate the dark corners. Just a few thick but meager candles tilted in their braziers, wax pooling in the bases and trickling down to create smooth formations similar to those Cheshire has seen in abandoned caves. This hallway was meant to be forgotten.

He stares at the blank stone wall across from him, as he has for the past three hours. He ignored this area of the castle for fear of what he would discover, but after a fortnight of mapping out the passageways of the castle and the city, he gave in to his curiosity.

The stone work is precise—mortar lines run uninterrupted across the wall, stones cut to match the others perfectly— to make it appear as if a door never stood here, and any memory of it could be considered a figment of someone's imagination, or a mistake in their mind, with each castle hallway appearing so similar. But a door was here, it existed—the door to his mother's room—the last place he saw her. But the door, and presumably the entire room, like many other memories and truths, has been lost, or rather kept from everyone. The Duchess's way of controlling the narrative and keeping the shallow level of power she possesses.

Cheshire stands, his legs sore from sitting so long in the same position, and rubs his hand across the stones where the door frame once was. Lingering will do him no good. Though the Castle Guard patrols on this level of the castle are infrequent, it is best Cheshire move on. There is much to explore, much to uncover, much to destroy.

It has been a week since Cheshire released the Gryphon from imprisonment. In doing so, he discovered his mother, for whom Cheshire has spent more than a millennium searching, has been dead almost as long. He allowed this news and his grief to consume him for three days. Without food and barely any water, Cheshire concealed himself within the hidden passageways of the castle, laying on the cold stones clinging to memories of his mother.

He thinks back to one of his favorite memories when he was in his sixth year in this world. He and his mother would escape the confines of the city and play in the catacombs beneath Wonderland, where she would let him explore to his heart's content. In this memory, he returned from exploring the tunnel behind the smallest door in one waypoint of the catacombs, only big enough for him to crawl through. As he emerged, his mother scooped him up in her arms and twirled him around the room, dancing on the beautiful black and white tile floor under the undulating light of the chandelier. She tickled him, hugged him and pressed her cheek to his, and settled down with him on her lap to sing him to sleep.

But now when he conjures the memory, he emerges from the small door to an empty room—his mother is nowhere to be found, not even the faint smell of her lilac perfume. The silence of the waypoint without her laughter and song is deafening, maddening, and Cheshire can feel the hurt burrow a hole in his chest so deep he could fall for an eternity into the darkness and the pain would never lessen.

After those three days, he wiped the dried tears and dirt from his face, the slobber from his cheek, and shoved every emotion deep within. All except his rage.

Once up and about again, he spent the next four days mapping out the entire passage system within the castle walls, every hidden entrance behind tapestry, painting, or false wall, and each two-way looking glass and spy hole. There was no area of the castle beyond his reach, though many doors are locked, for now. There are nights he knelt behind the looking glass and stared into the Duchess's bedchamber, watched her with a vacant stare and fantasized about the multiple ways he would kill her. She will answer his questions, then she will answer for the suffering he has endured all his life.

Late one night, while exploring one of the lower levels of the castle, Cheshire happens across an otherwise unassuming set of double wooden doors made of thick oak held together by wide wrought iron plates and hinges. He would have passed by completely and left it for another night if not for the intricate lock upon them with wheels, gears, and tumblers. No, not a lock. A puzzle box.

Curious. His fingers itch.

Fortunately, there are no holes, which means there are no keys to be found. On the other hand, this type of lock is unknown to him and he has no clue how to open it. There should be roughly three hours left until the Castle Guard patrol this corridor again. He pulls, turns, and fidgets with every piece able to move, but nothing works. The runes upon the tumblers do not correspond in any way, and he is sure several are scribbles with no meaning whatsoever.

It is well into the second hour before he concludes the gears, wheels, and tumblers may all be for show—decoys and traps to confound unskilled thieves and prowlers. Cheshire ignores the obvious and explores the smooth metal surface with his fingertips. He discovers a grid upon the face of the lock—six squares high by six squares wide. Every plate indistinguishable from the others except for a small, beveled notch cut out from the four outer-most corners. He picks at the plates with his fingernails from every possible corner. None budge. On each side of the lock, nearly unnoticeable, are two circles no larger than the tip of his small finger. He presses them. The left does nothing, but the right depresses and then juts out to reveal a silver pin narrowing to its tip. Once he removes it, one of the metal squares on the front face of the lock recesses, creating a sliding puzzle with no image.

Damn it all.

Cheshire shifts the squares quickly in every direction, looking for a pattern, but plain brushed metal stares back at him beneath each square, taunting him. The only clues possible at all to align are the notches. He slides the metal squares, feverishly, now with an end in sight, until each notch meets in the center of the lock face to reveal a hole at its center—a hole just big enough for the tip of the pin to slip into. It clicks halfway inside. An unseen door on the back face of the lock flips open and dangles.

The fuck is this?

He sits on the floor, back against the door, to inspect the underside of the lock. The back flap reveals a central, stationary, golden disc and four turnable concentric circles growing ever larger, all covered with etchings made up of overlapping lines of four various widths—each with hash marks facing different directions. At first glance, it appears to be the image of a knot made of several ropes. He twists the outer circles, growing more and more frustrated because nothing aligns, there is no image to be seen. It is a jumbled mess with no solution.

He hears the grind of guards' armor approach from farther down the corridor. It is a risk, but he must leave the lock as it is, hanging partially open, with the back flap kept shut by the door. He jumps to an iron brazier imbedded in the wall and then to the timber supports and wiggles into the tight space between a beam and the stone ceiling. Despite the rush of excitement he feels solving the puzzle, his frustration builds, wanting, needing to find the solution. The guards take their Time, their silent pace a saunter more than anything, tired at this late hour. Their eyes never break from the path in front of them and they continue on, thankfully, without noticing anything amiss.

Once they round the corner and silence fills the corridor again, Cheshire drops to the floor and resumes work on the lock. He looks at the tangle of four ropes again and notices one of them has a curious curve, meets itself, and ends inside the edge of the central disc.

The design is purposeful. Each rope is separate from the other, though their paths cross and overlap. Perhaps there is not one image, but four.

He turns the innermost ring to match the thin rope with horizontal lines to the center plate, then the second, third, and fourth. The letter P appears off centered in the tangle.

Four ropes, four letters.

His eyes follow the different paths, and he understands the four letter word to solve the puzzle—something so complex to conceal something so simple. This is Wonderland. He scrambles the circles again and follows a new path. The wide rope with diagonal hash marks forms the letter O. *Click.* A tingle races up his neck. The thin rope forms the P again. *Click.* A single line with no hash marks creates a rounded E. *Click.* Then the last thin rope with opposite facing diagonal marks forms the N. *Cluck.* The body of the lock falls free from the iron shackle with a final deeper click. Cheshire catches it before it hits the ground, its weight impressive. He removes the shackle from the door handles, cracks open the door, and slips in with the body of the lock.

By his count, he has just over two hours to be in, out, and reset the lock before the guards pass again. Cheshire takes the striking stone from his cloak and ignites the candle on a nearby table, revealing a surface cluttered with various instruments strewn on top of faded sketches of architecture and other oddities on aged parchment. He picks up a measuring compass by the knob at the end of its hinge and dangles it in the air while he walks.

The large chamber appears ordinary compared to what Cheshire expected to be concealed with such a lock. Its height must take up two more floors of the castle. This, he presumes, must be Pat and Bill's workshop within the castle. They seem to be the only two who are in charge of the creation and repair of architecture in the city, at least from what they have said, not to mention their knack for puzzles. Cut lumber ranging from the size of Cheshire's forearm to planks twenty feet in length lean against an otherwise bare wall. Boxes of hinges, handles, metal pins, nails, and what look like nails with a serrated spiral running from its head to its point, and other hardware fill shelves as tall as the stored lumber.

A strange construction resting on a table covered with detailed sketches of high walkways in Mirus catches Cheshire's eye. He pockets the compass and picks up what appears to be a forearm and right hand made of metal and iron, as if Pat and Bill were building a life-sized, no, larger even, oversized marionette. Cheshire holds the hand against his to compare the size, shakes it as if greeting a stranger, and then waves it back and forth. Each finger hinges with a small catch and thin metal wires to keep it from flexing past the point of a real joint.

He holds the arm by the round iron elbow joint and carries it over his shoulder, as Jonathan would walk with a sword, while taking in the rest of this curious chamber.

Dormy would consider herself among the heavens if she ever found her way here. She would leave this room weighed down four times her own weight with everything she would stuff into her pockets.

Piles of half-constructed wood, iron, and copper contraptions, counterweight systems, rolled sketches, and small metal boxes the size of loaves of bread, each with a unique style of lock fill every corner of the room. They call to Cheshire's curiosity—as the main lock on the door did, their secrets need to be revealed. But these all require keys, and he does not have Time.

Cheshire returns the arm to its position and angle where it sat, not to arouse suspicion yet. Though he doubts Pat and Bill would be the two who would announce his presence, otherwise they would have the first night they saw him. He pockets a handful of nails as well as a handful of metal balls no larger than his thumbnail.

Before he leaves, he rubs his thumb and forefinger together and snuffs out the candle he lit. The tiniest wisp of smoke twists its way up into the darkness, but to Cheshire's surprise, the candle comes to life once more. He thinks nothing of it and pinches the wick between his fingers, returning the room to darkness, but the flame, yet again, tauntingly returns. This time he blows the candle out with a hearty breath, and again it reignites.

Hello.

Cheshire has seen his share of magic candles in his lifetime, and this he does not count among them. He leans close enough to feel the heat against his face and inhales the slightest odor of something foreign, something alchemic. Just as the candle sparks back to life in the dark, an idea sparks in Cheshire's imagination. He searches every shelf, drawer, crate, even rattles the locked boxes to hear their contents, but none hold candles. At last, tucked away beneath one of the worktables, he finds a simple crate with wax upon its edges. Empty. A single candle will not suffice for the plan he has, and without knowing how long these particular candles last, he will need Pat and Bill to make more, or get more, depending on their source.

He licks his fingers, making sure they are thoroughly wet, then pinches the wick firmly a final time to extinguish the flame completely. After wiping his fingers on his trousers, he pockets the candle with the rest of the items in his cloak and resets the lock on the workshop door as he leaves, making sure to wipe the smudges his fingers left on the metal.

Over the next several days, while Cheshire waits for Pat and Bill to replenish their stock, he bides his Time waiting for the Gryphon. The gossip and whispers amongst the servants, at least those who speak, say the Gryphon is on the road to recovery, both physically and in sobriety. Cheshire can hear the moans and wails through the hallways as the physicians wean him off the bottle he had become so dependent on for centuries.

The Gryphon holds more information about Cheshire's mother. Cheshire tried on multiple occasions to pay a visit to the Gryphon in the castle's infirmary, but no less than six guards patrol outside and inside the room at all times. Cheshire could have dispatched them with ease, but it would draw too much attention and would not have given him sufficient Time to get the answers he seeks. They are not for protection of any kind, but rather for the Duchess's own paranoia, which in this case is valid. She feels Cheshire is near, and she will know his presence soon enough.

While he waits, he continues to reacquaint himself with every twist and turn of the hidden pathways in the castle, and then branches out to the adjoining catacombs beneath the city of Mirus. They span from the top of the Crest, through the breadth of Stonehaven, to the bottom of the Boroughs. Entrances hide in plain sight disguised in brick walls, shops and residences, and beneath the cobbled streets.

The catacombs beneath the city are not like those throughout the rest of the country, which are soothing, cool in temperature, and silent as the grave. In Mirus, the same stale, warm air seeps into the cracks of the city and the noise of its thousands of citizens permeate the stones. Cheshire likens it to what it must feel to walk in the constant, bustling hum of an ant mound. Even the castle's passageways are quiet by comparison, except for the kitchen staff who sing and hum at all hours, and the rest of the servants whose long dresses brush along the floor as they walk otherwise silently.

He is careful on his quest, keeping to the night and shadows, but there is the odd, unfortunate pair of soldiers who happen upon him or who are in the wrong place when Cheshire opens a hatch or door. They are dead before they even realize his identity. "Queen Slayer" or "Demon," is all they can mutter before Cheshire snaps their necks. He has become quite adept at the practice with either his arms or his legs, often at the same time. It is a pain to deal with the dead bodies, however. There is the option of pulling them into the catacombs, but he would rather not deal with the clutter or the eventual stench from their rotting corpses. His actions will draw attention, even though the dead bodies appear sporadically. With Lysander and Uriah's presence within the city set on inciting rebellion, Cheshire hopes the corpses will be added to their number instead of his own.

On the eighth night, deep within the catacombs, far on the western side of the city, he discovers a hidden door made of thick walnut panels and iron lattice. The door resists him when he tries to open it. Something extremely heavy placed on the other side keeps it shut. It is a risk to push any farther without knowing what is on the other side and where he will appear. It could be a storefront, home, alleyway, or just as easily be a den of soldiers. There is also a chance there will be someone, or someones, on the other side he will need to kill immediately and then deal with their bodies before moving any farther. He places his shoulder against the door and pushes hard, but it barely makes a sound. Thankfully, this narrow passage of the catacombs allows him to position his feet against the opposite wall while his shoulders rest against the door. With a strained grunt, he stretches his body, his thighs and backside shaking under the weight, and pushes the door open wide enough to squeeze through.

Large barrels of oil, the culprit blocking the door, slosh as they resettle from the move. He enters a long, thin room and finds double racks of archer's bows and shelves of quivers packed with arrows along the wall to the left. In the center of the room sits a towering pyramid of casks filled with oil to be boiled in the large iron cauldrons upon the wall. Small barrels in rows stacked four high run along the length of the room with the distinct odor of black powder—the armory for the outer wall defenses.

The idea which sparked into existence in Pat and Bill's workshop now takes form, its flame burning bright, pulsing in his eyes. When the Gryphon sobers and leaves the infirmary, Cheshire will need a way to reach him and speak to him undisturbed. There is little chance of this happening in the keep or on castle grounds. The Time has come for Cheshire's presence to be known, and in doing so, bring the Gryphon to him in the city. He can accomplish it all in one fell swoop. What better way to reintroduce the Queen Slayer and usher in the fall of Mirus than with a literal and earth-shattering boom.

CHAPTER 2

JONATHAN

High in the castle, Jonathan wakes, his face nestled in the back of March's pink hair, inhaling her like the finest of teas, warming every fiber of his heart and body. His bare back is cold from the chill of the predawn air gently meandering through the large open archway of the balcony. He wishes Cheshire had laid with them last night. Jonathan would feel his radiant warmth upon his back as he feels March's upon his front, from his chest to his toes.

They lie in the same position where they fell asleep—he wraps around her from behind, and she clings to his forearms, holding them to her chest. However, this morning, like almost every morning for the past week since they arrived in Mirus, he sleeps in this position for more than just comfort. Her sleep is not peaceful. He can feel her muscles tick and twitch sporadically during the night.

The sun is yet to crest over the mountains, so he does not wake her yet. If they were in the Hollow, he would kiss her gently on the neck, slip out of bed, and make his way down to the kitchen to prepare tea for them both to begin their day. Such a luxury is not afforded to them here. He waits patiently, all the while listing the teas in his apothecary cabinet back home, first in descending order from where they live, beginning with the top left corner to the bottom most right. Once finished, he begins in the order in which he first tasted each and the region where he found them.

Before he can finish the second list, March gasps as if finally emerging from being held beneath the surface of a body of water. She jolts from her slumber and thrashes in Jonathan's arms. Her breathing becomes erratic, and she tries to reach for the belt of daggers on the side table near the bed. He holds her tight, never squeezing, but hardens his muscles and his grip on his own forearms to keep March in place. She grunts and screams through gritted teeth, shaking and kicking away the linen sheets.

"It's me," Jonathan says softly in her ear. "I'm here." He bends his knees towards his chest and bends March's as well, curling both of their bodies. "You're here with me."

After several moments, the fight finally leaves March. She stops struggling and her body falls slack in Jonathan's arms, though her muscles still spasm randomly. Her breathing slows to match his own. Jonathan places his cheek upon the back of her shoulder and waits motionless. It is nearly a half hour before she presses her backside against him, her sign she is back without using words. It is then he hugs her and kisses the back of her shoulder.

Mornings such as these are few and far between when they sleep at the Hollow—once or twice every five or six years. Even when they sleep under the stars in some distant corner of Wonderland or in Dormy's wagon, her dreams and thoughts are peaceful, at least to Jonathan's understanding. When they travel somewhere different, somewhere unknown—a city, any city, in an unfamiliar bed—a nightmare crawls its way into March's dreams, and she wakes thinking she is somewhere she is not. This is why Jonathan changed the bedding to a coarser linen like their own sheets from home, instead of the original silk sheets which came with the chamber assigned to them by the Duchess. He hoped it would be helpful, but it made little difference. Everything in the capital is unmistakably different. Even the air, especially within the castle, is strange somehow.

March has always been his rock, his anchor, in this world and in his turbulent mind, and he will forever and always be hers in return. If only Cheshire were with them, then and only then would they all be complete, at least in some fashion—complete, but not free. March turns in bed, kisses Jonathan quickly, and then tucks her head to his neck. Her breath fills and warms the small space between their bodies. She hooks her leg over his thigh to pull him closer and folds her arms between them and nestles against his chest. Jonathan wraps his arms around the small of her back and runs his cheek on top of her head. They remain still, breathing in unison, feeling each other's heartbeat pulse with one another, wishing they were far away.

"It is this place," she whispers. "These walls."

Jonathan kisses her gently on her forehead, tilts her head up to his, and kisses her closed eyelids. "Then I think perhaps we need to find alternate accommodations. Sleep under the stars or by the water."

Eventually, her breathing slows, and March falls asleep in his arms once again, and Jonathan follows soon thereafter. A reoccurring dream returns to Jonathan, more colors, sounds, and sensation than images. In the darkness, pink and purple flames dance to the rhythm of his heartbeat. He looks at his hands and discovers he has no corporeal body. Instead, turquoise flames twist and turn in their place. As he moves what he believes are his hands, he can hear a comforting dull rumble, as if a torch were passed back and forth. Jonathan wills himself closer to the purple and pink flames and intertwines with them both until they can no longer separate, and their glow is a brilliant white. The cold Jonathan felt on his body while awake melts away and a warmth washes over him, starting in his groin and spreading outward until it is all-consuming.

In the distance, an orange flash erupts over a sea-green horizon. The warm light swirls as paint on the surface of an artist's container of water, and finally the sun takes form, and then the sparkling sea. It stretches and fills the surrounding darkness as far as Jonathan can see. His ears fill with the sound of lapping and crashing waves against the bow of a ship, the muffled songs of seagulls high overhead, the yawning of timbers, and the flapping of canvas.

The creek of timbers transforms to knocks upon wood, first three, then four following a brief pause. These are not in his dream. Jonathan opens his heavy eyes as the third set of knocks pound against the other side of the heavy wooden door of the bedchamber. It creaks open and Mary Anne's handmaiden, wearing her golden half-mask, peeks in and then wheels a small trolley into the room. Upon it, a plain white teapot, piping hot, and tea service for two. Sadness hangs off the corners of her pressed frown. She nods and closes the door behind her.

Jonathan feels a sick swell of guilt in his stomach, but before it can grow, March wakes again and stares into his turquoise eyes, quelling any other feeling except his devotion for her.

"I must be off," he says. "The council meeting will start soon."

She lowers her eyes, nods, and slides from the bed, in all of her morning glory. She rummages through one of the large wood and iron trunks she packed with their clothing to find proper attire for this day. Jonathan kneels at another enormous trunk with blue paint flaking off in areas. He rubs his hand along the top edge before opening it to reveal the wooden boxes of tea March packed while Jonathan and Mary Anne were off in Rookridge.

One hundred and seventy-four, he calculates quickly from their stacked configuration. None of the boxes have any writing on them or distinguishable marks to the unfamiliar eye.

March walks over, moves a few boxes, stacking them on each other, and grabs one from deep within. She holds it away from Jonathan and awaits his guess. They all look identical, save for scratches and scuffs in the wood from wear and tear over the centuries, but even though they are not in the drawers back home, Jonathan knows each by smell, no matter how intermingled they are.

He inhales slowly through his nose, blocking out all the other scents rising from the trunk, focusing, summoning the singular drifting fragrance from the box in her hand.

"Butterfly Pea and Lemon this morning, darling," he says to March. "Wonderful choice."

"Damn you. I had to try."

He takes the box to the trolley and carefully pinches the dried leaves with three fingers, drizzles them into each cup, and fills them halfway with water. While they steep, Jonathan and March help each other dress —both in leather trousers and heavy boots.

March takes a sleeveless linen shirt and slips it on Jonathan, then holds up his blue longcoat. He slides his arms in with ease, turns, and allows March to straighten his distressed collar and fasten his timepiece inside. From a different trunk, she pulls a brown leather jacket cropped just below her breasts, with gambeson sleeves, and three buckles to cross the open space across her chest.

Jonathan presents both cups of Butterfly Pea and Lemon tea, in all its wondrous blue and purple glory. March takes the flask from the table on Jonathan's side of the bed and pours several drops into his cup.

They sit on the stone railing of the balcony and sip their tea as the sun creeps over the mountains. Jonathan looks past the city walls at the lush canopy of the Queenwood—its auburn and deep juniper canopy stretching far into the distance between the rising gray and blue mountains, with a hint of purple on their slopes. He refuses to look down into the dull gray and brown buildings of Mirus. Out of the corner of his eye, he can see March peering down into the Crest, calculating scenarios. Once they finish their tea, she kisses him one more time, her free hand caressing the back of his neck and ruffling his hair. The way March licks her lips with a sly grin after their kiss always brings a flutter to Jonathan's heart.

"Every step away is a step back to you," he tells March. "We will find each other later, but first we must play the parts expected of us."

She takes his cup along with hers, returns both to the small trolley, and then opens the long trunk containing the swords she brought with her, all thoughtfully wrapped and oiled.

By the time Jonathan opens the bedchamber door, he barely catches a glimpse of Mary Anne's handmaiden turning the corner to descend the stairs. Fortunate, to avoid the long, awkward, silent walk to the council room. He thinks of March to keep himself from counting the number of stairs as he walks, even though he already knows there are one hundred and eighty-nine, having counted every time he walks up or down them. His mind drifts to Cheshire as well. The last he saw of him three nights ago in his bedchamber, Cheshire was lost—even more so than usual. There is no other word to describe the forlorn gaze in his lavender eyes. But at least Jonathan knows Cheshire is alive and somewhere in the city or in the castle, which is not much, but it—along with the knowledge he will see Cheshire again— brings some comfort to him.

In the council chamber, the walls, oak table, chairs, and the scarlet runner the length of the table, show no sign of the previous battle between him, March, and the Red Knight. All evidence has been erased as if it never happened, even the holes in the table where March plunged her swords.

Mary Anne waits alone in the room, seated in what would be March's chair if they sat at his table in the Hollow. She straightens her posture and smiles from ear to ear at first sight of him. She wears a floor-length, burgundy hooded gown, with jacquard embellishments a shade lighter in the fabric. Her black hair is pulled tight and held back by an ornate silver pin, and tendrils of hair cascade down the back of her neck. She wears just a hint of makeup—rouge to brighten her cheeks, and a slightly darker color on her lips and around her eyes, accentuating the blue in them.

"Good morning, Jonathan," says Mary Anne.

"Good morning to you as well, Your Majesty. You look lovely this morning."

"You are quite dashing, as always. And, Jonathan, do not be silly," she says, suppressing a laugh. "Please, do not call me that."

"I must stand on ceremony," says Jonathan. "When you are queen, everyone must acknowledge you as such. It is simply the way things are, were, or rather will be."

"Well, such a time seems far off still. So, let us hold off on such formality until then?"

"As you wish." Jonathan pulls out one of the high-back chairs and sits across from Mary Anne. He longs for his plush wingback chair from home, or any of the chairs from his table which are familiar, instead of this rigid and uncomfortable piece of oak.

She may not realize she does so, or perhaps hopes Jonathan does not notice, but where Mary Anne's eyes used to stay fixed on Jonathan's or bashfully lowered, now they roam to different parts of his body with a relaxed gaze—a look he knows well from March. They have grown more frequent every morning they meet, and even now, her eyes drift down his chest and back up his arms.

"How are your studies progressing?" he asks.

Her eyes snap back to his. "I wish I had more encouraging news," she says, disappointment heavy in her voice, "but despite the hours I spend in the afternoons and evenings trying to decipher and understand the runes in this blasted book, they are as foreign and cryptic as the day I first saw them." She places her hand on the large tome sitting in front of her on the table. "Except, I believe I have learned the Wonderlandian runic symbol for *Queen*, since it appears repeatedly ad nauseam on every page."

"My daily lessons with Chamberlain Weiss and what he translates for me are the sum total of my learning. What we cover is all for naught until I can come to terms with the second Tenet." Mary Anne becomes heated. Her eyes grow wide and tighten. "I cannot progress any further until I do, and therefore, I am no closer to returning home to my mother. Chamberlain Weiss will not translate any more chapters in the book after the second Tenet until I complete it." Mary Anne catches her temper and calms herself. "Forgive me."

"No need for apology."

The door to the room swings open, and the Duchess enters, followed by Weiss, Pat, and Bill. The Duchess takes her place at the head of the table, chair scratching heavily upon the stones as she slides it back and forth. Weiss, with his thin frame, slips into the chair to the right of Mary Anne without pulling it from the table. Pat and Bill sit opposite one another halfway down the table. Weiss's brow twitches at the sight of Jonathan.

"Good morning, everyone." The Duchess nods at Jonathan and smiles at Mary Anne, placing her hand upon hers. "Let me begin with encouraging news. I am happy to report the castle physicians say the Gryphon is responding well to treatment, and his condition improves every day. With a continued regimen of elixirs and leeches, he should be on his feet by week's end."

Mary Anne winces at the thought.

"Then," the Duchess continues, making eye contact with everyone in attendance, "perhaps we can all concoct some strategy to combat and expel the pests within our beloved city walls."

Jonathan sighs slightly, unnoticeably, relieved to hear the Gryphon will join their ranks soon. He reaches into his coat and circles the crystal face of his timepiece. On any other occasion or location, he would consider half a fortnight no time at all. But with enemies on all sides, any time can feel like an eternity.

"Speaking of which, Chamberlain, what news have you?" the Duchess asks.

"Yes, madam." Weiss shuffles through a handful of parchments he brought with him. "I regret to report"—he sucks on his teeth—"there is no additional information to add as far as the cult members are concerned. We have searched, re-searched, sought out as best we could, but there is nothing."

The Duchess flares her nostrils, Mary Anne lowers her eyes to her lap, and Pat and Bill trace the grain of the oak table with their fingernails, all frustrated but not surprised at Weiss's lack of anything useful.

Jonathan softly taps his fingertips on his wrist. He cannot be sure—but he is almost certain, from Weiss's self-pampered appearance and his silk and woolen robes—he hardly ever sets foot outside the castle grounds on a normal day, let alone when the city is filled with dangers. How could he know unless he walks the streets?

"The soldiers throughout the Crest," Weiss continues, "have kept copious notes, including the goings on of Lysander and Uriah. They leave the Crest every day and journey into Stonehaven where they congregate at Far Side with various citizens."

"Far Side?" asks Mary Anne.

"It is a tavern in the Quadrangle on the eastern side of Stonehaven. Their meetings there have grown in number as the days pass. At first twelve, the day after your arrival."

"And the count now?" The Duchess massages her hands.

"Well over one hundred," says Weiss. "They have moved from the tavern to the pillories in the Quadrangle."

"These are not meetings," says Jonathan. "These are rallies. We saw their numbers when they first confronted us in the Row, and their numbers grow still. Can nothing be done to stop them? Issue an edict or proclamation?"

"Against public gatherings?" snaps Weiss. "We cannot expressly forbid all gatherings, let alone specific gatherings. That will accomplish two things: Anger those who are not part of their rallies, and it will show our hand."

"What hand is that?" Jonathan asks.

"The truth," says Weiss. "That we hide from the public, with a new candidate for queen, and we dare not show our faces outside the castle walls for fear of retaliation."

"We have already shown them our cards." The Duchess huffs. "I guarantee our absence in the city has been noticed and noted by all. Especially Lysander and Uriah. Let us move on. Anything else?"

"Yes, madam." Weiss straightens his spectacles. "There has been an increase in deaths among the remaining soldiers. Nine in the past week. Five suicides and four accidental drownings or suffocations."

The Duchess throws her hands in the air. "Nine? They must presume us fools. These are not suicides. They are coordinated attacks by Lysander and Uriah to weaken us. This is the only explanation."

Mary Anne's face pinches with worry.

Jonathan knows better than to believe Lysander and Uriah are responsible for these deaths. If they conduct peaceful gatherings in public, they would not risk such obvious attacks, especially if they want to win over the citizens of Mirus. It is Cheshire. The news, though morbid, is well received. As long as the mischief continues and the bodies continue to pile, he knows Cheshire is still in the city and alive.

"What are we to do, then?" The Duchess waves her hand at Weiss and Jonathan. "Come now. There must be a single thought between the two of you."

Weiss scowls at Jonathan over his spectacles. His eyes twitch and his head rattles back and forth like the top of a pot boiling over a fire and spilling onto the hearth. Jonathan knows this expression well and can describe in detail every crease and line from memory.

"It is obvious she needs to spend her time in self-reflection. Every waking moment," says Weiss. "The second Tenet is all that matters at present. Because once she reaches the Second, then she will reach the Third, then the Fourth, and then all of our worries can be put to rest. We all know this to be true."

Mary Anne's shoulders sink, though her face remains unchanged. The sails of her spirit lose the wind and sag in doldrums so carelessly created by Weiss.

"What say you all?" asks Weiss.

Jonathan looks to Mary Anne, downcast. The Duchess squints at

Weiss. Pat and Bill both scratch at the table with their fingernails. Weiss looks to everyone's face at the table.

"What say you," the Duchess asks Jonathan, "her advisor?"

"I believe..." He thinks of her words before everyone else came into the room, and of her frustration. "I believe we should ask Mary Anne what she believes will help her."

Mary Anne raises her eyes to Jonathan.

Weiss scoffs and looks to the Duchess. "His answer cannot be serious."

"If I may speak honestly?" Jonathan asks Mary Anne.

She pauses for a moment, studying Jonathan's intentions plain on his face. She nods. A simple smile growing upon her face.

"Mary Anne has been ripped from her world, the life she knew, her loved ones. Everything she cared for gone in a blink. Think of all she has faced since her arrival in our strange land. Now she is expected, no, commanded to be something, someone she could never have imagined in her most ridiculous dream. Her heart, her spirit, her mind must rage out of control, adrift, lost in a turbulent sea, impeding her path forward." Jonathan looks to Weiss. "No matter how hard you wish it, you cannot force calm waters. They must come to rest themselves. Then, and only then, will they, and she, know peace."

The Duchess's jaw drops with a closed mouth, impressed at Jonathan's words.

"Do not always remind her of the shut door," Jonathan continues. "Tell her what waits beyond it."

Tears pool in Mary Anne's eyes. She does not have to say a word. Her quivering lips and the several sparkles in her eyes say, "thank you."

Weiss leans against the back of his chair, withdrawing himself from the conversation.

"What say you, Mary Anne?" asks the Duchess.

Mary Anne uses the cuff of her sleeve to wipe away her tears. "I know the second Tenet is what matters most, and I am trying. But while I

wrestle with my own struggles, please allow me to learn everything else."
She locks eyes with Jonathan. Her shoulders raise again with a newfound
sense of purpose. "But in the meantime, I must not be idle. I cannot be.
Teach me as much as possible."

In some ways, Jonathan sees a kindred spirit in Mary Anne. He, too,
cannot sit alone with his thoughts. Focus too long on them and they pull
him down a spiral from which he fears one day he may never recover. The
longer he allows himself to stay there, the stronger the shadows in the
corners of his mind grow, waiting to strike. Fortunately, and
unfortunately, he does not see a moment's peace in his near future.

CHAPTER 3

MARCH

The nightmare from this morning leaves a phantom, lingering film beneath her skin. She sits on the edge of the bed and cradles one of her swords across her lap, admires the craftsmanship, turns it in hand and tilts it ever so slightly for the morning light to catch the full length of the smooth blade. For a moment, it is as if a light shines from within the steel and illuminates her face, lifting the film from her body. She looks to the ceiling and watches the reflections of the coming day dance upon the stones and wooden timbers. Her fingers pass over the blade, drifting up and down through the air, transforming the sharp slice of light into a wavering gentle reflection, as if the dawn bounced on the surface of a calm pond or brook in the Rookwood. But she is far from the Rookwood, far from her home, and even farther from being safe, in the last place in all of Wonder she wishes to find herself. But at least she is with Jonathan.

They have not seen the Hollow in well over a week's time, and almost a week since she and Jonathan last saw Cheshire, though their time apart always seems longer. They were together in this room in the middle of the night when he was beyond consoling. He has not made himself known to them, but March overhears whispers of incidents throughout the city from the servant girls. As horrid a place as Mirus is, the number of deaths and suicides are suspect and scream of staged murders—at least to March. After all, she has orchestrated her fair share in her lifetime. All these and more chaotic mischief keep Cheshire away and out of her and Jonathan's arms.

Hurt and anger cloud Cheshire's mind and fill his heart, ever more so than the pain he normally hides behind his eyes and rakish smile. Cheshire will never share the cause, and March will never ask, but she understands the need to lash out at the world before the well of emotions inside overflows, becomes all-consuming, and drowns him from within.

She lays eight swords side by side on the bed, pommels facing her. Each sword as different as the men she slew to win them. She points at them from left to right as if playing the keys of an organ.

"Seamus. Absolom. Aeron. Turrell. Monpart. Caisyl. Burke. Flynn." Her memory with her swords is as sharp as Jonathan's with his teas. She can recall every detail—location, weather, season, and the names of their previous owners—of how all two hundred and forty-seven came to be part of her unique and prized collection. Not counting the random swords of lesser quality she picks up from the odd skirmish and nameless brigand.

March slips her arms through the harness of her back scabbards and tightens the buckles on her shoulders. She selects and sheathes two of her swords—Absolom, the copper-colored blade with a slight curve at its end and barely a cross guard, and Burke, the thinnest blade of the eight, with a looking-glass finish and acid-etched hilt. She has the need to stab something.

As she descends the winding stairs, the castle servants hurry to and from whatever repetitive daily labors and chores to which they must attend. The elderly women, dressed in their worn wool dresses and aprons, greet March with a half-smile and a nod of respect, which she returns. Younger servant girls in their fresh linens and kerchiefs dare not meet her eyes. The young women in the gilded gowns and half masks, however, like Mary Anne's handmaiden, stay at a distance or turn to walk away as soon as they catch sight of her.

She searches for the title they are called in the castle. *Sarafan. The Sarafan Courtiers.* Their appearance and their presence make March's skin crawl, as if hundreds of unwanted fingers groped at her flesh. If it were up to her, none of these servants would be in the castle.

March weaves her way through the west wing to one of the many interior courtyards surrounded by stone arcades. Old willow trees sway in the breeze, which drifts down from the opening high above. At the center of the courtyard stand two straw men—sparring dummies with stuffed sackcloth bodies and heads held together with rope from ship rigging—to represent Lysander and Uriah with a bullseye painted on their chests and faces. Wooden posts, which also look as if they were salvaged from discarded ship parts, form the spines and outstretched arms. At their ends, fat wrought-iron blades are shoved into the wooden wrists. Cleverly, each straw man is positioned at the center of a wheel. March pushes on the left arm of Uriah's dummy and it spins completely around. She lowers her head to avoid the blade. Pat and Bill's construction is swift and accurate. She gave them the request the previous day, after Weiss lost his wits about the branches of the willows being nicked by her swords.

She takes position between the straw men and unsheathes her swords. The sharp ting as the tip of the blades lick against the edge of their scabbards sends a shiver from the back of her neck down to between her thighs. She shifts the weight to her left foot, outstretches her right leg, foot pointed, angles both arms down, swords palm up. March takes a deep breath through her nose and blows out slowly, tickling her gently parted lips. The rustling of the willow branches and leaves fade, and the soft twitter of greenfinches in the courtyard become distant, until her breath is the only sound which remains, preparing for the music to begin.

With an upward swing of her right sword, she clangs against one of Lysander's and dodges the return attack from his other sword while she strikes the sword in Uriah's left. Each metallic clang resonates in her body. She reaches over her shoulder to lay one of her blades flat against her back to deflect the slash from Lysander. With a spin, she bats away a blow from each straw man in opposite directions. The harder she strikes, the faster they spin on their wheels, the quicker she must respond. Each note of iron on iron builds the song in her head. Beautiful. Echoing.

A shadow stirs in the corner of the colonnade. It does not distract her from the battle, but she notes someone is watching from a distance.

The song and fight intensify. Her sweat flings through the air with every turn, and her hair sticks to her forehead, cheeks, and neck. While she ducks under Lysander's blade, her blades run along his neck, slicing the sackcloth. Straw drizzles down to the ground all around her. Though entertained, music played on wrought iron, wood, and straw is not the same as bone, steel, and flesh. With one final flourish, she spins and stabs the points of each of her blades through the center of each bullseye on Lysander and Uriah's faces. But what she thought would end the fight only elevates further.

Her strike triggered something within the straw men. A smaller set of arms burst forth and uncoil from within the sackcloth bodies of both dummies at their waist, each with a long iron dagger at their end. March turns sideways and narrowly escapes them slicing into her torso.

What a remarkable invention.

The shorter arms stick out perpendicular to the larger, giving her less time to plan, but also the spontaneous thrill she would find in open battle. The arms force her to crouch lower to the ground, deflect quicker, move her lower body and upper body contrary to one another to avoid each attack. Her footwork becomes furious and quick, as do the notes and strikes all around her—a swarm of metal stings. In the flurry, she blinks to expel the sweat from her eyes. In those fleeting moments, the faces of Absolom and Burke flash in the darkness. The bullseye on each straw man transforms from the visage of Lysander and Uriah to their likenesses, smiling, taunting, laughing.

The song turns sour. The muscles of her thighs, back and stomach become weary. She knocks Lysander away to her left, Uriah to her right, giving her less than a second, but it is all she needs. She thrusts her swords down into the wheels, snapping the wood in half, ending the fight once and for all. The song fades. The trees and the birds resume their lives, as if they paused just for her. She breathes heavily. The muscles of her abdomen flex hard with each exhale. The breeze against the sweat of her face, arms and torso grants a much-needed chill to her heated skin.

Gloved applause draws her attention back to the shadow. A young soldier in full armor, except for a helmet, steps out from the arcade. Sweat covers the brow of his olive skin. At first, March believes his hair and eyes to be black as pitch, but once he steps into the sunlight, they are a deep moss green, the former in tight curls.

"That was truly an amazing display," he says. "Truly. The speed of your attacks, your defense, your recovery. Each movement took no longer than a blink. I had to strain to keep my eyes open to make sure I missed nothing. Oh, the tales of your skill pale compared to watching you in person."

"Why are you here?" March asks, not amused with a voyeur, eyes pinched from the sting of her sweat.

"My apologies." He approaches her with a wide smile, but stops suddenly. "I should not draw so near. In these times, I know it is difficult to know where loyalties lie."

"You may approach." March pulls her swords from the wheels and steps out from between the straw men. "If I am as fast as you saw and say, do you think I fear you?"

"Not at all." He walks to March with quick steps. "It truly was an honor to watch you."

"From the shadows."

"Yes. I do apologize. But how could I distract you while in the midst of such an exhilarating session?"

"You give yourself too much credit." March scoffs. "Yet here you are and still have not told me what your business is. Simply to watch a woman sweat. There are brothels for such activities."

"Forgive me."

March treats him harsher than he deserves. She senses the truth in him from the mere fact his eyes never lower from hers. But she trusts no one other than Jonathan, Cheshire, and Dormy.

"To my purpose." He reaches for his belt. "I have this—"

March's swords cut the air with such speed the soldier does not hear or see them, until they press against his skin, stopping his words. The point of one sword finds the small triangular cutout at the wrist of the thick Mirusian leather gloves he wears on the hand reaching for his belt. It hits the fleshy bit under the wrist between the bones which, with a flick, could sever the veins. The other sword point presses against the soft underside of his jawbone.

"Remarkable. Truly remarkable." His neck stretches, head back, face twitching as the steel tip breaks his skin. "But you have nothing to fear from me. Though this sounds suspicious as well. I have a letter for you. This is what I was reaching for. This is my purpose."

March darts her eyes to the small, rolled parchment protruding from his belt and back again. She steps back three paces and keeps one blade pointed at his throat.

"A letter from whom?"

"Oh, from the Gryphon's hand. Written this morning." He holds the scroll out for her to take.

"Impossible. He has not fully recovered."

"No, he has not. This morning he asked for quill, ink, and parchment, and wrote to you, specifically to you. I was standing guard outside of the infirmary when he called upon me. I was to deliver this to your hand, and only you." The soldier lays the scroll on the short grass and steps away. "The contents are not for my eyes. I shall leave you to it." He bows at the waist, turns in place, and leaves the courtyard.

She walks to the edge of the grass and watches him disappear far down one of the interior castle hallways. The scroll waits for her on the grass, innocent in appearance and size. The contents, however, could be more harmful than any wound from a blade. She is tempted to leave the courtyard and pretend she never saw it, never received it, then she cannot be held accountable for whatever it reads. She could easily track down and dispose of the soldier before he can tell anyone else.

There will be enough deaths in the days to come. No need killing someone for delivering a letter. Not yet anyway.

The grass crunches as she returns to the scroll. She circles it three times, then flips it over with the point of her sword to examine further. To be sure, the Gryphon's seal—the talon and the sword—pressed in crimson wax stares up at her.

"Damn it."

She sheaths her swords and picks up the scroll, turning the thin crinkling parchment in hand over and over again to delay opening it. Though light as a feather, something foreboding weighs the parchment down. The snap the seal makes and the rustle of the parchment are unnaturally loud as she unrolls it, as if purposely trying to bring others' attention.

Inside, the runes are unsteady at best, and the ink smeared by a heavy hand. "'Audrianna March,'" she reads. "'Word has reached my ears that you are in Mirus. Advantageous. You shall train this new army of Wonderland in the old and new ways. Accepted without exception. Cordially, Gryphon.'"

"What in all the nine hells?" She examines the other side of the scroll as if there were some other instruction, but three sentences are enough. "Fuck."

Her skin turns to goose flesh and feels cold all over her body. She does not know how to take this request, or rather, this command. She has never commanded anyone, held any position of leadership or mentorship. There are thousands of men in the Castle Guard and Mirusian army combined. If this be true, this is high praise, the highest praise for her skill, which she fought her entire life to master. But despite the honor, she does not want this.

The crunch of quick footsteps on grass draws her attention behind her. "I thought you said the contents were none of your business," she says, expecting the soldier. "Is there something else you need of me?"

"Madam?" The Doorman from the front entrance of the castle walks toward her, the corners of his wide mouth permanently downturned. He carries a scroll in both white-gloved hands, as if a servant would carry a silver tray.

She rolls the scroll from the Gryphon tightly in hand and points at the new scroll with it. "Is this another from the Gryphon as well? Why did he not send it with the soldier?"

"No, madam," he says, confused. He presents the new scroll to her. "Not from the Gryphon. A messenger delivered this to the main gates this morning. A soldier brought it to me, and with no servant in the vicinity, I brought it to you. Please take it so I may return to my post."

As soon as March has it in her hands, the Doorman turns and leaves in a hurry, arms bent, elbows pointed, and swaying side to side with each step as he walks away.

She turns the scroll in hand until the unmistakable purple wax seal stares her in the face—crossed swords on a coin, the crest of her family. The Gryphon's letter made her skin cold. This letter makes her blood boil. March's mother has finally sent word for her.

CHAPTER 4

CHESHIRE

During the past four days, Pat and Bill have proven more elusive than Cheshire believed they would. It was only by chance he saw them, or rather they spotted him for the first time outside the hanging cells. He admires their intelligence, but not their stealth. Even if he catches up to them, confronting them in the city during the day, while they work in public places surrounded by soldiers would be problematic, but then they retire to their home outside of the city walls at night, beyond Cheshire's reach. His plan hinges on finding them, but he cannot allow them to monopolize his Time.

He leaves their pursuit and continues his map of the catacombs under the city and castle. There are three routes which connect the passages of the castle to the catacombs of Mirus, each to a different tier of the city. Underneath the cobbled streets of Mirus, tunnels run from the Row to the Forge, from the poorest dwellings of the Boroughs to the most opulent manors in the Crest. Storehouses, feed houses, granaries, stables, Cheshire has access to them all. And most to his liking, he can disappear without a trace and reappear anywhere across the city or castle in a matter of minutes.

A thought crosses his mind. *The purpose of the catacombs beneath Mirus is to provide an escape should anything befall the castle. But every path leads into the city, which would in theory be under siege as well. I missed something. Somewhere in the dark, there must be a way out of the city.* He never gave thought to it before because he had no wish or reason to leave now that he is inside, but if there is a need to escape, this path would be his way back.

It takes him two entire days of walking through the lowest tunnels until he finds what he hopes he is searching for. In a barren stretch of tunnel with inset alcoves along both sides of the wall, one alcove in the middle of fifty disappears into darkness. Cheshire steps in and walks cautiously, hands on both walls and feet sliding along the dirt-covered cobblestones. After thirty paces, his toes curl over a ledge—the beginning of an exceptionally narrow spiral staircase barely wider than his shoulders. Should someone Jonathan's size ever traverse this way, he would need to walk sideways.

Cheshire follows the stairs down, down, and farther down still, until they end in moist dirt, not stones, and the walls give way to a void of darkness. He waits at the edge of the stairs for his eyes to adjust, and to his surprise, the natural lines of rock take shape in front of him—the wall of a cave, damp to the touch. Cheshire turns to his ears and listens past the silence. He hears distant drips and the buzz of rushing water bouncing from his left and his right.

He leaves the stairs and follows the wall to his right through the soft muck, not quite dirt, not yet mud. A cavern takes form before him as his eyes adjust as if the darkness wafts away like smoke. Large stone points hang from the ceiling, dripping water onto the earth. Boulders the size of small houses line the curved walls, and small, lonely puddles reflect the unrequited love of the darkness. If this is the way out, a door must be somewhere in the walls, but not a spec of light from the outside penetrates through. He follows the sound of the water to the far end of the cavern and presses his ear against the cold, damp rock.

He searches with hand and foot until he feels wood where there should be none. Swollen timber beams, almost as wide as his body, mark the doorway. Between the timbers, the door itself, made of stone, is too heavy for brute force to have any effect. If this is the exit in the case of siege or other emergencies, the release should be easy to find in a hurry. But the posts hold no secret, no lever, or button. The roots around the door are merely roots, and stones merely stones.

Perhaps brute force is the key.

Cheshire digs his heels into the cold slurry near the door, ready to push with all his strength, but as soon as he lays his hands on the stone door, it rumbles and slides into the cavern wall.

Perhaps not. He looks at his hand. *Curious.*

Another rock wall, hugged by daylight on both sides, stands on the other side of the door. Seconds later, the door rumbles again, and the mud slurps as the door pushes its way through it. The door closes, the light disappears, and the rumble stops.

Cheshire holds his hand out again and places it on the door—first his fingertips, then his palm. The door obeys and slides open.

"What sorcery is this?"

Soft daylight pours into the cavern. Cheshire looks to the staircase at the back of the cavern, carved into the back of one of many large boulders, completely invisible to the eye. If any intruder were to gain access, it would take thorough exploration in the dark to find it. A few seconds later, the door rumbles shut, returning the cavern to the peaceful dark. The door opened at his touch from the inside, but would it do the same from the outside? To find out, he must willingly risk not being able to enter Mirus again, at least not in the same way.

He places his hand on the stone face of the door a third time, and watches it open and close. Before it reaches the halfway mark, Cheshire touches the rock again, and the door reverses back into the wall, proving it will listen before it fully closes. He steps through the doorway and waits, heart racing, ready to pounce back through, waiting for the door to reach the halfway mark again. When enough room remains for his body, he touches the door. It pauses, then opens as it has every other time. Having this knowledge centuries ago would have saved him years of turmoil and searching. Then again, the catacombs this far down were never shown to him, and the soldiers and the Ace made sure to keep Cheshire from ever getting this close to the capital.

His thighs shake as he lets the stone door close fully, making a deep and final *thoom* when it seals. He closes his eyes, hoping he has made the right decision, and places his hand on the rock face one more time. The stones ease his fear as the door opens again.

Thankful, he still must question. *Why? Does this happen to any who lay hands on the stones? Or is it just me?* He hopes for the latter.

Once the door shuts again, he walks around the stone wall hiding the entrance. On the other side, Cheshire discovers a rocky, serene grotto at the edge of a river. A light dusting of vibrant green moss covers the dark gray rocks, along with creeping marshwort and fen violets sprouting between them. A gentle waterfall creates a curtain separating the grotto from the shallow, crystal-clear river.

He strips off his clothing, hides them behind the stone wall, except for his purple sash which he drapes around his neck, and stands under the waterfall, losing his breath to the brisk cascade of water. He cherishes the sensation washing over him, scrubbing his entire body clean. He wipes the water from his face and steps past the waterfall, into the chill of the river. His toes dig into the soft silt, and the current takes it away around the bend to his right.

Both sides of the river have narrow sandy shores covered with long grass and black bog rush. Above him, sheer, steep cliffs on both sides rise high to make the sky look like a single blue band, a reflection of the river below. *This is the river which circles the city.* He trudges through the shallow waters following the current, and as he suspected, far in the distance, the river opens up to the bustling harbor on the back side of Mirus. At the mouth of the river, four archers stand sentry on a wooden bridge across the water, and beyond, soldiers no larger than whirligig beetles patrol the docks between large and small merchant ships.

Centuries ago, Cheshire tried to enter Mirus by way of the docks, but security measures are even more elaborate at the harbor. Archers take position at every level of the docks, soldiers inspect every piece of cargo and transfer their contents into new containers before being raised up the lifts to the city, and any merchant or visitor who arrives by water are escorted by no less than six soldiers up the stairs, separate from their cargo.

There are several places Cheshire could hide in the small wooden buildings which make up the port stacked against the cliff, but he could go no farther. The cliffs themselves are nearly smooth to the touch, as if the gods cut into the earth with a sword fresh from the forge and burned away any imperfections. And the back of the castle grounds loom high above, jutting out from the mountain like the wide beak of a great bird.

Cheshire travels back upstream, walking against the current, wondering if anything different lies on the other side of Mirus. As he trudges, he notices a small peculiar black object at the top edge of the cliff keeping pace with him, naturally out of place among the verdant bushes and undersides of tree canopies.

"You son of a whore."

Even from this distance, the black object is the unmistakable onyx ax blade of the Ace, which has almost claimed Cheshire's life on multiple occasions. The Ace, the butcher of Wonderland, Death, stalks him even now, waiting for the moment Cheshire leaves the city. He can see Cheshire but does not jump down the cliff, which would not be a difficult feat for him. Once, centuries ago in the Draughts, the Ace plunged his ax into the mountainside and used it to slow his descent to continue his pursuit. Cheshire wonders if there is a barrier surrounding Mirus which keeps him at bay. Regardless, he knows within the city walls and in the surrounding river, there is one less enemy to worry about, at least for now.

45

He leaves his clothes behind, enjoying this fleeting Time of freedom in the daylight and continues to explore. The river and the chasm widen the farther Cheshire travels upstream until the support pillars of the long bridge into Mirus—the towering viaduct—come into view, each one wider than ten elder trees and made of bricks taller than Jonathan. Underneath the arch on the city side cliff, water pours from rocks, feeding the river and splitting the current. Not far around the bend in front of him, Cheshire stumbles upon a small dock, less than six feet in length, with a single, masterfully constructed dinghy tethered to one of its posts. A worn path in the reeds and sand leads from the dock to a rocky shore, on to a precarious wooden staircase, and up to a small cabin perched halfway up the cliff face like a bird's nest.

Dormy's words jump to the forefront of Cheshire's mind. *They live in a small cabin on the cliff side below the wall, just outside the main gate.*

It is not often Cheshire can celebrate victories in his life, no matter how small. He relaxes from his constant state of tension, and savors gaining entrance to Mirus, discovering a new secret entrance to the city, being safe from the Ace at least for a Time, and now Pat and Bill presented to him on a silver platter without the need to search for them any longer.

As the sun sets, Cheshire lies along the large beam at the point of Pat and Bill's roof and waits, watching the dark silhouette of the Ace, ever vigilant, pace back and forth on the opposite cliff. The sharp curve of his ax blade catches the moonlight every few steps, and Cheshire swears from this distance he can also see the tiny white glints under the nothingness of his hood.

It is well past twilight when Pat and Bill return home. Pat leads the way, her large hammer over her shoulder, and Bill follows carrying two sacks. Cheshire lies flat against the point of the cabin's roof and watches them grow in size as they descend the long staircase and near until they disappear through the cabin's front door below him. He drops from the awning and enters through the front door of the cabin without hesitation.

They glance at Cheshire and go about their business undressing for bed as if they expected his eventual visit. Bill hangs their leather aprons from wooden pegs on the wall, and Pat sits on a bench and kicks off her boots and trousers.

"Hello, again." Pat stretches her arms across her body.

"However did you get out here?" Bill uses his feet to pry off his boots, drop his trousers, and then he collects both his and Pat's clothing and folds them on a table against the wall.

Do they know of the catacombs? It would stand to reason, since they are the caretakers of the city and know every plank and stone. Then again, if they knew, they would not have asked. If they do not know, the catacombs will remain Cheshire's secret. But, if he is to get answers from them, he must not start by ignoring their questions.

"I have learned to walk through walls." Cheshire straddles the bench Pat sits on. She spies the sash around his neck and reaches out for it. He instinctively grabs her wrist to keep her from touching it.

"Hm," is Pat's reply, without changing the enigmatic expression on her face.

Bill sits behind her, legs on the opposite side of the bench, and looks over Pat's shoulder at Cheshire. "What can we do for you?" he asks with the same mysterious, calm look in his eyes.

"What happened to my mother's room?" He forgets the candles. Cheshire will not miss an opportunity like before.

"Sealed," says Pat.

"Filled," says Bill. "But not by our hands."

"Filled?"

"There is no room on the other side of the wall," says Pat. "It is solid brick and mortar from where one wall stood to the other. Try all you like to break in, but you will find nothing because nothing is there."

Cheshire's nostrils flare. The pure evil of the Duchess knows no limits. He asks the question that should have been the first out of his mouth when they met. "What happened to my mother?"

"We don't know," Pat answers plainly.

Her answer seems suspect, rehearsed, too quick, but it is impossible to know if she tells the truth or lies. Both of their faces reveal nothing. Their tone and eyes appear sincere, but Cheshire knows better.

"How did she die?"

"We don't know," says Bill. "We were all of fourteen years at the time, and that was an exceedingly long time ago."

"But you were working in the castle. You were there during the attack."

Pat and Bill look at each other, then to the ground. "Yes," says Pat. "A great number of people died that day. We never saw her body among them. All we remember is the screaming, the echoing in the halls, impossible to escape them."

"We ran," says Bill. "We ran from the castle that night. We came here. This was a side project of ours, but after that night, we never slept in the castle again."

The thought of his mother screaming, be it from rage or pain is beyond what he can bear. It feels like Cheshire swallowed a stone that will stay in his stomach forever. There will come a Time when he will press them further, but they may tell the truth and know nothing more. If not, he knows where to find them.

"Though we have not seen each other in quite some time, it looks as though not much has changed," says Pat. "Even in your youth, your mother had the most difficult time keeping you in your clothing. She would chase you through every corridor from the moment you were able to walk until you were eight."

Another memory comes to Bill. "When we were small, we would

chase each other through the gardens. You would scatter pieces of your clothes around to lead us in contrary directions to prolong the game."

Cheshire smiles despite himself. Someone remembers him. Someone remembers his mother. He wants to hear more but cannot for fear he will break here and now.

"Two more questions, and then I shall leave you be."

"Ask as many as you like." Bill stretches his back.

"The Gryphon is set to leave the infirmary soon. When exactly?"

Pat looks at Bill to answer. "If it were up to him, it would be this night," he says. "However, the physicians attending him say it will be four days more."

"At least or at most?" asks Cheshire.

"At all." Pat chuckles. "He will not stay a day longer. He has made it quite clear."

"Last question," says Cheshire, "this night, at least. The candles in your workshop—"

Pat turns to look at Bill before Cheshire can finish the question. "I told you."

Cheshire expected some level of surprise, or disbelief, but they knew he was there poking around.

"Where do you get them?"

They both squint and furrow their brows at Cheshire, sensing no good to come from his request.

"A candlemaker. In the Crooked Market," says Pat. "Look for the sign with the raven and three flames. Can't miss it."

Cheshire leaves without word or ceremony. As the door closes, he turns back and sees Pat and Bill climb into the single bed they share in the cabin. He walks down the stairs, lit by moonlight, upstream, and back downstream, and all the while the Ace follows him above. When he reaches the door, he tests it one more time to make sure it opens at his touch—it does—but he does not enter. Instead, he gathers his clothes and uses them as a pillow. Here, there is neither soldier, guard, nor Ace to

49

bother him this night. Tomorrow night he will journey to the Crooked Market, but tonight he will sleep undisturbed in the open air lulled by the water and cooled by its spray.

The last thought before he drifts to sleep is the sound of his laughter as a child, the feeling of the short grass in the garden underfoot, and his mother calling to him. When all is done, he will see her again, and then he will at last know true peace.

CHAPTER 5

MARY ANNE

Chamberlain Weiss drones on, as he does every afternoon, about the importance of Mary Anne's journey and transformation. There should be inspiration in his words, but they amount to nothing more than dates, populations, regions of Wonderland, and his own contributions during the reign of queens. This is the fifth time he has covered the same topics. She can recall the towns of the Wetlands and the Warrens, the number of citizens in the Crest, Stonehaven, and the Boroughs, and the locations of all six Pinnacles of Wonderland. None of these have any bearing or weight to Mary Anne because it is simply information and no connection to her journey.

During the hours spent in his study while he lectures, her eyes explore the chamberlain's study. She believes clutter to be a sign of intelligence—after all, her own study at home has a fair share of ledgers, receipts, schedules, and charts stacked around the room, and she knows exactly where everything is. This study, however, is beyond excessive. Perhaps Chamberlain Weiss believes the same and has taken the idea to an extreme. Three of the four walls are covered with floor to ceiling bookshelves, each filled with an inordinate number of books crammed on each shelf. A random assortment of scrolls and parchment, which could have no possible catalogue, fill every open space between books where one could see the back wall.

Glass windows with dark metal diamond-shaped frames cover the fourth wall. A dingy filth envelopes them, changing the light of the room from daylight to that of parchment. Stacks of books, from knee height to what must be ten feet tall, with papers between every one surround Mary Anne. Chamberlain Weiss wanders throughout the room while he lectures, and often she loses sight of him through the parchment forest.

The real jailor, but also savior, is the intricate hourglass mechanism which rests on a paper covered table in the middle of the stacks. Three wooden gears suspend a single hourglass within each—one large to measure a day, one medium to measure an hour, and one small to measure a minute. It took Mary Anne the first day to understand how to read them, but she does not know how they function. Once the sand of the smallest empties, the mechanism clicks, and the glass flips upside down on the wooden track to begin anew. The same with the hour and the day. The incessant faint sound of sand running over glass, the ticking, and the crank of the gears, keep Mary Anne prisoner, yet also tick away to her freedom. She is not sure which sound is worse, the glasses or the Chamberlain.

She has learned the exact time at which to return to her room, otherwise she would miss Jonathan and March, and Chamberlain Weiss would continue to speak until dusk or even well into the night. The first time happened by accident; she had forgotten her book in her room. She overheard Jonathan and March in the midst of passion in their bedchamber as she passed by during the early afternoon and so stayed to watch. Mary Anne had been watching them in the mornings before they leave and in the evenings before bed, but she did not know they found their way back to their room during the day. Unable to pull herself away, she learned their schedule and committed it to memory. Just the sound of Jonathan's moans, his roars of pleasure, his labored breathing, make Mary

Anne's body tingle and crave his touch. The way he makes March moan, scream, and pant fills Mary Anne with curiosity and jealousy. She enjoyed every time she and Thomas would make love, but he would never sound like Jonathan, and Mary Anne most certainly never made the noises March does.

She should focus on her return home, her studies, but what use is studying a book she cannot understand when there are other, more interesting, bodies of work to study, like Jonathan.

Each day, at the exact same time, she creates a new reason to excuse herself and return to her room. Today, Mary Anne stops Chamberlain Weiss mid-thought to explain the fruit from breakfast has unsettled her stomach. He waves her away, and she gladly takes her leave and races back up to her room, not to miss a single moment.

Her hands press hard against the stones of her washroom wall, and she peers through the tiny spyglass embedded within and waits. Even though the film on the other side of the glass distorts their image with a slight haze, she can follow every movement, every position of Jonathan and March in the sunlight from their balcony. Throughout the days since their arrival, Jonathan and March find every chance to be with each other. Four times a day, like clockwork. Morning, twice spread in the afternoon, and at twilight.

Through the spyglass, Mary Anne has seen March straddle Jonathan, hands behind her head, grinding her hips against his while his hands explore and massage every part of her body. Other times Jonathan lays March on her back beneath him, her legs hooked over his elbows, while his hips thrust into her long and hard. Or Jonathan stands in the middle of the room with March in his arms, her legs wrapped around his waist, his muscled back pinched to support her while he pleasures her.

After nightfall, he carries March out to the balcony where he sits her upon the railing and kneels, then nuzzles his face and laps at her most sensitive spot between her thighs. March brings his hands to her breasts. Mary Anne touches her own breasts while she watches, imagining it is

Jonathan's hands and not her own. Other times, he sits against the railing, and March kneels at his feet, her hands gripping his thighs. Jonathan runs his fingers gently through her hair as her head raises and lowers, swallowing him, pleasing him. His own head leans back as he huffs out quick breaths.

Often, they face out to the open air. March leans on the rail. Jonathan stands bare and beautiful behind her, inside her, with his hands around her small waist. The candles from within their room paint Jonathan's back muscles and backside in warm hues against the dark sky and stone. The bathroom window is too close when they venture outside, so Mary Anne lies on the floor of her own balcony to watch through the balustrade and risk a peek of Jonathan's buttocks as it flexes and relaxes with every thrust when he stands behind March. She arches her back and reaches her arms behind her to hold on to Jonathan's neck as if she were the carved figurehead of a ship. Jonathan's brawny arms surround March to press her against him. Mary Anne tries to catch a glimpse in-between them, to know Jonathan in full, but his body casts a shadow which keeps his secret from her.

After Jonathan and March climax, Mary Anne feels a crawling sense of guilt in the pit of her stomach. She should think of Thomas, and does when she lies in bed and touches herself, but as the days go on, it becomes increasingly difficult to envision his sweet face, hazel eyes, and thin mustache. Every time they would make love, she would lie on her back, and he would look down upon her with his kind smile. Now Jonathan's face takes his place—his turquoise eyes, his strong jawline. She tries to shake the image from her mind, but Jonathan grows more and more ever-present, and she stops fighting.

Over the past week, Mary Anne has wondered what Thomas thinks of her disappearance. Is he concerned? Has he gone to notify the authorities? Or has he returned to his wife, to his loveless marriage? How easily Mary Anne could fall out of his mind, as he has in hers. She is not destined to stay here. Mary Anne will, she must, return home to her life, her mother, her industry, her love. However, if she must wait to see England again, there is no sensible reason not to indulge this fantasy, knowing it is not permanent, and she will once again feel Thomas's warmth.

The day escapes her, and their room remains empty. By this hour, Jonathan has stripped his clothes away, leaving his boots and hat on, which for some reason excites Mary Anne thoroughly. She tiptoes to the door of her bedchamber and peeks out. Grace startles her. Her maidservant does nothing more than stand in the hallway and wait patiently.

"Forgive me," says Mary Anne. "Have you perchance seen Jonathan or March this afternoon?"

Grace shakes her head, eyes to the floor. At least, Mary Anne presumes her eyes look down since the half mask of her gilded uniform hides them from the world.

Mary Anne walks to Jonathan's bedchamber door on the off chance they positioned themselves beyond the spyglass's scope. Her hand pauses in the air before she knocks. What is to happen if they are within the bedchamber? They are not modest in the least. Would it be possible for Jonathan to answer the door without his clothing? Mary Anne's heart thumps in her throat, and heat washes over her ears as if someone cups them. She knocks. There is no sound on the other side of the door, sexual or otherwise. She knocks again. Nothing.

At dusk, after Grace helps Mary Anne into her silk robe, Mary Anne looks through the spyglass again and then through her washroom window to their balcony. The moon bathes their room in soft, cold blue light.

Where are they? A horrible chill overtakes her again, one she has not felt since the Inn in Briarwell, the thought they may have abandoned the city—abandoned her.

She rushes into the hallway to ask Grace, "Is there a lock upon their door?"

Grace shakes her head.

Mary Anne knocks three times. Once the silence builds, she pushes the door open and walks in as if it were her own room. Her racing heart slows. Everything they brought with them remains in the room—their large wooden steamer trunks hug the wall, and March's coats hang over the single wooden chair in the room, while Jonathan's coat is tidily folded and stacked on a thin table. A few of March's swords lie in an arch on the floor, and Jonathan's shabby top hat made of carpet pieces, the one Mary Anne first saw him in, hangs on the corner of the chair.

They have not left the city. But why are they not here?

Mary Anne must suppress her worry until the morning at the next council meeting. Jonathan should be in attendance, and if not, Mary Anne will wait near her bedchamber. She returns to her bed, feeling the chill of the night air on her body which lacks the warmth Jonathan would provide. Her foot shakes beneath the satin sheets. She has grown accustomed to watching Jonathan and March each night, touching herself, releasing the pent-up energy from the course of the day. Her hands slide through the opening of her robe, fingers massaging herself in small quick circles, but it is not the same. She tries to imagine Jonathan but feels no arousal without watching them, hearing them.

She kicks the sheets off, takes the small silver candelabra from her side table and lights the three half-melted candles. Since there is no lock on Jonathan's door, Mary Anne decides to explore to know more of them, of him. The door to her bedchamber creaks open into an empty hallway. Mary Anne walks cautiously, placing each foot down as if the patter of her feet would ring through the castle like an alarm.

"Jonathan," she whispers. She knocks softly and pushes the door open without waiting. The candlelight dances in the room and catches the blades of March's swords, the porcelain teacups on a side table, and the locks of all the trunks. She places the candelabra on the floor at the center of the room and opens the trunks at the top of the stacks against the wall. Their colors blend together, all appearing orange and yellow in the candlelight.

The first trunk holds what Mary Anne assumes to be March's wardrobe, since every piece of clothing is cropped, has cut-outs, or is no more than strips of silk, linen, or leather held together with copper rings. The second trunk holds Jonathan's clothing. She picks up a sleeveless shirt and holds it to her nose to breathe in his scent—a mixture of wood and fruits and herbs. She folds the shirt over her arm to take back to her room, to hold and inhale Jonathan as she falls asleep.

There are two trunks on the ground, open for all to see. The first is filled with small wooden boxes, an overpowering amalgam of smells coming from the containers. She wafts the air away from her face, but the odor remains. The second trunk is full of what Mary Anne believes are March's swords, all wrapped neatly in cloth and tied with twine.

In the trunk's corner, a small, simple book pokes out from beneath the wrappings. With slight rearranging, Mary Anne finds there are layers of books concealed underneath the swords. She stops a thought before it takes form. She wants to believe the idea of March as a scholar to be preposterous, since she so clearly relies on her body rather than her mind. But those are the thoughts of the men and women who surrounded Mary Anne in England, assuming a woman, no matter how well dressed, could not be educated.

The spine of the book crackles as Mary Anne opens it in hand. Her heart races again. She kneels on the floor next to the candelabra to make sure what she sees is true. There are no distinguishable marks on the cover of the old book but inside are the same runes as the Book of Queens—Old Prodigium, the first language of Wonderland—runes she cannot understand, cannot read, but apparently March can.

Mary Anne's stomach free falls. Chamberlain Weiss will not read any farther in the Book of Queens until Mary Anne completes the Second Tenet, and he wants her to spend her time alone without a way of learning. Now, however, she sees she must spend as much time as possible with Jonathan, her advisor, and March, who will hopefully be her tutor. She places the book back in the trunk, arranges the swords back to the best of her memory, and retires to her bedchamber and her bed with Jonathan's shirt tucked to her nose.

This is no time for both of them to disappear, not when she needs them most. After a week of feeling as though the wheels of her carriage spin but do not carry her any closer to home, at last she finds hope. Hope in the most unlikely, and most unwilling, of places.

CHAPTER 6

JONATHAN

As dusk falls, Jonathan climbs the eastern wooden stairway to the top of the castle's outer wall. Soldiers and the Castle Guard, armed with spear, sword, and longbow, stand watch every ten paces along the parapets. The silver finish of their helmets catches the reflection of the braziers, and it makes them all appear as if their heads spout flames.

"Good evening," he says as he passes each. Some reply, others ignore him.

He walks to the midpoint of the curved wall and looks to the east to catch the last glimpse of the sunset slide behind the mountains. Wonderland's hearth slumbers and gives way to a sky of blue, then black filled with a multitude of stars, dancing in their celestial home.

Below, lamplighters busy at work on the streets of Stonehaven and the Crest bring the city to light with an ember glow. All except for the Boroughs, which appear a dark chasm between Stonehaven and the outer wall of Mirus. The tops of the meager buildings sit below the pavers of Stonehaven, sunken by design to keep from view.

Jonathan takes position at the exact center of the wall where a long brass spyglass perches on a swivel. He presses his face to the eyepiece and positions it to look down to the row of torches cutting through the darkness over the Boroughs—to the Long Bridge. From this distance, it is difficult to make out individual figures. Just movement like shifting sand.

"Here," Dormy's pleasant voice says from behind Jonathan.

He takes a step back for her to adjust four brass rings in the middle of the spyglass. She turns them to the right. They sound like knives being sharpened on a whetstone until they click to a stop.

"Look now."

"Good heavens," says Jonathan. The townspeople's faces are clear as day. "Thank you. What ever are you doing up here?"

"I saw you walk up, so I followed." The only truths more constant and refreshing than the sunrise are Dormy's simplicity and honesty.

"How are you fairing?" he asks. "Away from the Market and all."

"Well, the first night I nearly pulled my hair out." She reaches into her pocket and shows Jonathan a small tangle of frazzled orange hairs. "But then I asked Pat and Bill to help me think of a way to keep my business going, safe like, without risking anyone. And they built me this." She takes Jonathan by the cuff of his jacket and leads him farther down the curve of the wall. "They call it a treadwheel crane. At first they built it where the winch had to be turned by hand; they used an old ship wheel. But let's face it, I ain't got the arm strength. So, they built this version, where I can get it and use my legs instead of my arms to turn the wheel. Run one direction and the bucket comes up from my wagon while another bucket lowers outside the wall to collect their coins. Then I run the other direction and lower the goods to them." If her face could shatter from smiling of pride, it would.

"Dormy, this is extraordinary." Jonathan examines the craftsmanship of timber and iron. "But wouldn't you need to be all places at once?"

She giggles. "At first it was fucking hard work, is what it was. Running all the way down and back. But then this friendly guard started running the wheel for me, so I could ride the bucket down, get what's what, then ride it back up. Then I got another one to be at the wagon. I shout to him where things are. He gets them, puts them in the bucket, then the other soldier wheels them back up while I take the next order."

Jonathan leans closer to Dormy. "You mean to tell me you have the Castle Guard working for you?"

"Yes," one of the nearby soldiers says dryly, without turning his head.

She smiles and perks her eyebrows up three times. "What brings you out of the castle this night?"

"I need to settle a suspicion." Jonathan walks back to the spyglass to peer down at the Long Bridge again. His suspicion is correct. At this late hour, travelers from across Wonderland flood into Mirus. The silk robes over their traveling clothes give away the highborn from Adamas. Those from Clypeus wear their copper-colored armor proudly. The common folk, farmers, and traders from the Wetlands and the Warrens wear the best, albeit worn, browns and blues, and their long coats which drag along the ground.

"I have never seen so many on the Long Bridge at once, and at this hour," says Jonathan.

"You're correct," says the soldier nearest the spyglass. "Numbers have increased by the day. More men had to be sent to the main gate to keep the inspections timely."

"Thank you," says Jonathan.

"Do you think they are here to see Mary Anne?" asks Dormy.

"I fear they are here *for* Mary Anne. Word has spread since we left Briarwell, maybe even Rookridge. And it takes little time for a message, a scribble, to travel, at least as the raven flies. Couple that with as many days as we have been here, over a week. The numbers could be staggering. But somewhere out there, within the city walls, there must be someone who leads them, instructs them. They cannot all act on their own accord."

"Who?" asks Dormy, enthralled in Jonathan's words.

"That, my dear Dormy, is what I must discover. Someone pulls the strings. If I find them, perhaps we can uproot the weed which spreads beneath our feet." His tone shifts to a whisper. "Tell me, do you still have—"

Dormy pats one of the many bulges beneath her long corduroy jacket, just below her hip. The knife, the identifier of the cult of The Mother, must hide on her belt among the bellows, dented silver chalice, box of herbs, collection of keys to nowhere, other bobbles, and no less than two pistols.

Jonathan motions with his head for Dormy to join him on the backside of the wall in the hopes facing away from the soldiers and guards and the evening wind will lessen what falls to their prying ears. He leans over and rests his forearms on the parapets. Dormy stands shoulder to shoulder to him and mimics his pose.

"The soldiers at the main gate were instructed to search all who enter the city," he tells her, "but these blasted knives are too easily concealed. No matter how thoroughly they search carriage and wagon, unless they have every man and woman who enters the city strip, there is no way to know completely. And there is the off chance some soldiers and guards are members of this cult. Those who defected with the Red Knight are in hiding somewhere either inside or outside the city, or both, and can be easily identified. But this cult can hide in plain sight."

"Speaking of which." Dormy walks back and repositions the spyglass into the Crest and motions for Jonathan to peer through again.

"What am I looking at?" Jonathan squints, looking at a dark blurred image.

"Sorry." She turns the four brass rings back to the left.

A wide window of a stone manor in the Crest comes into focus. Inside, most of a dark, round oak table is visible, a silver candelabra with twelve candles its centerpiece. Tall black, jade, and gold vases line the back wall.

Jonathan is not one for peeping into windows, but he will not question Dormy. After two minutes, Lysander and Uriah, without armor, dressed in white and green silken robes, sit next to each other at the table. A naked woman sits on each of their laps. Jonathan pulls away from the spyglass and motions for Dormy to follow him. They walk quickly, silently, down the stairs back to the bailey.

Even though they are a good distance away from any of the Castle Guard, Jonathan speaks in a hushed tone. "How long have you been watching them?"

"Only three nights," Dormy whispers. "I wish I had known sooner. I mean, I am not a fighter. Cannot handle a sword. I am fair aim with a pistol. Quick with my hands. In the fight to come, I doubt I will be of much use. What I can do is watch."

"Dormy, you can do much more than—"

"And take notes." She pulls a small, crinkled scroll from her belt and holds it out for Jonathan.

Jonathan clasps her hand before the parchment can be seen by anyone who may look upon them. "You are truly a marvel. Do the guards on the wall know?"

"No," she says. "They think I'm spying on the vendors who try to steal my loyal customers, since I have to stay within the walls. Which is still true, but..."

Jonathan chuckles. "Keep it so. And do not hide the next scroll on your person."

"Can we... can we not trust the Castle Guard?" asks Dormy, worry growing in her eyes.

"We survive as we always have," says Jonathan. "Our trust remains within our small circle."

Dormy nods once and hastens back to her wagon. Her head darts from guard to guard as if they would try to sneak up behind her. None pay her any attention, which is fortunate for her own safety. She is also the most unassuming of Jonathan's band and will therefore get away with more than the rest.

Jonathan waits until she is inside her wagon and the lantern within the upper compartment glows through the rear window. He slides his hands into his coat pockets with the scroll and walks back into the castle, never taking his eyes from his next step, through the castle hallway, past the kitchen, out the back door to the gardens, and into the hedge maze, counting the entire way—the only way he can recall the twisting path to the center.

As soon as he walks into the lush green, the temperature of the air drops, a slow breeze brushes against his face like cobwebs, and the soft crunch of the short grass underfoot drowns out the ever-present drone of the city and constant metallic scratch on the night air from Castle Guard and soldiers. None patrol the interior of the maze because an intruder would need to enter the castle grounds first in order to make their way into the garden. This would be the safest place for Cheshire to join them... if Jonathan could contact him at all. For now, this verdant wonder will be his and March's alone.

At the maze's center, the path opens to a sunken sprawling field with purple and pink primroses, white lilies, bluebells, and foxgloves in large basins around the perimeter. In the middle of the field, March lies on her stomach upon a linen sheet, propped up on her elbows enthralled in one of her books. The single candle dances across her face and shoulders in a warm flickering ombre, while the moon bathes the rest of her bare body in tender blues.

She turns to look at him over the spectacles she wears to read, smiles coyly, licks her finger to turn a page, and returns to her book. Jonathan undresses and folds his clothing at the corner of the sheet, lays his timepiece upon them, chain coiled in a circle, and takes one last sip from his flask before placing it softly as well. It disturbs the chain, and Jonathan curves every link to reform the perfect circle. He takes the scroll and lays on his back, arms behind his head, next to March, making sure not to disturb her. The night air of the garden chills the sheet enough to send a welcome shiver through Jonathan's entire body.

Occults of the Old World. Jonathan reads the top of the page over her shoulder. He was mistaken. This is not one of her books, but one from Weiss's study, no doubt.

Her mind swirls with the same fear as Jonathan—the unknown. In all their years, all their times in the capital, they have never encountered anyone from this cult. They know the tactics and schemes to prepare for when dealing with the Red Knight, Lysander, and Uriah, but not knowing what to expect from this mysterious opponent worries them both. To be of any use as an advisor, Jonathan will need to venture outside of the walls, back into the city, to discover more.

March finishes reading for the night and uses a small blue ribbon to keep her page. She sets her book and spectacles at the edge of the sheet and blows out the candle before swinging her leg over Jonathan's waist, straddling him, flexing her muscles playfully. The moonlight drips down her body and frames her silhouette, every muscle, every curve. Even in the night, he can see the strain in her eyes. Seven other books as thick as the one she laid down sit just off the sheet.

She locks her fingers and stretches upward welcoming, calling, Jonathan's hands. He slides them slowly down her body from her shoulders, down her waist, to her hips, and then thighs. She smiles at his gentle touch. He hates the thought of interrupting this moment, but before he makes love to her, he holds up the scroll between them. To his surprise, she leans over to the edge of the grass and produces a letter and a scroll of her own. He leans closer to her and rests his chin on her shoulder, wrapping his arms around her, pressing his body against hers. She wraps her arms around his neck, nuzzles her face against his, and sighs. They do not know the contents of each other's scroll and letter— they do not need to. They will read them in the morning. He and March should be side by side always, but they know in their hearts, because of the simple words written on these parchments, their paths will soon have no choice but to diverge.

CHAPTER 7

CHESHIRE

There are four doors from the catacombs into the Boroughs, as opposed to the five dozen in Stonehaven alone. To reach the Crooked Market from the closest door requires a walk measuring a quarter of the city's circumference, almost four miles. The narrow paths and roofs between the crowded, dull gray wooden shanties of the Boroughs allow for easier exploration for Cheshire. At the least, this trek will prove less tiresome. Where Stonehaven and the Crest are built on the steep slope with winding streets stretching from one side of Mirus to the other, the Boroughs sit on flat yet uneven ground under Mirus's foot—out of sight and mind.

Well past twilight, Cheshire jumps across the gaps between buildings and steps across others. He notices the absence of soldiers, or rather, the lack of their numbers. Over the past mile, he has seen all of four pairs grumbling as they patrol. They trudge through the moist and muddy streets without torches, for fear a single carelessly waved torch would ignite the city of kindling. Not a single structure in all the Boroughs is built from stone.

On his way to the Market, Cheshire pokes his head in windows and doors to learn all he can. The scent of stew and vegetables from suppers hangs in the air. Mixed with the wet earth, it makes Cheshire feel at home, as if he were outside the walls. In most dwellings he finds townspeople asleep on beds made of rough cotton and hay or hand-woven blankets on the floor. In others, a few families still stir at this late hour—children who should be asleep play simple games with pebbles and a circle of rope, a mother nurses her infants while she sings, and a man carves a stool from a tree stump. On all their faces, a smile. Those who live in the shadow of the city do not need the light because their hearts burn brighter than any other in Mirus.

When Cheshire finally reaches the edge of the Crooked Market, he hangs his head and lets loose an exasperated sigh. The Market must be a mile in length at least and stretches from the granite base beneath Stonehaven to his left to the outer wall of Mirus on his right. And worse, every stall except for a dozen, at least from what Cheshire can see, are canvas tents in all shapes, angles, and configurations. High overhead, large panels of stitched canvas stretch from tall, weathered posts to the cliff face and to the city wall, similar to those in the Row. These, however, serve the purpose to keep out the prying eyes of those above rather than the sun.

If he is to search through the Market, it will have to be on foot while stalls and vendors sell to all manner of customers at this forbidden hour. The Crooked Market never sleeps. It received its moniker from those who live in Stonehaven and the Crest and would never be seen in the dregs, the slums, of the city, at least in broad daylight. The impoverished found ways to survive, either by working the hardest manual labors in and out of the city or selling the more peculiar wares often frowned upon by most.

Below, two men leave a shabby dwelling with crates of tools in hand on their way to some job in Stonehaven. They wear boots caked with mud and patched capes dragging in the mud and hoods over their heads. Cheshire is tempted to do the same, but soldiers step out from the shadows between buildings, camouflaged in what little light from the moon reaches down this far. They order the men to remove their hoods and identify themselves before the soldiers will allow them to continue. There are more soldiers in the Boroughs than he first thought.

Oddly enough, another man leaving the Market approaches the same soldiers. He wears a scarlet half-cape and hood, linen shirt, black gloves, and black boots soiled halfway up the shin. He keeps his head lowered and passes by with a box under his arm, unbothered by the soldiers. By his garb, the man in the scarlet cape is from the Crest, and the soldiers did not stop him in order to protect his anonymity.

Cheshire wishes he could walk unbothered, unmolested, by soldiers in these streets, but to do so he would have to be invisible, which is not in his power. He follows the soldiers out of instinct, turning sharply when they reach the border of the Market, continue for some time, and then turn down another side street. Several streets over, a pair of soldiers walk the line between shops and homes, but never enter the Market.

They do not enter the Market. Perhaps there is a way to walk unseen, at least within its confines.

He pulls his mother's sash up over the back of his shoulder and wraps it securely around his mouth and nose, keeping his hood up over his head. His feet squish when he drops into the ankle-deep mud. He walks toward the Market, every step making a wet sucking sound.

"Hey, where did you come from?" a voice from an unseen soldier calls from behind.

Cheshire's heart jumps to his throat.

"Leave him be," says the second soldier. "Let the degenerates alone."

He walks faster, in case they change their mind, and does not slow until he turns several corners into the Market. Even if they followed, they would have a difficult time picking him out of the crowd since every customer in the Market wears their hood—some also wear scarves around their faces to further conceal their identities. Cheshire passes gilded-tipped boots from the Crest, stained overalls of the Forge workers, and the heavy cotton dresses and shirts of the men and women from Stonehaven. No one looks each other in the eye. The Crooked Market is the great equalizer.

He picks a row of stalls and begins the search, passing shops who sell questionable meats and animal parts, teeth and bones from every animal across Wonderland, portent runes, forbidden roots, snake oils and potions claiming to cure the pox, hair grow, and make-a-man's-cock-hard-for-days, and others who dabble in darker oddities. Cheshire's eyes keep a careful watch of every sign he passes. Weasels, letters, fish, swords, but no raven or flames. After four rows, weaving back and forth, he is no closer to finding the one candlemaker he needs. He is not used to searching on foot. The tents and the other swags and canopies limit his sight.

Cheshire makes his way to one of the few wooden structures in the Market, two-stories tall, piercing through the waves of canvas four rows to his right. The structure is derelict at best, and from the look of it, there are remnants of other parts of a building, a home. He looks around and sees the footprint of other structures jutting out of the mud—a piece of a doorframe, a wooden flower bed, a half sunken window. The Borough has eaten itself to make way for the ever-growing Market.

After waiting for a customer in a white robe and hood to pass, Cheshire slips into the jagged hole where a door once stood. Inside, the wood creaks as the building uses the last of its life to remain upright. He climbs the loose planks where the memories of stairs used to be and through a hole to the second floor, and another to the roof, all while the building growls at his added weight. From his perch, a sea of undulating candlelight laps against the dark wooden structure.

It stands to reason these candles may all come from the same candlemaker. And if he or she sells candles this late, their stall would be the brightest. He softens his focus and passes his eyes over the entire Market from end to end. *There.* Half a Market away, the largest and brightest aura shines against the base of Stonehaven.

When he reaches the shop, he finds hundreds of lit candles dancing back and forth unattended, the candlemaker nowhere to be seen. Instead of a canopy, this shop has two wooden walls made of reclaimed wood, lined with shelves. Old crates sit where tables should be, and on them, smaller boxes filled by braided wick candles with a unique wax body— thin powder blue with old runes on them, fat amber with embossed antlers, thin crimson with swirling designs, and pale green with vertical lines. Cheshire pinches the wick of a candle on a shelf. It hisses out, then a second later, flickers back to life.

A workshop area extends into the stone wall, dug out crudely by shovel and hand. Curing candles hang overhead from small hooks imbedded in the rock, while short iron cauldrons of wax bubble and steam in the corner. Dull iron spikes, bent forks, and blunt knives lean against the back wall, and squat glass containers filled with black powders line the back edge of a makeshift table. Unused wicks lie covered in the same black powder in a shallow wooden tray. The scent in the workshop is sharp and stinks of alchemy. It smells different from the black powder from the armory. Though he has had little experience with it, Cheshire has inhaled enough from carrying it around the past few days to recognize the difference.

"What do you think?" asks the elderly candlemaker. He smiles with half a mouth of teeth. Wild sprigs of gray hair jut from the sides of his bald head and from beneath his chin. Scars from burns, an occupational hazard, cover his boney hands and forearms.

Cheshire waited too long. He should have taken a box and walked away, with no one the wiser. The candlemaker must be near eighty years at best. Cheshire could drag him to the back room, smother the old man, and leave him propped up in the shop's corner until someone finds him the next day. At his age, no one would suspect any foul play.

A young boy, no more than ten, peeks out from behind him. The same burn scars cover his fingers. An apprentice.

"Yes," says Cheshire, "they are quite extraordinary."

"Ha," the candlemaker chortles. "Quite extraordinary. Those are fancy words. From the look of you, I would've guessed you were one of us, but that tongue of yours is a dead giveaway." The apprentice fetches a rickety chair from the backroom. The candlemaker holds onto his shaking knees and grunts as he sits. "Gets harder every time. If I didn't have to get up to take a shit, I'd sit all day." He laughs.

The apprentice clears his throat.

"Fine, fine," says the candlemaker. "What can I do for you, you contradiction of a boy?"

Cheshire could still grab a box and run. The old man or his apprentice could not catch him on their best day. But he cannot bring himself to do it.

"Candles."

"No shit." The old man laughs, too loud for Cheshire's liking. After he settles down, he asks, "How many do you need? Height? Color?"

"A half dozen," says Cheshire. "Three inches wide. Color does not matter."

The apprentice walks to a crate behind Cheshire and piles six candles into an empty box, falling apart at the sides.

"Wait." To be clear, Cheshire points to the candle he tested earlier. "I want those candles."

The apprentice looks to his mentor and waits for approval. The candlemaker squints, studying Cheshire's face, then nods, sending the apprentice into the back room. He returns with six plain beige candles stacked in his hands and places them with care into a burlap bag then cinches the top with twine and sets it on the candlemaker's knee.

"Tell me, how do you plan on paying for our work?" He holds onto the sack, hand trembling.

Cheshire has no intention of paying. Even if he wanted to, he has nothing to pay with—nothing the old man would want, anyway. However, perhaps he can pique the interest of the apprentice. The candlemaker's hands shake constantly, too much for the intricate details embossed in all

71

the candles. Perhaps he had the skill in his younger days, but not in his twilight years. The artwork comes from the apprentice. Cheshire glances to the table in the back room at the spikes, forks, and knives used for his artwork.

"From the look of you, I doubt there's any coin in your cloak," says the candlemaker. "So what is your plan?"

Cheshire reaches into one of the inside pockets of his cloak and pulls out the shining compass he took from Pat and Bill's workshop. He holds it point up so the surrounding candlelight can catch its fine point.

"What am I supposed to do with that trinket?"

The apprentice walks closer, eyes wide, as if Cheshire holds a gold piece in his hand. He cautiously takes the compass from Cheshire and inspects the needle-sharp point. He holds it in front of the candlemaker's face with an outstretched arm.

"Damn it." The candlemaker sighs. "Though I'm not sure it's worth six."

The apprentice gently slaps the old man's shoulder and points to the instruments in the backroom.

"Fine, fine. It's a deal," says the candlemaker.

The apprentice smiles at Cheshire, ecstatic, and runs to the back room to place his new tool with the rest.

Cheshire grabs the sack and throws it over his shoulder.

"You know, I've seen many people in my day," says the candlemaker. "From the Boroughs, Stonehaven, even the servants of the rich pieces of shit in the Crest. I've seen repeat customers for years. You, however, are new to me. And your eyes. Your purple eyes... are different."

The hairs bristle on the back of Cheshire's neck, worried he has been discovered. "What of them?"

"I'll say it again." The old man straightens his back. "You are a contradiction. I see both sincerity and ill intent behind them."

"Ill intent. Those are fancy words."

The candlemaker laughs. "You plan to use my artistry for something villainous?"

"And if I am?"

"You'll have no objection from me as long as it takes place outside of the Boroughs. I couldn't give two shits about the goings on of the upper tiers. I have no love for those who live and lord above us. Kill them all. I would see the entire city burn, that is, if stone burned."

"Trust me, stone can burn. And it will. I promise you that."

The candlemaker studies Cheshire's eyes intently then waves his hand to get the apprentice's attention and flashes different sets of fingers, twisting his hands front to back. The young boy brings out seven more candles and holds them out for Cheshire. He unties the sack and lets them drop in.

"Make it an even baker's dozen, then," says the candlemaker. "Make them count."

"Thank you." Cheshire does not know why, but he pulls his mother's sash down to reveal his face.

"Is that supposed to mean something?" The candlemaker wipes his nose.

"No." Cheshire laughs. "But you may see my face again. Commit it to memory."

"Oh, I know who you are, Queen Slayer," the old man says under his breath. "I've seen your face more times on parchment than I've seen mine in a looking glass. Look around. Do you think any of us care? No queens for you to kill down here. Handle your business, but leave us out of it."

Cheshire walks away with the heavy sack slung over his shoulder. He cannot tell if the churning feeling inside his stomach is guilt, pity, or responsibility. Perhaps it is their shared hatred for Mirus which makes Cheshire feel a kindredship toward them, or maybe it is his fondness for broken things. The Boroughs was never an intended target of his vengeance, but if the city burns, all of the city burns. There just may be two fewer people in it when it does.

He hurries back to the same passage which brought him into the Borough, hidden in an old storm drain with a partially bent iron grate. He slides his body back through one of the holes and disappears into the catacombs. Two days remain before the Gryphon's return, and the distance between the wall's armory and the hanging cells is great. He will not sleep the next two nights. Time ticks away, mocking Cheshire. As if he still could. Cheshire will show him. He will show them all.

CHAPTER 8

MARCH

While the morning sun peeks over the mountains, March strolls across the bailey to Dormy's wagon, a double-edged sword on each shoulder and a long dagger strapped to the inside of the leather bracers around both wrists. She climbs through the backdoor and then up to the second level where Dormy sleeps curled on sacks of flour, hugging her knees to her chest.

March kneels beside her and pets the back of Dormy's head. "Wake up, little mouse," March whispers. "I am in need of your company today." A snort and grunt are Dormy's only response. "I shall wait for you outside."

March climbs back down the ladder, grabbing a handful of ripe, crimson strawberries from a basket sitting atop a stack of books. She holds the stem of one, bites it just below the neck, and swirls it in her mouth. Her tongue massages the fruit before crushing it, savoring the tart juice before she chews. She hops from the back of the wagon, and before she can lean against it and eat her second strawberry, Dormy bursts from the back door, impossibly awake.

"I'm ready." Dormy smiles, out of breath. "Where are we off to?"

"The Crest." March holds out the letter for Dormy and watches her read. Her neck jerks forward when she reaches the bottom.

"This is from your mother." Dormy hands the letter back to March. "How exciting."

March's stone expression does not falter.

"How not exciting." Dormy notices the swords on March's back. "Do you wear swords because we are leaving the castle or because you are going to see your mother?"

"I have not decided yet. It depends completely on what happens when we arrive."

Four soldiers stop them as they approach the main gate. The two large simple gatemen are nowhere to be found. The soldiers make a line in front of the small door built into the castle's tall wooden gates.

"We are under strict orders not to let anyone in or out of the castle grounds," says one soldier. "Kindly turn around and return from whence you came."

"No," says March coldly. "Open the gates. We are leaving."

The soldier who spoke looks March up and down. His eyes stop at the belt line of her trousers, low on her waist, then travel up her bare torso to the simple leather top she wears, held on by a single strap around her neck and one around her back. The soldier walks around her, and March can feel his lustful eyes on her back.

"Perhaps you did not hear—"

"I heard. Open the fucking gate before I pin you to them."

"What's a pretty tart like you want to go outside for when you can stay in here with us?" He and the other guards snicker.

"What do you say? Flash us a little tit and we may be persuaded to let you through."

Once the soldier completes his circle, March reaches behind her as if to unbuckle the lower strap of her top. The soldiers jeer and elbow each other with sad little giggles. Unfortunate for them they spent all of their attention on March's breast and stomach instead of the blades on her arms. It all happens before any of the soldiers can react. She unsheathes the daggers at her wrists and thrusts the heel of her boot into the soldier's chest. He stumbles back and clatters against the gate with a great metallic *crack*. March dives forward and buries both daggers deep into the wood, the edges of the blades grazing the soldier's skin, drawing blood. Their hilts press against his neck, trapping him against the wood, restricting his air. The pinned soldier tries to scream, but any flex of his neck causes the daggers to cut deeper.

The other soldiers try to unsheathe their swords, but Dormy's hands are quicker—two pistols from her jacket are pointed at the soldiers' heads before they can break their seals.

March leans closer to the soldier on the door, her mouth next to his ear. "I told you, did I not?" she whispers. "Now, open the door, or I will cut all four of your cocks off and watch you run bleeding through the bailey. Would you like to see if I make good on that promise?"

"Open the door," the soldier says through a shallow inhale, unable to catch his breath. "Open it now."

Two soldiers move quickly and lift the three thick lock bars, while the third pulls the door open, all with shock painted on their faces. These are the men the Gryphon wants her to train. The idea gains favor in her mind. She will remember them and look for them when their training begins. March pulls the daggers from the door and returns them to her wrists. The soldier collapses to his knees, finally taking in a full breath. Dormy returns her pistols to her holsters and follows March through the door without a word, leaving the men confused and embarrassed.

The pair take the first staircase down into the Crest and emerge into opulence, decadence, and sloth. Women and men dressed in their finest white and gold silks and furs gawk at March with shock or disgust, circling wide and whispering as they pass. None have any actual place or purpose to go except to be seen by the others in the Crest.

They follow the curve of the city to the left, pass through the central, small shop area which deals in jewels and clothing too expensive for the Row, and into the white-stone residential manors. Light-gray cobblestone streets, swept to unnatural perfection, lined with tall, slender Juniper trees—this may as well be in a different world. The Crest reminds March of Adamas, the gilded city of Wonderland, secluded on its own island. A city without slum or working class because they are made to live off the mainland, out of sight.

Every step closer to her mother's house releases a nest of hornets inside March, stinging at her gut, infuriating her, pushing her to the point of nausea.

"Are we really going to your mother's?" Dormy asks, failing to hide her excitement.

"Yes."

"Are you... are you going to have tea with her?"

"Absolutely not."

"Are *we* going to have tea with her?"

"Dormy."

"I had to ask. Why, then, would you ask me to join you?"

"I did not want to be alone," March answers simply. She stops shy of the short golden gate at the base of the stairs to her mother's home—the gargantuan white-stone manor, taller and wider than any other in the Crest. The only one with blue domed roofs adorned with golden statues. A palace unto itself for all to see and to let all else know where the real power lies in Mirus.

She hesitates at the gate. *Gold. Wrought iron painted gold.* March takes one of her daggers and chips away a large gold fleck, if for no one else's eyes and satisfaction but her own. She lifts the latch, steps through, and wipes her hand on her trousers. Dormy waits at the threshold, staring up at the roof, mouth open and one nostril snarled.

March walks up the narrow, polished, marble stairs to the front door she wishes she never had to look upon again. She takes hold of the knocker and swings it with as much force as the gold hinge will allow. Each knock echoes in the open hallway on the other side.

Dormy scurries to the side of the manor, a curious look on her brow, and examines something on the second story. "March, wait. You mustn't go inside. Mustn't knock."

The chill in Dormy's voice hits March like the sour note of two dull blades. But it is too late. March already knows what Dormy will say, and the latch pops within the door.

The door swings inward to reveal not her mother, but Uriah, wearing only an ivory silken robe tied loosely low on his waist. He holds a glass bottle of wine in one hand and leans against the door with the other. "I am so glad you received our invitation."

Out of the corner of her eye, March can see Dormy clasp both hands over her mouth. "Where is Bronwen?" asks March.

"So formal." Her mother's voice triggers a sudden urge to stab something. "Is that any way to greet your mother?" She slithers in front of Uriah and ushers him away with a nod. "Thank you for coming, my dear. I see you have come dressed... for tea."

Her mother looks no different from the day March left. Silver hair with pink at her temples in an immaculate bun, even at home. It burns March to the core how much she resembles her mother—the eyes, cheeks, jawline, and full lips, though her mother's must be painted to keep their shape. This would be what she looked like in thirty years if time had not stopped. Even after a thousand years, her mother's beauty has not faded. Neither has March's malice.

"What do you want?" March asks firmly.

"Can you not step inside and have a cup of tea?" Bronwen opens the door wide and holds out an arm.

"No. Never with you. Never with them," says March, with an unwavering stone expression, though her innards twist and jump in all directions. She will not allow her mother to see how much she affects her. "I will not step foot back in this house."

"Oh, I think you will." Every sickly-sweet word from Bronwen equals another hornet's stinger in March's gut. "You will if you want all of this to end."

"Yes, you said this in your letter. Let me help shorten this conversation. No, I will not return home. Nor will I work for you. And I will not accept any charity from you. Just, no."

"Then why did you come, Audrianna? You could have ignored this letter like you have all the others." Her mother plays with the pearl necklace wrapped tight around her neck.

She could have stayed in the castle, burned the letter, and never thought of it again, like all the rest. But she knew Uriah and Lysander were with her mother. Plotting, Scheming. If she and Jonathan are to return to their life together, they must contend with all their adversaries. And she will not cower from them.

"I have a simple proposition for you," her mother says as she reaches out a hand to touch her daughter's shoulder, but March steps out of her reach.

"Like the propositions you and father used to make?"

"Will you at least step in and hear what I have to present?" asks Bronwen. "No one will harm you or touch you in any way inside our home."

"Your house."

"Yes." Bronwen raises an eyebrow and loses her painted smile. "But your friend must wait outside."

Against her better judgment, March concedes. "She will." She glances at Dormy. "And she will raise alarm should I not leave in a timely manner."

Dormy runs down the stairs and waits outside the gate, beyond their reach.

Bronwen sighs. "And what is a timely manner to you?"

"Five minutes." March looks down at Dormy, who nods confirmation.

"Five minutes?" Bronwen clutches her chest and feigns a laugh to cover up even more fraudulent hurt. "Is that all my estranged daughter will allow me?"

"Your candle is burning."

March walks past her mother and into the vast sitting room to the left. Twenty swords, polished and untouched, hang from velvet-covered plaques in the sitting room. Below them, porcelain, silver, gold, and jeweled trinkets cover every inch of hand-carved tables, shelves, and sideboards. The representation of both her father and her mother. The faint chatter of women drifts down from upstairs.

Uriah sits on a couch, one leg propped on his knee and an arm outstretched on its back as if March would sit next to him. Lysander sits opposite, leaning forward, his elbows on his thighs, wearing the same silk robe with nothing underneath. Both do not take their eyes off March's body.

"Have a seat, dear." The foyer is beyond spacious, yet Bronwen chooses to pass by uncomfortably close to March and sits in a gaudily carved chair between the two couches and men. "Sit wherever you like."

"I will stand. Four minutes."

"A lot can be done in four minutes," Lysander growls in an obvious yet failed attempt to be seductive.

March chuckles. "I am sure four minutes is how quickly *you* are done. A combined time between the both of you."

"Perhaps you will find out." The words ooze from Uriah's tongue as he continues to undress her with his eyes.

March turns her attention back to her mother. "What is his proposal?" she asks, but she already knows. This is the reason Uriah and Lysander are present.

Uriah leans forward and pushes his long hair behind one ear. "You wish us to leave the capital."

"You wish us to leave Mary Anne be," adds Lysander. "We will gladly do so."

"If..." says Uriah. A sinister smile grows on his face.

Here it comes.

"If you honor your father's arrangement with us," Uriah continues. His eyes finally raise to meet March's.

"Gods rest his soul," says Bronwen.

"You were meant to be ours after all," says Lysander. "That was the deal struck."

Bronwen sits back in her chair, ankles crossed, holding her tea and saucer in one hand, stirring with the other. The tiny silver spoon clinks out of rhythm against the porcelain. Though her head tilts down, she stares daggers into March from below her brow. This was her plan all along. Every letter sent was not to inquire about March's health or wellbeing, but to complete a business transaction.

There should be some feeling in March, but the stings, the anger, the nausea, are gone. She is numb. This house taught her how to turn off every emotion, and now she must do so for her own sanity.

Lysander leans forward. "Your father—"

March will not let Lysander vomit up another word. "Your business dealings with my father were for weaponry. Four hundred pounds worth of gold, if my memory serves me correctly."

"From the best weapons dealer in all of Wonderland," says Lysander.

"Warmonger," bites March.

"That is what we paid for," Lysander continues. "In addition to you. You were to be the gift your father gave us for our purchase."

"Sure, it was only to be one night"—Uriah leans back on the couch again—"but how could we only have a taste of your beauty, your body. We made arrangements with your mother for our time with you to be extended indefinitely, to uncork your cask and drink our fill of you every night. And our thirst is insatiable." He unties his robe and lets it hang open, revealing his entire body, his cock growing.

March wants to laugh outright at his arrogance, his conceit. "You speak as if I do not know this already," says March.

"Of course not," says Uriah looking at Bronwen, "but if I am not mistaken, the night we were to take you, bed you, was the night you ran away from Mirus, never to be heard from in this city again."

"I am sure you can see why we would take offense to this." Lysander sits back, matching Uriah. "Since your father gave you to countless other dealers before us, we only expect the most reputable family in all of Wonderland to hold true to their word."

"So, leave with us. Now. This day," says Uriah, "and we will turn our backs to this city and whatever dealings the Duchess tries to keep hidden in the castle."

"Or just let them both bed you here and now. They will still leave Mirus." Bronwen sets down her tea. "The choice is yours. The choice is simple."

"Your time is up." March turns and walks to the front door.

"Do you really want to do this?" Lysander asks without standing. "Do you really want to be responsible for what will happen to this city if we stay?"

March turns back. The numbness fades, but she clings to it like a piece of driftwood, as if she were lost in the open ocean. She calms the shaking muscles of her neck. "Do you think I care what happens to this repugnant city? I turned my back on this city and this family long ago. Burn it all down. Start with this house." She looks at her mother one last time. "And make sure she is in it when you start the blaze."

She turns, but she does not remember opening the door, descending the stairs, or opening the gate. She becomes aware as she walks through the streets of the Crest. Dormy has a tight grip on March's hand and arm.

Was it worth it? March asks herself. She now knows for certain Uriah and Lysander are in league, and probably in bed, with her mother. They already have their claws deep in the city; no telling how many citizens of Mirus honor the old line of kings. And her mother has sway over most of, if not all, of Stonehaven and the Crest since she holds the biggest purse strings which keep the city and treasury funded. Combined, their influence will prove problematic.

She does not speak or look anywhere except her next step the entire climb back to the castle. Once through the gates and in the bailey, she tries to pull from Dormy to return to her bedchamber, eyes filled with tears, jaw shaking. But Dormy keeps a firm grip on March's arm and pulls her into the wagon, knowing March will not make it back to the main doors, let alone her bedchamber.

As soon as the rear door shuts, March slumps to the floor, back against it. She knocks the back of her head against its wood and raises her eyes up at a net full of fruit hanging above. She tightens her lips to keep them from quivering. Tears pour down her cheeks like freshly melted snow on a mountainside. However, she will utter no sound for her mother, for her father.

Dormy sits next to March and gently lays March's head on her shoulder.

But was it worth it? she repeats. This day will be another hurt, another scar, she will shine away like the blemish on any one of her swords. The swords of the men her father sold her to. The same swords she killed them with. The very swords she will use to train the new army of Wonderland.

CHAPTER 9

MARY ANNE

Mary Anne follows the Chamberlain down a staircase to a lower level of the castle she has not yet ventured, devoid of windows, art, and fresh air. This area of the castle seems older, less frequented than others. The heel of her boot slides off a portion of a missing stair broken long ago, and she catches herself on the wall, almost dropping the Book of Queens, but she cannot stop the quick gasp from escaping her mouth.

"Of all the things I will ask you to do, Mary Anne"—Chamberlain Weiss, several steps ahead, turns back to check on her, pointing their only source of light, a candelabra, at her—"first and foremost is to not die whilst on my watch." He starts his descent again once Mary Anne has collected herself. "Do so with Jonathan or anywhere else in the castle, but not with me. The pain would be too much to bear," he says, the slow sarcasm in his tone as obvious as the candles in the darkness.

The Chamberlain has made every effort, against his own preference, to move Mary Anne's lesson out of his study. It all amounts to a grand tour of the castle, but it is a welcome change compared to the boredom she has endured.

"Gods take you," Chamberlain Weiss screams in a high octave.

Mary Anne's heart jumps, thinking it could be any number of enemies or dangers. She peers around the Chamberlain's tall thin person to discover Pat and Bill waiting by a set of hammered, wrought-iron doors. Upon them must be dozens, if not hundreds, of keyholes and etched lines covering its surface. The stones of the ceiling, floor, and walls around the door are darker than the rest of the corridor. The remnants of black scorch marks, scars from something in the past, explode out in jagged points.

The Chamberlain takes the fan from within his robe to air his face but grumbles when the candles flicker. "Can you not skulk in the darkness, at least?" Weiss adjusts his collar and pockets his fan. "Wear a bell or something."

"You instructed us to meet you here," says Pat.

"Here we are," says Bill.

They regard him with little expression, ceremony, or circumstance, treating the Chamberlain as an equal rather than a superior. They walk farther into the candlelight, and their sweat and dirt-covered arms, shoulders and chests shine. Mary Anne has not yet grown accustomed to the clothes they wear while they work in the castle, though to see them is a sporadic occurrence. Today they wear what looks like dirty corduroy overalls cut low at the waist, tucked into their clunky boots, and belts with several leather pouches hang around their waists. Neither wears any kind of shirt, not even Pat, with the sides of her breasts exposed to the world. Mary Anne blushes, embarrassed for her choice of clothing.

However, Chamberlain Weiss does not bat an eye. "Come on, come on." He waves at them with his left hand awkwardly then switches the candelabra to free his right hand and hurry them properly.

Mary Anne watches the clunky ring of keys which hang from Pat and Bill's belts and wonders which will open such a door. To her surprise, they use none.

Their hands glide upon the metal work of the door, synchronized but mirrored with each other. Together their fingers find and press buttons concealed within the designs of the metal work. If Mary Anne saw this door in the brightest sunlight, she doubts she would see them. Pat and Bill move their hands slowly over the door, almost caressing it, together but always opposite. Thirteen movements, twenty-six buttons in all. With each press of the invisible buttons, the dull sound metal grinding against metal builds within the door until the last rings with a deep metallic clunk.

Pat and Bill push the door open and a burst of wind, the castle's breath, hits them all. Mary Anne's dress and the Chamberlain's robes flap for a moment and then fall back to stillness. They both grab a candle from the candelabra and light torches with metal cages around them hung from the wall. With each additional torch they light, the room, no, the museum, before Mary Anne takes shape. Wide stone staircases lead down to different stone platforms, disappearing into the dark. Dozens of square and circular pedestals line the perimeter of the section she stands on alone, and they continue on each platform below, as far as she can see. Most are empty, but there are some artifacts on a select few.

"Behold. The Reliquary," Pat and Bill say together.

"There are three types of magic, as you so commonly put it, in Wonderland." Chamberlain Weiss walks farther into the room. "First, you have potions and alchemy. More science than magic, but what can be done with the correct mixture of chemicals can be quite astounding. Second, and most potent, are the powers of the queen. A queen possesses what we refer to as the Grand Arcana—the old magic. She is the only one who can wield it. No other person in all of Wonder, man or woman, great or small, can access it."

Mary Anne remembers the Duchess's words on top of the castle's highest tower. She said the first queen gained magic to overthrow her grandfather who sat upon the throne. With the previous attacks on her life, the talk of magic faded from Mary Anne's thoughts, but since the Chamberlain brought it up, she wants to know more.

"No one? What of the kings before?" asks Mary Anne. "What made the queen different?"

"No one. And no one knows. This makes a queen unique, powerful, and dangerous. Queen Dinah was the first. She stumbled upon the Book of Queens in this very chamber some levels down. By doing so, she found the means to become queen, depose her grandfather, overcome his armies, and usher in a period of great peace and prosperity for all, despite those who speak to the contrary."

A single woman changed the country. And they praised her for it. At least by most. How different a world this is than my own. A fleeting idea drifts into Mary Anne's thoughts. *Why should I return to a world where I face resistance at every turn, when I could be a queen here?* She shakes the thought from her head. She cannot leave her mother, Thomas, and everything she has built. Besides, even though she faces her fair share of opposition in England, there is no one there trying to kill her.

"What will I be able to do when I become queen?" she asks.

"I cannot say. The Grand Arcana manifests differently to each queen. But this is all the fourth Tenet." Chamberlain Weiss sniffs the air sharply to punctuate his point. "Pointless to discuss it any further until you at least complete the second Tenet."

March. If Mary Anne can convince March to aid her, to translate the latter chapters in the Book of Queens, perhaps this would expedite the process to become queen and the journey home. If the Chamberlain will not help her, she will make her own way.

"What of the third?" she asks, rather than rebuffing his uncalled-for snide comment.

"The third is why we are here. Long before our time, in the first Age of Wonderland, the Old Ones reigned. Some call them divine, while others say they were merely sorcerers. Either way, they vanished without a trace except for one or two mentions in ancient tomes, and their Arcana remains in the relics they left behind." He picks up a purple and gold mask from its wooden stand on one pedestal. "They created these objects and imbued them with power. Some are simple, some more complex. Some meant for good, others... debatable." He places the mask over his face and disappears completely from sight.

Mary Anne's jaw drops. Never has she seen a sight so beautiful yet so frightening. The candles on Jonathan's table were simple yet unexplainable. The Duchess's words made Wonderland sound like a fairytale or a book of fantasy. But to witness magic, real magic, with her own eyes, defies all logic and proves nothing can be impossible here.

The Chamberlain removes the mask from his face, and he reappears as if a mist cleared the room. Then he places it back on its pedestal. "Each and every one of these relics has a different use. Many are lost to time, but the ones we do have in our collection are kept here, their power too dangerous to let out into the world. As you may have noticed from the marks on the face of the door, attempts at forceful entry have been made in the past before the castle was as secure as it is now. Thankfully, to no avail. The Arcana protects this chamber as well, it would seem."

"We can get rid of the marks, but he will not let us," says Pat as she walks down the stairs to a lower platform veiled in darkness.

"No," says the Chamberlain with a dramatic spin. "They must stay as a reminder to anyone else who dare try to enter the Reliquary. Many have tried and failed."

"Silly," says Bill under his breath.

"Our lesson today is simple, Mary Anne," the Chamberlain continues. "You want something to work toward, a visible, tangible goal instead of a far-off fantasy. The Grand Arcana is very real." He walks to a different pedestal and picks up a white feather quill. With a flick of his wrist, letters made of light appear and hang in the air.

"Wondrous," says Mary Anne. She looks around the room at each pedestal. Every relic appears to be a normal trinket or everyday item. Across the room, a golden necklace hangs from a wooden cross, a dusty book lies flat five pedestals to the right, the base of an old broom made of twigs farther down, and a plank of wood farther still. She wonders what other items lie even farther down in the depths of the Reliquary.

The Chamberlain waves his hand through the letters to erase them as if they never existed and replaces the quill. "Hopefully, this will serve as inspiration enough. Let us return to the study to continue your lessons."

"Wait, please," says Mary Anne. The light from the candelabra catches the curves of two identical pearlescent rings, one white and one black, on the pedestal neighboring the quill Mary Anne thought empty until now. "These are more than beautiful."

"Yes," says Chamberlain Weiss. "Quite deceiving. They are not mere bobbles. They are tools for interrogation, methods of torture."

"How?"

The Chamberlain huffs, wanting to continue the lesson elsewhere. "From what we have learned," he points to the white ring, "this ring is to be worn by the prisoner to be tortured. The second goes on a separate person, separate prisoner, to whom the torture actually happens. The wearer of the white ring feels any sensation, any pain inflicted on the wearer of the black ring. Quite ingenious, actually. Torture can last hours, days, or weeks without killing the prisoner. It may not end so pleasantly for the person on the other end. Then again, that person could just be replaced with another should they happen to die, as long as they wore the ring."

Mary Anne has given up trying to use logic in Wonderland, but perhaps this time her logic could be to her advantage. *The Chamberlain said the ring wearer would feel every sensation, which does not mean the rings are limited to pain. Pleasure is another sensation altogether, but a sensation none-the-less.* She positions herself with her back to the pedestal with the quill and leans in for a closer look at the rings. Her hip grazes the pedestal behind her and it begins to wobble. The quill rocks back and forth, about to fall to the floor.

Chamberlain Weiss spins and wraps a long arm around the pedestal to keep it from toppling. Mary Anne quickly sets the Book of Queens down on an empty pedestal and slaps the quill to keep it from rolling to the floor. A small spurt of light spits from the end like ink.

"You clumsy woman." He stands and straightens his robe. "Of all places. You can maneuver through the stacks of books and parchment in my study without incident, but near a pedestal half your height, you become inept?"

As Pat returns, the Chamberlain orders her and Bill to douse the torches, which they do expeditiously, starting at the far end and waiting by the chamber doors.

"I am sorry," she says, clasping her hands in front of her. "The thrill of this place overpowered my better senses. You took the time and effort out of your day to show me something wonderful, and I did not show the proper respect to these relics or to you. I apologize thoroughly."

The Chamberlain raises an eyebrow at the unexpected compliment. "Yes. Yes, I did. Be sure to do better on our next excursion. If there should be one." He turns with a dramatic flap of his robe and exits the Reliquary.

Mary Anne follows quickly, her heart drumming against her chest. Before she follows the Chamberlain up the stairs, she watches to make sure Pat and Bill pull the heavy door shut and listens for the locks to clang shut.

"Forgive me, Chamberlain Weiss."

He hangs his head at the tone of her voice, like a father pushed past the limit of patience with his child.

"I placed my book down to save the quill..."

The Chamberlain's eyes grow wide, and his neck stretches toward Mary Anne. "And you left it? How careless can you be?"

"I leave it in my room all the time or the dining table when I eat. I always keep it with me. This is the first door I have encountered which is locked."

He gestures frantically to Pat and Bill to open the doors once again.

"I do apologize," Mary Anne tells them.

"No need," they say together, and begin their dance upon the door again.

This time, Mary Anne studies their every movement, height, distance from the middle seam, arm length and angle, which finger they use to press each button. Upon closer study, the markings on the door are identical yet mirrored, so it would stand to reason the location of a button on one door would be the exact same on the other. Thankfully, they move slowly, allowing Mary Anne time to repeat the pattern in her head to commit it to memory.

Mary Anne steps inside as soon as Pat and Bill push the door open again. "I will retrieve it."

"Do you not need candlelight?" the Chamberlain asks.

"No, sir. I do not want to trouble you anymore." The dim light from outside is not enough to spot the black book in the dark room. However, the light from the pin, though fading, still hangs in the air and shows her the location of the pedestal with the quill. She walks quickly, her footsteps matching the rhythm of her racing heart. With her left hand, she picks up the Book of Queens while she grips the rings with her right. The loose spine of the book and its missing pages allows some extra space, so she drops both rings inside the front cover, and holds the book tight under her arm.

All she can hear as she leaves the Reliquary is her heartbeat and her swallows, which stick in her throat. But when the doors shut and lock again, she lets out a sigh of relief.

She has never stolen anything in her life, but some primal urge took control of her faculties, and she was helpless to stop her actions. While Chamberlain Weiss saw nothing, there is the chance Pat and Bill might have, though they have said nothing. Mary Anne hopes her theory about the rings is correct, and she can feel every pleasure March experiences. If not, she knows the pattern to the doors and can return them without anyone the wiser.

CHAPTER 10

CHESHIRE

T he ninth day. In the hanging cells.

The soldier regains consciousness. His groggy bloodshot eyes struggle to open—one then the other—until his pupils focus on the wavering darkness before him. He grits his teeth and squints, veins thick on his temples from the pressure of blood rushing to his head. He chokes on the dirty, bloody gag in his mouth as panic sets in and thrashes in his binds, but the coarse ropes only dig deeper into his wrists and ankles. Bound and suspended upside down, naked, from one of the Mirusian hanging cells, he cranes his neck backward to look down into the abyss where the pit full of centuries-old piss and shit festers in a thick quagmire far below. Its putrid warm air wafts up and gags him.

His eyes dart above his feet to the platform with the control levers to look for aid, his companions, any soldier still standing, but there are none. When he notices the black shadow hanging from the cell in front of him, he jerks his head back and locks eyes with the dark figure in the dim warm candlelight.

Cheshire hangs down also, without clothing, feet hooked through the square holes of the iron cell's grated floor, to welcome the soldier to his upside down world. The world he knows he controls. He holds a candle right-side up in one hand—the thinnest trail of smoke snaking its way down past their feet—and plays with a handful of silver coins from the soldier's purse in the other, shifting them in his palm. Cheshire drops one coin after another until none remain, each spinning up past his head and into the darkness. The soldier's eyes follow them upward and watch as the small glints of light reflecting off the silver disappear into the pit above.

Even in the darkness, Cheshire senses the look of recognition in the soldier's eyes, stretched wide with horror. The soldier tries to scream but only mumbles through his rough gag.

"Queen Slayer," the soldier gargles, almost incoherent. The veins around his eyes and neck bulge like worms under a thin layer of soil.

"There really is no need to shout," Cheshire tells the struggling soldier. "Anyone who could hear you and come to your aid is already in attendance." Cheshire turns his head to the right to lead the soldier's gaze. Fourteen other soldiers, still dressed, bound in the same fashion, hang from the other nearby iron cells; twelve by their feet, two by their necks, dead. Each lured in one by one throughout the night.

Cheshire pushes against the soldier's forehead with a finger and starts him swaying back and forth. "You are the fortunate man to be closest to my measurements. Or unfortunate, depending on how you view the situation."

The soldier tries to reposition the gag in his mouth and whistle with his tongue to alert the hounds outside the jail, but he only manages a few feeble, garbled puffs of breath, saliva dripping up his face.

"No good either, I fear," Cheshire says. "They are streets away, gnawing on a choice cut of beef from a butcher in the Row. It seems hungry mongrels are not so loyal. Never cared for dogs."

Had Cheshire thought of this plan weeks ago, there would not have been a need to walk miles in the shit-filled tunnels beneath the jail. But on the other hand, had he not, then he would never have discovered the secret entrance built by Pat and Bill, which granted him access this second time. He never thanked them for their help. When he sees them again after today, Cheshire will need to apologize for what he is about to do.

The bound soldier twists side to side as he sways, trying to call to the other unconscious soldiers, but soon realizes his attempts are futile and turns his attention to the out-of-place lit candles dangling through the bottom of each cell floor, including his own.

"Admiring my work?" Cheshire smirks. "Curious, is it not? I have no doubt this will impress you. I impressed myself when I thought of it." He tosses the upside-down candle he holds back and forth between hands. The soldier squirms. "You see, from what I gather, the cesspool beneath us would be quite flammable, and the centuries of putrid fumes down there would probably cause quite a fire if a stray flame ever made its way down into the depths. But a fire is not enough. Not nearly enough. Which is why I have carefully spread twenty-five barrels of black powder down there amongst the shit, piss, and bones."

Cheshire tosses the candle into the air, catches it between his thumb and forefinger, and gently swings it back and forth.

The soldier screams but gags himself on the cloth in his mouth. He thrashes side to side, wrenching his shoulders and contorting his entire body as he tries to pull his arms free of their binds. The cell he hangs from jerks violently as he struggles. The large metal chain rattles and grinds against itself.

"I have always thought this world to be a cruel place," says Cheshire. "So I say it is high time we departed this miserable life. Consider this me setting you free. Ironic, is it not?" He lets the candle slip from his fingers. Both he and the soldier follow the flame into the darkness.

The soldier screams at the candle as if he could will it to stop its descent. But his outburst is for naught. The flame of the wick puffs out from the fall, and the candle tumbles into the darkness.

What Cheshire first thought to be sweat turns out to be piss trickling up the soldier's face. He shakes his head to keep it from his nose and mouth, then weeps, his chest and head bobbing back and forth.

"The candles you normally use would never survive the fall. Same with the braziers," says Cheshire. "They blow out before they ever reach the bottom. Smart." Cheshire does not give the soldier Time to relax. "So I brought my own."

He points to the candles dangling from six other cells. Each has two rusted nails pushed through the smooth wax with a length of twine running up through two square openings of the cell floor, to two more nails pushed into another candle sitting within the cell.

"All these candles are special and do not extinguish so easily, no matter how hard you try to snuff them out," Cheshire says, eyes full of playful ferocity. "Once the candles in the cells melt past the point of the nails, the hanging candle will fall and twist and flip through the air all the way down to the muck and mire. Then *boom*. From my measure, I believe there is less than half an hour remaining in the wax. Give or take. It took me some Time to get them all lit; no telling which one will fall first," says Cheshire, to torment the soldier.

The soldier's body falls slack, resigned to his inevitable fate, and he sobs through the cloth gag, trying to speak.

Cheshire huffs, swings over to the soldier, and pulls the gag from his mouth. "What do you want? Make it count."

"Please," the soldier says, choking on his own snot. "I have a wife."

Cheshire tilts his head and studies the soldier's face. For a moment, through the tears, swollen brow, and dried blood, he sees the man for who he is: handsome, clean cut, more than likely in his third decade on the earth, give or take a millennium. Cheshire imagines the soldier walking down an exterior staircase to the rear door of his small basement dwelling in Stonehaven. The soldier's wife opens the door to greet him with a warm smile, though her face blurs in his mind. The soldier removes his helmet and sits with her at a meager wooden table to enjoy a warm meal of chicken stew while they laugh and smile at one another. But as they speak, the wife's face twists, stretches, and contorts, transforming into the face of Cheshire's mother—her soft face solemn, her deep purple eyes holding back reservoirs at their edge.

To his horror, the skin on his mother's face dries, cracks, and deteriorates. The purple hair on her head falls to the ground, her lips peel back, and her eyes shrivel and disappear into the dark sockets of her skull. Cheshire blinks and shakes his head violently to rid his mind of the horrifying image.

"Please. I have a wife," the soldier repeats.

Cheshire resurfaces, reaches up, and grabs onto the bottom of the grate to turn himself right side up. A tingling sensation like pins and needles pours down from the top of his head and travels to the rest of his body with a shiver. He looks the soldier in the eye with cold, hard resolution.

"And I had a mother," he seethes through a grin dripping with darkness, the same darkness filling his eyes. "And you lot did nothing to prevent or stop her death."

"Please," the soldier weeps. "Please. This isn't right."

"No, it isn't."

"You... you are a monster."

Cheshire shoves the gag back into the soldier's mouth. "I am what you created. All of you."

He leaves the soldier to his muffled cries and climbs up the cell, its chain, and across the ceiling of wooden and metal gears back to the platform with the control levers. Before he leaves, he gathers the soldier's armor, helmet, clothing, and boots, which he left wrapped tightly in a black wool cape on the platform. He slings the bundle over his shoulder, walks from the room, through the short stone hallway, and pushes open the main black-iron doors of the jail.

The city air feels heavy and warm, even on a crisp morning. A hint of dawn brightens the sky over the mountains on the other side of the city wall. The hard caw from crows somewhere within the city, and the distant, nearly inaudible, clangs of hammer on anvil from the Forge are the only signs of life. There are no nearby leaves to rustle, nor birds to sing, not even the scampering of a rodent, as if Mirus itself stifles all life from everyone within its walls.

He crosses the cobblestone road and follows a narrow alleyway between the rear of two stacked wooden houses. The woman of the house to the left, dressed in her night shirt and kerchief, opens the top half of her rear door to empty a chamber pot into the street and gasps when she lays eyes on Cheshire. She does not scream, cry for help, or signal she has encountered the Queen Slayer. It would be impossible for her to recognize him either way since her eyes never leave his groin. He snickers and continues down the alley, still feeling her eyes watching him walk away.

After turning down two more corners, the alley dead ends underneath a stone staircase leading up to the next level of Stonehaven. After making sure no eyes are upon him, Cheshire places his hands on two smooth hexagonal stones in the wall—one at the height of his eyes, the other near his waist, invisible to anyone else who does not think to look for them—and presses them both at the same time. A series of muffled clicks emanate from behind the stones and a thin door a few paces down the wall springs open. Cheshire slips into the city's catacombs, pulls the door closed behind him, and listens to the tumblers reset and lock.

He drops the soldier's armor next to the bundle of his own clothing and a bucket of water and scrub brush he stole from the city stables and left here before venturing into the sewer to sneak into the jail. The hard bristles leave his skin red and raw as he washes the layers of shit off his legs. He scrubs the rest of his body to get rid of the lingering smell, using his hands for the more sensitive areas, then unfurls his clothing, laces his tattered trousers back around his waist followed by his mother's purple sash, dons his cloak and vest, and finally straps his fingerless leather gloves back to his wrists.

Cheshire stares at the soldier's bundle and snarls his lip, dreading the thought. He unties the soldier's cape and quickly lays the armor and clothing out on the floor, as if the body within them vanished. Dark leather pants, heavy black boots, unpolished greaves, a rough linen shirt, long-sleeve chain mail, breastplate, gauntlets, helmet, and the cape underneath it all. This is more clothing than he has worn in over a thousand years. And the boots. There is little Cheshire cannot recall, but the last time he wore shoes or boots of any kind is a memory lost to Time. He licks the roof of his mouth, as if to get rid of a foul taste, huffs, and slips the soldier's clothing and armor over his own. He shifts and stretches, unaccustomed to the weight of armor and the texture of the long trousers and shirt, a foreign layer of skin against his own.

"Two rights, one left, and up," he says to himself as he races down the dark catacombs beneath Mirus.

He runs through the empty tunnels, his hand following along the wall on his right side, and wishes for some form of discarded decoration or ornament—a painting frame, candle holder, or even a boot, like the catacombs outside the city—to break the monotony of the blank stone walls. But these tunnels functioned as escape routes, not for casual travel, so there is little to be found within them.

His path stops at a circular shaft leading skyward, and an iron ladder rising high, stabbing the dark. He climbs what he figures must be at least two hundred feet, fighting against the soldier's clunky boots, which both almost slip off and get caught on the rungs of the ladder. In another scenario, he could have dressed after coming down, though Time would most assuredly be against him then. Cheshire suffers the clumsy climb until the ladder stops next to a small alcove in the stone wide enough for a large man to stand in. He steps in with room to spare. He pulls at the collar of the guard's tunic and breastplate and stretches his neck in all directions.

"Fuck it all," he shouts. His words echo as they bounce their way down the stone cylinder.

He searches the wall with both hands and finds a thick stone latch the size of a normal mason's brick. Cheshire turns it, stone scraping stone, then pulls open a porthole just larger than his head high in the city wall disguised as bricks. From this vantage point, he will be able to witness the fruits, the chaos, of his labors with no one the wiser. He gazes up at the castle, its looming visage, and his heart aches, and his body yearns for Jonathan and March's touch. It has been torture to know they have been so close, staying in the castle, where he could have so easily visited them to satisfy all three of their needs and desires, be they emotional or physical.

Cheshire grips the edge of the porthole and waits. If the Gryphon has indeed recovered, he will have no choice but to respond to the blow about to be dealt to the Duchess. This city, the city which turned a blind eye to him and his mother, the city that forgot the truth, will soon taste his grief, and afterward, the Duchess shall choke upon it.

CHAPTER 11

JONATHAN

M arch fastens each buckle and secures two leather belts with four scabbards and swords around her waist. She wears the teal fustian top she wore in Briarwell—the small triangles centered on each breast and tied around her with thin leather straps—a sign to Jonathan she will not escape a fray. He holds her brown leather gambeson jacket, cut high under the arm, for her to slip into, then helps secure the final two scabbards to her back.

Jonathan, with her taste still on his lips, drinks in her strength and beauty and continues their morning escapade for a fourth time.

Though she will not show any reaction, Jonathan has enough excitement for them both. This morning, the Gryphon will make his triumphant return to the public, with March at his side to introduce her to the battalions she will train, and Jonathan will be there to support her in any way she desires.

"Wipe that silly look from your face," she says.

Jonathan cannot keep his pride for her contained. He does share the concern she tries to hide behind her jeweled eyes. March has never wanted to be the center of attention, unless she places herself there for a strategic purpose, and now she finds herself thrust into it.

Jonathan slips on his blue gambeson tunic, and March buckles the leather straps on his left side from the bottom up to his neck, except for the top two. She fumbles through another large leather trunk and brings Jonathan a thin metal vial, smaller than his little finger, and slips it into a hidden pocket on the inside of his trousers, since there is no place for his normal flask on his person and no telling when he will have time to come back to their room.

It is bound to be one of those days. She shrugs.

He kisses her on the forehead. "I will meet you downstairs, my love. You will be marvelous." He looks to her lowered eyes and does not move until she meets his gaze and nods.

Jonathan steps outside his bedchamber where Mary Anne waits for him, poised, relaxed, and with a genuine smile. The sharp sound of iron and steel clattering together rings from within the room. He finds humor in the little ways March shows her distaste for Mary Anne.

"Shall we?" Jonathan extends an arm toward the end of the hallway. He walks by her side as they descend the spiral staircase. Jonathan notices her movements are smoother, regal, almost to the point of gliding down the stairs. Her training with Weiss has actually proven beneficial.

Out of the corner of his eyes, he notes Mary Anne continues to glance at him out of the corner of hers. Jonathan chuckles and twists the tip of his pommel with his fingers. As they walk, he can see the thoughts churning in Mary Anne's mind clear on her face. There is a thought held at bay on the tip of her tongue, wishing desperately to take the leap past her lips.

"Is something on your mind?" he asks.

Mary Anne blushes and looks down one of the long corridors, not knowing her face would betray her thoughts.

"Forget I asked," says Jonathan. "It was not my place. I should not pry."

"But it is your place." Mary Anne sighs and stops on the stairs. "You are my advisor. And dare I say, friend. Yet, there are thoughts and issues of my own I fear I cannot tell you."

"Mary Anne, do not be silly. Anything you wish to ask, ask it."

She takes a deep breath as if preparing to impart some terrible news. "You and March," she begins slowly, "have not slept in your room these past nights." Her fluster overtakes her words. "Not that I pay attention or mind."

"Ah," says Jonathan. "Forgive me. I should have mentioned. March and I needed fresh air, so we have slept outside. We are not used to sleeping surrounded by stone walls, you see."

"Will you return to your room tonight?" she asks.

"I think March fairs better outdoors, away from the confines of the castle. But I promise to meet you every morning."

"Oh," is Mary Anne's only response. One word, one sound, dripping with disappointment.

Jonathan hides his smile better than Mary Anne. He wants to feign ignorance, but from the blush on her face and the way she looks at him, he can see the longing in her eyes, the void she must feel without physical touch. She spoke of a man she was intimate with back in her world, but if Mary Anne wants to speak more on the matter, she will do so on her own time and of her own accord.

"I have something to show you before we join everyone." He steers the conversation back to today's events to pull Mary Anne from her own thoughts. He offers his arm and escorts her to the front doors of the castle, by the longest route possible, first passing by the kitchen.

The warm aroma of freshly baked bread and the sweet scent of sliced fruit fills the hallway, and Jonathan can feel the heat from the ovens before he even reaches the door. He pops his head around the corner to see the women who work in the kitchen, eight in all, kerchiefs tight and faces and hands covered with flour, humming as they knead mountains of dough. With the head cook nowhere in sight, Jonathan walks in and swipes two scones brushed with melted butter, still hot from the oven, from a table near the doorway. He winks at the women and raises the scones up to say thank you. They laugh and shoo him away to carry on with their work.

Jonathan and Mary Anne walk through one endless hallway after another, one of hundreds which look identical to every other passage in the castle—towering stone walls with ribbed-vaulted ceilings high above, silver candelabras as tall as any man, polished to perfection spaced out along their lengths, thick vibrant woven tapestries held up by iron bars with swirling knobs at their ends high overhead. On the walls without tapestries hang grand paintings by Wonderland's premiere artists. But be they countryside, shore, mountain, castle, or forest, all are painted with a mysterious and melancholy chiaroscuro technique. Pathos fills every brush stroke.

Out of the corner of Jonathan's eye, he notices Mary Anne slyly glance up to his mouth every time he takes a bite of his scone, and then quickly returns to her own. He cannot help but smile more and more with each bite as they walk. Perhaps it is a bit wicked of him, but if something as simple as eating can bring a smile to her face, why not continue?

They reach a large hexagonal chamber, which has not seen visitors in some time. The torches and oil lamps on the white pillars hang cold, and if not for the dawn creeping down diagonally through the small arched windows high above, the room would sit in darkness.

Jonathan finds a striking stone on a small marble pedestal next to the entrance and ignites the torches. One by one, the room fills with warm amber light. Cracked looking glasses placed behind the torches spread the light and illuminate the three towering marble statues—the reason for this detour.

"As thrilling as Weiss's lectures are, I thought you might enjoy a change. Behold," Jonathan says with dramatic flair and a deepened voice, pointing to the center statue of the Gryphon. "This morning, you will see the Gryphon returned to all his glory. He is one of the three legendary heroes of Wonderland's history. We are fortunate to have him with us now."

The stonemason's work is impeccable. They captured each detail of the Gryphon's fearsome appearance—the scowl concealed within his thick braided beard and long mustache, the long hair cascading over his pauldrons, the raised points of his eyebrows, and his height. Even in stone, he towers over the other two statues.

A reverent silence overtakes the chamber, overpowering the small crackles and pops of the torches. Jonathan finds a knot growing in his throat. The Gryphon has returned. Perhaps this trip to Mirus was fated to happen. If he did not stumble upon Mary Anne, Cheshire would not have followed them into the city, and the Gryphon would have remained imprisoned and presumed dead. Despite Cheshire's unexpected meddling, he may have changed the tide for them all, though it is too premature to tell, and Jonathan will give no hope to the thought just yet.

"Who are the others?" Mary Anne whispers, scared to break the silence.

"Wonderland did not have many heroes, but this triumvirate, Duncan the White Paladin, Quinn the Rook, and the Gryphon, general of Wonderland's armies, were enough to defend the Queendom and inspire hope in the people of Wonderland. The Sword, the Shadow, and the Stratagem are how they are referred to by the common folk like myself in song and tale. The White Paladin was the weapon to cut down any enemy, Quinn was unrivaled in infiltration and reconnaissance, a ghost, and the Gryphon was, is, a master strategist. Their feats are as countless as the leaves on every tree in Wonderland."

"Where are they now?" asks Mary Anne. "If the Gryphon is one of this trio, could we call upon the others to fight at his side, our side, once more?"

"Gone."

Jonathan raises his eyes to the statue of the White Paladin. He stands a full head shorter than the Gryphon, but his powerful jaw, short wild hair, and intense gaze rivals the Gryphon's. The sharp corners of his armor—his pauldrons, gauntlets, and chest plate—catch the firelight and shine as if they were iron instead of marble. And his sword, the Vorpal sword, whose point touches the floor, stands twice Jonathan's height.

Quinn's statue and smooth visage match the Gryphon and the White Paladin's in severity, except with sad eyes, immortalized in stone. The stonemasons captured the soft curves of this sleeveless cloak he wore over his armor. The wavering light almost gives the illusion of the stone moving as if it actually were fabric in a breeze.

"The Age of Heroes in Wonderland ended a long time ago," Jonathan continues. "From the stories spread through Wonderland, they all disappeared on separate missions and were thought dead. But this is all rumors. No one knows for sure."

"How can the Age of Heroes be over if one is in this very castle with us?" Mary Anne steps forward to bring Jonathan's eyes back down from the statues. "If one lives, then perhaps it is possible the others are alive somewhere as well. Nothing is impossible. Is that not right?"

As often as he has told Mary Anne these words, it helps to hear them as well from someone who has grown to believe them truly.

The thought of the White Paladin and the Rook's return, reuniting with the Gryphon, sends a shiver down Jonathan's neck all the way to his tailbone. To have all three here would mean a bright future for Wonderland. Over the centuries, soldiers searched the country one hundred times over to look for them, to no avail. Or at least those were the lies intentionally spread.

"News will travel of the Gryphon's return, and if his two compatriots are somewhere in hiding, perhaps they will make themselves known," says Jonathan. "For now, one hero must suffice."

"Two," says Mary Anne. "You may not be a legend, that I know of, but you are a hero. You have proven yourself time and time again in the short period I have known you. And for no other reason than to protect me." Mary Anne smiles. "You are my hero. And that is enough."

The sick swell in Jonathan's gut returns, guilt twisting his insides. He will not rebuff Mary Anne's compliments, though he feels they could not be further from the truth. He is no hero, and his motives have little to do with Mary Anne. His father, the gods rest his immortal soul, taught Jonathan to be two things: a hatter and a gentleman, and he will keep his father's legacy and memory alive with his own life. Then there is March and Cheshire, who are at the center of every decision he makes. Every step away is a step back to them both, and once Mary Anne is gone, he will return to the Hollow, to his teas, to his table, to days and nights lounging, wearing as little clothing as possible, with March and Cheshire, forsaking the outside world once more.

"Thank you. You are very kind." Jonathan nods. "Shall we depart? It would be best not to keep the day waiting."

Mary Anne smiles, and they walk in silence to the main doors of the keep, where March stands, pensive.

Jonathan cannot deny Mary Anne's transformation thus far, this new woman in place of the terrified one he met in the forest. If he bumped into this Mary Anne back then, he could have passed her by and thought she was any other woman of Wonderland, except for her mismatched hair and eyes. She has become more comfortable in Wonderland, which is both reassuring and at the same time cause for concern. Whatever follows, Jonathan must remain hopeful Mary Anne will make the correct decision when the time comes, for all of them.

CHAPTER 12

MARCH

The rattle of the wooden scabbards against each other, two on her back and two on each hip, marks a beautiful overture for what March hopes will be a remarkable symphony. The doorman, nose upturned as she walks down the hall, finally jumps into action and grabs one of the iron handles of the door to open it for her.

"Wait, damn you," she says.

"Pardon, madam?" The doorman recoils from the door handle, as if it were red hot, and clenches his entire body into a sad, crooked stance.

"Wait," she repeats.

It is not insecurity or nerves that give her pause but rather the familiar, sick, foreboding weight at the base of her spine. She's felt it several times recently—the night Jonathan returned to their table under the oak with a woman, a stranger, Mary Anne, in his arms; the following morning, when she watched him walk away into the wood with her by his side; when the looming silhouette of Mirus first rose into the sky on the horizon; and finally the moment she smelled the sticky sweet perfumes as they crossed into the Crest. Each time, the sensation screamed through her bones to let her know, just like the present, there is no turning back.

"Are you ready?" Jonathan's soft voice says from behind her.

He dispels the sick feeling within her as if it were a waft of smoke from a candle on their table. It lifts away through her back and leaves her body in a welcome shiver. Even though she and Jonathan spent the waking dawn in each other's arms less than two hours ago, his voice finds its way into the deepest part of her being and settles her spirit, no matter the length of time they are apart.

She turns, and her pink eyes lock with his turquoise gaze, brighter and more beautiful than any jewel, shimmering in the daylight reflected through the hall. She fastens the loose leather toggles of his blue gambeson tunic and runs her hands down his arms, able to feel his muscles fight against the thick quilted fabric.

He takes his right hand and gently circles her cheek with the bend of his fingers. If March could decide how they spend their morning and afternoon, she would drag him back upstairs, drop both their leather trousers down to their boots, rip open their tunics, and continue their morning escapade, or find some other secluded corner of the castle or gardens as they have these past two weeks. The moment spoils as Mary Anne walks forward from behind Jonathan.

"Good morning, March," she says.

March hangs her head to hide her tightening lips and flared nostrils. Another feeling fills her gut. The inexplicable need to take one of her swords and shove the blade up through the bottom of Mary Anne's jaw and out through the top of her skull. Her dark-crimson blood would ooze out of the top of her head, coating her full brown hair, and her dull blue eyes would gloss over, and March and Jonathan would be free to return home—if they moved quick enough. She would be justified. It is, after all, Mary Anne's fault they are in Mirus.

March raises her head to look Mary Anne in the eyes and manages a pitiful excuse for a smile. "Morning."

Jonathan stares at March with a crooked grin, knowing the exact thoughts running through her head.

I know, her raised eyebrows and the small tilt of her head tell him. "Shall we?" she asks both Jonathan and Mary Anne then turns back to the door where the doorman has his hands on the handle, waiting. He swings open the door proudly and lowers his head as they pass.

The dissonance of scrapes of armor and hundreds of conversations of men of all ages and experiences reverberate across the stones. By March's count, at least four thousand men stand shoulder to shoulder with very little room between, filling the entire bailey. The Castle Guard and soldiers still loyal to the crown assemble in the bailey awaiting the Gryphon, their once-upon general, making his triumphant resurrection. The guards anxiously scurry about and try to form columns and rows in the crowded mass to prepare for his return. The soldiers and guards do not know the Gryphon sent word for March to be in attendance. They will learn.

A few men closest to the steps stop mid-conversation, though the majority continue unbothered, and glance up to the top of the stairs, to Mary Anne, the strange woman from another world. They study her with a mixed expression of curiosity and disgust—a feeling March knows well. They are aware Mary Anne is the catalyst of the impending insurrection.

A loud, rough cough echoes from the hall behind them. The Gryphon steps through the doorway and shields his eyes from the sun for the first time in hundreds of years. March wonders if there was a window in the infirmary he recuperated in, or if this is the first time since his release that he has seen the sun. Either way, he now stands before the soldiers and Castle Guard, who for centuries believed him dead, and a hush ripples through the crowd. The sun reflects off his freshly polished chest plate, gauntlets, and greaves. He chooses not to wear the rest of his armor but instead a green and brown patchwork coat long enough to drag on the ground behind him. March recognizes it as the disgusting, crusted frock caked with centuries of grime and filth he wore when Cheshire first appeared with him, but thoroughly laundered now. He positions himself between March and Jonathan and towers over them, standing at least a full head above Jonathan.

"Carter. March," the Gryphon says under his breath in a voice not yet recovered to full strength. "It's refreshing to see you're both still in the game."

"Not for lack of trying," says Jonathan.

"How long has it been?" the Gryphon asks, looking down at Jonathan and scratching at his chin through his freshly trimmed beard. "How long has it *really* been? The bloody nurses kept saying the best they could tell I was imprisoned for ten years, but we know that's not the truth."

Both Jonathan and March look sharply at Mary Anne, who does not understand the question. And for now, they wish to keep it a mystery to her. There are many more pressing matters she will need to burden herself with rather than how time works in Wonderland.

"Best leave this conversation to a more private location," says Jonathan.

"Right," says the Gryphon. His eyes jump to Mary Anne. "So, you are our queen-to-be."

"Yes, sir," says Mary Anne. "Mary Anne Elizabeth. I am grateful for your aid."

"My loyalty is forever and always to the crown." The Gryphon straightens his posture. "Never doubt my word, madam."

"Thank you," she says in the sickly naïve tone March has hated since Mary Anne arrived in Wonderland.

"On we go." The Gryphon walks to the edge of the castle stairs and clears his throat. His sheathed longsword raises the end of his coat. "Good morning."

Before he can say another word, the crowd erupts with thunderous cheers and ovations, welcoming their hero, Wonderland's hero and General, back from the dead.

March's eyes dart through the crowd, distrustful, and up to the Castle Guard standing watch atop the battlements of the outer wall, looking for any sign of treachery or attempt at assassination, but she can find nothing suspect or out of character. From what she can see, there is only genuine relief and admiration amongst the soldiers and guards.

The Gryphon raises his hand, and a hush falls again, almost immediately. "Thank you. Thank you all for remaining loyal through these trying times. But we have much work and a hard road ahead of us. A great number of your brothers, over half, have chosen treason and sided with men who would see our queendom toppled. And as I stand here before you, resolute, I promise they will not succeed."

The soldiers and guards all raise a fist into the air and cheer.

"But," the Gryphon continues, "every soldier and guard present must be prepared to fight and kill your brothers, your friends, your neighbors. They know you. They know your training. And they already know how to defeat you. So you will need to be better, stronger, fiercer."

A shiver runs up March's body as the Gryphon's hoarse voice becomes the roar of legend.

"Complacency and comfort will have no home in your hearts any longer," says the Gryphon. "Soldiers and the Castle Guard trained separately in the past, during my absence, but you will be one brotherhood. The only difference is on what side of the castle wall you will stand. Either way, you stand for the crown. For the Queendom."

The crowd erupts again with a hope and vigor long missing in the hearts of these men.

"So, you will train under the tutelage of the most skilled sword in all of Wonderland." The Gryphon nods, his heart filled with the same invigoration.

"We're ready, sir." An older soldier unsheathes his sword and points it skyward, followed by a raucous contagion of cheers.

"Teach us the old ways, your ways," a younger soldier shouts.

But before the responses boil over, the Gryphon raises his hand again. "You misunderstand. I am your general, your commander, but as I stated previously, the best sword in Wonderland will train you." And with an upturned palm, he ushers March forward.

She wants to step forward, but her legs feel as if they have turned to stone. An uncomfortable emptiness fills her chest. She is confident in her skill and her reputation as the finest sword in all of Wonderland, and she has fought tirelessly to prove it—the swords on her hips and back are evidence—but to have the title given so freely and proclaimed so certainly, and to be given the authority to lead men, fills her with an awkward and unfamiliar sense she does not know how to comprehend.

She looks to Jonathan, who tries to tame his smile, pressing his lips tight, but he cannot hide the pure joy and pride he feels for her.

Several soldiers scoff, and the slick sound of the sucking of teeth from soldiers scattered throughout the crowd change this unfamiliar feeling in March to pure, burning hate—and hate, she understands.

"Are you serious, sir?" a gruff, weathered-faced soldier asks from within the crowd.

"What can some pink-haired woman possibly teach us?" another asks.

The shorter soldier next to him elbows him in the side. "Do you know who that is?"

There are other soldiers with smiles on their faces who look around to others near them, excited at the opportunity to train with March. Their mouths move, but she cannot hear their words—only those who flout her.

"You mean, best sword since you're still recovering, sir?" a younger soldier asks from the front of the crowd.

"No, I do not," says the Gryphon. "Even in my prime, she bested me. If you are to have any chance in the battles to come, you will need her skill."

"In the bedroom, perhaps," the gruff soldier snickers, causing a ripple of laughter throughout the rest.

"Are you going to accept that?" the Gryphon asks March without moving his lips.

She laughs. Their words cannot hurt and are incapable of piercing her skin. Her stone legs, keeping her frozen before, shatter, and she walks to the edge of the stairs and down to the cobblestones of the bailey with a confidence which shakes most of the men to their core. The men push back against each other, as tightly fit as they already are, and form a circle around her.

A few of the older soldiers at the circle's edge nod their head.

"It is quite evident," the Gryphon roars again, "many of you are ignorant of the reputation, or rather legend would be a better term to use, of March, here."

"You mean Lady Audrianna March," a snide soldier says from within the crowd.

Those specific words together bring a blood curdling impulse to kill the person standing nearest her. She is proud of and loves her name, but putting *Lady* in front of it—albeit an attempted insult to her skill—cuts deeper by linking her to her mother, her father, and their sordid family history and dealings, which she left behind long ago.

"Make no mistake," says the Gryphon, "she will be the one to train you."

Most of the soldiers and guards remain silent, but a smattering of grumbles continues to carry through the men.

"If you feel you are better suited for the job," the Gryphon bellows, "best her, if you believe you can. I know you do, since you have made your thoughts vocal. Beat her and you will train the armies of Wonderland." The Gryphon takes his long coat in his right hand and flaps it for emphasis. It ripples in the wind like an open sail upon the mast of a great ship. "Those of you who will accept my terms and March's instruction, take a knee. Now."

March turns and watches all but one hundred men by her count take a knee without a second thought at the Gryphon's command. She spots two of the soldiers who tried to stop her from leaving the castle days ago on both knees with their heads bowed low, not to meet her eyes.

Whether it be because of genuine respect for her or more than likely just the Gryphon's command, the sight and the sound of rolling thunder as nearly four thousand men take a knee brings a smile to her face and turns the hatred inside her into spite. Spite she can harness. Spite is an old and welcome friend.

The Gryphon's eyebrows furrow, and the lines on the outside of his eyes become more prominent. "You men who remain standing. Thank you for your honesty. I take it you accept the challenge to face March, here? Now?" With a small flick of his right hand, the men around March get up and widen the circle to thirty feet in diameter.

Some of the standing men look across the bailey at one another, shaking their heads and holding their swords up in the air. While others, less confidently, look around to the men on their knees to see if they made the right decision. Ten decide against their initial choice and take a knee.

"Step forward," the Gryphon commands the soldiers. "If you are as confident as you think you are, prove your worth and take March's life. Then you will train our armies."

March raises an eyebrow at Jonathan. *One sword or two?* she asks without words.

He stands properly, with both hands clasped in front, straightens two fingers, and winks to say, *show them all.*

She unsheathes two of the swords from her back and flips her wrists, swirling and slicing the air around. The high-pitched *ting* the swords make as the tips of their blades leave their scabbards echo in her head and prelude the orchestra about to unfold.

Out of the corner of March's eye, she can see Mary Anne reach for Jonathan's sleeve and tug, trying to understand what is about to happen. "This seems a bit excessive," her lips mouth.

Twenty more soldiers stop in their tracks at the prospect and slowly take a knee.

"To be fair, I will hold March to the same expectation," the Gryphon continues. "March, are you ready to fight and kill your brother, neighbor, and friend?"

She looks to the Gryphon for permission to take the lives of these men, and he grants it with a single sideways nod. "I see no brother, neighbor, or friend of mine standing before me. Let them come." March holds her right arm out, the cold steel in her hand an extension of her. "These are enemies, and I will treat them accordingly." She turns in a circle so the tips of her swords pass the heads of all who will oppose her, no matter how far they stand. "If you step into this circle, and face me as an enemy," she tells the soldiers, "you will die in this circle as an enemy."

Thirty more take a knee, sensing the conviction of her words, not ready to die this day.

"There appear to be fifty men who believe they will take your life, March." The Gryphon rests both hands on the pommel of his long sword. "How would you like to face them?"

"This is war," says March without hesitation. "Let them face me all at once." She widens her stance, positions her back toward the Gryphon and Jonathan, shifts her weight back to her right foot, and rolls her left shoulder forward. She holds both blades outstretched down, matching the angle of her legs.

Shaken, twenty more soldiers decide to take a knee rather than face her.

The first several men, fifteen to be exact, reach the perimeter of the circle, and the way they shift their feet, twist their necks to crack them, and swallow audibly, betray the cowardice easier for them to hide at a distance. Some of the kneeling soldiers tug at their tunics to pull them to their senses, but their attempts go ignored.

March cannot help but smile at the men wavering on the edge looking at one another wide eyed, trying to formulate some crude, silent plan. Once they cross into the circle, they will die. She knows this. The Gryphon knows this. Perhaps the soldiers believe they will be victorious together. They will learn.

Ten. Ten deaths is what it will take for the rest to take a knee, she tells herself.

"Attack," the Gryphon commands.

After several quick breaths, the soldiers release a collective battle cry amounting to little more than strained grunts, more fear than courage, and enter the circle, charging with swords drawn. But instead of their screams, March only hears the lingering *ting* from her swords, now all but diminished, crying out for the song to continue.

March turns and, with a single swipe, swats away two attacks from overhead with the sword in her left hand and follows through to slice the throats of their owners with her right. New notes to add to her symphony.

She spins and ducks under a slash from another soldier and stabs her sword up through his ribs and out his back. With a blood-filled rasp from his burst lung, he falls to his knees and crumples to the floor. She leaves it firmly planted to retrieve later and pulls another sword from her left hip just in time to parry an attack from both sides. Note after note, the music swells in the air. Before the soldiers have time to recover, she spins again, extends both arms, and punctures both of their throats, hitting their spines with the tip of her blades.

Four more soldiers box her in on all sides. She dodges and defends against their every attack in a flurry of steel and beautiful music, and once her song crescendos to its peak, she decides it's time to stop playing.

She dashes behind one soldier—evidently unnerved by her speed—and plunges one of her swords through his thigh to the hilt. He collapses to the ground, howling and clutching the gushing wound. She circles around him and thrusts the heel of her boot into the chest of one of the other soldiers. He stumbles back, unable to catch his footing, and falls on top of the dead soldier with the sword protruding from his chest, impaling himself through the middle of his own sternum.

While sidestepping another slash, the soldier's sword clangs a sour note against the stones. They try to ruin her sweet melody. She grabs the ankle of the man with the sword through his thigh, jumps over him, and slams his foot to the ground, shoving the blade through his skull. It clinks a bright note as it bounces off the cobblestone.

With a single sword, she clashes with two more soldiers, backing them up to the edge of the circle. A barrage of metallic beauty fills the air, her song reaching its end. One falls back into the kneeling men, escaping her blades, but the other receives double slashes diagonally from cheek to sternum. As the other soldier rises back to his feet, the tip of March's blade plunges deep into his left eye socket, sending him to the ground for the final time.

The largest soldier yet attacks wildly, with great power behind each swing of his broadsword. He comes dreadfully close to cleaving the kneeling soldiers. March dodges, unsheathes another sword from her back, and runs him through the abdomen. He keeps swinging, fueled by the pain. While he draws his sword overhead with both hands, she takes the other sword from her right hip and plunges it upward through his gut. Blood gurgles from his mouth. His limp arms fall, and the point of his sword drops to the ground with a resounding clang, but he refuses to fall. He vomits streams of blood through clenched, defiant teeth. March pulls another blade from her right hip and plunges it into his back, sending him to his knees and, finally, to the ground.

The older soldier who spoke out previously is the last man standing in the circle. He is the last man standing at all. Every other soldier who had intended to face March has taken a knee some time during the fight and looks on with sheer bewilderment. The old soldier waits en garde, ready for March to attack. His eyes glance at his fallen comrades and the blood-soaked cobblestones, face twitching with frustration.

"What is your name?" she asks.

"Ewan," he replies.

She attacks first, only using one sword and matching his form and footwork. They travel around the entire circle, steel biting against steel. Each clang vibrating through her body. A thrilling outro. He fights with experience and grace and returns her attacks strike for strike, parry for parry. But despite the glorious hum of the swords as they clash, March knows the song must come to an end. With a final upward swing, she knocks the soldier's sword into the air, and while his arms rebound into the air from the strike, she spins one final time and plunges her sword into one of his armpits and out the other, honoring him with a quicker death than the other soldiers.

His sword falls to the ground, followed by his body. The hum fades from her ears. A motionless silence fills the bailey, and the remaining soldiers look on with wide eyes, some in awe, others in fear.

Mary Anne applauds out of nervous excitement but stops once she realizes she is alone and hides her hands behind her back.

March lets the metallic tune finish in her head before she addresses the crowd. "First lesson. The brave are always the first to die." She collects her swords, wipes the blood on the fallen men, and re-sheathes them. "A more accurate way to phrase this is the stupid are always the first to die. You will face many adversaries who are larger, stronger, and braver. To win, you must be more than the sum of these. You must be smarter. You will be smarter. Or I will kill you myself."

She picks up and examines the sword of the older soldier and admires the silver carvings of the hilt and the weight of the tang. *Ewan. She will add him to her collection.* She keeps it in hand as she walks back up the stairs and stands between the Gryphon and Jonathan and finally takes a deep breath in and out through her nose.

"Well said," the Gryphon says to March, and then addresses the soldiers and guards once more. They all rise to their feet with newfound respect.

"Well said, indeed," says Jonathan, with the same beautiful, pressed smile. But this time there is a hint of sadness behind it. He has known what she has since Mary Anne arrived, and with every passing day and occurrence, it becomes clearer to both of them, and it terrifies them. There is no turning back.

But their shared melancholy moment of triumph is cut short. The tremors in the ground reach their feet before the deafening crack assaults their ears. The earth below their feet jolts violently and knocks everyone in the bailey to the ground, except for the Gryphon, March, and Jonathan, who are quick enough to catch themselves. Jonathan grabs Mary Anne around the waist to keep her upright. A great tower of billowing black smoke erupts from the city like a hellmouth assaulting the heavens. Mary Anne cowers and hides her face behind Jonathan.

The Gryphon instinctively unsheathes his sword. His eyes dart through the air, assessing the situation. "Stonehaven," he says. "There is an attack on Stonehaven."

March and Jonathan share a glance, and swallow at the same time. They wish it were Lysander and Uriah, or even the Red Knight's retaliation, but deep within themselves, they know the sad truth.

Both of their eyebrows pinch to say together, *Cheshire*.

CHAPTER 13

JONATHAN

The Gryphon stands tall, sword pointed to the heavens. "To arms! Be ye men of Mirus. Stand!" The Gryphon roars almost as loud as the blast, mouth tall, face muscles straining. His last word turns into a growl, which terrifies the soldiers and brings them to their feet. The Gryphon of legend has returned.

The soldiers scramble and clatter against each other, disoriented, holding their heads and opening their jaws wide to regain their hearing.

Jonathan, distracted by the power of the Gryphon, did not realize Mary Anne clings to his chest, fingers twisting in his tunic, until he feels her breath. When the explosion happened, his left arm instinctually wrapped around her waist and pulled her in. His right arm snaked around her back and his hand cradled the back of her head. Her blue eyes now look up to meet his, inches away.

"I am unharmed," she says before Jonathan can ask. A question he found himself repeating when they first met. "Jonathan..."

March glares at them over her shoulder.

Before Mary Anne can continue, Jonathan rights himself and gently grabs Mary Anne by the shoulders to pull her away and look her over. She is shaken, quick of breath, but otherwise uninjured.

The Gryphon brings his sword down as if to slice through the crowd. "Twenty men to the fire wagons." A cluster of men run through the small door in the castle gates and into the city. "Twenty tend to the fallen. Two hundred with me. The rest of you, positions. Ignite the oil canisters. Archers, to the walls. No traitor steps foot inside the gates." He commands them as if he has never left the battlefield.

Jonathan cannot let him know there is no need for such a response. The enemy will not come, at least not in the way the Gryphon expects.

"You three—"

Jonathan interrupts the Gryphon, knowing what he is about to suggest. "Allow me to accompany you, sir."

"No." The Gryphon walks down the stairs without a look in Jonathan's direction.

"Please, sir. Let me help," says Jonathan, following at his heels.

"You are the future queen's advisor, are you not?" The Gryphon continues to walk across the bailey. The soldiers scatter as he passes. "Your place is by her side. Not out there."

"Sir—" Jonathan can barely finish the word. The Gryphon spins around, forming an impassable wall in front of Jonathan, glaring down at him, nostrils flared.

"I... I know I can be of assistance," Jonathan stammers, afraid to meet eyes with what could very well be the mythical beast of the Gryphon's namesake. He lies. He is not sure what use he could be except to protect Cheshire if need be.

"I will stay with her," says March from the top of the stairs. "His sword work is shit anyway." She winks at Jonathan. "As much as I hate to admit it, and I do hate it, she is better off with me."

The bottom of Gryphon's eyelids raise to contain the piercing annoyance in his canary yellow eyes.

"It is alright. Let him go," says Mary Anne. "March will escort me inside and assure my safety."

"As you wish," the Gryphon grumbles loudly without moving his lips. "Now, enough of this. The city burns while we waste time." He turns on his heel and joins the soldiers pouring through the castle gates pulled open by the two behemoth gatemen.

Jonathan turns quickly to March and Mary Anne to give them both a wink. *Thank you.*

He gives chase after the Gryphon, pushing through the bottleneck of soldiers. Jonathan turns sideways to slip and jump through spaces where he can to keep up, but the Gryphon's gait is mighty. His head and shoulders stand taller than every soldier and Castle Guard. His hair and longcoat whip behind him like the cape of a rider on horseback galloping at full speed.

The soldiers descend the steps of the city like a crashing flood, cutting through the Crest and into Stonehaven. Citizens scream and yell from their windows, pointing to the black sky from the streets. Infants cry, and dogs bark and howl from all directions. Bells toll throughout the city. Above it all, the Duchess's voice rings out.

"Citizens of Mirus," she says, a metallic reverberation in her voice. "Remain calm at all costs. Show strength and compassion to one another. The soldiers of Mirus and the fire brigade wagons are en route to render aid."

As he runs, Jonathan's eyes dart around the streets erratically trying to find the source of the explosion, but the multiple echoes bounce off the stone buildings and walls making it difficult to pinpoint its origin. He presses his palms to his ears, eliminating the sense which has failed him, and relies on his sight.

The townspeople in the streets stare at carved stone statues of nightingales and skylarks in flight perched at the corners of rooftops and the tips of awnings.

"The Long Hall will be open this day," the Duchess's voice continues from another set of birds. "Those affected by this travesty, please make your way to the castle. And for anyone else in need, please come as well. The Queendom is strong and will provide."

Jonathan gives no more thought to the birds or the Duchess's words —the rumble ahead of him swells to a roar, and the sight before him is worse than he could imagine. Jonathan stops in his tracks. An uncontrollable inferno bursts from the pit where the hanging cells once stood, like dragon's breath to scorch earth and sky. A noxious black column of smoke rises into the air and creeps across the sky, blotting out the sun. Jonathan turns his back to shield his face from the intense heat bubbling up from the pit in waves. He presses his eyes with his sleeves to relieve the stinging tears.

The adjacent houses and buildings around the jail have collapsed in on themselves from the blast. Shattered stone and the splintered remains of wood lie in mounds, like pebbles and dried pine needles on the forest floor. A chunk of Mirus, just gone in an instant.

Townspeople from the surrounding areas of Stonehaven, men and women alike, join the soldiers and rush to help where they can, hauling buckets of water to douse the buildings still ablaze, clearing the street, and searching the rubble to pull neighbors from their collapsed homes.

Within seconds, six horse-drawn wagons approach. Jonathan joins the soldiers and clears charred debris from the burned cobblestone street. With both hands, he grabs large timbers—which were once part of someone's roof or floor—one after another and flips them to the side of the street. The wagons thunder past and stop just shy of the pit. In the back of each, hundreds of blue glass orbs are suspended apart from each other by twine and rope. Heavily armored soldiers positioned in the back of the wagons carefully remove the orbs from their nests and hand them to soldiers.

"Positions," the Gryphon screams above the cacophony filling the streets.

Soldiers run and form three rows in front of the crater. The first row of soldiers lob their orbs into the bellowing plume of smoke and down into the crater. The Gryphon yells again. Like archers, the rows of soldiers throw their orbs, make way for the line behind them, then return to the wagons to grab another. Other soldiers launch orbs at the sections of the nearby building, still on fire. The orbs shatter, and bursts of white and blue powder extinguish the flames.

Jonathan grabs an orb in each hand and throws them into flames high in a nearby building, and out of range for the soldiers hindered by their armor. He takes two more in hand and almost drops them both, jostled by the crowd of soldiers. He takes another and throws it far down an alleyway to a stack of crates which have gone unseen. The other is stolen from his grasp by a soldier who runs toward the pit. Another soldier, escorting an elderly man on his side, trips on a splintered post. Jonathan reaches around both, grabs them by the ribs, and hoists them to their feet again.

If only it were possible for him to lose track of time, but the minutes and seconds race in his mind incessantly. He checks his pocket watch to make sure, even though he is never wrong. The rescue efforts carry on for almost an hour. Jonathan helps who he can, lifts what he can, and listens to the Gryphon when called upon, all the while searching for any hint of Cheshire on rooftops.

The smoke thins and shrinks in width. Gradually, the sun pierces through its dark veil. The soldiers continue to race back and forth from the wagons and escort townspeople to safety. Now, screams overpower the dwindling fire from those who suffer burns, broken bones, and discover the bodies of their dead. The flames will soon be contained, but the devastation is insurmountable. The city is chaos.

Jonathan blinks the sting from his eyes. He focuses on the sound of his breath. He fills his chest, despite the stench, and exhales slowly to calm the pounding of his heartbeat in his chest, throat, and fingertips. All around him, soldiers, townspeople, cinders, and smoke fly by in blurs.

However, in the middle of it all, half a block away, a soldier stands still in the madness and stares at Jonathan. His heart races again, beating against his chest like the initial blast. In the cross-shaped opening of the soldier's visor is the unmistakable glint of lavender eyes. The eyes Jonathan sees every time he closes his own.

Cheshire.

Never would Jonathan have thought Cheshire would be so brazen to stand for all to see, though his visage concealed, hiding in plain sight. Hundreds of soldiers swarm around him, inches away, with no idea at all the Queen Slayer is within their grasp.

Jonathan blinks, and Cheshire is gone, lost among the crowd. But he knows well enough Cheshire meant for himself to be seen and means for Jonathan to follow. He pushes through the soldiers, away from the wagons, up the street where the crowd is thinner, and reaches the point where Cheshire stood. Jonathan tries to look into the helmet of every guard who passes, but then realizes like before, he should seek the soldier out of place, the soldier who is still in the chaos. Finally, half a block away, he spots Cheshire leaning against the door frame of a weaver's shop, waiting for Jonathan to find him.

He looks back over his shoulder to see the Gryphon continuing to order the soldiers. Whether it be through inspiration or fear, the soldiers heed his every word and keep the fire from spreading, and tend to the injured and dead, under his leadership.

Jonathan turns back to the empty door of the weaver's shop and makes his way slowly, not to arouse suspicion. Images of the destruction and death in Rookridge flash through his mind like lightning illuminating the dark and revealing the dead. He saw the pain and hurt in Cheshire's eyes the last he saw him a fortnight ago. Jonathan and March sat with him, held him through the night, his tears running down their chests. But like clockwork, he disappeared without a word when they all finally slept. Cheshire's reputation has always been one of murder, destruction, and chaos—Jonathan has witnessed it firsthand—but this is different.

The weaver's shop is shallow at first glance, with no place to hide other than a thin wooden countertop. Tall shelves of folded tapestries and rugs line the squat room on three sides and cover most of the front window. Jonathan looks behind and finds himself alone but does not believe it to be true.

He examines the shelves along the back wall again and finds a section, barely the width of his shoulders, where each shelf from floor to ceiling, sits just below the rest of the length. Jonathan moves stacked rugs and discovers two sets of hinges running along the left side of the offset shelves. Even in a place as unassuming as a simple weaver's shop in Stonehaven, nothing is ever as it seems at first glance.

He takes a firm hold on the shelf and pulls. The entire section swings forward from the wall with the lower shelves barely tucking under the others, to reveal the door disguised as part of the wall on the second set of hinges.

It takes little effort upon the door for it to push open. The dim sunlight through the smoke and obscured window barely catches the first few shelves of the long, narrow storehouse. A single aisle runs down the middle and disappears into the darkness.

For a moment, Jonathan wonders if this is instead a trap laid by Lysander and Uriah, and he only thought he saw Cheshire because he longs for him. He draws his sword and walks into the dark, point first. The commotion on the street, his footsteps, and even his breath become muffled the farther Jonathan walks, all sounds absorbed by the thousands of yards of rolled fabric. Eventually, the tip of Jonathan's sword clinks against the wooden rear wall. He searches it with his free hand for any sign of another door but finds nothing. Behind him, the front door to the storeroom is far enough away that his outstretched hand can cover it from sight, and the edges of each shelf are backlit by the sun.

Forty-eight.

If this is a trap laid for him by the Red Knight, and a soldier stepped from concealment between each shelf, Jonathan would find difficulty making it from the room unscathed.

"Do you think I meant to harm you?" Cheshire whispers from the dark to Jonathan's left.

"Of course not."

"Why is your sword drawn?"

He returns his sword to its sheath. "On the off chance I conjured you in my mind, as I do every day you are gone, and I followed some random soldier in here to my death."

Cheshire steps from the darkness, without the helmet, and stands between Jonathan and the door. The light halos the sides of Cheshire's face—soft jaw, bedraggled hair—and catches the corner of his cheek perked up with a grin.

Jonathan has so many questions, and Cheshire so many things to answer for, but in Cheshire's presence, he cannot deny the love and the desire he feels, or the mere gratitude to be able to look upon him again. He is powerless. Outside, the world burns, but nothing matters more in this moment than Cheshire.

He seizes the moment, fearing the next will never come, and grabs Cheshire by the nape of his neck. He brings him close and leans down into a rough, passionate kiss. Cheshire rubs his chin, lips, and cheeks against Jonathan's face as they both breathe heavily. Jonathan welcomes the pressure and swells in his trousers.

His hand slides from Cheshire's neck to his jaw, to hold him in place, to savor the taste of Cheshire's lips. His other hand frantically searches Cheshire's chest, back, arms, and stomach for any bare skin to caress, but the damned armor he wears covers his body completely.

Sensing his frustration, Cheshire slides his hand up the front of Jonathan's tunic—his touch tickles—then slides it down the front of his trousers, gripping Jonathan firmly. Jonathan flexes against Cheshire's grasp as his hand squeezes at the same time, and a half-moan half-laugh slips from his lips.

"Give me your tongue," Cheshire commands in a whisper.

Jonathan will not fight the urges of his body and opens his mouth.

Cheshire takes Jonathan's tongue between his lips and slowly slides as far into Jonathan's mouth as he can and back to its tip, sucking and pulling on it slowly and tenderly over and over again. Jonathan stretches his tongue forward as far as he can, surrendering completely.

There is nothing else outside of their two bodies, their two spirits, the purple and turquoise flames. Jonathan wants so desperately for Cheshire to turn him to face the wall, pull his trousers to his boots, and take him here and now. Jonathan's ass and legs twitch at the thought, but with neither able to control themselves, they would lose the rest of the day, if not be caught.

He pulls his tongue from Cheshire. "Wait," he pants, lips dry, and grabs Cheshire's wrist to keep it from moving any farther inside his trousers. Jonathan unlaces his trousers and pulls them to his thighs. The tepid air in the storehouse feels good against the heat of his body. He forces the soldier's trousers Cheshire wears down to his knees and pulls open the stitches of his codpiece, allowing Cheshire to spring free, solid as stone and dripping with lust.

They both look down to watch as they twist their hips side to side, playfully sliding, grinding, and pressing their bodies back and forth against each other. Jonathan takes them both in one hand—his on top with Jonathan being the taller of the two, though Cheshire's endowment bests his own. Jonathan's grip barely makes it halfway around as he holds both their cocks in hand. Cheshire's arms hang by his side as his body quivers at Jonathan's touch. Jonathan strokes the full length from Cheshire's body back to his own.

"Yes," Cheshire pants softly, pushing his hips forward again and again. "Yes."

They kiss wildly, their tongues matching the speed of Jonathan's hand. He can feel the end nearing, but they both pause, not ready to let it end. They bring each other to the edge, the precipice of their desires, three more times. Each time their breaths grow quicker, air daring to escape their mouths, and it becomes increasingly more difficult to stop. Jonathan wants to hear Cheshire's moans fill the room, feel his body shudder against him. The fourth time, Jonathan pulls back and awaits an answer from Cheshire. With a quick nod, Jonathan knows he is ready as well. They angle themselves toward the dim light and stand side by side in order to watch their collective climax. Cheshire takes hold of Jonathan, matching the vigor of his strokes, while Jonathan grabs the back of Cheshire's neck and presses their cheeks together. Cheshire slips his free hand down the back of Jonathan's trousers, squeezing with the force to crush rocks, and then slides farther down between his buttocks.

The first touch from Cheshire is all it takes. Their long breaths become pants, become moans, and then they stop breathing for a second and an eternity. Their bodies shake, and together they release their pent-up passion, their lust, their love. Jonathan breathes again in quick bursts of moans. Cheshire lets loose one long, glorious roar until he is spent. He is always the more vocal out of their trio. Fortunately their sounds are muffled within the storeroom, otherwise he would be heard all the way in the Crest. Before letting go, they stare into each other's eyes and share gentle kisses while they both play with their sensitivity. Jonathan's only regret is they are not somewhere in the sun, to drink in every inch of one another.

"Whatever do you do while I am away?" Cheshire jests.

Jonathan wets his dried lips. "March has a harness she wears around her waist with a..." Jonathan motions to his groin, muscles bouncing outside of his control.

Cheshire's eyes grow wide at the thought. "I like the sound of this. Did she bring it with her?"

"Of course."

Cheshire pulls away, grabs the loose end of a bolt of fabric from the nearest shelf, and wipes himself clean.

"Cheshire," says Jonathan. "That is uncalled for."

"What?" He laughs. "How else do you expect to clean yourself? You plan to shove your cock back in your trousers like that and go about your day? I'm sure the stains through your leathers would not be evident at all. Besides, look at the dust back here. The owner has not ventured this far in some time."

Jonathan looks down at his crotch and at his hand and can see no other solution. He pulls the fabric from Cheshire's hand and attends to himself. Cheshire kisses Jonathan on the cheek once more before tying his trousers and then Jonathan's. As Jonathan cleans his hand and folds the fabric back over itself, the crushing guilt and weight of reality presses on him, hearing the muffled screams from the streets and washing away this beautiful moment.

"Cheshire," says Jonathan, "what have you done?"

"Pleasure you, if I am not mistaken."

"Do not be aloof." Jonathan turns Cheshire to look him in the eye. "The city burns and it is your fault. Again, with the needless destruction and death."

"Nothing is ever needless." His voice is calm, reassuring. Unnerving.

"But what are you doing?" Jonathan pleads. "What are you trying to accomplish, and why?"

"I warned you weeks ago to leave. I warned you this was coming. You stayed."

Jonathan thinks back to the night he last saw Cheshire and his words. *I will be responsible for what comes next.*

"Fuck," says Jonathan. "I did not think you meant this."

"Did you not?"

In truth, Jonathan hoped his words would never come to pass, and it is not as if Jonathan has seen Cheshire since to discuss their meaning further. In his heart he wanted to believe Cheshire fled the city, but in fact, he has been planning this all along.

"Are you finished? Is it done? Is this the end?" asks Jonathan.

"Not in the slightest." There is no sign of guilt or remorse in his voice.

"Cheshire."

"Jonathan," Cheshire snaps.

"You are insufferable," Jonathan says. "I see how tormented you are by the past. You are shackled to it. Do you not see what is wrought from clinging to it?"

"All of us are shackled, chained, tethered to the hurts in our past. Whether you choose to believe it or not, our past is what defines us. There is no way to escape it," says Cheshire. "It is what pushes me forward."

Jonathan knows he is a hypocrite for the words he says. Cheshire embraces his past to the point where it consumes him. Jonathan and March choose the lesser of two evils and ignore their pasts, knowing they follow behind like a ravenous wolf ready to devour them at any moment. And each bears the consequences and side effects of their decisions. None are on the right path, yet they walk it together.

"Is there not a chance," says Jonathan, "you can let go of your suffering? Your rage?"

"I find comfort in my suffering," Cheshire says with confidence. "It is familiar. Constant."

"But it does not need to be."

Cheshire snaps again. "Do you expect your words to deter me from a thousand years of work?"

"I would hope March and I would be enough." Jonathan caresses Cheshire's cheek.

Cheshire sighs heavily and hangs his head. "You are. You will be. When I am through." He turns his head and kisses the inside of Jonathan's palm. "But I am here now. I am not leaving. And to answer your question about what I am doing…the less you know, the better and safer you are. We do not ask questions, Jonathan. Do not start now. I would rather you and March be out of the city altogether, but you refuse. All I ask is if you are to remain in the city, you help me where you can."

"I propose a bargain," says Jonathan.

Cheshire narrows his eyes.

"Two conditions. Firstly, March does not fare well in the confines of the castle."

"Do any of us?"

"She needs you," Jonathan whispers. "I need you. My first request is for you to not keep yourself from us anymore. Times being what they are, the three of us need to remain close. Especially close. If we are to be trapped here, let us make the most of it, even if they must be fleeting moments such as this. Though I hope there will be many more. Do you know a way to the center of the hedge maze without coming through the garden?"

"Of course."

"March and I spend our nights there now. Away from prying eyes and attentive ears. Jonathan gently pushes his fingers between Cheshire's. He caresses them, plays with them, strokes them as he talks. "No guards patrol within." Jonathan leans close, his lips brush Cheshire's ear. Cheshire's breaths become long and heavy. "The three of us, under the moonlight again. Take me while March watches and strokes your hair. Let me lay you on your back on the grass. Allow March to ride you while you lean back against my chest. These could be our days and nights, as they should be."

"I... I have other—"

Jonathan licks the curve of Cheshire's ear, stealing his thought. "You need us. Do not pretend otherwise. You will meet us this evening. I will not go another night without your taste in my mouth or your scent upon my skin." He takes Cheshire's silence as a 'yes,' says thank you with a kiss, and then leans his chin against Cheshire's forehead.

Cheshire rubs his lips on Jonathan's chin. "And the second condition?"

"You want us out of the city." Jonathan thinks wisely about his choice of words. "I make you this promise: we will leave once I have kept my word to help Mary Anne return home. You know Wonderland more than anyone. In your quest, find some time to help *me* get her home. Then March, Dormy, and I will depart the moment after."

"Of all the fucking foolhardy, idiotic, asinine, outrageous requests you could ask." Cheshire swipes at several bolts of fabric and kicks every bolt from the bottom two shelves. "It does not matter what I say, you will continue on with this fool's errand in service to your honor."

"Are you worried?"

"Of course I am." Cheshire leans his forehead against Jonathan's chest. "You are not me. You are the one last bastion of hope and goodness in Wonderland. I do not want your honor to cost you your life."

Jonathan steps back, puts a bent finger to Cheshire's chin, and lifts his face. "Every step away is a step back to you. I say this to March every time I walk out the door and face danger without her or you by my side. I have always wanted to tell you the same, but you never stay long enough to hear it. You love me for who I am. I cannot be anything else. So when I walk out of this door, I do so with the end goal of living a full life with you and March, undisturbed by the outside world. And in this instance, I could not be more grateful to have you and her by my side. I fear this danger may prove too much." Jonathan leans into Cheshire, their noses so close he can feel Cheshire's breath upon his lips. "Please, will you help me?"

Cheshire swallows. "You know I will, damn it. What does this all entail?"

"Mary Anne must become queen in order to leave Wonderland." Jonathan expects an outburst or any kind of response from Cheshire, but he stares back with an eerie stillness, breath held, processing Jonathan's words but keeping his thoughts to himself.

"It seems a misguided path to ask the Queen Slayer to aid you in this endeavor." Cheshire steps back. "But I have already given you my word, haven't I? So I will. But this will not stop what I have planned, and you do not get to stand in my way."

"Agreed," says Jonathan. He knows he could not stop Cheshire no matter how hard he tries, but while they are together, be it with March or helping Mary Anne, he can delay his plans.

"Since we are making requests," says Cheshire, "I need your help presently. Since you are here, you have made the next part of my plan much easier."

"Name it."

Cheshire smiles wider than he has in ages. "I need you to bring the Gryphon to me. Here. Now."

CHAPTER 14

MARY ANNE

Once Mary Anne and March are inside the keep, the doorman, hands trembling, turns four lock bars, two on either side of the door, into place. The metal snaps together with horrible finality. Mary Anne glances from ceiling to floor to the end of the hall several times over, unsure why, except as a way to process her panic. She covers her throat with her hand, fearing her heartbeat makes her look like that of a toad. A nervous whimper escapes her. March guffaws.

Mary Anne removes her hand after she realizes the foolishness of the thought and straightens the front of her bodice. March leans back against the wall, arms crossed and one leg bent with her foot upon it as well, calm as a pond at sunrise. One eyebrow is half-raised as she studies Mary Anne. Despite the commotion and threat of danger, March remains in control, strong, unbothered, except for the tightness in her full lips and her eyes, different from her usual sardonic expression.

"What is next?" Mary Anne fiddles with her fingers unconsciously.

"About time you said something," says March.

"You were waiting for me?" asks Mary Anne, confused.

"Yes." March circles the silver ball at the end of one of her pommels with her middle finger. "You are to be queen, are you not? I wanted to see the strength of your mettle. I am pleased to report you fulfilled my every expectation."

"How dare you speak to me in such a manner?" Heat rises in Mary Anne's face, both out of anger and embarrassment, because she knows March is correct: Mary Anne acts like a scared, naïve, young girl. "I am a grown woman," she says with biting articulation. "I am a woman of industry."

March pushes off the wall and stands uncomfortably close to Mary Anne. "Not here, you're not," she says with the same crisp inflection. "No wonder the throne room doors will not open for you." March walks away, silent, except for the clack of her boots upon the stairs and the shift of her leather belts and occasional clink of the swords she carries upon her back and hips.

Mary Anne's nails dig into her palms. She wants to lash out, list every accomplishment she has ever achieved and recite the inscription on her diploma from university. Then, the sober realization that March is correct, yet again, quells her emotions, relaxes her fists. Mary Anne stretches her jaw from side to side, unaware of how hard she clenched her teeth, and chases after March, who is halfway down the corridor.

"What do we do now?" she asks with a forced, calm tone.

"Get to your room. Close the door. Stay there," says March. "I am going to the cellar for a drink."

"Will you not accompany me?"

March stops.

Mary Anne asks the question about to leave March's lips, and answers in the same breath. "Do I need to be accompanied? No. No, I do not."

"I will be along shortly." March grows smaller as she walks farther down the long hallway and then disappears around a corner to the left.

As Mary Anne climbs the spiral staircase alone, she cannot stop herself from pausing when she reaches the landing of each floor. She peeks around the corner in case some unknown foe lies in wait for her. If the attack on Stonehaven was indeed orchestrated by Lysander and Uriah, she must expect anything at any time. The odd servant girl dressed in the same ornate wardrobe as Grace hurries somewhere in the distance.

The voice of the Duchess reverberates through the tower, muffled, distant, but from all around Mary Anne. "Citizens of Mirus. Remain calm at all costs. Show strength and compassion to one another. The soldiers of Mirus and the fire brigade wagons are on their way to render aid."

How is this possible? Where is her voice coming from?

"The Long Hall will be open today," her voice continues. "Those affected by this travesty, please make your way to the castle. And for anyone else in need, please come as well. The Queendom is strong and will provide."

"Remarkable," she says to herself.

Her voice, the strength in her words, brings Mary Anne a sense of comfort.

"The Queendom is strong," Mary Anne repeats. "The Duchess is strong. March is strong. My mother is strong. All without trying. They have no one to impress. They just are." This is one of many lessons Mary Anne must learn, but she wonders how she can compare to any of them.

At the thirteenth floor, her handmaiden Grace waits on the landing, hands clasped in front of her, tighter than usual, bouncing slightly on her toes. Her shoulders relax when Mary Anne comes into view, and she greets Mary Anne with a simple, pressed smile.

Has she been worried? About me?

"Thank you," Mary Anne tells her.

Grace tilts her head as if to ask, "For what?"

"For being here. For being a friendly face." Mary Anne stops herself before she continues speaking. *At least half of one* almost slips out, commenting on the golden half-mask which covers Grace's eyes, whether by choice or duty. She will not risk offending her.

Grace opens the door to Mary Anne's chamber for her, head bowed.

"Will you wait with me?" Mary Anne asks.

Grace declines with a respectful shake of her head and steps away down the hall.

"Please," Mary Anne calls after her. "After this morning, I would rather not be alone. Your company would mean quite a lot."

She hesitates, looks both ways down the hallway as if someone watches her, then follows Mary Anne into her chambers and shuts the door. She stands next to the door, hands clasped in front of her, but fidgets toward the door handle, reconsidering her decision.

"Sit with me." Mary Anne gestures to a basil-colored chair reminiscent of Louis XV's design. "Who knows for how long we will be here? I would like for you to be comfortable."

Grace's head tilts sharply to the door and shakes so slightly, yet quickly, it appears to vibrate. Her trembling hands fall to her sides and pat her long black and white dress she wore the day Mary Anne met her, thinking she had dressed for a masquerade rather than a service.

Mary Anne approaches her. "May I?" she asks, seeking permission to examine her dress.

Grace wrings her thumbs and bites her maroon-painted bottom lip but gives no objection.

Mary Anne kneels and runs her fingertips down the slope of her dress. "Thick, quality damask. Heavy." She twists the edge of the goldwork at the bottom of her dress. "I have half a mind to believe this is actual gold thread. Well, now I understand why you are reluctant to sit. I would hate to wrinkle or crease a dress, or rather a gown such as this."

Grace nods her head with a false smile, which looks to bring pain to her face, then turns to the door to leave. Mary Anne's intent was never to insult or offend Grace, though she does not know how her comment could. Perhaps it is because she is a servant and the extravagant dress she wears is only out of duty and will never be hers. But the faint muffled sound of metal clicking against metal surprises Mary Anne. She only heard it because her ears were inches away from Grace's dress.

"Grace, stop," says Mary Anne, with the concerned tone of her mother. "Turn around, please."

She does so cautiously, hand still tight on the door handle.

Mary Anne reaches out again and presses on the dress with a heavy hand. It sways back and forth as a dress with a hoopskirt beneath would, but the give is different, rigid. She twists the fabric between her fingers to feel the metal frame used to keep its shape and follows the metal up the dress. The piping does not match a hoop skirt at all. There are breaks in the metal with sharp points every eight inches or so. The reluctance and worry on Grace's face, her simple movements, the way she kneels, all make sense now. If she were to sit down, the dress would bend with her, but the sharp metal frame would stab at her legs and cause severe discomfort, if not pain. She may be a servant, but this is inhumane, torturous.

"Grace..."

She runs from the room before Mary Anne can finish her next question. Although dressed in splendor, Grace does not wear a gown, she wears a cage. Mary Anne will not follow or question her anymore today. She hopes Grace will return, and she will apologize for her curiosity and for causing her any embarrassment. Though Mary Anne feels justified in her concern. But the lingering question of *why* remains. There are several other servants throughout the castle in the same uniform.

Why? What have they done? Is this punishment? Or just the cruel ways of a strange land?

The sky outside is too dark for morning. Mary Anne walks to the balcony where the ominous, dark veil of smoke twisting out of the city consumes the western sky. She looks east—mountains and a clear sky. Below, Mirus's main gates and the Long Bridge point northward.

The sun rises in the west. It should not rise in the west, yet there it is. Obscured by the smoke, the faint glowing orb taunts her, reminds her she is a stranger in a strange world, a land full of contradiction and danger.

The clatter of metal from the next room signals March's return to her room.

She and March will be alone, and there is no better time to ask March for her help in translating the Book of Queens. At least thirty feet separate the balconies to their rooms—the length of the large washroom between them—but any conversation is better than sitting with her thoughts, even if the conversation is with March. Though, from this distance, for their words not to be carried away by the wind, they would need to raise their voices beyond civil conversation. She walks into her washroom to the window closest to Jonathan and March's room. Mary Anne moves the gossamer curtains and waits.

March walks onto her balcony, wordless, and with two frosted blue bottles full to the neck.

At first, Mary Anne thought March still wore her already all-too-revealing top, but to her shock, March walks onto the balcony without any top at all, as if it were a casual practice, as if she were Jonathan. She places one bottle on the stone railing and takes a lengthy drink from the other, then turns her back to Mirus, leaning on the balcony with both elbows.

Mary Anne immediately averts her eyes, looking to sky, stone, the horizon, her stubbed fingernails, anywhere but March. She cannot fathom why March could be so tawdry, so vulgar with no thought to Mary Anne at all.

"Must you?"

"Must I what?" March says after a long drink from the bottle. A drop of her drink trickles down the curve of her breast.

"Please, do cover up," says Mary Anne, adjusting her own gown as if it hung open as well.

March places the half empty bottle on the railing with a dull clink. "Am I not allowed to air myself after the battle I had moments ago?"

"Was what you were wearing not airy enough?" asks Mary Anne. "Have some respect for decency."

"Whose decency?" March stands and stretches her arms upward, arching her back and making her chest more prominent. "Yours? You do not remark when Jonathan walks around shirtless. Why am I any different?"

"Because you are a woman, and women should not—"

"The women of *your* world do not. If you are any representation of them, the women of your world are weak, repressed, focused on modesty when it has no bearing of what or who you are. Here, in my world, I can do whatever the fuck I please. No one will tell me how I should act or present myself. You can always go back into your bedchamber and leave me be, because I will not change who I am. You are here for such a brief time, after all."

The truth stings. In London, women were chastised or publicly humiliated if they dared show too much of their leg or shoulder. Mary Anne looks to her own gown. Its scooped neckline would be considered indecent by most, even though not the slightest part of her breasts are exposed. She can also not give away she has seen March without clothing numerous times and thought nothing of it. This is where Mary Anne positions herself every night after dusk and almost every morning at the first glimmer of sun on the horizon, in the thralls of heated and carnal passion. Even though March is nude, Mary Anne hardly notices, since Jonathan is the object of her lust.

Mary Anne's mind drifts, and Jonathan takes the place of March on the balcony. He wears no shirt nor pants. The muscles of his chest and shoulders shift and tighten as he crosses his arms and smiles at Mary Anne. Her eyes travel down his arms, the muscles of his torso, to his groin.

"Is there something wrong with your chest?" March stares at her with a quizzical look.

Mary Anne flutters her eyes, and her heartbeat drums in her neck, ears, and face. She snaps back to the present.

How long have I been daydreaming? How could I daydream at a time such as this? How long has she been waiting?

Mary Anne did not realize she had been dragging a finger in circles on her chest between her collarbones.

"Forgive me. I had a random thought of home," she lies. Mary Anne wishes it were true. She thinks of her mother often and worries about her health. But when she fantasizes about Thomas above her while they lie on his bed, Jonathan's face flashes in her thoughts. At first she felt guilty, but after a week, she welcomes Jonathan's intrusion.

March sips from the second bottle. The first sits empty on the rail. Her eyes trace the lines on the stone floor of the balcony rather than look at the darkening sky or the fire. Mary Anne glances to the hundreds of soldiers running in the courtyard below, out into the city, and somewhere among them Jonathan runs headlong into danger.

Always the hero. Her hero.

She does not hide the worry on her face. Neither can March, even with her steel exterior.

"He will be alright," Mary Anne tells March to try and comfort her.

"You think I don't know that?" March says without raising her eyes. "Jonathan and I have been on countless adventures together long before your shadow came across our path. And we will continue to do so long after you depart this world."

Mary Anne is unsure if March means when she leaves Wonderland or when she dies. What she is certain about is the fact March could not care less either way, as long as Mary Anne is gone.

March drinks again. A trickle escapes her mouth and runs down her neck.

"Tea?" Mary Anne asks, unable to climb back out of the pit she dug. "Juice?"

"Rum." Her eyes meet Mary Anne's for the first time. "Drink?"

"No, thank you. Is it not too early for liquor?"

March approaches the corner of the balcony and extends the bottle to Mary Anne. "Drink."

Be strong, or at least pretend to be until you are. She takes the bottle, closes her eyes, and tilts her head back. The liquor sloshes against her pressed lips. Hesitant at first, fearing its potency, but finally she takes her first drink. The taste matches the aroma—woody, molasses, and a hint of vanilla. A dangerous drink, for she knows it is liquor, but the flavors around it mask its severity. She hands the bottle back to March, who finishes its contents in a matter of seconds.

"You certainly can handle your liquor," says Mary Anne.

"Indeed, I can." March wipes her cheek with a sleeve. "It has proven useful in the past. I remember once I had to entertain several soldiers to get Cheshire and Jonathan out of a pinch." Her expression softens, lost in the past. "Years ago, they dared each other to steal a damned crest from the captain's tent in a camp on the northern shore. But the barrack tents surrounded the captain's. Two hundred soldiers, at least. They waited until the dead of night, went in, got the bloody golden crest, but cut their escape too short and did not make it out before the rotation change of the guards. I held their attention for more than an hour, until the lot were all stone drunk, and Jonathan and Cheshire got away."

Mary Anne catches the particular word choices March uses. *Entertain. Held their attention.* March may be skilled at drinking, but she must have used other methods to hold the guards at bay.

"I do not have a tale anywhere near as interesting," says Mary Anne. "I drank wine, sometimes champagne, always with Thomas. I would sneak next door and he would have two glasses waiting. We would sip and discuss our days before we would—"

"Thomas. The married man you were sleeping with." March chuckles. "You must fancy yourself quite the catch to steal him from under his wife."

"Not at all. We found something in each other. He found something in me he was not getting from his marriage. There is nothing wrong with that," Mary Anne says to convince herself as much as March.

"No judgment at all on my part." After a long inhale, March continues. "Since we are sharing a moment of honesty between women," says March, "you should know, I have thought about killing you several times over since you intruded on our lives."

Mary Anne is dumbstruck. This information does not surprise her, but she is shocked March would dare utter it out loud. This is the first time they have been alone since Briarwell.

"The night you first slept in our home," March continues. "A quick blade to the temple and you would have continued on in a dream never-ending. Then at the Inn in Briarwell, while Jonathan and Dormy were out gathering provisions. By then, my patience had waned, so I thought about slitting your throat. Not as elegant a death. Quite horrible, really, drowning from the inside. Then, during the battle with the mercenaries, I knew where you cowered in the wagon, and I could have easily thrusted a single sword through its wooden hull and found your heart. No one would have been the wiser."

Mary Anne's mouth dries and her eyes grow wide. The prospect of asking for help shrinking in her mind. "Why did you not?"

"Jonathan." March plays with the inside of her cheek with her tongue, licks her lips, and stretches her jaw. "I will do anything for him. And Cheshire. Just thought you should know."

"Why are you telling me this?"

"I am a killer. It is what I do. It is what I am good at. I have buried thousands of bodies in my time, and there are several thousand more graves yet to be dug for the foolish fucks who dare threaten me and mine." Her eyes turn as sharp as her blades. "Do not for a second believe I do not notice the way you look at him. Infatuation. Lust. I know the look, and it is painted across your face like a beacon."

Mary Anne's face flushes. Her heartbeat sends wave after wave of humiliation through her body. The small amount of liquor turns in her stomach, and she instantly feels the need to vomit. *Does March know I listen to them? Does she know I watch them? She has to. Or she is not as astute as she believes. Look down, Mary Anne. Look down.*

She lowers her eyes, as if March could see her thoughts if she gazed into them. "And now?" Mary Anne asks warily.

"Oh, I still have thoughts of killing you every now and again." March smiles. "But I won't. I want you out of Wonderland as badly as you want to leave yourself. So, at Jonathan's behest, I will do all in my power to get you the fuck out of here and out of our lives."

"I understand." She looks to the city below once more to avoid March.

"Bravo," says March, her tone brighter. "Your reaction was much better than I expected. I had thought you would run back into your bedchamber, bar the door, all that nonsense."

"You mean to tell me this was some sort of charade?"

"Oh, no. I meant every word. But you are learning. Perhaps there is hope for you."

At last, a moment of calm between the two. "March." Mary Anne swallows her nerves. "I need your assistance. I need your help." March arches her eyebrows, as shocked at the turn of events as Mary Anne. Mary Anne must choose her words carefully to not reveal her intrusion into their bedchamber. "The book I am to study is written in a language I do not understand. The Chamberlain will not translate any further until I pass the Second Tenet. So I find myself no closer to returning home. He said the language was called Old Prodigium, and it is only taught to the highly educated. I am not a fool. I can see the woman you are—strong, intelligent. Is there a chance you know how to read it?" Mary Anne waits, hoping March will not lie.

"Yes," she says slowly. "But I do not think—"

"The more I learn, the sooner I learn, the sooner I will leave." Mary Anne can see the interest grow in March's eyes. "Wait, before you answer." She decides the old adage may hold true. In this moment, she may be able to kill two birds with one stone. She rushes to her bed, lifts the corner of her mattress nearest the headboard, and retrieves the black ring. The white ring remains hidden. She walks back to the washroom window, pulse throbbing in her chest and hand. "I apologize for what I said earlier. I want to return home more than anything, and your help would be invaluable." She holds the black ring out to March. "Here. Take this as a token of my sincerity and appreciation."

March waves her head slowly from side to side mulling over both requests. "Fine." She takes the ring from Mary Anne. "On both accounts, against my better judgment. If this will rid you from my hair, so be it." It takes March a moment to realize Mary Anne stares at her, waiting for her to put the ring on. She rolls her eyes and slips the ring on to the middle finger of her left hand.

Mary Anne sighs with relief. She has a new tutor with the same goal. And if her theory about the rings is correct, she no longer has to wonder what it would be like to lay with Jonathan. A knock on Mary Anne's chamber door interrupts her thought and startles her.

"March," she says. "What do I do?"

"You answer the door." March collects the first empty bottle in the same hand as the other.

"But what if they have come for me? Should you not open the door?"

"You expect me to jump to your room to answer your door? Not likely."

Mary Anne jumps at a second knock. "March, please. You said you would protect me. Could you look through your door?"

"Do you really think if someone were to come and abduct you, they would knock?"

"Please, March."

March lets out a huff which sounds more like a creaking door. She disappears into her room.

Mary Anne tries to drown out the sound of her own heartbeat to listen. The slide of metal on leather. March unsheathing a sword. Her boots clack across the floor. The high-pitched whine of the door's iron hinges. Then nothing. Foreboding silence. Her heart rages.

They have come. If March is the best sword in all of Wonderland and she was defeated so swiftly, so easily, there is no hope for me.

March emerges from her room again, third bottle in hand and to her mouth. She waves Mary Anne away with the other, telling her to open the door, dispelling her worry.

She expects Grace when she opens the door, but the Duchess stands in the hallway, eyebrow raised, an uneasiness in her eyes.

"Follow me," the Duchess says. "We have much to do this morning."

CHAPTER 15

CHESHIRE

urious. Mary Anne must become queen.

Cheshire once again finds himself grateful he did not allow Mary Anne to die in the Rookwood—or kill her himself. If she is to become queen, there will be information the Duchess must share with her. There will be knowledge he can use once he sifts through the Duchess's lies. Like his entrance into Mirus, Mary Anne's path aligns with his own for now, and he will help her as much as use her to get closer to his end goal.

He lifts the long-forgotten trap door hidden in the back corner of the weaver's storehouse. The cobwebs between boards stretch and tear like sinews in a fresh gash. He peels off every layer of the soldier's uniform and rubs and massages his arms, legs, chest, and abdomen to rid himself of the lingering phantom sensation of fabric. After tying the clothing and armor back into a bundle, he drops it into the hole for later use. When he closes the trapdoor, its edges disappear into the wooden planks of the floor. Above the shelves and stacks of fabric, there is a space, roughly two feet, between the top shelf and ceiling where Cheshire climbs to, swats away cobwebs, wraps himself in his cloak, and lies motionless across the dusty wooden boards to wait for the Gryphon.

Cheshire thinks of the moment he shared with Jonathan, the Time he could share with him and March if he were not so hellbent on his quest. He cannot deny the relaxation he felt in his body, the clarity in his mind, the rejuvenation of his spirit. Every time he is with Jonathan, March, or both of them, it is as if they push away the darkness. Although he loathes the idea of helping Mary Anne, it will offer more opportunities to indulge and experiment with Jonathan and March.

Four quick, heavy thuds from the front of the weaver's store send a sudden chill through his body. He fidgets his toes and rubs his lips with his thumb. Facing the Gryphon while in a thousand year drunken stupor, out of his wits, was one thing, but confronting him now, fully recovered, is quite another. It is not fear which causes Cheshire's heart to race, but the anticipation, the exhilaration of the unknown, having never faced the Gryphon as an adult. Now Cheshire can fight him properly.

The door shuts with a rattled bang. Heavy boots continue to clunk against the wooden floor. Their pitch lowers and softens the closer the Gryphon approaches, then vanishes as if the Gryphon decided he could float the rest of the way. Cheshire strains his ears, squints his eyes, but he cannot find the Gryphon, the tallest man in all of Wonder, in the darkness. He has felt first-hand the weight of the Gryphon bear down upon him—twenty stone, at least. How could a man almost seven feet tall in armor disappear from all of Cheshire's senses?

There is a brief rustle of fabric, a puff of air, the instant pain from the crack of the Gryphon's palm against his chest, the breadth of his hand wide enough to grab both sides of Cheshire's vest. His world spins upside down as the Gryphon yanks him from the shelf and slams him against the back wall of the storehouse, forcing the air from Cheshire's lungs in a rasped, painful grunt. The Gryphon holds Cheshire against the wall with a straight arm, three feet from the floor, as if he weighs no more than the clothes he wears.

"You received my invitation," Cheshire wheezes. He tries to manage a laugh but coughs instead to reclaim his air, fighting against the pressure of the fist crushing his chest.

"What are you playing at, boy?" The full circles of Gryphon's yellow eyes pierce through the dark. "I told you to run."

"You are a fool to think I would." Cheshire struggles, punches, scrapes at the Gryphon with his toes, but he cannot free himself.

"The first time was a warning. Take this one as a threat," the Gryphon says with biting clarity. "Leave this city tonight. Do not return."

"What do you have to threaten me with?" Cheshire croaks out mockingly. "Will you kill me? Doubtful."

"I do not need to kill you to stop you. I can break your legs, snap your arms." The Gryphon grabs Cheshire's right wrist and squeezes.

Cheshire can feel his bones shift and screams from the pain. His fingertips feel as though they might burst.

"I doubt you will be able to accomplish whatever plans you have without them," says the Gryphon. "You will heed my orders, or you will suffer the consequences."

"Have I not suffered enough?"

The question and its truth take the Gryphon by surprise. His brow squeezes, his eyes dart down, and his hold relaxes for an instant from the thought of the guilt he must carry with him.

The eternity held within the half second the Gryphon is distracted is all Cheshire needs. He wrenches his hand free of the Gryphon's crushing vice hold, digs the fingers of both hands into the Gryphon's hand at his neck, raises his knees to his chest, and kicks downward with all his strength. Cheshire slides down the rough wall of the storehouse, pulling the Gryphon's arms with him. With his full weight keeping Cheshire against the wall, once Cheshire falls, the Gryphon loses his footing and stumbles forward, crashing into the wall and then to the floor.

Cheshire scrambles into the dark a quarter way through the storehouse and ducks between shelves.

"Foolish boy." The Gryphon grunts as he gets back to his feet.

"Do you think I lasted a thousand years against soldiers, guards, assassins, and the Ace without knowing how to handle every adversary? You do not intimidate me." Cheshire waits for a reply, but the Gryphon has disappeared from him once again.

Fuck.

"I am unsure if it will be your hubris or your mouth that will be your undoing, boy," the Gryphon says from the left. "You want my attention? You have it," his voice says from the right. "What is it you want?"

"Answers," says Cheshire, before slipping through an empty bottom shelf to the next room. Even in the darkness, the faint silhouette of the Gryphon, darker than the room, stalks without a sound. No, not stalks. *Hunts.* Although Cheshire's eyes are attuned to the deepest of shadows, the unfamiliar surroundings and the unpredictability of the Gryphon causes his hair to stand on end.

"Did you not care for the answers I gave while you attempted to beat them from my semi-conscious head?" The Gryphon reaches through the shelf, his fingers grazing Cheshire's hair.

Cheshire bolts across the small aisle, jumps through four more shelves, kicking fabric in all directions to throw off the Gryphon. He perches silently between two shelves while the bolts thud and settle to the floor.

I could lure the Gryphon between the shelves and push them on top of him, trapping him. But with his strength, he could hold up several shelves without struggle, if not push them back and pin me. If I shift—

Before Cheshire can continue his thought, a thick bolt of what feels like brocade swats him across the face with the force of a punch from Jonathan. He can taste the blood from his cheek. Dust from years of neglect explodes into the air. Cheshire tries to suppress his coughs, but his lungs resist him, and puffs of air and spit burst from his lips. He wraps his sash around his mouth and nose, wincing at the scraping pain on the side of his face, and sits balled, back to the storehouse wall between shelves.

"Is this encounter not going the way you envisioned?" The Gryphon chuckles with a show-rolling growl. "You did not run before when you struck me beneath the castle. Yet you hesitate now." The Gryphon coughs. Whether it be because he is not fully recovered or from the dust, it is a sign none-the-less and gives Cheshire a bearing of where he is. Two shelves to the right.

The sudden urge to move fills Cheshire's legs, muscles twitching. He scales the shelf inch by inch, making sure not to make the slightest noise, rub against any fabric, or press too hard on the wood for it to bend and creak. Once on top, he stretches across the gap to make his way toward the trapdoor. The shadow of the Gryphon walks directly underneath him and waits. Does he see Cheshire? Does he stand there in order to toy with him? He holds his breath.

"You freed me, spared me from the torrent of the bottle. For this, I am grateful. But I must ask myself, to what end? To help you destroy the city, the country, the Queendom I swore to protect? Have you even seen the damage and death you have brought to Mirus? What do you intend to change? Will you build the future on the blood of the innocent?"

The shadow shifts, and the Gryphon's arms burst upward, clawing for Cheshire. Cheshire throws himself to the left, narrowly escaping his grasp, then rolls over the shelf, falls to the ground with a thud, and continues to roll through the bottom shelves toward the trapdoor. He has fought the Ace for hundreds of years, knows his tactics, the way he thinks. The Gryphon, however, is completely unknown to Cheshire, except for the fleeting memories he has from childhood. In his arrogance, Cheshire thought he could outthink the Gryphon, but it is all he can do to outmaneuver him.

"Every civilization, past or present, has been built on the blood, bones, and misery of its people," Cheshire says. "Mirus is no different." He darts across the walkway again, but the Gryphon's boot catches the end of his cloak with a deafening thump. It catches under his arms and slams him to the floor. He recovers quickly, curls up, and kicks backward at the Gryphon's knee. The Gryphon is formidable, but no matter his skill and experience, he cannot avoid his age and the weight bearing down on his joints from his size. The Gryphon drops to his knee, growling in pain like a distant storm.

Cheshire pulls himself free and runs for the trapdoor. "Once I am done with the city, I will turn my gaze to the Duchess and cut her candle short. You can aid me or oppose me. The sooner my questions are answered, the sooner she dies. But until that happens, blood will be spilt, I promise you this. And that blood will be on your hands."

"I will thwart your every effort, boy."

"So be it." Cheshire reaches for the trapdoor and tries to open it, but debris from the shelves weigh it down. He braces himself, expecting the Gryphon to grab him by the neck, punch him across the jaw, or to slam his boot on the trapdoor. Nothing.

"I tire of this game." The Gryphon's voice sounds distant. "I gave you your answers the day you rescued me. Do what you will with the information. But come for me again, destroy another part of the city, take another life in this futile quest of yours, and you will not need theatrics to find me. I will seek you out. If I lay eyes on you again, then like my namesake, I will descend upon you with a fury you have never known. You will not see me coming, and I will make sure you will rue every decision you have made thus far." He opens the door to the storefront on the other end of the storehouse and pauses. The tone lifts in his voice but not the severity. "Remember, there are many who have tried to oppose the Duchess, and they have all, every one of them, failed." He sighs. "It was good to see you again. To know you are alive and well. Stay that way. Take care of yourself." He closes the door behind him and returns to the blaze.

Cheshire squats, out of breath, and looks to the faint rectangular light outline of the door. He rakes his fingers against his scalp, swirling them around his head, trying to make sense of this paradoxical encounter. Regardless, the Gryphon's warnings will not deter Cheshire from his quest, nor will they stop his pursuit for answers. The Gryphon knows more than he lets on, and Cheshire must know everything.

There are two more locations planned for Cheshire's opening salvo before he turns his attention to the castle and the Duchess. If the Gryphon wants to stop the impending destruction, he will tell Cheshire what he wants to know. He thinks back to the answers the Gryphon gave him as he spit up blood in the catacombs beneath the castle. Cheshire needs to know if the Gryphon can be trusted, if his words were indeed true. But to do so will break him to his core. He will confront the Gryphon again, get the exact location of his mother's grave, and see it with his own eyes.

"You tire of the game," says Cheshire, "but it has only begun."

CHAPTER 16

MARY ANNE

Mary Anne follows a step behind the Duchess at a hastened pace. Their heeled boots echo in rhythm against the floor as they walk through the lofty hallways of the castle. The journey is silent until the Duchess leads Mary Anne down an unfamiliar corridor.

"Where are we going?" Mary Anne asks.

"The Long Hall," the Duchess says without a look back or missing a step. She stops in front of a large, arched, oak door. "Tell me," the Duchess says, "where is your advisor? Should he not be by your side?"

Of all the questions to ask. Jonathan should be by her side. She wants him by her side. But she could not deny the look in his eyes, the call to help others, as he did for her.

"He asked to accompany the Gryphon into the city to render aid. The Gryphon denied his request, but I allowed him to go. I could not in good faith stop him. I am sorry."

The Duchess huffs as if to laugh but keeps an unbreakable stare with Mary Anne. "No, you are not," the Duchess corrects her. "Queens cannot afford to be sorry. They do not apologize or show weakness. You will not win over anyone with platitudes and courtesies, let alone a crowd. Collect yourself. We have work to do."

Crowd?

"We have hidden within the castle long enough. The attack this morning has forced our hand. I need to make an appearance, and there is no point in hiding you any longer." The Duchess dusts the front of her gown with both hands to straighten any lingering wrinkles, pulls at the lace around her neck to increase its volume, and smooths the hair at her temples, hiding any stray gray curls under her bulbous hat. She pulls on the large iron ring of the door, and its hinges groan as it swings open, releasing the muffled roar of what must be hundreds of voices beyond the door.

Mary Anne wishes she could retreat to thoughts of Jonathan on the balcony or one of the paintings behind her to hide in their darkness. She smooths the front of her dress, mimicking the Duchess, but presses hard against her thighs to keep her hands from trembling. She tries to swallow again, to keep the fear at bay, but the knot the size of an apple refuses to budge from her throat.

She steps through the door and onto a wide mezzanine with thick, spiral, wooden pillars. The distinct smell of old cedar hangs in the air. Short wood panels of carved trees, deer, and decorative curves create a short wall around them, and through tiny holes, Mary Anne can see the throng of Mirusian citizens, out-of-focus shapes and colors, squirming and shifting back and forth.

The Duchess turns back and extends a hand to call Mary Anne by her side.

Mary Anne tucks her hands behind her back and looks over the railing at the crowd inside the ridiculously lengthy hall. Most of the townspeople continue their conversations, but within the crowd, Mary Anne catches the eyes of several who look upon her. Some raise their eyebrows and widen their eyes, others sneer and press their lips together, and others express some facial expression in between.

Upon searching the crowd, Mary Anne notices a thin walkway divides its length and the townspeople. The more elegantly dressed citizens of the Crest stand to the right with room to spare, while the rest—those of Stonehaven and farmers, dressed in working linens and cottons—are on the left, packed like sardines.

"Do not bite your lip, Mary Anne," a voice says from beside her. Chamberlain Weiss speaks through barely parted lips.

She releases the grip she has on her bottom lip, feeling the divots with her tongue.

He sniffs and shrugs his tiny spectacles back from the point of his nose. At first appearance, Mary Anne thinks him to be completely at ease, but his gloved hands say otherwise. Chamberlain Weiss holds them clasped in front of him, but the middle finger of the clasped hand taps incessantly at one of the silver buttons of his long robes. "Confidence," he reassures her.

The thought of both Chamberlain Weiss and the Duchess unnerved sends a cold snap through Mary Anne's marrow. Though no one else in the room would be the wiser.

"Is it safe," Mary Anne whispers to Chamberlain Weiss, "to have all these people in the castle?"

"The Long Hall was specifically built and designed for the queen to be able to speak to the people. You will notice there is no way leading up or down from the mezzanine."

"But with all that has transpired—Uriah and Lysander— is it wise?" Mary Anne asks without a glance in Chamberlain Weiss's direction.

"Every citizen was searched by the soldiers and Castle Guard at the gate and the door to ensure no weapon entered," says Chamberlain Weiss. "Besides, we cannot ignore the people now."

"That will be enough of that," says the Duchess. "We have hidden from the people long enough." She takes her place at the center of the balcony on a mauve rug with holes the exact size of her boots worn down to the wood beneath. She raises a hand, and the people from both sides of the hall form a line down the middle walkway.

"We are here for you." The Duchess addresses the crowd. "What happened this morning is an absolute travesty. Make no mistake, we will discover if this was an accident or assault against our fair city. Please step forward and the crown... the Queendom will render aid. I know there are those among you with simpler requests, but please let those affected by this morning's events step forward first."

Over the course of an hour, the Duchess listens to the requests of more than four dozen pleas. Shaken townspeople with wiped soot marks covering their face and arms humbly ask for help, having completely lost every possession as well as their home. Grief-stricken wives, mothers, and fathers ask for the whereabouts of their sons and husbands who worked the morning shift in the jail, fearing the answer. But there is nothing to report yet; the Gryphon and Jonathan are yet to return from Stonehaven.

The Duchess remains calm and collected no matter the state of the townspeople speaking or screaming at her. She offers funds to help replace what can be, and soldiers—which she knows she cannot spare, but does so anyway—to help in the efforts to rebuild.

Once the townspeople asking for aid and repair leave, most satisfied, some furious, but all still in bewilderment, a new line forms with townspeople from both sides of the room. A farmer with odd-shaped overalls and cinnamon-colored hair steps onto a small, raised platform covered by a deep-crimson rug.

"What can we do for you today?" the Duchess asks.

"My cattle... they are... that is..." He tries to speak, but his eyes dart back and forth from the Duchess to Mary Anne.

"Please, there are many of you today," the Duchess continues. "Be brief."

"Your pardon, Your Grace," the farmer says. "I run a farmstead with my family between here and the Queenwood. There have been beast sightings again."

Mary Anne looks up to Chamberlain Weiss without turning her head and tries her best to speak low, without moving her lips as he did. "Are all of these people in need of something?"

"Of course," he replies. "Did you think we just sat here in our lofty castle and ignored the people below? The morning after every new moon, the doors to the Long Hall are open to the public to air any concerns, needs, or grievances. It is taxing. Without a queen, the burden falls on the Duchess to tend to the people. Having a queen on the throne means as much to them, and us, as it does to you, different of course, but just as important."

Mary Anne searches the faces of the crowd. Every one of them, high or low born, has a sense of longing in their eyes, though the citizens from the Crest have learned to mask theirs better.

"Yes," the Duchess answers the farmer. "The Queendom can replace the four oxen you lost to the beasts."

"Thank you, Your Grace," he says. His eyes continue to bounce back and forth from the Duchess to Mary Anne as he bows and steps off the platform.

A woman in a long amber robe with a thick plumage of feathers around her collar steps onto the platform and asks for justice against a neighbor who broke a vase by the gate to her house. After her, a man covered in soot tries his best to wipe his face clean with a dirty sleeve before he steps onto the platform and asks for aid to rebuild the furnaces in the Boroughs. The line continues with more requests, some life threatening, some mundane minutia. The needs of the people and the generosity of the Duchess compel Mary Anne forward. She stands beside the Duchess and places her hands upon the rail, smiling and nodding at every citizen after they speak. There is nothing more she can offer them. At least for now.

After at least two dozen more townspeople have made their requests, two figures appear at the entrance at the far end of the Long Hall, distorted by the sunlight behind them. But as they walk toward the platform, Mary Anne recognizes them immediately. Even though she has only seen them on horseback, the sheer arrogance in their stride is unmistakable.

"Uriah and Lysander," she says under her breath.

A murmur grows within the crowd. Those from the Crest haughtily straighten their posture and lift their noses higher into the air, watching for the Duchess's reaction, while the other half of the room grumble in confusion.

"Yes," the Duchess whispers back, never looking away from their approach.

Mary Anne lifts her heel, ready to move back to the door.

"Do not retreat. Never. Not to these two," says the Duchess, sensing Mary Anne's apprehension. "Do not give them an inch."

Uriah's white robes, with their gold, braided lining, almost float behind him while he walks down the aisle, appearing angelic—smooth skin with a gentle expression upon his face, sunlight gleaming, radiating off his golden belt and single pauldron. But from what little Mary Anne has seen of him, nothing could be farther from the truth. His brother Lysander walks beside him, as different in appearance as a bear is to a swan—hulking, bearded, with a charcoal cape with the fur of some animal upon its collar draped long over his left side. The citizens of the Crest make room for them close to the platform. They wait and watch as the Duchess attends to two dozen more townspeople.

Mary Anne's eyes bounce from one to the other, waiting for them to cause a disruption or lash out, but they never so much as look in her direction. She knows they feel her eyes upon them, and they willfully ignore her. Mary Anne's heartbeat thumps in her entire body at the sight of their smug faces. A heat fueled by both fear and resentment courses from her chest to the tips of her fingers and toes. They feel as though they are about to burst. She should let no one have such a hold over her, but these two men are here with the sole purpose of keeping her from becoming queen. Keep her from returning home.

She wonders if they would be open to a reasonable discussion. If they knew her plan to leave Wonderland forever and return home, perhaps they would be amenable to terms to allow her to become queen, knowing she will leave the throne vacant soon enough.

As if on cue, they both look at Mary Anne without moving their heads—their stares void of any hint of diplomacy or peace.

Despite the aid of the Duchess, Chamberlain Weiss, and Jonathan, her fate balances precariously on the edge of their sharp tongues. Upon their first encounter in the Market, a few words from them were enough to incite a riot, which could have overtaken her and Jonathan if not for her escort of soldiers.

Mary Anne relaxes her forehead, unsure of how long she has scowled at them. Once the short merchant on the platform bows his head and steps down, Mary Anne grabs onto the rail like the Duchess and addresses her opponents. "And you two gentlemen? Do you have anything to say?" Mary Anne embraces the heat flowing through her skin, holds her chin up, and calls them by name. "Uriah. Lysander."

Chamberlain Weiss suppresses his gasp behind pressed lips, and the corner of the Duchess's smile wavers.

Uriah and Lysander smile, their innocence a charade, and approach the platform.

Lysander steps up first. "Hello, Your... Grace," he says to the Duchess, the pause in his words full of detestation for her, for Mary Anne, and the simple fact he must stand beneath them.

"I heard you and your brother returned to Mirus," says the Duchess, confidence unwavering. "I am sure Adamas misses their prized sons dearly. It has been almost two weeks, if my count is correct. I wondered when you would officially call upon us."

"I assure you, other business has taken priority," Uriah says sweetly. "But it would appear an audience with you is necessary. You see, my brother and I have enjoyed the luxuries of the Crest for this past fortnight, relaxing, catching up with old family acquaintances, yet your soldiers stalk us at every move, prowl outside our temporary residence while we entertain guests, and question them as soon as they leave."

"Trust us," Lysander says, stoic and severe, yet still calm, "the whores who leave have nothing worthwhile to tell, save for the experience."

"So what is it you require?" Mary Anne asks, biting the inside of her cheeks.

Uriah looks at her again and tilts his head. "Why, all we want is the freedom to conduct our business without such harassment."

The Duchess inhales deep and then sets upon them. "You come here and ask for what? Leniency? When there are multiple attacks on the loyal soldiers of Mirus as well as acts of sabotage throughout the city? All of which started with your arrival. We by no means make any accusations, of course, but understand we must pay close attention to coincidence."

"Of course," says Lysander, stepping onto the platform next to his brother. "And as you can see, we come before you to simply talk. No weapons. No malice. Just talk."

Though they carry no sword, Mary Anne knows in this moment their words are more dangerous than any other weapon they could wield. It would be prudent to expel them from the Long Hall before their words can poison the masses further. Surely the Duchess has given this thought consideration? But treating them as hostile when they have done nothing wrong would transform them from aggressors to victims. Mary Anne must wait to see what unfolds, hoping they do something to require the soldiers to forcibly remove them from the castle grounds.

"As you and your soldiers have observed," Lysander continues, "we have not left the comfort of the women we keep, let alone the Crest. These attacks, fires, and murders have happened throughout the city. They could not have been orchestrated by us. There are many who will account for our whereabouts and activities."

Mary Anne can see the deceit swirling in their eyes and seeping out from between their teeth, the schemes twisting in their minds, and she wonders how their blatant actions could bewitch anyone.

Uriah turns away from the Duchess and addresses the crowd. "Her concerns are admirable. But there is another alternative that should be addressed since our involvement in these matters can easily be disproven. The matter of the Queen Slayer's return to Mirus."

The room falls silent—no shift of fabric, no breath—only the breeze whistling through the archways at the far end of the Long Hall.

Queen Slayer? The thought makes the muscles in Mary Anne's neck twinge. *What or who do they speak of? Is this yet another adversary I must add to the growing list? Uriah and Lysander bent on not seeing her take the throne. A murderous cult who believe I am some goddess and want to drink my blood. Now there is someone in Mirus branded a Queen Slayer?* She wants to back away, run through the door, and find Jonathan. This congregation does not feel safe any longer.

Uriah methodically paces along the perimeter of the platform as he continues. "If we were your primary concern, what would be the purpose of the increased patrols in the Boroughs and Stonehaven? Ladies and gentlemen, the harsh truth of the matter, whether or not the Duchess wishes to divulge this information, is the Queen Slayer has indeed returned to our fair city and is at this very moment wreaking chaos."

Townspeople whisper among themselves but not quiet enough to avoid Mary Anne's ears. "He is within the city walls?" a well-dressed woman from the Crest asks the gentleman next to her.

"What of our children?" A woman from Stonehaven wrings her hands in her linen apron.

"He killed my father," says a farmer toward the front of the crowd. "I'll not see him take anyone else."

"How will we be able to sleep at night knowing there is a murderer on the loose?" another voice calls out, louder than the others.

"How are we to go about our lives fearing the worst?" a young woman asks the Duchess softly.

"Is this true?" Mary Anne asks the Duchess under her breath. "There is a queen slayer? And in the city, no less? When was someone going to tell me about this?"

"A discussion for later," she whispers back, her voice hard as marble. The smile she painted on her face to entertain Uriah and Lysander melts away, and she fights against the tugging muscles in her face to keep them from a scowl.

"It is a logical assumption," says Lysander. "Wouldn't you say? Perhaps if you ordered your soldiers to spend less time following us, they could work to find the murderer hiding within the city walls."

The Duchess inhales deep through her nose, but Uriah cuts her off before she can respond.

"Perhaps his apprehension should be your priority, considering who stands by your side." Uriah's eyes shift slowly to Mary Anne.

He is correct. And they speak the truth. He must. Mary Anne waits for some sign from the Duchess, a rebuttal, or some condemnation for their lies. But instead—

"Do you think the patrols throughout the city are for naught?" The Duchess smiles again. "Soldiers search day and night throughout the entirety of Mirus."

"We understand you are shorthanded," says Lysander, poking at the Duchess for a response. "Several hundred soldiers deserted, if we heard correctly, maybe thousands."

"Nothing we are worried about," the Duchess says confidently. "With the Gryphon's return we will all soon rest easy." She turns her attention to the crowd. "I assure everyone in attendance, your wellbeing is of the utmost importance to us. To me. If the Queen Slayer is indeed within the city, it is only a matter of time before we deal with him, and the nightmare will be over once and for all."

The crowd on both sides of the aisle nod to their neighbors, encouraged to hear her reassurance.

"So," the Duchess continues, "Uriah, your request this morning is for fewer soldiers to patrol the Crest?"

"Precisely," says Uriah, "And if—"

"Though I will take your suggestion under consideration," the Duchess continues, "I am sure with the Queen Slayer in the city, the citizens of the Crest would want more soldiers to patrol their streets, to quell any attempt on their lives or damage to their property. Would you not agree?"

The townspeople all nod again, vigorously. Mary Anne smiles at the masterful reversal by the Duchess, thwarting Uriah and Lysander's attempt to diminish the townspeople's confidence in her with a smile and only a few words.

I can learn much from her during my time here.

"So, if that is all," says the Duchess, "I will bid you and your brother a good day."

"We thank you for your audience," says Lysander.

"Is there anyone else who would like to make a request?" Uriah asks the crowd.

Since they stepped foot on the platform, those in line behind them dispersed and joined their respective sides of the Long Hall.

"I have one," the voice of a woman echoes from the entrance.

Uriah and Lysander exchange a glance, then a smirk, and step down from the platform.

The woman's heels click against the stone floor in silence of the now hushed hall as she approaches. Her steps keep time like the slowest beat of a metronome. She wears the most elegant white coat Mary Anne has ever seen, with a full collar of white fur and cuffs to match.

As she nears the platform, the details of her face become clearer to Mary Anne. The lines on her cheeks and around her eyes suggest she is near Mary Anne's mother's age, though there are more around this woman's lips when she presses them together. Her silver hair is up in a proper bun high on the back of her head, and the deep, carnation-pink hair of her temples swirl into it like a peppermint.

"Bronwen March," says the Duchess. "I am surprised to see you here. What could I possibly do for you?"

Immediately, Mary Anne can see the resemblance, not just in the face but the confident air, though her mother's seems to be at an extreme. Questions about March erupt in Mary Anne's mind like embers in a fire. She is from Mirus? Did she leave willingly, or did her mother reject her for her choices? Her mother is wealthy beyond measure, so why choose to live in seclusion? It is the same question she asked herself about Jonathan and his decision to ignore his reputation.

"I never thought to find myself here as if I were a beggar or had need of anything," March's mother scoffs. "But here I am."

"What can we do for you this day?" The Duchess smiles warmly.

"Audience," March's mother replies and points directly at Mary Anne. "With her. I know the past few weeks have no doubt been stressful, but it is time to introduce this young girl, our future queen to us, yes?" She does not let the Duchess respond. "I propose a small gathering here in the safety of the castle, nothing extravagant, conversation over tea and cake perhaps, in order for us to know this young woman better."

"That sounds marvelous—" the Duchess tries to say.

"To see if she is fit to rule," March's mother continues. "Not today, of course, but soon. You can manage this, can you not? I will invite some of the prominent families of Mirus and Wonderland to attend." She glances back at Uriah and Lysander. "I await your response."

Her arrival was not by chance. She is in league with Uriah and Lysander and the three of them orchestrated this meeting, and Mary Anne cannot help but feel the sinister intentions behind every word she speaks.

Be strong. Do not retreat. Not to them.

"I accept," Mary Anne says, to the dismay of Chamberlain Weiss.

"Excellent," the Duchess says before Mary Anne can add another word. "But we must observe one of the oldest traditions for this auspicious occasion. Croquet. Give us time to make the necessary preparations to the grounds, roughly two weeks' time, and you will be welcome."

"Until then." March's mother smiles without her eyes, turns, and walks back down the aisle and out of the Long Hall, with Uriah and Lysander following at a distance.

"My apologies for certain people taking up most of your time," says the Duchess. "We will conclude for today. Chamberlain Weiss will stay behind and record any other immediate needs which must be met. Thank you for your time today." And with a small raise of her hand, she turns and pushes the door open to exit the Long Hall, Mary Anne at her heels.

Once on the other side and the door shut behind them, the Duchess releases a long sigh and sits back against one of the stone walls, letting her rigid posture melt. She hangs her head and slowly massages her temples with the thumb and middle finger of her right hand, muttering something too quiet for Mary Anne to hear. This is a much different woman than Mary Anne has grown accustomed to following around the castle—vulnerable, affected, human.

"Madam," Mary Anne says after a lengthy silence. "Are you well?"

"Yes, my dear. Quite. Thank you for asking." The Duchess sounds like Mary Anne's mother resting in her study chair after a long and weary day. "Surprising, but not unexpected. I knew it was only a matter of time before those wolves came sniffing."

"Did I make the right decision?" Mary Anne asks. She has hidden in the castle for the past two weeks and now she has initiated a croquet game—a game which she knows nothing of—and invited prominent figures from the city. From the looks they shared, if March's mother is in attendance, Uriah and Lysander will be as well.

"A queen always makes the right decision," the Duchess says as she stands and straightens herself again, with a small groan and pop of her back. "Whether they are smart decisions is quite another matter entirely."

Mary Anne and the Duchess share a laugh for the first time since their introduction—without pretense, or meant as deflection or punctuation, but a genuine laugh between the two women. They begin their long walk back through the castle.

As they walk, just as before, Mary Anne notices a difference in the Duchess's stride. On the way to the Long Hall she floated regally, hands in the air at her sides, gown swishing from side to side, chin gracefully raised, pointing her direction. But now she walks in step with Mary Anne, slower, as if they were perhaps taking a stroll in a garden as acquaintances instead of the positions they find themselves in. Find is not the right word. Trapped. The Duchess gets no honor, glory, nor praise for her work, yet she continues tirelessly because someone must, and keep up appearances whilst doing so.

Despite this shared moment, a comment from earlier scratches at Mary Anne's thoughts, and she must know more. "Madam, if I may ask a question. Who, or what, is the Queen Slayer?"

PART II

STONEHAVEN

CHAPTER 17

JONATHAN

Every afternoon for the past week, since the explosion of the hanging cells and Lysander and Uriah's proclamation in the Long Hall, Jonathan walks through all of Stonehaven, tipping his hat to those who meet his eye and smiling, even, to those who do not, while his other hand rests on the hilt of his sword. For the most part, his greetings are genuine, and he keeps his concern subdued, but he wishes he did not have to worry about who will strike first: Cheshire, Lysander and Uriah, or this cult.

Thirteen. Thirteen more knives peek out from the backs of belts, within jackets, and out from boots this morning alone, bringing the total to two hundred and thirty-seven. These people who carry them, unlike when he first arrived, are not from Mirus. They slowly trickle into the city at someone's behest.

There must be someone. A mob cannot move of its own accord, can it?

The Row is crowded this day, ever more so than usual, from the laborers going to, coming from, or on break from the reconstruction of the hanging cells. The faint scent of shit from the pit below trails them.

Jonathan stops by one of his favorite merchants, who frequents the

Warrens to the southwest. The animal pelts he wears around his collar and hanging from his belt, along with his wild yet matted pumpkin-colored beard, make him appear double in size. The teas he brings, while common and sweet, always soothe Jonathan's nerves.

While perusing through his collection kept in squat glass bottles, low giggles from behind Jonathan reach his ear over the usual haggling of prices and barking of demands. Three young women shop at the fishmonger across the thoroughfare, covering their mouths to hide their smiles, and stare at him through the corner of their eyes. Their thoughts are plain as day on their faces. When Jonathan meets their eyes, the woman with hair the color of a blue sky with whips of high clouds elbows the one with the pale yellow of a Blue Tit. He tips his hat to them and drops his eyes quickly to see if any sign of a knife protrudes from their long shifts or corsets. They misunderstand Jonathan's intentions and walk away, whispering and laughing even more. The third with hair the bright pink of an apple blossom, close to March's color, lingers for a moment and raises her eyebrows to Jonathan before following her friends, or rather her sisters in trade. From the garments they wear, and the way the surrounding townspeople avoid their gaze, they must work together at the Corolla Garden—the brothel in the west end of Stonehaven.

Jonathan's eyes follow them as they weave through the crowded market, turning back every so often, wondering why they stared—out of some misguided attraction, or could they be in league, spies, with any of their enemies. Even if they are innocent, a man they pass by is not.

Far in the distance, four streets away, through bonnets, kerchiefs, torques, wide-brimmed leather hunters, skullcaps, chaperons, tricorns, hoods, and an assortment Jonathan or his father hand crafted themselves, an all too familiar bald head and film-covered eye stands out like a gleaming white stone in a sea of volcanic glass. One of Lysander and Uriah's men, not seen since they took part in the Red Knight's escape. The man watches Jonathan with his good eye but turns frantically and disappears down the alley behind him when Jonathan meets his gaze, almost knocking over a stack of baskets.

"Terrence," Jonathan says under his breath, "or something." He never learned his or his companion's name all those weeks ago in the Rookwood.

The soldiers who defected with the Red Knight have not been seen since. Whoever turned them was cunning enough to select men who had no wives, children, or parents left alive to question. Their homes in the city and countryside sit abandoned, their belongings and livestock claimed and sold for their treachery. But Terrence, and no doubt his partner, walk freely among the people, because only a small circle knows their true involvement.

Jonathan pays three silver coins for a jar of Vermillion Wild Flower and of Long Stem Honey and tells the merchant he will return to pick them up shortly.

"Thank you kindly, Carter's son," the merchant says while setting the jars aside. "I'll be sure to look for you."

Lysander and Uriah have their spies watching Jonathan. Every day he has walked through the streets of Mirus focused on searching for the damned knives of the cult, but he did not give thought to look for anyone watching him. March and Cheshire are much better in these situations.

How would they think? What would they think? The three times Jonathan has seen these two men before, they have always been together, so it stands to reason the other is close. Jonathan casually walks through the street toward the alley where Terrence fled.

"Good afternoon, Jonathan." A soft-faced old woman waves to him from behind her apple cart.

Not even three paces farther, a small boy with a homemade stitched leather top hat runs up to Jonathan and stops at his feet. He says nothing. Instead, he smiles from ear to ear, with one of his front teeth coming in. He laughs and runs back into the crowd, his hat falling over his eyes.

At the corner of the alley, Jonathan overhears two older women talking to each other as he passes. "Carter's son has certainly turned into quite a man, hasn't he?" one says. "The arms and chest of a smith and the midsection of a knight."

"What I wouldn't give to have those hands touch me the way he touches them hats," the other says.

He ignores their comments and looks down the alley for any sign of Terrence. It turns sharply after the shadow of the first building, and in the short stretch he can see, there are three doors, one cellar entrance, and four sets of tall, shuttered windows which could easily be used for escape. Even now, he could watch Jonathan through any of them, or he could have simply escaped to any other part of the city.

"What's he looking at?" one of the women says. "What's he staring at him for? Like he's got a chance in the nine hells."

"We've got a better chance at getting fucked by Carter's boy than he does," the other cackles.

Jonathan strains his eyes to look at the women without turning his head, curious as to the *he* they speak of. One of them continues to laugh silently and gestures across the street behind Jonathan. The time for subtlety is over. He has never been any good at it anyway. Jonathan turns his head quickly. Across the street, through the crowd of unsuspecting townspeople passing between them, he locks eyes with the second bandit from the Rookwood—Marcus, or whatever his name is. His voyeur wears a pale blue hood and scarf to conceal his identity, but his pronounced nose is visible under the wrapping, and the scar on his cheek running up to his brow betrays him.

Jonathan stares intently at the good eye of the bandit, waiting to see who will move first.

"Damn," one of the old women says behind him. "Guess I was wrong."

The bandit looks down the street, perhaps in search of his partner, and gives Jonathan the opening he needs. He lunges for Marcus, trying to navigate the torrent of townspeople shopping in the market without shoving any of them, but loses sight of his target through the people. His eyes jump to every blue hood in the crowd—seven to the east alone, six to the west, nine of which face his direction. There is no way to follow and know which direction Marcus fled. And now Jonathan is the center of attention.

A group has gathered at the corner of one of the high wooden walkways running through the city, smiles and curiosity beaming down on him like the afternoon sun. Most who pass smile or walk by wide-eyed. Merchants he knows well beckon to him to join them at their stores.

He realizes the unsettling and uncomfortable truth. As much as he has used it to his advantage in the past, everyone in Mirus knows who he is. Even those he does not recognize, travelers who have entered the city for Mary Anne, at least know of him, which adds great complexity to his search for cult members. He could learn from his last encounter with Cheshire, as he walked unseen as a soldier in the wake of his attack on the city, but because of his lineage and reputation, Jonathan does not have the same luxury. He contemplates a disguise as well but then realizes he does not have to be the one who is invisible, or the spy at all, if the price is enticing enough.

A smile and a wink buys Jonathan a small piece of parchment and use of a quill from the tanner in the Row. He scribbles a quick compass rose and note to March.

Read your poetry. Fourth volume. When will the next be ready? Catherine is impatient. Fourth is the best by far. Third was thought to be the best, but this is incredible. Need of your next work soon. Signed, *E.*

Over the centuries, March and Jonathan have created numerous codes and ciphers for games. Today, he uses the simplest to convey his meaning.

The first letter of the first word of every sentence signify the consonants in the cypher, except when a number. Each written number corresponds to a specific vowel in their alphabet. The signature in this case indicates a cardinal direction, hinted by the compass rose. He wishes for March to meet him at the east end of the Row with coin for their next endeavor. He knows March will understand, though in the past they use this code in conversation and with snaps or taps instead of written numbers.

He enlists the help of three youths—two girls and a boy with no shoes and dirt to their feet and shins from the fields—to be his couriers with strict instructions to deliver the note to the front gate of the castle. He pays them with the three silver coins in his pocket, and they disappear into the woodwork, giggling as they go. If Terrence and Marcus still watch him, they will face a choice—pursue the children, who could outrun them on their best day, or stay and watch Jonathan. On the off chance they catch them and retrieve the note, there is no way in all the heavens they will understand its meaning.

As dusk approaches, March meets Jonathan at the west entrance of the Row where the canvas canopies between buildings end. She rests one hand on the hilt of her sword and clutches the pouches tied to one of her belts. The coins inside jingle louder as she descends the last few stairs.

"Could you not have returned to the castle yourself?" Her fingernail taps the iron ball at the end of her hilt twice. "Vexing is what you are." Another two taps. "Return to the castle with me this instant."

He kisses her on the forehead and rubs the end of his nose along her hair line.

"Haven't used that one in a while," she whispers to his chest, referring to the coded message. "We will have to dust off many more, I fear."

Jonathan wraps his arm around March's exposed waist, under her cropped jacket, and together they make their way west, snaking through back alleys and shadowed underpasses beneath the twisting highways, limiting their interactions and doubling back four times in case Terrence and Marcus still watch. The two bandits are not capable combatants nor skilled trackers, but Jonathan made himself easy quarry earlier, walking in plain sight, focused so intently on his search for knives.

The farther west they travel in Stonehaven, the more cobbled streets, dwellings, and businesses transform to wide rocky streets crunching beneath their feet, and towering storehouses and granaries loom overhead. Jonathan sips from his flask as they emerge from the alley across the street from the Corolla Garden. Its lush yard and pristine exterior are out of place, belonging to the Crest rather than Stonehaven. But its location is strategic, on the only street from the port entrance of Mirus, which is a stone's throw away.

Jonathan looks to March with raised eyebrows. *Ready?* they ask.

Always, says the twinkle in March's eye.

He swoops her up in his arms and wraps her legs around his waist. They kiss furiously for a moment against the weathered grain storehouse before walking across the street through the Garden's iron fence, meant as a funnel more than protection. March runs the fingers of both hands through Jonathan's hair while they kiss, sending shivers down his body. She exhales hard through her nose against his cheek at the pungent miasma of spicy perfumes and oils forcing itself into their nostrils the closer they draw to the wide, open front doors.

Inside, it may as well be twilight. Dense purple and crimson damask curtains blot out every window on the main floor, allowing the sun only a voyeur's peek through the main doors. Sculpted bronze fixtures made to look like arms cut before the elbow poke out from the wall and pinch small hanging lanterns between their fingers. The farther Jonathan and March walk in, the darker the world becomes, bathing everything in hues of oranges, purples, and reds. The constant moist humidity of Mirus doubles as they step away from the door. Jonathan can feel his trousers stick to his thighs and his shirt suction to his body. The clunk of his boots on the wood floor draws the attention of the Madam Rose. She bursts through the opening between two thick embroidered curtains and closes them swiftly behind her.

She saunters to them, poking her cheek with her tongue, annoyed at the display of affection, but once Jonathan sets March down, her mood improves dramatically. "Well, well, well. Never did I think the strapping Jonathan Carter would grace our establishment." She straightens her curled wig, and her eyes drop to Jonathan's groin. "At least, not outside of my personal fantasies. May I handle you personally? I'm not as limber as I once was, but with your arms, you can bend me any which way you see fit. And I assure you, I can pleasure a man better and with more skill than any of my girls." The muffled sound of laughter, moans, and screams of feigned ecstasy punctuate her words. "I can handle you both if you wish?"

Jonathan laughs and nods as he bites at March's ear and runs his hands upon her back. "No, madam. But thank you."

"Worth a shot," she says, walking away. "And, Lady Audrianna, fancy to see you here. Whatever will people say, seeing you enter or leave this establishment?"

"Nothing more than the rumors already spread through the city," says March, sliding her hand down the front of Jonathan's trousers.

Rose raises an eyebrow and shrugs her shoulders. "As long as you're aware. But I must say, it is a grand day. It's rare we get visitors from the Crest here."

March guffaws. "You're having a laugh. I can name at least three dozen men and women who frequent here on the daily." She turns to the main salon where prices and terms are negotiated. "I can point out eight to you right now."

"I don't have a clue what you speak of." Rose sniffs and closes the partially open curtain to a salon where both men and women are entertaining drinks with the *flowers* of the Garden, as they are called. She models her business on the tales of the secluded, idyllic garden of Wonderland far to the west, mocking its majesty and beauty. Few have laid eyes upon its outer wall, and fewer still have entered. Jonathan and March have the honor of including themselves in the number. "What brings you two to my humble establishment?"

"A room," says March, massaging Jonathan.

"For the both of us." Jonathan grabs March around the waist and kisses her temple. "Cannot seem to wait until we get back to our own accommodations."

"We are not an inn." Rose tugs at the bottom of her whalebone corset. "You don't pay for the room, you pay for the flowers."

"Trust us." March slides both hands up Jonathan's linen shirt to rub his chest, exposing his torso. "We will gather a few along the way."

Rose, distracted by Jonathan's body, mutters a few incoherent words and circles a finger on the rose tattooed on her ample cleavage. She shakes her head to gather her wits. "Most of my flowers are already busy with other tenders. I would be more than happy to pick a select—"

"There were three," says Jonathan, "who were in the market earlier this morning. They will do nicely."

"My pansies?" She taps her fingers of her right hand on her thumb. No one else would notice such a slight movement, but Jonathan knows counting when he sees it. She is calculating the price. "My pride and joys. Can't have all three. Doubt you could afford even one. They are in high demand, and I just so happen to have several gentlemen lined up for them this evening. Hardly fair to hog them all to yourselves, no matter who you are, or how scrumptious you look."

March ignores Rose and pulls Jonathan's shirt off over his head in one swoop and bites at his chest.

"Fuck me," says Rose. "And I don't mean that as just an exclamation. Fuck me, for the love of any deity in the heavens what will listen. Fuck me."

Jonathan chuckles. He taps March on the small of her back with a finger twice. She pulls a sizable leather pouch from her belt and holds it out for Rose. She bounces it once in her palm for the coins within to perk Rose's ears.

"We are sure this will cover all three women, as well as several return visits," says Jonathan.

"Done." Rose snatches the pouch from March and snaps with her other hand. "But the shirt comes off immediately every time you step through those doors." A woman with a young face jumps from a small closet door in the hallway. "Weapons, if you please." Rose gestures to the swords around Jonathan's and March's waists. "Customary. Rules and all. Can't have any shenanigans, if you get my drift, with any of my flowers or other customers."

March and Jonathan unbuckle their leather belts with their scabbards attached and hand them to the woman, who lays them on a shelf among an assortment of other swords, daggers, and knives. Jonathan is tempted to peek within to see if any blades of the cult lie with the rest, but if there are, he would not know who they belonged with. March adjusts the thinner, studded belt with several smaller coin pouches secured to it on her waist.

"All your weapons," says Rose with a false smile. "I hear about more than just your escapades, Lady Audrianna."

March smiles, pulls a long dagger from each boot, and hands them to the woman. Rose waits, unblinking. March huffs and pulls a short-bladed dagger from inside her trousers below her hip.

"That is the lot," says Jonathan. "I know. I placed them on her myself after we fucked for the third time this morning," he adds before Rose can argue. "Now, our room?" He winks.

"End of the hall, up the stairs, fifth floor, door with three bronze rings. And should you stray, I will still charge you extra."

Jonathan can feel Rose's eyes traveling the lines of his back as they walk away until they reach the end of the lengthy corridor. A large stained-glass oculus window in the ceiling rains down heavy, warm colors from the top of the angled corkscrew stairway. Once out of Rose's sight, Jonathan pulls his shirt back over his body and kisses March on the temple.

Well done, darling.

They make their way to the fifth floor, past rooms and dimly lit hallways full of muffled laughter, moans, and screamed compliments far too outlandish to be true. Where the second through fourth floors have eight rooms and four hallways, the fifth has only three doors, the middle the one with three bronze rings.

"How many?" asks March, as they circle around to the room.

"Sixty-four," says Jonathan, knowing she means the stairs. He looks down into the well of flesh below them. Half-naked women and men scurry back and forth, laughing, growling, and grunting.

March pushes it open with her boot to reveal a spacious octagonal room with no bed or chairs. Instead, a sunken pit filled with pillows takes up most of the room with a few upholstered benches around its perimeter. Overhead, swaths of violet and burgundy fabric sweep out from a central point where a golden chandelier hangs from an iron chain with all of its arms formed to resemble a woman's open, bent legs.

"Charming," says March. "Do not sit anywhere. I would say not to breathe if it were an option. No disrespect to the women who work here, but their customers probably bring the pox from every corner of Wonderland."

In less than five minutes, the trio of giggling women walk through the door wearing only four panels of sheer lace attached to a golden embroidered collar—their petals. They bite their lips and slink to the center of the pillows and beckon to Jonathan, who waits on the far side of the room.

"We saw you in the market. Saw us and couldn't resist," says the pansy with blue hair. "Have we been the fantasy running through your mind all afternoon? Running through your trousers?"

"If we would have known," says the pink-haired pansy, "we would have left with you then and there, found an alleyway, lifted our shifts, and let you sniff the flowers, Lord Carter. We would give our bodies to you freely."

"Tend to our gardens," says the pansy with yellow hair. "Spread your seed. Here, we can take our time. You can take your time. Tell us what you want, and we will fulfill your every fantasy."

They lower themselves to their knees among the pillows and writhe and press against each other, their voices becoming indistinguishable from one another.

"Call us yours, Lord Carter."

"Grab us by the hair, turn us, flip us, fuck us in every position, Lord Carter."

They work themselves into a heated frenzy, grabbing at each other's breasts through their petals, sliding their hands between each other's legs, whimpering when they do not speak, licking their necks.

"Tell us how badly you want to fuck us. Show us your mighty prowess, your power."

"Command us to tell you how badly we want you to fuck us. How good it feels to have you inside us."

"Use us, Lord Carter."

Their attempted temptation comes to a sharp end when March slams the door behind them and chuckles in low, dark tone. Their veneer drops from the shock, and the faces of the women in the market return, though confused.

"Mar—" the blue-haired pansy begins to say but swallows and corrects herself. "Lady Audrianna."

Jonathan laughs, unable to help himself.

March leans against the door. "Is this what passes for seduction? Do the men and women you entertain fall for this nonsense? *Fuck us. Command us. Lord.* What a load of horse shit."

"It truly was a marvelous performance," says Jonathan. "But we have other business to discuss with you."

March unties her trousers and reaches between her thighs.

The blue-haired pansy tries to recover. "Oh, I didn't know this was going to be a party." She looks to Jonathan. "Do you want to watch us with her while—"

"Shut your simple mouth, you sod." March pulls a knife of the cult from a holster she wears against her inner thigh and tosses it to Jonathan.

"You're not supposed to have weapons of any sort in here," says the pink-haired pansy as she and the others clump together in the middle of the pit, shrinking like wounded animals. "We will scream."

"Forgive us," says Jonathan. He lays the knife at the end of the pit. "No harm will come to you by our hands. We have many requests of you, and none of them include violence or sex."

"Least not with us," adds March.

Jonathan kneels on one knee at the end of the pillows. "We will compensate you handsomely for your time and efforts. What we need is information, and you have means we do not."

"Compensation," says the pink-haired pansy. "You mean the purse you gave to Madam Rose? We won't see a quarter of it."

March takes the three pouches from her belt and tosses them onto the pillows with muffled clinks.

"We keep our word," says Jonathan.

"We know you will," says the blue pansy. "Everyone knows the reputation of Jonathan Carter. It took us by surprise when Madam Rose said you were here and requested us. Didn't think you would ever find yourself in this place."

"To your point," says Jonathan. "Everyone knows me or knows of me. I wish it were not so, but it is a truth I cannot dodge. There are currently groups in Mirus who would do irreparable damage to all who live here."

"The Queen Slayer," says the yellow pansy. "I heard he's been lurking around the city."

"Not him," says Jonathan, though he knows Cheshire poses his own threat. "There are two other groups we need help gathering information on and from. I dare say some of them may frequent your establishment, or you might spot them when you run your errands to the market once you know what to look for. We are too easily recognizable in public. Every few days, March, myself, or both of us, will visit with a brand new purse for each of you, as long as you have information for us. True information. Mirus and your future Queen are in need of friends. We search for allies to keep Mirus safe."

"We care little about keeping Mirus safe," says the pink-haired woman. "Doesn't matter who is in charge or if there is a queen or if there is not a queen. We get customers either way. It was the same way in Adamas and Clava before we settled here. But if you keep us in coin, off the books, we can be convinced to help you. With one other condition. You saw through our facade and all, but that doesn't mean we are not excited at the prospect of bedding Jonathan Carter." She looks to March, who stares back with a raised eyebrow, waiting for her next word to decide her fate. "Can we watch you two?"

March shrugs, walks behind Jonathan, kneels, and ever so slowly peels his shirt up and tucks it over his head. The tight linen presses into the skin between his chest and shoulders and causes the veins to show slightly. She slides her hands down his chest to his stomach and leans her head against his.

"Perhaps," says March with dark glee.

The pansies swallow and release their bated breath.

"Do we have an accord?" asks March.

"Yes."

"Completely, yes."

"Fuck."

"A common word today." March lowers the shirt back to Jonathan's waist. "But then again, look at where we are. We will take the last as a confirmation as well."

"How much time do we have?" asks Jonathan, trying to raise the women's eyes back to his.

"Three hours," says the yellow pansy.

"Brilliant," says Jonathan. "We have much to discuss. But first, would you three mind securing the room?"

They nod, grab their purses, and climb from the pit. The yellow-haired woman collects the purses and puts them in a hidden compartment beneath a bench. The blue-haired woman grabs a key from a small shelf and locks the door.

The pink-haired pansy, however, approaches Jonathan and March. "Just so you're aware, we will need to make some noise, turn the act back on, scream, moan, all of it. Nothing more suspicious than silence in a brothel." She smiles and helps her yellow-haired friend secure their purses.

March studies the women as they move around the room. Jonathan can see a plan of her own formulate in her mind piece by piece. He will not ask. She will share it with him when the time is right, or if she sees fit at all.

Who else? he asks himself. *Who else in the city can be an ally? Odd, the people we must depend on are those whose loyalty is only to themselves. Perhaps it is best considering the history of Mirus, and the presence of Lysander and Uriah. This is why we appeal to them instead of their loyalties. Self preservation can be trusted much more. There must be others in the city who feel the same way and who Jonathan and March can use to get Mary Anne on the throne.*

CHAPTER 18

MARCH

The stench of the brothel clings to them like wet clothing and does not fade the more space they put between themselves and the establishment. March and Jonathan will need and enjoy a deep soak and scrub when they return to the castle. But before she makes the climb, there is one more destination March has in mind to visit while she is out of the castle—Far Side Tavern.

They walk clear across the curve of Stonehaven, almost two hours' time, stopping once to have tea Jonathan smuggled in his trousers with a new set of cups and saucers purchased from a pawnbroker outside of the Row whom Jonathan calls friend. They sit across from the shop in a small stone courtyard and rest their feet. March slides her boots off and cools the throbbing of her soles in one of the four giant water basins. She keeps watch of those who pass by while Jonathan savors his drink. Mothers walk by with their children, following behind like a line of ducks. Weary men and women trudge home after a long day of work. Soldiers patrol in pairs and pull down the hoods of anyone, regardless of age, who they pass.

Cheshire. You have made this harder on yourself.

"In your estimation, who is the bigger threat?" Jonathan asks.

"Uncertain. It would be easier if either group attacked the city instead of Cheshire. Then our compass could shift in one specific direction instead of spinning out of control." Jonathan reaches down into the pool and lifts March's legs out and across his lap. "Lysander and Uriah are the present threat. Or at least the threat we know. I hate to admit it, but I fear for all our sakes that we must focus on the most pressing matters. While we wait, you advise Mary Anne, I train the soldiers, and we both keep Cheshire from destroying the city."

"Agreed," says Jonathan.

She cannot help but smile at the joy on Jonathan's face. He stares at the ripple of tea in his cup after he sips until it is calm and still once again. The simple things in life bring peace to Jonathan.

He winks at her over the curve of his cup. *So do you*, it says.

After tea, she kisses him, and they part ways for the evening.

"I will find you in the garden," she whispers, savoring the tingle he leaves on her lips.

Jonathan retires to the castle, and March crosses through the Row as merchants close for the evening, locking their doors, dropping their canvas awnings, or pulling their carts from their stalls while customers try to haggle to save one last coin for the night. The crowd of the Row should thin at this late hour, but at the far end of the market, a mass of people gather, clogging the thoroughfare. Men and women forcefully push against each other and squirm through the other townspeople like worms in soil to gain closer audience in the Quadrangle, closer to Far Side where Lysander and Uriah hold court. Cheers surge through the crowd like a stone dropped into a pond—grand and loud at its start but the farther the ripples travel from the center, the energy dies.

"What are they saying?" one man asks.

"I can't bloody hear a damn thing," grumbles a woman next to him. "I want to see them. Been trying for a week to get close but can't seem to get here early enough." The woman, along with all around her, cheers with the crowd in front of them, albeit halfhearted, unaware of what transpires in the crowd ahead, but follows Lysander and Uriah blindly.

The clatter of shutters draws her attention high overhead. Those who live in the stacked houses leading to and surrounding the perimeter of the Quadrangle hang out of their windows to gain a better view over the sea of people. March finds the nearest door to her right, takes a dagger from her belt, and slides it through the small crack between door and frame. With a flick of her wrist, she pops up the short wooden lock bar within and climbs to the fourth floor of the structure, stairs creaking with every step. The fourth floor, like the three below, is an annoyingly long and crooked corridor with apartment doors running down its entire length on both sides. These hallways were constructed as an afterthought to join two separate buildings together. Marks of crude masonry work, not of Pat or Bill's hands, line the edge of each door.

The constant noise, not a hum but a nauseous drone, fills the air, as does a meandering odor. She cannot tell if it's some forgotten meal left out to spoil or just the unpleasant aroma of people. Her skin crawls at the thought of living, sleeping, or doing anything so close to so many people.

The raucous cheers from outside grow louder the farther she follows the uneven hallway. Finally, it takes a sharp turn to the right, then after a length back to the left—the corner of the Quadrangle. Most of the doors along this stretch hang open to varying degrees. Those who live on the outside of the square cross over to share the windows of their neighbors, which look down into the crowd. To March's relief, most of the conversations she hears are complaints rather than praises.

She slips into one of the empty apartments, empty except for a small boy who sits on the floor and plays with two wooden figures. The room, the only room of this apartment, is smaller than Dormy's wagon but still as crowded with what must be four generations of trinkets, furniture, and memories piled to the ceiling. The young boy gasps at the sight of March and her sword and holds up one of his figures with an outstretched arm—

carved in a woman's shape with small swords in both hands, no bigger than a large splinter.

March grabs a scrap of thick linen from a table covered with various fabrics and sewing needles, no doubt a blow to the child's mother. She wraps the fabric around her head and shoulders as a shawl and hood to conceal her pink hair, then smiles and winks at the boy and climbs through the open window to the backside of the Quadrangle. She hangs from the windowsill, jumps, catches the edge of the eaves with both hands, and flips her way to the roof. The loose wooden shingles clatter with every step up to the ridge. Two slip from their place and slide to the ground below.

She sees why Cheshire prefers this view of the world. There is a peace to it, even with commotion below. The apartment windows on the other three sides of the Quadrangle match the one she perches on, she believes. Most shutters are closed in a vain attempt to block out the noise of the crowd. A few frame the heads of men and women curious at the sight below.

From here, March takes in the full spectacle. Townspeople pack the Quadrangle so tightly they can barely move, the discomfort clear on their faces, yet they still cheer, ignoring their own well-being. At the mob's center, Lysander and Uriah stand atop the small pillory platform, drink in hand, shirts undone and hanging open while tucked into their trousers.

"We will never keep secrets from the people of Mirus," shouts Lysander, "from the people of Wonderland. Our people. Our family, unlike others. The Duchess would have you believe the attack on our beautiful city is not the work of the Queen Slayer. She hides the truth of the destruction of the hanging cells as she hid the truth of the women she tries to make a new Queen from."

The crowd hangs on every word and erupts into uproarious applause after every sentence, quieting only when Uriah raises his bear-like hand into the air.

"You deserve honesty," Lysander continues. "We do not come here with sword and spear to tear down the once great city which was our forefathers. We come with a pledge to return Wonderland to the glory of old, when all prospered. We will hunt down and see the Queen Slayer answer for his crimes, a promise the Duchess has never made. But we will."

March sits, resting her forearms on her knees, and shakes her head at the folly of the townspeople below. Lysander and Uriah's offers sound appealing, almost inspiring, though hollow to the core. They want nothing more than to regain the castle, the crown, the power in Wonderland, and look down the hill at everyone as they always have, as they do now.

The shingles clack behind her. She breaks the seal of her sword, ready to strike, but Cheshire's hand stops her elbow. He squats behind her and drapes his arms over her shoulders, along with his cloak concealing him, his cheek nuzzling her ear. The heat of his body presses against her back. She has missed his touch. This is his first appearance she knows of since the explosion of the hanging cells. The faint hint of black powder mixes with his natural scent, and something else she cannot readily identify, but it is on the tip of her tongue.

"See anything of interest?" Cheshire asks.

"They spout the same contrived dribble they have peddled for years." March reaches up and runs her hand through his tousled hair under his hood. The shiver of his body ripples into hers. "Yet people continue to listen. It is the crowd I have come to see. By your count, how many would you say are down there?"

"Two thousand packed in the Quadrangle alone." Cheshire makes clicking noises with his tongue out the side of his mouth. "With the rest clogging the streets, I would triple it. Six thousand."

"Shit." Their numbers have grown more than she expected. Cheshire's attack on the city probably drove more townspeople to them, looking for someone to act, to protect them. The Duchess does little except offer kind words with false sincerity to soothe, and gold to placate—not so different from Lysander and Uriah. Soldiers who remain loyal to the crown number roughly four thousand, and deserters nearly two thousand at the last estimate. They have double the numbers. The people below may not be soldiers, but they will lay down their lives for a cause they do not understand. Put a sword in each of their hands and Lysander and Uriah will have gained the upper hand with thousands of pawns to lead the charge and die. The soldiers of Mirus will tire, overrun by their unskilled numbers, just enough for Lysander and Uriah's troops to lay siege. This is what March would do.

She leans her head against one of Cheshire's arms. His muscles are taught, larger, and the veins in them much more prominent. "What have you been up to?"

He brushes his lips against her neck and chuckles deeply as a response.

"You've become quite brazen. Out in the open. Are you not fearful the soldiers will see you?"

"Look down," he says. "There are none. The crowd does not let them in. One or two soldiers trapped within the tavern have resorted to drinking until the crowd disperses."

A thought ticks away at the back of March's mind. *Why is he here? Lysander and Uriah are of no concern to him.* She reaches behind her, hands searching his back, waist, and legs for a weapon or explosive of some sort. *Nothing.* While her hands are on his body, she gives into her temptation and slides them up his inner thighs and discovers Cheshire excitement. He rises well above the top of his trousers, a common occurrence around him, which Jonathan and March take advantage of often.

She teases his length with her fingertips while they talk. "What is your plan for the people below? Kill them?" she asks bluntly.

"Eventually," he says with stuttered breath, "but not this evening." He slides one of his hands down March's stomach—it jumps at his touch— and down the front of her trousers. His fingers, like Jonathan's, know every inch of her body. His touch causes March to grip him tightly.

"Why are you up here?" she asks.

"I had every intention of carrying on with my business," he whispers as he strums her. "But I spotted you earlier when you and Jonathan parted ways. I had a moment alone with Jonathan days ago and haven't yet had one with you. I thought I could catch you in the stairwell, but my curiosity got the better of me, so I followed and found you here." He slides his finger farther. "And here." Farther still. "And here."

"You risk everything for a moment out in public?"

"Should I deny the effect you and Jonathan have on my body?" he whispers with his lips pressed against her ear. "The hold you both have over my very being? I would risk everything. I would destroy the world for both of you."

She fights against the flutter of her eyelids but must remain vigilant, even watchful, of the crowd, but the temptation to succumb to Cheshire battles her reason. She pushes her hips forward against his hand, and his fingers return the force. March lets go of Cheshire and moves his free hand to her breast. His fingers slide underneath her jacket and find her nipple, ready for him. Jonathan's touch is strong, yet gentle. Cheshire's is gentle as well, but unbridled, animalistic. His hand shakes wildly between her legs, and she hates that she must suppress the scream building up, welling up inside her.

"Not fair." He growls in the back of his throat. He presses his body against her back. "I want more."

He intentionally kept his hands away from her breasts—his craving for them rivals a drunkard's lust for wine. On many occasions, Cheshire has spent hours caressing them, kissing and suckling at them. The same attention is given to other body parts of Jonathan. Their encounter must be quick or risk discovery, so she brings him to the precipice they both know he will not be able to stop once he crosses. A horrible tease on her part, no matter how badly she desires him.

She allows her moans to escape her gritted teeth when the crowd cheers below. The hot tingle, the flurry of butterflies in between her legs climax and explode and radiate through the rest of her body. She lays her head back on Cheshire's shoulder and tenses her entire body to lessen the spasms. She sucks in breath through her chattering jaw. His hand fights against the grip of her thighs and massages her until her body jerks its last and relaxes.

"Damn you." He kisses March tenderly on the lips while his trembling hand still grips her breast, attempting to keep his animal at bay.

"You are welcome." She chuckles, her mouth still pressed to his. "Find us in the garden this night or any night should you wish to continue. Or if you won't, since I know you skulk through the city after twilight, find me in a more private place and I will finish what you started."

Cheshire laughs reluctantly and rubs his face against the back of her head.

"You half answered my question truthfully. What brought you here?"

"Patterns," says Cheshire. "Everyone has a particular path they follow through the city—to work, their home, leisure activities. I watch to see where people are and where they are not. These gatherings have altered the pattern and I do not care for them in the least."

"Can you give us a warning before you strike again?" asks March, rubbing the muscles of his upper arms, trying to discern his schemes. Whatever it is has involved strenuous activity. She could feel it in his touch. She can still feel it. "Jonathan and I could have been in the city, near there."

"I would never put you or Jonathan in harm's way. Purposefully. Do you think I do not know where you two are every moment of the day?"

She believes him without a second thought. March has seen Cheshire accomplish no less than six impossible feats before the sun fully crests over the horizon. Cheshire knows almost everything, and almost everything is where his limit needs to remain.

"We can make use of your knowledge," says March, "to expedite our departure, if you are willing to share."

"You sound like Jonathan."

"Good. We are all of the same accord. I do not think you realize the yearning I have to leave this place."

Cheshire slides his arms, rolls away, and lies on his back on the slope of the roof behind her, hidden from view of the Quadrangle. He pants with frustration, his lust cut short, but he drips high above his navel, pooling in the muscles of his abdomen.

"What do you want?" he asks. "To help Mary Anne, as well?"

Her name claws at the back of March's neck. Even now, while she is here trying to find out information, Mary Anne might be with Jonathan. "I do not give two shits about her. I want your help and the patterns you collect." She runs her fingers through his hair once more. "And it would be much easier if there were some way for us to contact you when we have need, instead of hoping our paths will cross. Then again, if you just bedded with us during the night, it would all be much simpler."

Cheshire runs his fingers across his lips. "Whose pattern in particular? Lysander and Uriah are simple enough. They spend their mornings walking through the Crest, their evenings in the Quadrangle, and then retire to the largest manor in the Crest, with no less than four women with them."

"I know this already." March stares down at the crowd surrounding Lysander and Uriah, straining their arms to reach for them as if they were prophets. The misguided reverence on their faces makes March sick to her stomach.

"The hour is late," says Uriah. "To your homes, to your loved ones. Spread the word. We are here, and our voices will ring out over the city and over the country. With your support, perhaps one day soon, Mirus will be a shining city once more. Thank you, everyone, for your presence." He takes three young women by the hand and pulls them up onto the platform with him. Uriah brings up two more from the opposite side. The command to leave ripples through the crowd, and while those at the center wait for the outliers to disperse, Lysander and Uriah fondle their women, hands on their breasts and asses.

The small hairs on the back of March's neck bristle. Her mind shifts to a better way to make use of Cheshire. "There is a time to use a scalpel and a time to use a sword. But there are also times for the dagger no one sees."

Cheshire chuckles darkly, knowing she means him.

"Jonathan errs on the side of delicacy, but we cannot risk an outright war with so many unknowns."

"What do you ask of me?"

"We need information about their forces." She gargles a pained sound in the back of her throat. "And the damned cult. Do this for me, and I will shift the patterns of the soldiers to make your endeavors easier."

"Done. Congratulations on the appointment, by the by." Sarcasm drips from his tongue.

"Shut up. Before you go, I must give you a warning. I train the soldiers to fight Lysander and Uriah. The Gryphon has selected two dozen men, archers, to hunt for you. I have tried to dissuade him, but you have made his decision immutable. Your patterns will soon change."

"Noted. I will call upon you soon."

She reaches for him to run her hands upon his chest, then farther down to savor one last taste of him as well, but Cheshire vanishes without a trace, as if he left while she watched the sunset and only his voice remained. March watches Lysander and Uriah finally leave the Quadrangle, the women following behind them, never beside them, never their equal.

March has the reputation of the best sword in all of Wonder, but she has never faced the Twins in combat. Their reputation and skill are unmatched as well. If she, Jonathan, Cheshire, and the Gryphon fought them both, she could not assure their victory. It is not a matter of if she fights, but when, and before the day arrives, she will need to test their skill, see how deadly they are with her own eyes. The lingering question in her mind is who will she sacrifice to gain this knowledge?

CHAPTER 19

CHESHIRE

Damn the soldiers. Damn the Gryphon. Their patrols change, as March said they would after the explosion of the hanging cells. This new pattern, while simple, proves formidable when trying to navigate the city from above instead of the catacombs. Instead of in pairs, they walk alone carrying a torch, never out of sight of the soldier behind. Collectively they create a fire serpent in the streets of Stonehaven and the Crest, an impossibly long dragon the likes of the Jabberwock of yore, snaking through and strangling the city.

Cheshire waits and watches the parade of soldiers through the slats of a shuttered window on the top floor dwelling above the barber's shop in Stonehaven. The owner lies sprawled across the floor unconscious, a welt swelling on the left side of his forehead. If he had remained asleep, Cheshire would not have needed to slam his head against the wall, but it was the quickest solution, other than smothering him in his sleep, to make sure he raised no alarm. A pitiful, pained whimper escapes him every few breaths.

On the street below, the Gryphon grows in the distance, a nocturnal sentry. His longcoat billows behind his towering figure as he strides through the streets of Stonehaven. Two sets of archers, loaded crossbows in hand and longbows slung over their backs, flank the Gryphon. He walks slower than his usual gait to allow the archers to walk at their pace. This is the fourth night of their new patrol, and Cheshire has their timing down to the second.

Sitting inconspicuously in the windowsill of the neighboring house and the one across the street, two lit candles burn on scrap iron Cheshire stole from the Forge. Two long, thin iron nails wedged into each candle, cold two hours ago, now hang precariously from the melting wax. As the Gryphon and his escort reach the neighboring buildings, the first nail from the candle across the street slips and clinks against an iron plate behind them—a sound which would have gone unnoticed during the day but rings out of place in the dead of night.

The four archers draw their crossbows and loose their bolts with deadly accuracy. Shortly after the four hard thwacks of their bolts piercing centuries-old wood, the next nail from the building behind them drops and clinks. The archers turn and take aim again, firing without the need to load another bolt. Upon closer inspection, their crossbows hold several bolts. Cheshire has never seen such an alteration. Were he not on the potential receiving end of their iron tips, he would applaud Pat and Bill's invention.

The archers look down the shaft of their next bolt, surveying the rooftops, waiting for their target. The Gryphon, however, searches where they do not. His keen canary-colored eyes travel across every wooden beam, post, and shadow of the adjoining structures with the skilled steadiness of a painter's hand.

While they search, the second nail from across the street drops. They spin again and shoot. One of their bolts cuts the remainder of the candle in half. Whoever lives within stirs and lights a candle of their own. The Gryphon raises a hand to halt the archer's next volley. Then he turns and locks eyes with Cheshire through the narrow space of the shutters, as if he knew where he stood the entire time. The Gryphon nods—a signal—and the roof above Cheshire's head shifts and groans under quick footsteps.

"Fuck you." Cheshire scrambles to the side of the room, narrowly escaping the soldier who swings from the eaves and kicks through the shutters.

Over the centuries, the count of soldiers from across all of Wonderland dead by his hand number in the thousands. Except for the bellicose soldiers of Clypeus, Cheshire's adversaries, no matter their number, have proven disjointed and unorganized. A quality Cheshire exploits at every turn. But under the guidance of Gryphon and March, the soldiers of Mirus become a unified force.

The soldier drops to his feet, slips on the splintered fragments of the shutters, but still manages to draw the crossbow from his belt and fire three shots in rapid succession. All three sink into the wooded walls. One tears through Cheshire's cloak as he dives behind the body of the unconscious barber. Two bolts pierce his stomach, searching for Cheshire. He rouses for the briefest of moments with a curdling scream before a third bolt stabs through his skull and lodges inches away from Cheshire's face.

Click. Click. Click. The soldier grumbles at his empty crossbow. It seems nine bolts are the sum it wields. Cheshire should return some of them to the soldiers. He springs over the barber's lifeless, seeping body and pulls the two bolts from his gut. Another soldier climbs down from the roof and perches on the windowsill with a full complement of bolts. Cheshire spins in the air and launches the first bolt at the first soldier's groin. He unsheathes his short sword, and the bolt clanks sourly against the steel blade. The soldier smirks, proud of his skill. But unfortunately for him, the first bolt was only a distraction. The second finds its intended target—his right eye. The soldier howls in pain, rearing back.

Cheshire charges, jumps, and kicks him with both feet in the chest, propelling him into the soldier at the window. Cheshire grabs the red cloak of the speared soldier and pulls him back to the floor. The screams of the falling soldier end with a metallic crunch upon the stones below.

The thunder of soldiers' boots beat the staircase like war drums, quickening as they draw closer. Before Cheshire can take a step toward the window, two arrows whistle through the air, fired from soldiers with longbows on the rooftops across the street, and bury themselves into the planks inches from Cheshire's feet, cracking them in half. Cheshire runs to a window at the back of the house. A barrage of crossbow bolts shatter the shutters as soon as he reaches them. They have cut off his escape by rooftop. He would rather be back in the forest fighting the Ace by this point. At least then it would be one foe, a familiar foe, to deal with.

In utter shock, the first soldier kneels on the floor, tapping his fingers around his lost eye, dull to the pain.

"Do not move." Cheshire kneels in front of the soldier. "If you touch it, you risk your own life." He unbuckles his gorget and chest plate.

Frozen, the soldier holds his arms out obediently but shaking. "Do you think there is a chance I will survive this?"

Crack. Cheshire swings the chest plate against the soldier's face. The bolt stabs deeper into his skull, finishing him.

"You ask the wrong person."

Cheshire wraps his fist in the soldier's cloak and belt, drags him to the landing, and waits for the sound of boots to become clear, for the soldiers to be directly underneath him. He heaves the lifeless body over the edge, and the four archers from the street crumple underneath the unexpected dead weight. Cheshire jumps down, holding the breast plate beneath his feet. He skids over the pile of soldiers. Bolts clank against the breastplate. One flies a hair's breadth away from his cheek. Another nearly catches the wrapping on his right arm. When he reaches the bottom of the flight of stairs, he rolls, keeping the shield underfoot, deflecting four more shots. He pushes off the wall and rolls down the next long flight of stairs out of their aim. However nimble Cheshire may be, a fall down a flight of stairs, no matter how calculated, takes a toll. His right shoulder, left knee, and left forearm take the brunt of each stair edge until he careens into a narrow wooden table between him and the front door.

He does not stop his momentum. He slides under the table, hoists it onto his back, grips the legs over his shoulders, and bursts out the front door. Dogs bark in the distance. Townspeople stir and shift within their homes in what should be a silent hour. The iron tip of an arrow pierces and cracks through the tabletop inches from Cheshire's face, followed by the creaking of multiple longbows being drawn back. Beyond the arrowhead which almost claimed his life, the Gryphon stands at the center of the street—a towering shadow. He dresses the same as he did the last time Cheshire saw him. The only armor he wears is his pauldrons, gauntlets, and greaves. Dull chainmail fights to sparkle from behind the ties of his shirt. His massive longcoat, the same longcoat Cheshire found him in, drags across the ground, making it appear as if the Gryphon appears from shadow. He grips the handle of his sword slung over his back. His eyes reflect the moon in small glints. An eerily familiar sight. Cheshire backs away slowly.

"You wanted me. Here I am." The low, rolling, deep tones of the Gryphon's voice, fully recovered, could shake the walls of every structure on this street. "Yet, you run."

"Does it look like I run?" Cheshire speaks under his breath, too low for prying ears, but he knows his words reach the Gryphon. "I wanted an audience with you. And again, you give me exactly what I want."

The Gryphon huffs through his nose. "I warned you."

"I have done nothing more since last we spoke. Not yet anyway."

"Do you think I would give you a chance to destroy another part of the city?"

Cheshire raises his voice, provoking the Gryphon. "You already have, when you let me go in the—"

The Gryphon shoots toward Cheshire with blinding speed. His sword comes down with terrible force on the table, shattering it like a stale biscuit. Cheshire dives through the Gryphon's legs and under the length of his coat, which reaches the shadows cast by the nearest awnings. He darts from beneath the coat's end and disappears through a thin alley between two buildings, barely wide enough for him to pass through sideways.

"He's gone," says one soldier positioned on the rooftops, unaware of where Cheshire actually escaped to.

"He is a demon," says another. "The Queen Slayer is a demon. He vanished into your shadow. How in all the hells do we fight a demon?"

Cheshire pushes through the narrowing space to the lower street beyond. His feet find their way into slippery vile muck, no doubt several days of emptied chamber pots. *Why is it always shit?*

Half of the Gryphon's face appears at the end of the alley. "We will have words again, boy. Mark me."

"We have an accord." Cheshire wiggles from the alley away from Gryphon and spooked archers. However, three soldiers wait for him. They must have heard the commotion and gathered from their patrol. At least they wield swords instead of crossbows.

The middle soldier opens his mouth to spout some useless command. Cheshire wastes no Time. He shoves his middle three fingers into the man's open mouth, curls them, and pulls him to the ground by his jaw. Before the other soldiers can unsheathe their swords, Cheshire kicks both across the face, swiping the bottom of his shit covered foot across their mouths. One heaves repeatedly while the other vomits out right. He would kill them—should kill them—but more soldiers run to their aid from both sides. Arrows and bolts whistle as they cut through the air, from rooftops and streets. They shatter clay pots, *thunk* into the sides of houses, *clack*, *ping*, and ricochet off the cobblestones near his feet.

Cheshire runs for the next alley, jumps across streets, passing soldier after soldier as a shadow. They do not expect him, or he spooks them enough to delay the draw of their bows. But the archers on rooftops keep him in their sights, firing continuously until he reaches the lowest ring of Stonehaven and the broken storefront of the weaver's shop. It is the closest entrance to the catacombs not hidden in plain sight. But over a dozen soldiers, at least with swords and not bows, stand watch as laborers continue to reconstruct the hanging cells by torch light. If he moves any closer, they will notice him.

Fuck. Since the soldiers do not patrol in pairs any longer, their canvas, their reach, their hold on the city widens. *Canvas.* The catacombs are not the answer this time. The risk of their discovery too costly. Cheshire sprints and weaves up the streets and back down, confounding the soldiers on his tail, blending into shadows, until he reaches the arch of Stonehaven directly overlooking the Crooked Market. The scrapes and clangs of armor bite at his heels as the number of soldiers grows behind him, but the *thunk* of arrows stop, which means they search and cannot see him at the moment.

Cheshire slips through one final alley, skids to a stop, and grips the edge of Stonehaven with his toes. Dirt and small pebbles fly off into the air, the void, between Stonehaven and the Boroughs.

Candles from the Crooked Market undulate one hundred feet below beneath the giant swaths of canvas spanning the width of the Boroughs between rock face and wall. He does not wait for the soldiers to get any closer. He turns his back to the Boroughs, takes a deep breath, leans backward, and falls from Stonehaven. His cloak flaps and whips hard against his body, his stomach spins, the wind roars past his ears, and the beautiful rush of weightlessness is what he imagines death would feel like. Perhaps this is how it will happen. The long canvas catches him, cradles him, bouncing from the impact. The thick ropes tethering the canvas yawn at the weight of their unexpected passenger. Some stitches strain, but they hold. Even if the seams popped, he could survive the fall, unpleasant as it would be. He has survived worse.

High above, at the edge of the Stonehaven, in the same alley he jumped from, the Gryphon appears, as if conjured. His mighty silhouette no larger than the nail on Cheshire's little finger. He glares down, both impressed and annoyed. The tops of the buildings of Stonehaven appear nothing more than jagged teeth trying to bite the night sky. Cheshire indeed escaped the jaws of the Gryphon.

Cheshire thought he was safe for the Time being, in Mirus away from the Ace—cunning, ruthless, unyielding, a mad dog off its leash. Inside the walls, however, the Gryphon does not possess these qualities, but one far more problematic—stratagem—and proves just as formidable an opponent. His game remains unclear to Cheshire, but he will know all, eventually. The Gryphon believes he can stop Cheshire. Foolish.

He waves up at him with a wide grin. The Gryphon shakes his head, whips around, and disappears out of sight. Cheshire rolls to his hands and feet, ready for another volley of arrows, but realizes the Gryphon may have sacrificed his own men against Cheshire—endangering the denizens of the Boroughs would not fit his code of honor. Even if the soldiers pursued, it would take them nearly an hour to cross Stonehaven in either direction to reach the stairs down to the Boroughs.

Cheshire lifts his hands and rubs his fingers together. An oddly dry, viscous film covers his palms and the bottom of his feet. He knows the texture.

Wax. Curious. Useful.

He hops across the canvases, mindful of the seams, and climbs down the rock face above the old candlemaker's shop. Cheshire lets a hooded patron make her purchase and turn down another row of the Market before he drops, surprising the old man and his apprentice.

"The devils take your hands, your youth, and your legs." The old man stumbles back into a chair, exaggerating for Cheshire but not big enough to draw attention. "Not going to apologize for terrifying your elder? Look at my state. I'm short of breath. Heart thumping against my chest. My own candle is cut short enough."

"You certainly have a lot of breath to say you are out of breath." Cheshire slumps to the ground, finally able to rest his legs.

The young apprentice greets Cheshire with a smile and shows him several beautiful candles he carved with the tip of the compass.

"Remarkable work," says Cheshire.

The boy beams proudly, wipes his hands on his stained trousers, then holds a hand to his chest and extends it to Cheshire, with a roll of his wrist.

"He says thank you." The old man rises back to his feet, knees and back cracking. "I guess I should thank you as well. But I won't." He twists his face and looks skyward, then back to Cheshire. "Did you drop from Stonehaven?" Cheshire's silence is enough of an answer. "Will stupidity never cease? So, what brings the Queen Slayer back to my stall? Here for a proper purchase this time? Or another barter? Whatever it is will have to be better than that little trinket you pawned off on me. You got the better deal of the two of us."

"I had intended to visit you again, but not so early. But while I am here, I would like to make a request—a commission—as well as a few more candles."

The old man shifts boxes of candles onto the tables of his stall and turns the candles in them to appear busy.

"The canvases overhead are coated in wax to keep rainwater from soaking in. I require one. Coated in your best wax."

"You were up there. You could have just popped the stitches of a panel and taken off."

"And compromised the integrity of an entire swath. It barely holds together as it is. It could fall, catch fire, burn down, and destroy the market."

The old man gives Cheshire a knowing look out of the corner of his eye. "Were you not the one who destroyed the hanging cells? With my candles, no less." The apprentice bangs a heavy spoon against the workshop table. "*Our* candles, no less. Why would the destruction of the slums of Mirus matter to a Queen Slayer?"

"Does it matter?"

Another customer arrives, and Cheshire pulls his hood farther down his face while the candlemaker tends to him.

"As I said before," the candlemaker says, returning to Cheshire, "as long as your business takes place above the Boroughs, do what you will."

"Then will you help me?"

"Do you have the coin?"

"Not yet. But I will get it, I promise you."

The old man looks down his weathered, spotted nose at Cheshire. "How much canvas?"

Cheshire looks across the muddy walkway of the Market and spots the stall where a wood carver sells chairs, dolls, and walking sticks. "That should suffice."

"That must be nearly thirty yards."

"Can you do it?"

"We can. Our payment?"

"You will have it. How long will it take?"

"Two days."

"Done." Cheshire rises back to his feet, lowers his hood farther over his head, and leaves the stall.

"I did not tell you my price," the old man calls after him.

"I will sort it out."

While Cheshire makes his way back to the storm drain in the cliff face, he ponders this night's events. These tactics are more than for hunting Cheshire. The Gryphon fortifies himself from Cheshire. If there was no other information to divulge, why does he keep archers so close? Rooftops are one thing, but as a personal escort, for someone with his reputation, screams duplicity.

Now the Gryphon has discovered Cheshire's methods, half of them, so the nights and rooftops are no longer an option, no longer safe. The catacombs are the safest place but not for the next step of his plan. Since the Gryphon's strategy has changed, Cheshire must adapt also.

He thinks of the old candlemaker's face—weathered, thick beard crawling up his cheeks, almost to his eyes, and the hood he wears obscuring the rest of his face. The answer is obvious. To move forward, Cheshire will need to become someone else.

CHAPTER 20

JONATHAN

T he oak doors are twice the height of Jonathan, and the room within three times taller. He pushes them open wide, and they clunk on the bookshelves behind them. Inside, painted maps span the height and width of all four walls, and a full map of Wonderland stretches across the floor.

"Welcome," he says to Mary Anne who follows close behind him, "to the cartographer's chamber."

Mary Anne's mouth drops as her eyes travel and jump from map to map, following some path only known to her. "This is..." She stops herself as if her brain suddenly switched tracks. "I know this. Not Wonderland," she corrects herself. "But maps, routes, cartography, seafaring. This was my family business."

Her smile grows as she takes in every detail of the room. Drafting tables and wooden cubbies stuffed with rolled parchment—maps of all the distant regions of Wonderland, at least those able to be explored. The sun peeks in through the high arched windows and, coupled with the wealth of aged parchment, creates a warm glow which bounces off every wall.

"We are one of the leading shipping companies of import and export from England to Portugal, Spain, Scotland, Italy, and most recently to and from India and China, half a world away." Mary Anne notices the mesmerized expression on Jonathan's face. "I apologize. These are places you do not know of."

"No," says Jonathan, "never apologize. I am honestly enthralled. Sailing and exploring the strange countries far from Wonderland has always been a dream close to my heart, and yet I have never left these shores. Have you?" He forgets the reason they came to the cartographer's chamber and becomes the student to Mary Anne.

"Oh, yes." Though the maps on the walls are not her world, she holds a hand up to them and circles the entire room as if she knows the path she follows. "I have not been to the exotic countries such as China or India, but I have traveled the routes to Spain, Portugal, France, and Italy. Each country—their culture, their food, their people—so different from the last."

Jonathan catches himself holding his breath. "What is it like? On the ocean."

"Vast," says Mary Anne. "Empty. At times monotonous."

Jonathan's stomach turns at how Mary Anne can take such an experience for granted. He also fears there may be truth to her words. The dream he longs for may not be the idyllic vision he has in his mind. But to him, the open ocean means freedom, and he will not let his hope diminish.

"Yes, but what of your first time? How did it feel?"

Mary Anne's eyes lower, and she bites at her lip, blushing at Jonathan's choice of phrase. "I was fourteen the first time my father allowed me on any ship larger than a ferry in the Thames. I was terrified, but I wanted, I needed, to know what it felt like to break through the invisible barrier a mile out from the coast. There was no real barrier. Just the one my mind created."

Her eyes lose focus as her mind drifts back to a memory. "I remember the chaos of it all. Walking up the gangway from the dock and looking down to the water slapping against the side of the ship's hull. The sailors in the rigging overhead yelling to one another. The men on the deck rushing about, ready to make sail. And in all of this, I wondered what would become of us if we did not return, if the ship sunk, hit some reef or sprung a leak they could not mend. But once we were in open water, every worry subsided with the rock of the ship, the crashing of the waves, the yawning of the timber. And the horizon—the beautiful, endless horizon." Mary Anne inhales and pulls herself back from the memory. "Enough of that. We are here to talk of Wonderland, not of my world."

"You may talk to me about your world any Time," says Jonathan. "Your words painted a scene that would rival any masterpiece hung in the castle." He wants her to continue but knows he must resume their lesson before he is to meet March.

The *thunk* of the doors closing surprises them both. Cheshire leans against the door, head cocked to the side, an eyebrow raised. "Did I interrupt?"

Jonathan's heart leaps in his chest. He runs to Cheshire, throws his arms around him, lifts him into the air, and breathes him in. Cheshire tries to hide his smile, but, once in Jonathan's arms, he cannot contain himself and chuckles against Jonathan's neck. Jonathan sighs at the warmth of his bare chest, no longer kept from him by the soldier's uniform.

"Hello," says Mary Anne, wide eyed, fumbling her words. "You followed us."

It suddenly dawns on Jonathan, Mary Anne has not seen Cheshire since their tumultuous conversations in Rookridge and Briarwell weeks ago.

"Closer than you know," says Cheshire as Jonathan sets him back on the floor.

Jonathan turns the iron crank on one door to twist the lock bar into place. Cheshire takes a significant risk to be here, but Jonathan is pleased Cheshire kept his word, although he made him wait.

"The guards?" asks Jonathan,

"Just passed. I have a half an hour at most," says Cheshire with a grin Jonathan has not seen in weeks—a smile to melt his heart. If Mary Anne were not here, this would be quite a different rendezvous, though Jonathan cannot imagine Cheshire remaining quiet in the castle.

"Why... why are you here?" asks Mary Anne.

Jonathan shakes his head, pleading with Cheshire to hold the thought at the tip of his tongue.

"Well"—Cheshire laughs and cocks his jaw as if to shake the words from his mouth—"at Jonathan's behest, I am to help you become queen..." The inflection stays high, his thought unfinished. His eyes dart to Jonathan, unable to help himself, then back to Mary Anne. "So you can get out of my world." Before Mary Anne can argue, Cheshire walks to the center of the map of Wonderland on the floor and holds his arms wide. "Behold. The Queendom of Wonderland." Cheshire locks eyes with Mary Anne and points to Mirus on the floor—a dark red jewel with the name written in script on a flying banner above it. Mary Anne does not move, so Cheshire snaps repeatedly and points again, until she moves into place.

He motions with a sideways nod and sends Jonathan across the room, over the painted forests to the Rookwood. Jonathan passes close to Cheshire and brushes his fingers against his for a second. They both try to grab for each other. The small contact sends a chill through Jonathan's body.

"I feel backward." Mary Anne addresses Jonathan. "The Duchess took me to the top of the castle to look out over all of Wonderland, and it was magnificent. Somehow I feel as if seeing its magnitude with my own eyes would have been daunting, but I feel the weight now, having the entirety of Wonderland under my foot."

"Interesting choice of words," says Cheshire.

"Here I can see the edges of the map," Mary Anne continues

cautiously. "This place, Wonderland, is real. Its people are real. Becoming queen will mean something to every inhabitant of this land, and I'm to use it as a means to escape. It does not sit well with me."

Two things strike Jonathan as odd. This is the first he has heard her doubt leaving Wonderland, and his heart sinks. Second, and more immediate, there is something odd with the way Mary Anne regards Cheshire. She fought with him proudly in Rookridge, but now she watches him as she would a circling, snarling animal.

"If there were another option, we would take it," says Jonathan. "It may not be the best choice for the country but having a queen for a moment is significantly less problematic than having one for years and then disappearing."

"Disappearing?" asks Mary Anne, the white at the top of her eyes visible. "Or murdered?"

Jonathan can feel the air shift in the room. All he can hear is his swallow. Cheshire stands motionless, staring at her. Can he and Cheshire not have one normal moment together? As much as Jonathan wishes it, he realizes this will not happen in the castle, and never happen with Mary Anne present.

"Mary Anne—" Jonathan tries to deflect the conversation, but Cheshire will not allow it.

"No, no, no." Cheshire waves a finger back and forth at Jonathan. "Mary Anne has something on her mind," he says with pointed diction. "Let her speak."

"How many queens of Wonderland have there been?" Her voice trembles, but her body stands firm.

Cheshire raises an eyebrow, shifts his head slowly side to side, studying Mary Anne, then rolls his words in the back of his throat. "Depends on who you ask."

Jonathan cannot let this conversation continue, but as soon as he takes a step, Cheshire holds out a finger to stop him, never breaking away from Mary Anne's gaze.

"And how many have been slain?" She continues to dig.

The word hits a chord within Cheshire. He approaches Mary Anne, every step silent, purposefully stalking her. "Depends on who you ask."

"Cheshire, stop this nonsense." Jonathan puts himself between them to break their tension. He can feel Cheshire's breath on his chest. The brief jovial moment was fun while it lasted. "Please."

"Me stop?" Cheshire looks up at Jonathan, his purple eyes like daggers.

"He is here to help," Jonathan says over his shoulder to Mary Anne.

"Why would I accept help of any kind from the Queen Slayer?" Mary Anne's voice no longer wavers.

Jonathan's shoulders drop. The news was bound to reach Mary Anne's ears eventually, being in the capital and in the Duchess's presence. But the rumors of Cheshire as the Queen Slayer may have been prevented, or at least delayed in reaching her, if not for his attack on the hanging cells. At times, he is his own worst enemy.

"I knew I was right not to trust you from the beginning." Mary Anne backs away to the door.

"See, Jonathan," says Cheshire. "She does not want my help."

"She did not ask you for it. I did." Jonathan lays his hand on the back of Cheshire's neck and turns to Mary Anne to stop her. He can feel the urge within her to run and alert the guards. "Do you trust me?" he asks her.

"You, of course," she says, appalled at the question. "But how do I trust him? Jonathan, you are in league with a notorious murderer."

Cheshire looks out from around Jonathan. "Did you forget Jonathan killed just as many mercenaries as I did in Briarwell? Not just killed, split them from groin to gullet. Sliced through their necks. Crushed their faces with his bare hands. Funny how you can overlook killing when it is in your favor."

"Different entirely. They attacked us," Mary Anne stammers, caught off guard. "Jonathan, how can you expect me to trust him?"

"Because I do. Because he has saved my life countless times, and because he has saved your life twice already. Once in the Rookwood against the Ace, and the other in Briarwell. Mary Anne, people tell many tales in Wonderland, and many of them are not true."

"Do you know this truth?" she asks. "Is he the Queen Slayer or not?"

"Cheshire is branded the Queen Slayer, yes, but if he is guilty, I cannot say."

"Why would an entire country pose a falsehood if it were not true?" she asks. "Oh my God, he already threatened to kill me once." Mary Anne reaches for the lock bar.

"Mary Anne," Jonathan pleads, "you mustn't. The guards, the soldiers, the Duchess can never know Cheshire is in the castle. If they did, you would be under lock and key, under constant guard every waking moment, and while you slept. Not guards outside the door or patrolling the halls, but posted in your room, following you at all times. Your journey is hard enough. I ask you, please, not to make it more difficult."

"I cannot."

"But you must," says Jonathan. "There is no one in this world who knows more about Wonderland than Cheshire. I dare say with confidence even more than the Duchess. As your advisor, if you are to gain as much knowledge as possible, Cheshire is the one to teach you. He will not harm you." Jonathan looks for a response from Cheshire, but he picks at the dirt under his nails, unbothered by the entire conversation.

"I trust you." She turns and walks back onto the map of Wonderland. The pinch of her brow shows she searches for a question to prove Cheshire is of no use. "Since you know everything, then tell me this. How do I know when I am ready to become queen? Will there be a sign or will it just happen?" she asks smugly.

"You stand on the answer," Cheshire says without pause. Cheshire enjoys the humor in Mary Anne looking under her boot as if she squashed a tiny insect.

"I do not see what is so particularly funny about me wanting to know when I can get home, or how this map is an answer at all," she snaps. "You know nothing at all."

"If you believe I do not, then I do not, and we will leave it there. You can depend on the Chamberlain and the Duchess," he scolds her. "See how forthcoming they are with their answers."

Jonathan should interject, but it will do no good.

"To answer your question, I will give you all the information in one go, and it is a bit of a history lesson, so please save all of your questions until the very end." He squats and points to a large red jewel embedded in the floor in the middle of the Wetlands. "These large crystal shards represent the Pinnacles of Wonderland. Each marks a different region, but you knew that part already, I assume. What you do not know is their purpose is to serve as a beacon or conduit for the queen's magic. These same crystals are at the center of each spire—each Pennacle, or whatever people refer to them as now—and whenever a queen ascends to the throne, they glow a brilliant red through the runes. From what I know, the first time the Pinnacles came to light was during the ascension of the first queen. After her death," Cheshire looks pointedly at Mary Anne, "the light went out and stayed out until the arrival of the second queen, then the Pinnacles glowed dimly again. Then, after her coronation, they burst to life once more. Death, darkness, again and again and so on and so forth. So I believe you will know you are closer to being queen and departing our Wonderland when the Pinnacles glow again. Finished."

Mary Anne tries to sift through all the information dumped on her and looks to Jonathan for validation. "Is what he says true?"

"I cannot prove or discredit all the details," says Jonathan, containing his surprise. Jonathan knows Cheshire possesses infinite knowledge of the world and its people, their habits and goings-on, but had no clue he knew such sensitive, secretive information. "What I do know to be true is time," says Jonathan. "Time never lies, though she can be a cruel mistress."

"*He*," says Cheshire, under his breath.

"I was barely in my sixteenth year." Jonathan slides his hand into his pocket to feel the cold metal and crystal of his timepiece. "I recall the day the light within the Pinnacles went out."

"Snuffed out," adds Cheshire.

"Soon thereafter," Jonathan continues, "travelers to Rookridge brought news the queen had been—was dead. The years following her death, the world changed, became darker, colder, as if the glow kept every dishonest or devious urge and intention at bay. It was not until years later, during the reign of the second queen, that the glow returned. His connection makes sense."

"From the confounded look on your face," Cheshire says to Mary Anne, "I can see my work here is done." He walks to the door and releases the lock. "And I believe I have pushed my welcome a bit too long. Until next time."

Jonathan rushes to the door and holds it shut with one hand, almost pinning Cheshire between.

"Will we see you tonight?" Jonathan says in a hushed and tender tone.

"After my work is done, perhaps." With one swift motion, Cheshire slips through one door and closes it behind him.

Jonathan opens the door again to catch one last glimpse, but Cheshire is already gone, leaving an emptiness in the room and in his chest. "Shall we continue?" Jonathan asks Mary Anne, positioning himself on the Grayfield, the part of the southeastern coast of the main country, covered with marshes and swamps.

Mary Anne is slow to turn from the door, but when she does, worry fills her eyes. Jonathan would have thought Cheshire leaving would have the opposite effect.

"I feared to say anything while Cheshire was in the room with us," says Mary Anne, "but I must tell you now. When the Duchess spoke to me of the Queen Slayer, the way she told me of his deeds, I thought them despicable. When she described him physically, I told her the description reminded me of a young man I met in the forest on my arrival."

A stone lodges in Jonathan's throat.

"I told her he followed us to Rookridge and then to Briarwell." Mary Anne fidgets with her fingernails. "We discussed the matter in Chamberlain Weiss's study before he arrived. When I mentioned Cheshire by name..."

The stone falls to the pit of Jonathan's stomach.

"... her eyes grew wide and round for a single moment, and then she continued to tell me the vile acts of a horrific murderer. A murderer of queens. And what am I to think now that he has followed me here."

He did not follow you. He followed me. And March. At least, Jonathan hopes this to be true. Regardless, the Duchess knows Cheshire was in Briarwell when she was. She will come to the conclusion he has found his way into the city, and the deaths of the soldiers and the destruction of the hanging cells are indeed his work. From every angle a new complication arises, but Jonathan must push forward, for all their sakes. But the Duchess knows. She knows. He takes his flask from his pocket and takes a sip to calm his nerves, which he tries his best to conceal.

"Shall we continue?" Mary Anne dusts her skirt with her hands and rubs the side of her neck as if released from a stranglehold, ready to change the topic of discussion back to Wonderland's geography. "With just the two of us?"

Jonathan nods, offers Mary Anne his arm, and walks her around all of Wonderland, from Ilex to Adamas and back to Mirus. She studies the different terrains by their colors—whites, browns, and greens—while Jonathan thinks of the path ahead as he stares at the unmarked spot on the map for the Hollow. Cheshire's, Jonathan's, and Mary Anne's paths draw dangerously close to one another, like three horse-drawn chariots racing toward a finish line where there is only space enough for one to cross, and their wheels are beginning to scrape against each other.

CHAPTER 21

MARY ANNE

The following day, Mary Anne waits for Jonathan outside the tall arched doors nearest the kitchen, as he instructed. She hopes Cheshire will not join them today so she and Jonathan can enjoy a peaceful moment together. She watches both ends of the hall for any sign of Jonathan and fidgets with the corner of her book she carries under her arm. Instead of rounding a corner, Jonathan pushes open the doors from the outside. The morning sun bathes his shoulders and shines through his partially open linen shirt, silhouetting his body.

"Good morning," he says with a smile to make Mary Anne blush. She knows his smile is not from her. The scent of tea and sex drift off of him.

He opens both doors completely and steps aside to reveal the castle grounds beyond, where a lush, vibrant topiary garden awaits them. Emerald-green horses and unicorns frozen in time stand poised on their hind legs. Sea serpents crest in and out of the grass, along with giant eagles with spread wings bursting from the ground. Lions with manes covered with yellow marigolds engage in battle. Tall cypress trees shaped into spirals and stacked spheres tower over them. Beyond them, the arched entrance to a palatial hedge maze spreads as far as she can see.

Mary Anne rushes down the stairs and sits on the edge of one of the white marble fountains, water gently cascading down the three tiers. "I have never seen anything so beautiful in all my life. In the museums in London, I have seen masterful, beautiful paintings of Versailles. It is a palace in France, another country in Europe," she tries to explain to Jonathan. "But art, and I dare say not even the real Versailles, cannot compare to this, all of this. This is magical. Wonderful. I could use every word to describe its beauty in the English lexicon, but I would still fall short considerably."

"It is remarkable."

"Why have we not come here before?"

"All in due Time." Jonathan takes the book from her and offers his arm. "Shall we?"

"Are we going into the maze?"

"No. That is an adventure for another day. We are walking around to the croquet fields at the end of the castle grounds."

She takes his arm with both hands and feels his firm muscles through his sleeve—he normally wears thick jackets or coats when they walk arm in arm. The wide grassy lane between hedge and wall has no shrub or decoration of any sort and stretches and shrinks to a point in the distance. Mary Anne enjoys the peaceful, sweet crunch of grass as they walk.

"To be honest," says Jonathan, "March and I made a makeshift camp farther inside the hedge maze. This is where we have slept the past few nights. It is quiet, serene, one of the few places to hear the wind rustle through leaves, and it is cooler in temperature than any place in Mirus." Jonathan points to both sides of the garden. "And as you can see, nary a soldier or guard in sight. I suppose they believe if they guard the perimeter well enough, there is no need to guard the interior grounds. So it is two-fold. March and I get a sliver of the taste of home, and we can help secure the castle from the outside."

This explains their absence from their room. Their whereabouts every night matter to no one else in the castle besides Mary Anne. Though she lost the ability to watch and hear them as they have sex in the next room, she now has the power through the rings to feel Jonathan inside March, inside her, but she has not dared try it yet. March wears hers while Mary Anne's still hides securely underneath her mattress.

"Secure the castle grounds," Mary Anne mocks. "Is that your euphemism?"

"My what?"

"Your term, your code, for sex." Mary Anne laughs. She speaks with a confidence that shocks even her. Perhaps it is the anticipation of knowing Jonathan's prowess, at least secondhand, that allows her to speak openly to him. "You treat it as if it is such a secret. It is not as if I did not hear you two the first night I stayed in your home or the morning in Briarwell. Also, the castle walls are thin."

Jonathan's face grows flush. "My apologies. We, I, do not mean to offend you."

"Oh, come now, I am not made of glass."

"No, but from what I gathered upon our first meeting, and since learning more of the world you come from, this England, is..." Jonathan searches for the word. "...demure?"

Mary Anne remembers her conversation with March on the balcony. Demure would never describe her. "My world puts a rather large emphasis on modesty, chastity, and propriety, and those who deviate from what is considered acceptable are ostracized. Then again, I was sleeping with a married man while his wife was away. So, to judge you and March on your promiscuity, whether by your location or frequency, would be rather hypocritical of me, would it not?"

Her heart races with excitement. She has never talked to Jonathan, let alone anyone, about anything sexual before, but now with the barrier broken through, perhaps their conversation from now on would be more colorful.

"I miss his touch," she says after a long pause. She catches her thumb slowly rubbing his forearm but does not stop since Jonathan has not protested. "Thomas. You asked a few days ago what was on my mind." Mary Anne lies. She wanted to know where Jonathan and March were, missing Jonathan's body, not Thomas's. "I miss feeling him next to me, and I fear when I return, he will have forgotten me. Seeing the glances you and March give each other, when you stand next to one another or across the room, how she puts her arm around your waist and lifts your shirt to run her fingers against your skin, even sliding them just inside your trousers, or how you both—" Mary Anne stops herself and looks to the clear blue sky overhead.

"You are quite observant," says Jonathan.

Only of things which interest me.

Jonathan pulls his arm from her. Mary Anne second guesses if she spoke her thought aloud or if rubbing his arm crossed a line, but she realizes they reached the end of the lane and stand at the edge of the croquet fields.

"This, I am afraid, is where we must part ways." He hands her back the book and bows his head.

"Can you not stay longer? I am always more comfortable, more confident, in your presence."

"I was instructed to be your escort here. Nothing more. I assume the Duchess and Weiss want a private lesson for the ears of the queen only. But do not worry, I will return to escort you back to the castle when the time comes." And with a smile, he returns to the castle, never looking back.

Wonderful. Truly wonderful.

In all of England, she has never known anyone like Jonathan. Though a bit neurotic when it comes to his teas, he is the perfect combination of strength, charm, chivalry, and sensuality. He radiates them all without ever trying, which makes Mary Anne desire him all the more. Her thoughts of Jonathan take her to the opposite side of the field where the

Duchess, the Chamberlain, and several Castle Guard already have a match underway.

She picks up her skirt and rushes to the sideline where the Duchess leans on a mallet like a cane.

"I am sorry if I am late." Mary Anne curtsies as soon as she stops.

"*If?*" the Duchess questions. "Are you or are you not?"

"I was not sure, so I thought it polite to apologize."

"Mary Anne, do you recall the last lesson I taught you?"

"Queens do not apologize."

"Precisely. Nor are they late. Ever. Do you know why they are never late?" The Duchess answers before Mary Anne. Her tone reminiscent of her mother when disappointed. "A queen moves at her own time, therefore a queen makes her own Time. A queen is never late because she arrives precisely when she intends. So I ask again, Mary Anne, are you late?"

"No, madam. I am not."

"Good girl." The Duchess's tone abruptly shifts. "Just so you know, you really are not late, but I saw a teachable moment, so I took it. Tell me. Do you play croquet?"

"No, madam," Mary Anne admits. "I am afraid I never have. I never gave much time or thought to leisure activities."

"Oh, my poor child." The Duchess sighs. "Club her."

Mary Anne winces as if a guard would bludgeon her. Surely never playing croquet before should not require such a harsh punishment. But the strike never comes. Instead, Chamberlain Weiss approaches Mary Anne, relieves her of the Book of Queens, and hands her a croquet mallet.

"Do not be simple, Mary Anne." The Duchess laughs.

"I am sor—" Mary Anne stops herself before she can apologize again.

Even though Mary Anne has only seen other students play croquet at university, she should have known this game would differ from what she has seen in England. The mallet she holds is one continuous piece of carved wood. The top of the handle resembles a bird's_feet gripping a smooth sphere, and the club end resembles the head of a long-beaked bird. There are no wickets or stakes to speak of on the field. In their place, Castle Guard stand scattered around the field with polished armor and white tabards which look to belong in a grand ceremony instead of a back field, no matter how neatly gardened. Two soldiers with scarlet tabards and visors hold white poles with flags at both ends of the field.

The Duchess floats onto the field and beckons Mary Anne to follow. "Croquet is much more than a leisure activity. The game is not about scoring points—it is about making them."

"Are they not the same?"

"Not in the slightest. And you must prepare yourself if you are to face the likes of Bronwen, Lysander, and Uriah. Did I mention there would be an audience of the most elite from the Crest as well?"

The Chamberlain places a wooden croquet ball painted with a yellow stripe and covered in small, blunted spikes on the grass in front of the Duchess, then he shuffles to a bench to the side of the field but does not sit. The Duchess takes aim and knocks the ball with a loud *clack* and sends it through the legs of the nearest soldier.

Interesting.

Chamberlain Weiss claps softly from the sideline, his gloves muffling the sound, then brings another ball onto the field, this one with a white stripe, and sets it in front of Mary Anne.

Unsure how to position her hands, she tries her best to control the heavy mallet and swings. The ball skips a few times on the grass, but its aim is true, and follows the same path as the Duchess's ball. However, Mary Anne should have thought to look before she swung. The soldier in place of the wicket moved at least six feet to the right so Mary Anne's ball misses completely.

"Unfair," Mary Anne says under her breath, or so she thought.

"What is?" the Duchess asks with what sounds like genuine concern.

"The guard moved. Why?"

The Duchess stands behind Mary Anne and rests her chin on her shoulder. "Because I instructed him to. Did we discuss the rules prior?"

"No."

"Well, then." The Duchess strides to her ball and swings again without stopping or aiming. It skids off in a diagonal direction. She flicks her finger at the guard closest to her ball, and he shuffles to the side for it to pass underneath him. "Are you getting the point?"

"Are there no rules in this game?" Mary Anne clutches the club's handle longways in both hands. She does not understand how all this trickery will help her.

"Of course there are." The Duchess sighs and walks close to Mary Anne again. "What do you want to do in this moment? Do not think. Feel."

"I want the guards to pay you no mind for the rest of the game," she shouts out of frustration.

"Hm," says the Duchess. "Your shot."

She walks to her ball and prepares to swing again. "Turn," she says to the first soldier, who follows her orders, and then she knocks the ball gently through his legs.

The Duchess walks silently to her ball and looks to the third soldier, half a field away after her wild swing. She lifts the mallet high overhead and cracks the ball with enough force to send it across the entire field, but she aims wide again and misses the soldier completely. This time he does not move to aid her.

"Well done, Mary Anne," says the Duchess. "Is the point made now?"

Mary Anne tries to rationalize the reasoning behind this but reaches broader and thinks of what runs through the Duchess's mind instead of her own. "The queen makes the rules. I set the terms. I make the rules."

"Magnificent. All ways are your ways." The Duchess floats back to Mary Anne. "Now you think like a queen."

Chamberlain Weiss clears his throat from the sideline and taps the book. "Tenet three. We are not there yet."

"Give her something, Weiss," the Duchess says, not the first time he has piqued her annoyance with his compulsive observation of strictures. "Do you expect her to win a match as she is? No offense, Mary Anne."

"None taken," she says, excited at the prospect of learning more. She and March have not yet had their first clandestine lesson, but she will take any knowledge she can. "Please tell me more."

"Queens, for right or wrong," the Duchess continues, "must be able to instill both inspiration and fear when needed, without doubt. A queen does not rule or lead. She reigns."

A lingering shiver runs up Mary Anne's body, from her heels to her ears. "What is the difference?"

"In Wonderland, the queen has ultimate authority. Anything she decrees becomes law and reality. If you wanted everyone to walk around on one foot the third day of every month, if you commanded the flowers to bloom in winter, it would be done."

Mary Anne cannot help but laugh at the absurdity of it all.

"This is the extent of your power," the Duchess continues. "Her very words can move the heavens and all those below it. Which is why she must speak them carefully but with confidence. Therefore, under a queen's rule, we all observe a time of peace and prosperity."

They continue to play up and down the field, and Mary Anne moves the soldiers to her advantage as they continue their conversation. She hangs on the Duchess's every word, both astonished and a bit horrified to think a queen, she herself, has not only authority or sovereignty but dominion over the people and the land.

"Do the people do so out of fear of the queen?" Mary Anne asks.

"Fear and respect," says the Duchess. "I believe the proper way to rule is a healthy balance of both. And it depends on how you wield such responsibility."

Mary Anne notices she is three strokes ahead of the Duchess, since she controls the game. She points to the last three soldiers and calls them to line up one behind the next for the Duchess to catch up with a single hit.

"Well done." The Duchess places her hand on Mary Anne's cheek.

Mary Anne can feel the age in the Duchess's plump hand, and though tender as her mother's touch, it reminds her of home.

"I am not sure what I could accomplish in such a short time." Mary Anne speaks out of genuine concern. On her journey home she does not want to pass a law or give a command she and all Wonderland will regret.

"My dear"—the Duchess leans on her mallet—"there are many tribulations plaguing our fair land. You have seen and met some of them. And there are still many yet to encounter. Wonderland needs a queen. Wonderland needs a savior."

The word hits Mary Anne like an anchor on the water. She loses all taste in her mouth and her hands grow cold. *Savior.* The responsibility and weight associated with such a title is beyond comprehension. The Duchess must speak in hyperbole. From what Mary Anne has seen, there are only a few things needing to be dealt with, namely Lysander and Uriah. And the Ace, wherever the brute stalks.

"Perhaps I will make one or two decrees before I leave," Mary Anne says with a growing smile. "Simply out of curiosity about the scope of my magic, the Arcana, since I shall probably never be able to witness it again."

"Whatever you wish," says the Duchess. "But it all begins at your next croquet match."

"Mine? Will you not play?"

"Oh no, my dear. Bronwen's intention, as well as the others of the Crest, are to see if you are fit to rule or if you will crumble under the pressure, of which I will tell you there will be much. You will play against them. Why do you think I suggested croquet? Show them the woman you are. The queen you can be."

While the match continues, Mary Anne imagines the possibilities as if she were a child again. What girl in all of her world has not dreamt of being a fairy or some other magical figure? Mary Anne will be so much more. She wonders if she could change the colors of the castle walls daily or keep her garden in bloom year round.

She most certainly will change Grace's uniforms. Wonderlandians have such beautiful colored hair. Why in the world would they hide it? Then again, servants must not have any say in the matter, but wardrobe is a simple change requiring no magic at all. If the queen commands it, it must be done.

The Duchess joins in her excitement, as if she could read Mary Anne's thoughts. "There are stipulations, however," the Duchess cautions. "Although the queen possesses ultimate authority, she does not have unlimited power. But that will be covered when you reach the fourth Tenet."

Mary Anne can hardly hear what the Duchess says. She continues to daydream of the possible wonders she could, and can, and will create, and the good she could do for Wonderland, forgetting all else. For the first time, the *need* to become queen has shifted to *want*.

CHAPTER 22

MARCH

The clatter of armor and swords ring through the bailey like raindrops on stone. The soldiers' half-hearted grunts while training darken March's current irritated disposition.

One thousand men in the first battalion paired to practice the new forms and steps March taught them during the course of the past week. The victor of each pair kneels once his opponent falls, to give all a lesson and a view of those who are strong enough, smart enough, to still be on their feet. The first man fell in less than two seconds mere feet from March as she walked through the pairs.

This is the third of ten rounds with this battalion, and three more battalions will follow this afternoon. Four thousand men are too many to instruct at once and achieve any notable success. One thousand proves a challenge, but it is manageable.

"Again," March commands as the last soldier falls.

If only it were the skill of the victors or the incompetence of the those who fell that decided the outcomes, but neither is true. Some pick up the footwork easily while others are swifter to learn sword work. They have skill and discipline but lack desire and a sense of urgency. The soldiers who wait for the round to finish pick at pebbles on the cobbles, fidget with their armor or sword, look up at the passing wisps of clouds, or look anywhere but where the fighting still occurs, where they could learn something from the soldiers still able to stand. Where boredom and apathy are absent, frustration drips down men's faces like the sweat on their brows and cheeks.

She whips the sword off her shoulder and points it at the nearest kneeling soldier, its blade reflecting the sunlight in his eyes. This soft-faced young man has never seen real battle. Most here have not and are not old enough to remember the last rebellion. "You won. Why?"

"Because I hit him in the chest like you said to," says the soldier, squinting.

"Say it louder, for all your compatriots to hear."

"I hit him in the chest like you said to," the soldier says louder. His voice carries across the stones and armor. A smattering of laughter makes its way through the men.

She points to another soldier. "You lost. Why?"

"I don't know," he says.

"Simple enough," March says to all, "but not good enough."

"That don't make a lick of sense," another soldier to her right calls out, this one with a scar dividing his left eyebrow in two. "You tell us to do something, we do it. How is that not good enough. He won his match. He lost his. I won mine. The end."

"The end is death." March turns and strolls to the outspoken soldier. "If you survive the battle to come, what will you tell your sons? Your daughters? What will the bards sing and songs say about your victory or your sacrifice? 'I don't know'?" She couldn't care less about this drivel, but most soldiers carry on about legacies and such.

"We've been beating each other for a week straight," the soldier continues. "None of us have shown any marked improvement no matter what fancy or basic moves you show us."

"You are correct in this regard." March chuckles. "The truth is you do

231

not care about them or anything I have to say. Or is it you lot do not believe there is a threat? Your brothers deserted you and their oaths."

"You speak of the battle to come, but there is no proof. The only threat we have seen with our own eyes is the attack by the Queen Slayer."

A few men peppered through the soldiers mutter to themselves, agreeing. She wishes she was as gifted with her tongue as Jonathan, able to spin a tale so vividly and have his charismatic nature drive it into the minds and hearts of those who hear him. March may not be as gifted, but she picked up a skill or two. She does not need prose when logic and Cheshire's misdeeds will work to her advantage.

"Do you not think it coincidence the hanging cells were attacked days after Lysander and Uriah arrived in Mirus?" she asks the men. "And is it not also coincidence they blame this attack on the Queen Slayer immediately after it happens? Have any of you seen a trace of the Queen Slayer?"

"Soldiers have gone missing or are found dead," the soldier barks. "Who is to blame if not him?"

"You truly are simple," says March. "In all of Wonderland's history, what is the Queen Slayer known for? Killing three queens, four depending on who you ask. There are tales of slaughtered soldiers who pursue him through the country. But never here, correct? Never within the city. You fall for their words as easily as autumn leaves at the first chill of winter. Heed my words. Lysander and Uriah are the threat you must concern yourself with."

"Words," the soldier scoffs and stands, a head taller than March. "Their words. Your words. It all amounts to a pile of donkey shit. It's time to get the Gryphon back out here so we can get some real work done, lass."

March points her sword at the soldier, arm outstretched. Its tip hangs in the air, perfectly still, two inches from his face. "Speak out again in such a manner and I will give you four eyebrows instead of three."

Another ripple of laughter spreads through the crowd.

The soldier steps back to put more distance between them, smirking haughtily. March raises and lowers her sword to test the distance. He steps closer, but still out of range of her blade.

"You need us," he says. "We don't need you, unless it's to gawk at the half of your breasts on display on the outside of your top. How could you wear something like this and expect us not to be distracted by those plump—"

Before he can finish, March flicks her sword up again, slicing through the air unseen and splitting the soldier's full eyebrow. Blood pours from the wound in the heat of the sun and covers his face in a blink. "The hells!" he shouts, believing he lost an eye, spraying blood from his lips with every breath.

"How?" a soldier asks another near him.

"She didn't move forward," another says.

"Not an inch," says another.

"I did," says March. "You could not see it. He could not see it." She addresses the entire battalion. "He thought my arm was at full extension, but in actuality, I rolled my shoulder back. He thought he was at a safe distance, so he became confident, comfortable. I didn't need to step forward or even lean forward to strike you. I made one small adjustment. He thought I would not touch him, despite the fact I slaughtered ten of his brothers-in-arms on these very stones. He thought he knew what was right. He thought wrong. I have watched you *beat each other with swords* this past week because I needed to assess your skill level, your potential, and your mind set."

A soldier raises his hand four pairs away—the soldier who delivered the first scroll from the Gryphon. "What have you learned? What do we need to learn?" His confidence spreads through the men as easily as their laughter.

The men look to March, heads nodding, agreeing with the question and curious of the answer. The soldier March pinned against the gate weeks ago catches her eyes and lowers his head.

"I have learned no matter what technique or combination I teach you, it will not save your life or improve your skill in battle because you have forgotten the most fundamental part of battle. Win or lose. Kill or be killed. Live or die. Your comrade bleeding here thought he was not in danger. In your pairs, your matches, you knew you were not in danger, so your hearts, your skills, were not invested."

She breathes deep. The way to train them is the same way she trained Jonathan, though they had hundreds of years to practice. "Armor off," she commands. "Armor, chainmail, shirts, pauldrons, the lot. Lose them all and pile them against the outer wall. Boots, trousers, forearm guards, and belts are all you are allowed. Quickly, or I will have you fighting in only your boots, then your bare asses will enjoy the tang of the blade."

"To be fair and all," another soldier shouts as the men stand, "will you be taking your—"

Crack.

The soldier's snide words turn to a scream of anguish as his jaw breaks from one swift blow. The soldier from the gate shakes his hand from the impact. He nods at March solemnly and walks to the outer wall. The rest of the soldiers follow suit and do not tend to or even acknowledge the bleeding or broken men.

"Both of you get yourself to a physician and return without your armor before the day is done. If you are not back in time to train with the fourth battalion, you will not train at all," she says in a stern whisper.

"Is that all?" the bloody soldier says, his hands and forearms now stained as well.

"Your other option is to slit your throats here and now to release your suffering. I made good on my first promise. Would you like to test the second?"

The two large, bald gate men rise from their wooden seats, release a rolling grunt while their vacant eyes follow the two soldiers passing between them and exiting the bailey through the single door, then they sit again. Their size could be useful in a brawl—they stand nearly nine feet tall and as wide as any carriage. March has seen them replace carriage wheels with one hand while holding the carriage up in the other. Besides opening the gates, they are indolent to any who make requests of them, all except Pat and Bill. Two weeks ago, March saw them hold up the Duchess's carriage between them, one giant hand each, and replace the wheels. One finger of theirs is equal to March's wrist. Though their size and power would be advantageous, they move at the speed of melting wax.

The soldiers finally return to their positions. Bare chests and bodies of all shapes, sizes, and hues create a unique mosaic across the bailey, and a distinct, ripe odor wafts through the air without their layers of clothing and armor to keep it suppressed. March gains a clear view of each man she passes. Some are as thin as a signpost, ribs pronounced, looking as if they have not eaten in days. If this is the case, March will see it changed. Others are strapping men, both young and old. While others are larger, rounder, but stronger than the rest. Even the most confident man wavers, no matter their build, eyes darting to the other soldiers and puffing out their chests.

She motions for them to take a knee, and they do so without question. "I do not see soldiers before me anymore. I see men. You should see men. Brothers-in-arms. Flesh and blood. Not steel and iron. Steel and iron can be mended and reforged. Men, not so easily. Remember this." She walks through the crowd catching the gaze of all who look up at her. "New rules. Each man will find three partners. One larger than you. One smaller than you. One roughly your same proportions. You will learn to fight against each, because you must fight differently against each. A match is now won by landing a strike on the back and chest of your opponent with the flat side of your sword."

"What if we wound our opponent?" one soldier asks.

"We could get injured," says another. "What if we get hit?"

"Then you bleed," says March. "Life and death. You control the outcome."

Whispers spread throughout the men.

"Control your weapon," March commands as if she is with them on the battlefield. "You will no longer swing your sword like a child playing with sticks in the streets of Mirus. If you do not want to injure your opponent, then don't. You know how to fight, but you do not know how to survive. There is a great difference between the two. Contrary-wise, control your body. If you do not want to bleed or die, evade, block. I expect you to bleed. I expect you to hurt. I expect you to fail. This is how you learn. Rise and begin."

March points to the soldier who served as her messenger and the soldier from the gate and beckons them to follow her. The rest of the soldiers find partners and begin their matches with hesitant stances, afraid to hit each other at first but slowly realizing the thought it takes to control their blades. They hold their wrists firm, twist their arms as they should, adjust their stances. The thoughts click in even the most confident soldier—the forms and skills March taught them now make sense.

She walks to the main stairs of the castle and drinks from the glass bottle of water she left there this morning. The cold soothes her throat, rough from speaking so damned much. She surveys the fruits of her labors immediately; the men train with renewed vigor, competitive smiles, and even a smattering of laughter with one another.

The two soldiers stand at the foot of the stairs awaiting commands. Both men are of the same muscular build, fit, agile, though the messenger's frame is thinner.

"You two will train with me," she tells them, motioning to them with bottle in hand. "There are four battalions, and one of me. The Gryphon will command one, I the second, and you two the others. Should you survive."

Their reactions could not be more disparate. The messenger straightens his posture, an anxious smile spreading across his face, breathing heavy with anticipation. The soldier from the gate stands stock-still, his mouth slightly open in disbelief, eyes squinted.

"Make no mistake," March continues, "this is not an honor or compliment. You will train, you will bleed, and you will die for these men should the time come. You will serve me." She sets down her bottle and takes a stance on the stairs, sword pointed between them. "That is, if you survive."

CHAPTER 23

CHESHIRE

The Gryphon and his archers thought they could keep Cheshire from the rooftops, from continuing his work, his mission. They merely change Cheshire's methods with a slight delay. He uses the long-forgotten entrances to the catacombs hidden in the houses of Stonehaven and the Crest. Though few, they serve his purposes. It took Cheshire several days combing through every twist and turn of Stonehaven and the Crest, listening and peering through cracks in the walls to find the perfect location.

A lofty, thin, three-story house with five bed chambers, several streets lower than the Row, with a more-than-well-off owner, sits sandwiched between two similar homes, whose windows face the street. Upon thorough inspection, Cheshire discovered only one older man, near a half century, lives here—though there are five bed chambers with distinctive scratches from swords and armor along the floor and wall. All the soldiers who did not flee Mirus with the Red Knight have their own homes or small apartments in other buildings like this one scattered throughout Stonehaven. Yet only the owner came or went. Which means he had information for March and Jonathan, and ample room for Cheshire.

The owner occupies the topmost bedchamber to the rear of the house, bound, gagged, and unconscious. He will be the last. The other bedchambers are no longer empty. Cheshire collected various townspeople, a motley selection from Mirus, for his purposes and has given each new guest a room of their own.

During his lurking about, Cheshire could not help but notice the blades of the cult, identical to the one he first pulled from the dead body of the magistrate in Briarwell, peeking out from boots and dangling from belts under coats or aprons. Those he has seen walking through the streets stay clear of Lysander and Uriah's gatherings. Once the shouting starts, they walk the opposite direction to not be associated with them. Unfortunate for them. He caught two, and before Cheshire takes what he needs from them, he will gather what information he can for Jonathan and March.

He steps over the unconscious homeowner and fumbles through his wardrobe. Cheshire grimaces at the thought of wearing more clothing. Heavy black boots, an unnecessarily thick woven hood and cloak, and shirts and trousers which reek of cider. The thick clothes will absorb odors well—Cheshire counts on it.

Not yet. He will wear them only when he must.

Downstairs on the first floor, almost every item that shimmers or gleams in the house Cheshire took to the old candlemaker, who made good on his promise of the wax-covered canvas days ago. The last remaining trinkets he tucks in his cloak—a silver cream jug Jonathan would envy, a handful of silver forks, and four golden rings from the mantle to take for one last trip to the Crooked Market.

He slides open the wooden planks behind the kitchen cupboard that hid the entryway into the catacombs. When the burst of cold air hits his face, his head rushes and his eyes lose focus. The thought of sleep in the dark corridors calls to him, the cold stones beckon, but he must refuse. This side quest, as it were, serves as respite enough for his sore muscles. Ironic. Cheshire possesses all the Time in the world—he made sure of it—yet he acts as if Time runs out.

By the time Cheshire exits the storm drain into the Boroughs, night falls, and the candles burn in the depths of the Crooked Market, and his vision goes in and out of focus. It would be so easy to lie on the ground and sleep until tomorrow night, but he shakes the temptation. He wraps his mother's sash around his face and pulls his cloak closed as he makes his way through the shanty houses until he reaches the heart of the Market, the black heart, where the peddlers, merchants, and apothecaries sell, buy, and deal with the macabre, the dead, and the taboo.

Servants from the Crest trudge nervously through the soft mud, worried they will be seen. The working class of Stonehaven keep their eyes on the ground but are less worried. From what Cheshire has seen, they come here for harder spirits, opium, or other ways to make them forget their troubles.

Cheshire pushes through his exhaustion while he explores and discovers newfound energy in his delirium. Deep within the Market stalls, he finds one of many apothecaries—a woman almost out of place in the Boroughs, with golden hair and eyes and soft skin. Tattoos of animals and runic symbols cover her arms, the space between her breasts, and her neck. Masterful artwork. He trades the forks and a chance for her to rub the muscles of his stomach for a large bottle of hemlock essence. For her to use both her hands, he charges a bottle of her most potent spirit.

Deeper still in the maze of canvas and candles, Cheshire stops at a large tent covered with dried spray and splotches of blood, urine, and gods know what else on the inside. This is the best, the only, surgeon in the Boroughs. Cheshire pushes through the heavy cloth meant to keep prying eyes out and the odor of blood and rot within. Jars and bottles with questionable animals and body parts sit upon rusted shelves circling the perimeter of the tent.

The surgeon takes a single look at Cheshire, realizes he needs no attention, and returns to sawing off the black, bloodless toes of a man with gangrene. Fifteen other patients stand around the interior, coughing, crying, waiting to be seen. If he had the choice, Cheshire would sooner have the apothecary tend to him than the surgeon. He leaves the silver cream jug on a table and in exchange pockets two curved needles and a rusted surgeon's scalpel with no one noticing. For his purposes, it does not need to be clean. He hopes no one had need of them this night, but in the end, it does not really matter for what is to come.

One last stop before he departs. In the middle of the Market against the cliff face, he stops at the candlemaker's shop again, even though he was here not two, three, or four days ago.

The candlemaker's young apprentice greets Cheshire with a wide smile and wild wave. Small spots of red, orange, and yellow wax pepper his face and coat his arms.

"Where is the old man?" Cheshire asks by circling his finger in the air and tugging on an imaginary beard.

The apprentice pulls on his imaginary beard, closes his eyes, and points to the back of the workshop where a thin door made of old planks from the harbor, sea-worn with a few dead and dried barnacles scattered about blends into the stone wall at back of the workshop.

Cheshire puts a hand on his throat, sticks his tongue out, and points to the closet. "He died, and you have hidden him in the closet?" Cheshire jests. He taps on his temple and the forehead of the apprentice. "You are smarter than that." Cheshire pretends to dip his hands in the cauldron of lavender wax and holds his hand up, then shakes his head. "Cover him in wax. No one would ever find him." He wafts his hand in front of his nose. "Until the smell."

The apprentice smiles and laughs in his throat. He wipes his hand across his forearm sleeve and points to Cheshire, asking if the canvas Cheshire picked up days ago worked.

"Yes." Cheshire nods, and his eyes cross.

The apprentice rubs the soft areas under his eyes and points to Cheshire.

"I am tired." Cheshire nods again. In truth, he does not know the last time he slept. Two days, four days. It all blurs together now.

The boy points to the thin door and asks if Cheshire wants him to rouse the candlemaker.

"No, no." Cheshire shakes his head. He points to himself, then to the apprentice. "I need your help." He holds up two fingers, spreads his arms wide, then holds one finger up and mimics flames coming off of it with his other hand. "I need two of your best candles." He holds his forearm flat and circles his fist behind it. A horizon and the sun. "That can last for days."

The apprentice nods and rummages through a box at the bottom of a shelf hidden within the dark workshop. He unfurls layers of linen and pulls out two exquisite tall candles, a foot tall, with the finest filigree designs Cheshire has ever seen.

Cheshire points to the apprentice, then the candles. "You made these?" Cheshire points to the boy then scribbles in the air. "You carved them?"

The apprentice holds his head up proudly to reveal his thin neck which has not been washed in days.

Cheshire tussles the boy's rust-colored hair and taps him on the forehead again. "You are smart. Let no one tell you otherwise."

The boy holds the candles out for Cheshire to take.

"No." Cheshire shakes his head. He points at the boy and then points to the east side of Mirus. "I need *you* to take them somewhere."

It is as if no one has ever asked him to do anything more than carve wax. The boy's crooked smile grows no matter how hard he tries to conceal it. So many questions pick at Cheshire's mind about the boy—if his parents are alive or dead, is the candlemaker his guardian or just an old man who took pity on an orphan. The answers do not matter.

The apprentice holds out his hands to ask if Cheshire needs anything more.

Cheshire takes the candles from the boy, lays them down gently on the worktable, and kneels to be eye to eye with him, the smile gone from his face. He places his pointer finger on his chest, points to the candles, to the east, and then with slow severity points toward the main gate of Mirus, looming high overhead. He points again, muscles firm, to make sure the point is clear, then places the four golden rings in the apprentice's wax covered hands and cups them with his own.

"Deliver the candles, then leave Mirus. Please." Cheshire holds up his hand. "But"—he holds up a single finger and mimics a flame with the other hand again—"take one more candle with you."

CHAPTER 24

MARY ANNE

At long last, Mary Anne can sit with March and discuss the Book of Queens. In order to ensure their lesson, she sits on the stairs of the keep, book on her lap, and waits for March to finish with the soldiers. March never looks her way, purposefully, or so Mary Anne believes, but she is aware of her presence.

The sea of skin before her serves as a welcome distraction to occupy the time while she waits. Every man in the courtyard fights against one another without armor, without a shirt, bodies and muscles on display, sweat shining in the sunset. It is a veritable buffet for the eyes, though none compare to Jonathan in her mind, but the sight is enjoyable. March is the only one to wear a top, if it can even be considered such. She might as well be shirtless with the rest of them. It is little more than a square of leather across her chest held on by a strap around her neck and another across her back. Mary Anne wonders what Jonathan thinks about her wardrobe in such a situation, among such men, without him. Surely they stare and lust after her body. With her hair pulled up in a messy bun on top of her head, her entire back is on display, except for the two-inch strap and buckle.

Perhaps she likes the attention of other men. Whether or not it is true, Mary Anne will believe it to justify her thoughts of Jonathan. If March can parade around other men thusly, what would stop Mary Anne from doing the same, except for her thoughts of decency—which fade by the day. In Lyndhurst, she had the courage to undress in the window for Thomas to see, and eventually to touch herself while he watched. In the end, she won. Thomas was hers to claim.

When their training is complete, all but two men exit the courtyard, one with dark green hair and the other with a paler shade of orange than Dormy's hair. Mary Anne wishes she could hear what they speak of but watching is enough to fill her mind. March positions them, corrects their stance by running her hands over their arms and back, and stands curiously close to them—too close in Mary Anne's opinion—sometimes with her breasts pressed against their backs. Their movements are a graceful dance, and with the amount of skin showing and touching, Mary Anne cannot deny the sensuality either.

Jonathan deserves better.

Once done with their flirtation, the soldiers exit the courtyard, armor in hand, and the large gate men shut and secure the doors. March finally turns to look Mary Anne in the eye for the first time this evening. Her tongue presses against her cheek as she massages the back of her neck roughly. She intentionally climbs the steps slowly, to prolong the wait, and then sits on the step above Mary Anne with a loud groan.

"Let's have it," says March, hand outstretched.

Mary Anne notices the black ring on March's middle finger as she gives her the book with both hands, but March carries the heavy tome as if it had the weight of an empty serving tray. "Thank you. I appreciate this more than you know. You must be exhausted after such a long day. This is—"

"Get to the point." March cuts Mary Anne short, her irritation as plain as the sweat on her body. "What would you like me to translate for you?"

"Well, the entire book, if possible. There is so much I need to know."

March pops her neck and inhales deeply. "No. I am not a tutor. Weiss can do this as easily as I."

"Yes, but he refuses."

"Have you thought perhaps there is a reason? Or are you just an impatient child?"

"I am neither, thank you very much. I would think you would want to help me get home."

"I do. Therefore, I spend almost the entirety of my day training soldiers, four thousand soldiers. This is my lot. And you add to it."

This is the way every conversation seems to lean with March—Mary Anne succumbing to the guilt she knows too well, the burden she is. But she will return home, damn it, no matter what it costs.

"Yes, I do. My lot is to sit and wait for others, to which I am not accustomed. I have spent my time here at the mercy of everyone else but myself, and I will have it no longer. But to do so, I need help from another strong, intelligent woman." She waits in a thick, uncomfortable silence for March to respond. She must see herself as March's equal, talk to her as an equal, in order to be heard.

"I will not read this book to you," says March in a lighter tone. "For fuck's sake, look at the size of it. And I have thousands of soldiers, and Jonathan, to attend to. However, meet me here every evening and I will read until the sun has set. Then you can retire to your chambers for the evening, and I will sup with Jonathan and then return to the garden."

March cracks open the book without regard for its age or importance. Mary Anne's eyes follow March's as they scan the page. She reads the first line out loud in Old Prodigium and familiar, though still incomprehensible, sounds cause Mary Anne's ears to perk as well as her curiosity.

"Gaelic," Mary Anne says under her breath.

"What now?"

"Gaelic. Old Prodigium sounds very much like a language of my world. An older language of my world."

"Fascinating. May I continue?" With Mary Anne's silence, March continues to read, this time in the common tongue. "'Six Tenets dictate the once then and once future of...'" She has trouble forming the word. Her lips press out of her control the same way Mary Anne's did when she tried to name the Chamberlain as her advisor, the same way the Chamberlain's stuck when he read the same passage. "'Wonderland,'" she continues. "'The First Tenet—'"

"Would you mind terribly if we skipped farther?" asks Mary Anne. "According to the Chamberlain and the Duchess, I must complete the Second Tenet before I move on to the Third. Is there something in the pages of the Second Tenet that could tell me how to accomplish this?"

March widens her eyes and flaps through the pages, almost a fourth of the way through the book until she stops. "The sun is almost set," she says.

March flicks her finger on the large header at the top of the page then flips to the next with a similar heading. "Nothing. The Third Tenet follows. And the sun has set. We will continue this on the morrow." March hands the book back to Mary Anne and climbs the stairs back to the keep without another word.

Mary Anne wants to scream, to curse, at March for abandoning her when she needs her most. But she has no power. One harsh tone or word from Mary Anne may be all it takes for March to quit all together. She will wait on the steps tomorrow, and the next day, and the day after, adhering to March's terms, and will make the most of every remaining second of sunlight until she has consumed every page.

———

The following evening, March reads from the Third Tenet, but it mostly contains duties of the queen, more managerial than regal, listing out how to address delegates from the other cities of Wonderland, how to conduct meetings, and appointments of land and title. The third evening, Mary Anne learns the rules of the treasury. The fourth night she learns about the decorum held at court, at banquet, and abroad, none of which are useful in the slightest. These things she can learn at a later time.

The fifth night, March holds training until after the sun sets and walks by Mary Anne without even a glance.

"Bitch," Mary Anne utters as the doors to the keep shut behind her. She has never used this term in her life, never thought it, but March infuriates Mary Anne with every day growing longer. March has Jonathan, has armies at her command, a confidence Mary Anne could only dream of. The snide look on her face, the smug raise of her eyebrow, makes Mary Anne's blood boil.

The sixth night, Mary Anne asks March to jump forward to the Fourth Tenet. From what the Chamberlain and the Duchess have said, the contents of the Fourth are of more interest and importance anyway.

"'The Arcana'," March reads. Her lips press hesitantly. "'The queen has ultimate authority, ultimate power in Wonderland. The Arcana flows through Wonderland and thus will flow through her, granting her power overall.'"

"And?" Mary Anne asks after March pauses longer than her liking. A growing look of concern in March's eyes raises the same in Mary Anne's. A knot grows in her throat. "What? What comes next?"

March turns several pages, and her fingers stop at a smaller heading of filigree on the page. "'The queen's word is law under the Arcana'," she continues reading, "'and therefore incontrovertible.'" Her finger slides lower on the page. "'A queen cannot alter or negate her own decrees once spoken. She is bound by the Arcana in mind and the physical.'" March slams the book. "Mary Anne, these words are not meant for my eyes."

"Continue," Mary Anne says forcefully, losing all sense and craving more. She is a drunkard, and the book is her liquor. She will drink her fill until she is gorged. "This information is vital. I must know more. I must know everything."

March drops the book on the step beside her and raises her voice. "You do not command me. No one commands me." Her upper lip twitches and her eyes burn, even in the dying light of day.

"Not yet." The words slide from Mary Anne's mouth before she can stop them.

March grips the handle of the sword at her hip so tightly it rattles in its scabbard, and her arm shakes. Mary Anne has seen hatred in March's gaze before directed at her, but never this. Regret and murder are all she can see. Her eyes dart from Mary Anne's to her throat and back again erratically. If she utters another word, March will kill her here and now before Mary Anne can scream for help.

Mary Anne waits to know her fate, her confidence stripped, her thirst gone, and now only the scared woman who first arrived in Wonderland remains seated, trembling on the stairs to the castle. Her heart thunders so loudly, so quickly, she fears she will faint straightaway. Will March kill her while unconscious? Jonathan's face, Thomas's face, the face of her mother, all flash before her. Even though Mary Anne faced brigands, soldiers, and the Ace, she has never felt closer to death than this moment.

However, March decides to spare Mary Anne's life—this time. She walks away, climbs the stairs, every step fueled by pure hatred, and disappears into the front entrance of the keep.

Mary Anne did not mean what she said to March. Or did she? She spoke nothing more than the truth March read. If she is to be queen, she will have the power to command March. The Book of Queens says it. March cannot decide what she will or will not follow, especially since Mary Anne does not have any choice at all.

It is abundantly clear there will be no further lessons with March, and also uncertainty over what will happen the next time they meet. What will she tell Jonathan?

Not yet. How could two ordinary words have such an effect?

The night air slowly cools Mary Anne's skin and slows her heartbeat. The Castle Guard keep watch high along the perimeter of the outer wall. Did they hear? Did they witness? They must have. For the first time since she arrived, even surrounded by hundreds of guards, the icy feeling returns to her chest, never feeling more alone. She must return home, needs to return home. Not ready to return to her chamber, she pulls her knees to her chest and lies her head against them.

Not as alone as she first thought. Out of the corner of her eye, Mary Anne notices Dormy scurrying from her wagon around the side of the castle, lantern in hand, in an odd manner—half sneaking, half skipping— but in good humor. At least someone is.

A warm, genuine smile would do Mary Anne a world of good at this moment. The same smile Dormy shared at Jonathan's table. She follows her, both apprehensive and excited to see a part of the castle she has yet explored and can easily find her way back from. The farther she follows, the more dirt covers the clean cobblestones of the courtyard, hay soon thereafter, and then the unmistakable odor of manure. Dormy's path ends at the castle stables, rising high against three stone walls at a dead end. Fat wooden beams hold an arched roof aloft, and elaborate swirled carvings adorn every angle and joint.

Lantern light flickers out of the first stall. Mary Anne treads lightly so not to spook the horses or Dormy. She pokes her head around the corner to find Dormy brushing the coat of one pony and then the other while singing a tune under her breath, which sounds like something that belongs in a tavern or on a ship.

"Good evening, Dormy."

"Good evening back to you, Mary Anne." Dormy stops brushing and rushes to the edge of the stall. "What might I do for you this night? I have a sleeping tonic if you need. New pillow. Book on astronomy. Lizard skin. I'm not sure why you would need the latter, but I have it, should you need it."

"Nothing of the sort," says Mary Anne, amused. "I thought I would come and say hello before retiring for the night. With everything happening, you are the one I see least."

"I appreciate the sentiment. Would you like to look at my ponies?" She gestures to them as a child would beckon their parent.

"They are lovely." Mary Anne does not know what else to say. She is no expert on horses or ponies, except for those who drew the carriages in London and Lyndhurst, but they do indeed look well kept and well fed. Mary Anne obliges to Dormy's request to pet them as well. She strokes the short soft hair of the backs. "They seem quite good tempered and gentle animals."

"They are," says Dormy. "They are special."

A deep guttural whinny from several stalls over draws Mary Anne's attention. The mammoth black steeds that pulled the Duchess's carriage shift and reposition themselves. Their hooves clack heavily, deeply, against the dirt-covered stones. Their backs stand a head taller than Mary Anne, their heads four times more. Long, wide braids swing from their manes.

"How regal," says Mary Anne, which elicits a high-pitched scoff from Dormy. "I meant no disrespect to your ponies. I am sure they are quite exceptional..." Mary Anne trails off and glances back and forth between both sets of beasts. Jonathan and his band followed Mary Anne and the Duchess from Briarwell and arrived in Mirus only hours apart. "Dormy, perhaps your ponies are even more exceptional, considering they could keep up with those beasts, let alone pull your wagon."

The grin of a particularly juicy secret she should, but cannot, keep to herself envelops Dormy's face. "Would you like to see why?" The joy she radiates shines brighter than the lantern hanging above them. She rubs her hands along the right flank of one pony and pulls back its skin.

Mary Anne recoils in horror and shields her eyes with her forearm, expecting to see muscles or sinews, unsure how Dormy could commit such an atrocity.

Dormy giggles. "Move your arm."

Hesitant, Mary Anne lowers her elbow first, able to see the pony, still standing, unaware of what has just taken place. She lowers the rest of her arm. Horror turns to morbid curiosity. Mary Anne has learned Wonderland has many surprises but can honestly say she has seen nothing quite so intriguing. No muscle, no flesh, no blood. Instead, metal and wooden gears whir and click to the rhythm of a heartbeat within an iron frame, all undetectable to the touch.

"Clockwork horses?"

"Couldn't tell the difference, could you?" Dormy says proudly. "Ten hands or twenty hands tall, makes no difference if what's inside is the same."

Are they both mechanical? Some automatons that are impossible feats of engineering? Mary Anne glances back and forth between the ponies, no larger than Shetlands, and the Duchess's steeds, taller than Clydesdales. "I did not even know such a thing existed."

"Look and act just like the real things."

Mary Anne must ask, afraid to look naïve, "Are... all horses in Wonderland like this?"

"No, no, no, of course not," says Dormy. "I told you these were special. Two sets of horses were made especially for castle use. The black shires over there and the two dapple-gray at the farthest stall in the stables." She motions with her head.

"Two sets of horses," says Mary Anne. "But what of—"

"Which is why mine are even more special." Dormy secures the flap of skin back to the pony's side. "These were the first. Proto typical is what they called them. The design was improved upon quite a bit, so I'm told, and out popped the other two sets. But few people knew of these ones at all. So they were gifted to me. So, please don't say anything."

"My lips are sealed. So this is how we traveled without stopping from Briarwell all the way here."

"Correct. They can travel long distances without rest or water—just need a good wind every several days. But I tend to them and pretend to feed them to keep up appearances."

"Will wonders never cease?" A question pops into Mary Anne's mind like a soap bubble bursting but in reverse; something she never thought to ask and shrugged off because of the whirlwind of events after her arrival. She stood with Jonathan on a map of Wonderland but had no reference for scale, so thought nothing of it then, but knowing they traveled almost non-stop for four days at a steady speed, now she has to ask.

"How far did we travel, Dormy? That is, how far is Briarwell from Mirus?"

Dormy wiggles her fingers and her orange eyes jump side to side and then up and down, plucking numbers from the air. "Just under fifteen hundred."

The number does not register with Mary Anne at first. "Say again."

"Fifteen hundred. Miles."

A flurry of thoughts flood her mind. *How could I have traveled so far? No wonder Jonathan misses his home so. What if my way home is back where I entered Wonderland? Is there a chance? Should we return? No. We are here. I am here. And the Duchess's plan, no matter how outlandish it seems, is sound and plausible. If I return to the forest, I would wander aimlessly, not knowing what to look for.* Mary Anne shakes them from her head and focuses back on Dormy staring at her with pinched brows. "I am sorry," she says. "I never gave thought to it. Thank you."

"Anytime," says Dormy. "Though I'm not sure what I did."

"Your disposition is enough."

Dormy yawns and climbs the side of the stall to unhook the lantern from above and drops back to the floor with a soft thud of her boots. "Shall I walk you back to the keep? It is late. I would fetch Jonathan, but I'm sure he and March are already in the garden by now."

Mary Anne's thoughts continue to churn. "Do you think they are asleep yet?"

"Doubtful. It will take them a while to reach the center of the hedges, and then they will have a nightcap, and then have their nightly routine and all. So what will it be?"

"No, thank you. You are too kind, but I can manage."

Dormy nods again and scurries back into the courtyard in a zig-zag pattern, lantern clinking in her hand, and the orange pool of light makes it appear as if she floats across the night.

Routine. The temptation of the rings whistle to her like a distant ship off the coast, waiting for an answer. Tonight may be the last night the rings are even a possibility, especially after her encounter with March earlier. There is only one way to discover if March has taken off the ring.

Mary Anne hurries back to her bedchamber, running as if trying to escape the Ace. After Grace helps her dress for bed, she excuses her, and once sure she is alone, Mary Anne pulls the white ring from under her mattress and stares at its brilliance, the candlelight from her side table dancing in its curve. Her heartbeat quickens at the thought, the idea, this type of magic exists, and the possibilities if it does. She slips it on her left ring finger, and it fits snuggly, as if it were meant to adorn her hand. She lies back in bed, and clasps her hands over her stomach, turning the ring on her finger, and waits. Her eyes follow the mortar lines of the ceiling stones as they slowly shift in and out of focus. She tries to stay awake, worried she would miss the opportunity, but succumbs to her heavy eyelids and drifts into a deep sleep.

A pressure between her legs rouses Mary Anne. She is unsure of how much time has passed. At first she thought it a dream, but no, the rings truly work. Still groggy, she clumsily pulls the nightdress off over her head to feel the morning air on her bare skin. She can feel his hands wrap around her wrists, March's wrists, the weight of his body pressing down on top of her. There is a pressure behind her knees as well. Though she can feel every sensation March experiences, there is no way to tell what position Jonathan has her in, but Mary Anne will imagine.

Jonathan kisses her neck, just below her jaw, and swirls his tongue at her earlobe. His fingernails drag up her forearms. He teases her, rubbing himself against her sensitivity, and her body shudders with every throb between her legs. Wave after wave of hot pulses overtake Mary Anne's body, radiating from deep within her. She bends her legs, spreads them on the bed, and raises her hands above her head, pressing them against the headboard.

She can feel his breath, his mouth kissing its way down her collarbone to her breasts, lips dragging on her skin. Jonathan squeezes her left breast and circles her nipple with his fingers while the warmth of his mouth envelops the other, and his tongue matches the rhythm of his hand. She moans, no matter how hard Mary Anne tries to subdue them, but realizes Jonathan and March no longer sleep in the next chamber and, with no one else on the floor, there is no longer a need to fear being heard.

Fortunate timing. She is not prepared, not ready, for Jonathan to enter March, enter her. A long, lingering moan louder than any she has ever uttered escapes her lips like smoke rising from a bellowing fire—it might be her very soul.

Is he so much larger than Thomas? Or has it been so long? It doesn't matter.

Every slow, long thrust replaces the faint visage of Thomas with Jonathan. She can feel drops of his sweat fall on her chest. Her body feels as if she was at sea, rocking back and forth. Her legs kick wildly, her arms grasp and tear at the bed sheets as Jonathan quickens his pace, faster and faster still. Mary Anne tries to relax her torso, but her entire lower body from navel to toes remains clenched. His motions slow to a crawl as he pulls and pushes, his body shaking—Mary Anne can feel it—until he can restrain himself no longer and quickens again. Mary Anne loses focus of her eyes and tenses her body, the tingling, the fire building between her legs, until she cannot restrain herself. She climaxes while Jonathan continues to thrust, unwavering.

Jonathan grabs her thighs, pushes deep, and holds her there. Mary Anne climbs to her knees and grabs onto the carved footboard, believing their evening escapade finished. She is wrong, oh so wrong. Mary Anne climaxed, not March, and she is now at the mercy of March's tolerance, having Jonathan in her multiple times a day and night. She lays her forearms across the footboard and rests her head on them, backside in the air, unable to move, unable to think, only able to feel. Her fingertips dig into the wood of the footboard. Her fingers ache, but it does not matter. It pales compared to the pleasure she feels. Mary Anne climaxes twice more before March reaches hers, forcing Mary Anne's third, moments after Jonathan. Her body trembles, but her thighs shake uncontrollably, her heart thundering in her chest, stomach, and between her legs. She feels his warmth fill her, her warmth mix with his, and drops, beautiful drops, meander down her thighs.

To end off the perfect morning, her body jumps at the soft kisses between her thighs, the soft laps of a tongue over and over again, and then a long-lasting heated kiss on her lips. She can feel his lips, his tongue, consume hers, and she has no choice but to kiss the empty air as if Jonathan were really there. In the brief moment of their recovery, Mary Anne pulls the ring from her finger to escape the ecstasy for fear they will continue. Her body is not experienced enough to endure Jonathan's passion, at least not yet. She gasps for breath and collapses on the bed, her body and sheets covered in sweat. Her abdomen spasms randomly and she cannot help but laugh, delirious with jealousy.

March enjoys this multiple times a day. Multiple times in one go.

Mary Anne thinks back to her first weeks in Wonderland, terrified and full of worry at every turn, and now she lies on satin sheets, sleeps in a castle, and can have a dalliance with the man she desires every morning and night. She retrieves her nightdress, twisted and shoved into the crevices between mattress and headboard, and pauses before slipping it back on.

No.

She tosses it to the floor and embraces her newfound freedom. The exquisite brush of the silk sheets on her skin, her backside, her back, her breasts. She lies on her side, spent from the experience, and drags her fingers along her hip and torso until she falls asleep once more, ready to dream of what just occurred, ready to feel Jonathan again in the morning. The rift she caused between her and March needs to be mended, even if it is disingenuous—it must. Now that Mary Anne has felt what is possible, she refuses to give it up. She will have Jonathan every morning and night until the day she leaves.

CHAPTER 25

JONATHAN

T he blue pansy straddles the pink, holding one of her legs in the air, hips pressed and writhing together. They grope at each other's breasts, their moans a rising sea on a rocky shore, overpowering Jonathan's conversation with the green-haired pansy. Jonathan asked for them to provide cover, as they did during his and March's first visit, moaning and panting as they listened to their requests. But if they wish to make their subterfuge authentic, Jonathan will not deny them.

Screams crescendo and bodies jerk wildly in an attempt to entice Jonathan since March did not accompany him this night. Out of the corner of his eye, he can see them alter their position to display all and put on a show for him, no doubt an act out of their repertoire when dealing with other men and women. However, their efforts fall flat. Jonathan focuses on the green pansy seated on the edge of the pit of pillows, even though she wears the same sheer petals as before.

"There isn't one," the green-haired pansy says, one arm crossed over her body, pressing her breasts together.

What in all the hells have I put myself into?

"In the past week, we've had three men and two women come in here with the same blade you showed us," she continues. "We slipped our sisters, who share duties downstairs in the arms closet, a few coins to make sure they send us anyone who drops one off. Not one of them said anything about someone being in charge."

"Are you certain?" Jonathan has a hard time believing a cult with this many members has no leadership. Then again, from what little Cheshire told him, the men in Briarwell acted of their own accord. How, then, do they send word to one another? If, in fact, every member acts separately, there must still be some way of communication. There must have been another member in Briarwell or Rookridge. He cannot think of a single person in Rookridge, the village where he was born and spent his better years, who would be a member. He cannot recall ever seeing one of these blades in all his years, though he did not know to look for them.

"The three of us know how to get information." She smirks. "Six hands and a limited number of holes, you know? You'd be surprised what a man will tell you once he has a finger up his ass."

Jonathan suppresses a small laugh, thinking of the familiar sensation of March and Cheshire's fingers, and how helpless he is at their touch. "I can only imagine."

"One of them men, and one woman matter of fact, told us their whole life stories, almost screamed it at us between and during orgasms. In the heat of fucking, men and women blurt out all types of secrets without realizing it. Inhibitions dropped and all."

"I have no doubt. Did you figure out any other information that I may find useful and you may find lucrative?"

"Well, they didn't have to tell us, but from what they wore, only two of the three were from Mirus. The second woman was from a farmstead close to Breighton. One of the men smelled of the mines of Rutrum, and the other strode in here in the gilded robes of Adamas."

Three. Three out of how many hundreds? Jonathan stands. "Thank you, once again." Jonathan tosses another hefty sack of gold coins, secured tightly with twine, to the pansy. "I am unsure if March or I will pay you a visit next time, but either way, we will supply you with coin as long as you supply us with useful information."

"We would rather it be you," says the green-haired pansy.

"Speak for yourself," says the blue pansy in clenched breaths. "I bet she has the most remarkable breasts. Perhaps she will remove her top as you do."

"I am certain she will not take issue with such a request. And she does." He swings his short blue jacket on and straights the gambeson sleeves, leaving buckles undone—evidence of his fraudulent deeds with the pansies. "Until next time."

"You know"—the pansy stands and smooths her petals—"we will do this more, for much less than you are paying us. In fact, it won't cost you a single piece of gold." She gestures to her sisters who have paused momentarily, breaths heaving, all looking at Jonathan. "Join us just once. You can do anything you like. And we will do anything you command, day or night."

"I thoroughly appreciate the compliment, ladies." Jonathan tips his hat. "But gold will suffice, or it will stop finding its way into your hands."

The green pansy reluctantly hangs her head to the side and shrugs. "Can you blame us?"

Jonathan lowers his hat over his eyes and gives no answer. He waits with his hand on the wooden door handles for the women to climax. Not for any personal interest or curiosity, but if they are to continue the charade, it would look suspicious for him to leave their room while they continue to howl. Once they collapse, he slips through the door, closes it behind him, and descends the spiral stairs.

Sixty-four. He counts, knowing the answer, but unable to help himself. He collects his sword and scabbard from the arms closet, secures the belt around his waist, and drops two silver coins in the flower's hand tending the weapons, without Madam Rose's notice. Men and women howl from the large rooms behind the velvet curtains on both sides of the hallway—

dozens by the sounds. The lesser the price affords less privacy. A man and woman arm-in-arm from the Crest, dressed in gray silk cloaks with fur around the collars, pass Jonathan on his way out, their perfume more odorous than the incense burning in the Garden.

Jonathan saunters toward the closest stairway into the Crest—the quickest way back to the castle and to March. He checks his timepiece, cradling it in the palm of his hand. By this time, she should be finished with her training, or rather torture, of the soldiers. Now someone else can experience her rigorous expectations. Jonathan has endured them for hundreds of years and is still yet to match her. Despite the grueling training she has put him through, he is a swordsman and a better man because of her. When he meets her at the center of the hedge maze, they will have tea—Dandelion Melon—then he will bathe her tired body in the fountain and massage the knots from her shoulders and arms. The tolling of the city bells cuts his daydream. No. Just one, signaling for aid.

A man in a frantic state cuts in front of Jonathan, sprinting as fast as his legs can carry him. At first, Jonathan thinks nothing of it, until a second and then a third follows. They do not run from something; they run toward something. It is not his business, should not be his business, yet he feels whatever happens at the destination of these men is Cheshire's doing.

He follows them at a distance but still must run to keep them in sight as they race around the curve of Stonehaven and down the thin stone stairways between residents. They head toward the Forge, the row of smiths on the lower levels of the central tier of Mirus. Iron and steel crashing against anvils and the roar of the bellows should be clear between the tolls the closer Jonathan draws to the Forge, but all he hears are the shouts and howls of angry men.

A crowd of men at least fifty deep, all covered in soot, sweat, mud up to their knees, and leather aprons and sleeves covered with scorch marks, form a ring with two men at its center, one dead, face first in the mud, skull crushed to the point where it looks like he does not have a head at all. The second looms over the body, shoulders arched, heaving breaths, blood trickling from his nose, and gripping a bloody pair of smith's tongs as long as the man's legs. Soldiers try to push their way through the crowd but are squeezed in, unable to move.

A young man with a thin frame manages to slip through. He runs to the body, falls to his knees, tears running down his face, mouth agape, and screams for every god to hear him.

"Father!" the young smith cries. "Father. What the fuck did you do to my father?"

The larger smith walks away, drawing the tongs and wiping the blood from his own face.

"You will answer for this. Murderer." The young smith pulls two straight-peen hammers from his belt and charges his father's killer. He takes swipe after swipe at the man's head, fueled by blind range and grief, aiming nowhere else.

The larger smith uses the tongs as a shield, but one hammer slams into his fingers with the same force to forge a blade on an anvil and bursts them open. Two hang from the man's hands like bloody sausages dangling from a butcher's block. With a roar, he swings the tongs wildly with one arm and cracks the younger smith's jaw. Blood and teeth fly into the mud.

Pain does not stop the son. He charges once more while the larger smith recovers and swings upward, burying the hammer deep between the man's legs, surely shattering his pelvis. Jonathan cannot shake the image of the man's balls exploding like crushed plums.

"Such a shame," says an old man not far from Jonathan. He peers over tiny cracked spectacles balanced on his large nose. Along with the size of his nose, which barely surpasses the size of the Adam's apple on his crooked neck, his unkempt, scraggly, gray mustache, his oversized wool coat, and the way he holds his hands out in front of him, make him appear more rodent than man. "Such a downright horrible shame."

"Yes, sir," says Jonathan. "It is."

Soldiers push their way into the circle, but it is already too late. More smiths break through and attack each other and the soldiers. The young smith falls to his knees again as another smith, an older man, triple his size, kicks the boy square in the face, sending him into the mud to join his father in the hereafter. Some lunacy has set upon them. Men who stood by now become entangled in the brawl. First five, then twelve, then twenty men, not counting the soldiers, roar and swing at each other. The screams and crunch of iron on bone become palpable. The soldiers are overcome, knocked back and forth, shielding themselves from blows while trying to determine where this began and what must happen to stop it.

Jonathan is unsure what he can do, but he cannot stand idly by while the city descends into chaos. The anger in the crowd burns like a wildfire, consuming all those around it, and he fears the only way for it to stop is to let it burn out. But then how many more will lose their lives today? He climbs old crates full of potatoes and apples stacked as high as the nearby blacksmith's thatched awning to get a better vantage.

He wishes he could use his words instead of his sword, but no matter what he says, none will listen. They are past the point of reason. The air is thick with screams. Screams to stop. Screams for help. Screams to kill. Screams of terror. Innocent men and women caught in the fray reach out with hands stretched to the heavens, hoping for salvation. More townsfolk run from the surrounding dwellings, and with each new addition, an additional fight breaks out somewhere in the crowd. Jonathan can say nothing to stop them. The only thing which stops their screams, stops their fighting, are the cracks and crunches of bone.

One burly man tackles two more who stood by and watched next to the crates Jonathan perches on. The weight of all three men splinter the old boards, and Jonathan tumbles down over the men, into the mud, into the mob. Mud fills his right ear and nostril. He tries to get to his feet, but another man trips over Jonathan's back, sending both, and the nearby woman he clung to, all back to the ground.

Jonathan digs his hands deep into the mud and thrusts himself upright. He reaches for the man and woman who tripped over him, but the crowd separates them, their fingers just out of his grasp, eyes wide with terror as they disappear behind more bodies. Fed up, Jonathan grabs men by the collar and shoves and pulls them away to clear the area. He may not be able to save everyone, but he can save someone. He can pull these two innocents from the mire.

"Clear the way," a distant voice shouts. "Move," says another.

Jonathan could not hear them coming, his senses overtaken by the cacophony of wails, curses, and screams, and the mud deafening his faculties. Two pale horses plow through the townspeople, tossing them aside, leaving everyone stunned in their wake.

Their riders, Uriah and Lysander, command the people with voices to rival cannon fire. "Stop this at once," they shout. "Hold. In the name of the Old Kings. Throw your mistempered weapons to the ground. Or suffer swift justice at the edge of our blades." They snap the reins, gallop faster, and push through the crowd in a circle, three times until a clearing forms and all have stopped. The soldiers shift uncomfortably. The bell rings its last. All that remains are the sobs, heavy breaths, and the dead littering the muddy ground of the Forge. Thirty-seven by Jonathan's count.

Uriah holds his glaive along his arm and points the curved blade at those he speaks to. "What began this fray? This wonton loss of life? What brought this madness upon you?"

"Speak," roars Lysander, hand on the hilt of his longsword.

A smith steps forward, beard braided down to his gut, covering a blow to his forehead, face covered with mud and blood not of his own.

"Speak up," says Uriah. He tries to sound sincere but cannot hide the arrogance in his tone.

"An argument is how it all begun," the smith says confidently. "Accusation more like it." He points to the smith with the tongs first, then the first dead man, trampled beyond recognition. "The big one accused him of murdering his wife. Been at each other's throats for years.

Always threatening to kill each other but never acting on it. Next day, the day previous, he returns home from the Forge and his wife ain't nowhere to be found. Their home's in shambles. Don't return for the entire night. Soldiers searched for her, probably still searching for her. Then the morning came, one man confronted the other, and it all went to shit."

"Look at all of you," Uriah seethes, "the proud smiths of Mirus fighting one another like a pack of witless mongrels. What shame you have brought unto yourself and unto your city. Your brothers lie dead in the mud by your hands."

Lysander spits. "We should find every man responsible and behead them here and now for the vile misdeeds."

"No, brother." Uriah holds out a hand and calms his breath—a show if Jonathan ever saw one, but quite convincing. "We do not have jurisdiction, we do not have the power to make such judgement. But I assure you all, we would never let this happen in our beloved city."

Not good. Not good in the least.

"Who knows if the man's claims were true?" Lysander trots around the perimeter of the circle, glaring at the mud-covered smiths and townspeople, indistinguishable from one another. Silence. "You slaughter your kin, your friends, your neighbors," he continues in a low growl, "without reason or just cause? Fuck beheading. Too quick. Too merciful. This entire lot should be taken to the gallows to watch each other dance before it is their turn."

The circle widens, bodies press tight against one another to get farther away from Lysander's threats and the steely look in his eyes. If this is just a performance, every word is genuine.

"Do not retreat from us," says Uriah. "Never let the thought cross your mind. Had we known of this heinous situation, we would have found the man's wife and discovered the innocent parties, and the guilty, before the morning dew disappeared." The townspeople hang their heads. "But I do not blame you. I cannot. The hard truth is, you all took justice into your own hands, because deep inside you know the truth. You have none.

265

Those who reside in the castle look down upon you, the workers, the laborers, and deliver what? Nothing."

What he speaks of would not be possible in the timeframe given, if this all transpired within a day. But he wisely, albeit unfortunately, plays on their heightened emotions—their anger and their guilt. Jonathan would have done the same if given the chance, but with a different outcome in mind.

"There are soldiers among you now," says Lysander. "What did they do to end this travesty, this horrible loss of life?"

"We did what we could," a soldier says from within the crowd.

"And it was not good enough." Spit flies from Uriah's mouth as a shout. "Look at what the apathy has done to this city. To its people. You are as guilty as they are, protecting an old crone who hardly ever sets foot out of the castle. And who plots to put another queen on the throne. Lies. Lies and deceit."

The crowd mumbles and stares daggers at the soldiers pinned within. Jonathan's heart quickens, fearing for their safety. With a few words, Uriah has made them enemies, and if these people would kill their own, the soldiers do not stand a chance. Jonathan looks through the crowd for helmets, to count how many soldiers there are, but he can spot only five, though he knows the number is greater, their helmets knocked to the ground during the struggle.

"We can tell you for certain, the men who lost their lives today were indeed innocent," Uriah continues. The people ignore the promise he made earlier about finding the guilty parties and hang on to every new lie out of his mouth. "Do you see how lies and deceit fester and darken the mind? If only you had been told the truth. If only the Duchess did not keep secrets from the people of Mirus. Then the entire debacle could have been avoided. As we have said all along, the truth which has been kept from you—the Queen Slayer has returned to Mirus."

The crowd gasps and erupts in frantic and heated whispers.

"He has returned with his own dark designs," Lysander adds to the powder keg. "This man's wife was not the first taken. There have been several others who have reported other loved ones missing, kidnapped. She is only one of many. One of you. I fear no one is safe this time."

"It's true," a woman shouts. "One of the butchers disappeared days ago."

Jonathan hopes these claims are not true. If there were a way to contact Cheshire, he would do so immediately. He can no longer turn a blind eye. Cheshire's deeds endanger them all.

"We know of the trail of dead soldiers in Mirus," says Uriah. "Left behind as warnings to us all, but we did not heed them. We all are at risk. At the mercy of the Queen Slayer."

Whispers are now shouts of frustration and disgust.

"Answer me this." Uriah snaps at the reins and trots around the circle, hoping his energy will fuel their rage. "Would the Queen Slayer even have returned if the Duchess did not attempt to seat another queen on the throne?"

"Shit," Jonathan says audibly.

Lysander joins Uriah, and they both pick up speed. "If you had been told the truth from the beginning," he shouts, "your brothers would still be alive. The blood is not on your hands. It stains those in the castle and those who protect them."

The crowd roars, fists thrust in the air, and they turn on the soldiers, punching and clawing at their faces. Uriah and Lysander let the assault go on just long enough to prove their point, to prove their influence.

"No," Uriah commands. He raises his glaive in the air. "We will not spill any more blood this day. Let them go. Let them return to the castle to tell the Duchess and the queen-to-be that the people of Mirus have had enough. It is time for change. And change has come."

The silence of the crowd unnerves Jonathan. Not a breath can be heard. The soldiers, fear clear in their eyes, worm their way through the townspeople until they can run from the Forge.

Jonathan does not need to hear or see anymore. The longer he lingers, the more risk Uriah and Lysander will discover him. He backs away from the crowd and turns to leave. Thirty-nine. Thirty-nine bodies. Jonathan adds the man and woman he attempted to help up to the number, trampled by Uriah and Lysander's horses when they first arrived. A fitting testament to their hollow promises and lies.

He reaches into his trouser pocket for his vial and holds it to his lips. Empty. He loses all color and his legs tremble. The entire contents leaked through a crack in the bottom of the glass. Both legs felt wet, but he assumed it was a splash of water from the barrel earlier. He bolts from the Forge, up the nearest stairs, not caring if Uriah or Lysander see him. Nothing else matters now. He must return to his trunks high in the bedchamber, high in the castle, and receive a new vial or flask.

Must not stop. Panic hastens his steps. Seventy-three. One hundred eighteen. Two hundred forty-seven. He counts every stride toward the castle to keep his mind focused. Three hundred five. He counts every stride as if it were his timepiece ticking down. Four hundred thirty. He counts every stride because any one could be his last.

CHAPTER 26

MARCH

By the time March enters the chamber for the morning council meeting, the mood has turned, like milk left out in the sun for days. But instead of a rank odor in the air, it is as if everyone tenses their bodies and senses after a lighting flash, waiting for the boom of thunder to shake them. The Duchess sits at the head of the table, still and silent as a headstone, eyes focused far beyond the walls of the chamber. Weiss paces the length of the room wide-eyed and picking at the threads of his white gloves. Pat and Bill sit at the far end of the table. Exhaustion hangs heavy in their eyes from the extra repair work to the hanging cells added to their already mountainous workload.

March unties the belt of her scabbards and sits halfway down the table, in the exact center, twelve chairs on her left, twelve on her right. Jonathan will approve. She sits her swords in the chair to her left, to which Weiss twists his face, then keeps pacing, wearing a groove in the stones.

Out of the corner of her eye, March notices the sleepless worry in the corner of the Duchess's eyes, in her pressed lips which she tries to conceal with the paint she applies. March sinks down in her chair, rests her knee against the table, pulls a dagger from her boot, and picks the dirt from beneath two of her nails. Jonathan's vigor was more than usual this morning, and she ripped grass and dirt from the ground.

A few moments later, the chamber door opens and Mary Anne enters, escorted by Jonathan. She takes her seat at the left hand of the Duchess, and Jonathan at her right. Instinctively, he counts the number of chairs around the table, and when he notices where March sits, he winks, a sparkle in his beautiful turquoise eye. Curiously, Mary Anne's expression is more relaxed of late, though March has not seen her in almost a week since their encounter on the steps of the keep—a wise decision.

"Morning, all," says the Duchess. "Now with all in attendance, we may begin. We will be brief this morning. What news of yesterday?"

Jonathan clears his throat. "We are losing the people. The longer the castle remains silent, the further the influence of Lysander and Uriah spreads like the roots of a great tree we will not be able to unearth. Perhaps in the past, the citizens of Mirus could be left to their own devices, but now more than ever, they need a voice. They need to know they are seen, they matter."

"I shall write a proclamation at once and speak through the skylarks. Patricia, William, please make it ready."

"No. That is not good enough." His tone is firm. He pauses and waits for a reprimand from the Duchess, but a wave of her hand allows him to continue. "We hide while Lysander and Uriah parade through the streets unchallenged."

"What do you suggest?" asks the Duchess.

"As much as it pains me to say, and goes against every intuition I have, I believe you and Mary Anne must appear to the people... outside the castle walls."

"Preposterous." The Duchess scoffs and sits back in her chair.

"Jonathan," says Mary Anne, fear in her tone.

"Absolutely not." Weiss stops and grabs the back of the closest chair for dramatic effect. His long white hair swings side to side as he shouts.

"Of all the ridiculous ideas to come from your mouth. This is why you should never have been appointed her advisor. You will see us all killed."

"I am her advisor, Weiss. You seem to forget this often."

Before Weiss can reply, the Duchess waves Jonathan's suggestion away with her hand as if wafting the lingering smoke of a candle from the air. "We have the croquet game coming soon. We will officially present Mary Anne there, properly, safely, within the confines of the castle grounds."

"He is right," says March. Jonathan told her of what happened in the Forge last night as they laid together. He told March her voice would be needed. So she fell asleep playing out the game in her head. "Who will be in attendance at the croquet game? The elite from the Crest, Lysander, Uriah, my mother, dignitaries from the other *important* cities of Wonderland, no doubt. But they are not who you need to be convinced. They swim in my mother's pocket, and if you think you can convince Bronwyn of anything other than what she already has set in her mind, you are mistaken. Lysander and Uriah spend their days not in the Crest but in Stonehaven, garnering support from those who used to be faithful to the crown. Their followers number in the thousands."

"And you suggest we walk willingly into such a lion's den?" The Duchess slaps her hand down on the table, to a less-than-intimidating thud.

"Yes," says March. "With myself, Jonathan, the Gryphon, and a battalion of soldiers and guards if necessary. If our presence, if..." March does not want to acknowledge her. "If Mary Anne's presence, and yours, can slow their number or decrease them, we must try."

The Duchess bites at her lip. Her eyes bounce around the table, looking at the options before her like dinner plates.

Jonathan looks at Mary Anne and extends his hand across the table. "Do you trust me?" he asks her.

Hesitant at first, she reaches out and places her hand in his. "Yes. I do."

March's stomach turns.

The Gryphon enters, quiet as a ghost for a man his size, and stands at the door. "Fourteen." His brow furrows, and his gaze pierces through the stone floor. "There have been fourteen kidnappings these past few evenings, men and women alike. We have not found the bodies of any more dead soldiers. I fear his tactics have changed. Something is coming."

Jonathan and March fight the urge to look at one another, but they say his name in their minds at the same time. *Cheshire.* While March trains the soldiers, the Gryphon canvases the streets of Mirus, looking for any evidence of Cheshire and where he will strike next.

"I want the Queen Slayer found immediately." The Duchess bites out her words. Her veneer of confidence drops. Her cheeks shake and lips quiver out of anger. Or perhaps fear. "Do you hear me? Find him. Kill him." The Duchess takes Mary Anne's hand from Jonathan's and squeezes. "He will not claim another. He alone is the reason our beloved queendom teeters on the precipice of collapse, and wolves claw at our doorstep ready to devour us should we take our eyes away. If you send Mary Anne out into the city, you invite his wrath. You may as well strike Mary Anne down here and now, if you are so careless with her life." She realizes the volume at which she speaks and regains her composure.

I may as well, March repeats to herself. She will remember the permission given. However, March can sense the Duchess's concern is not for Mary Anne, but for herself.

"I will restructure the soldiers' training to have more men searching," says March.

"No." The Gryphon's voice could shake the stones from the room. His stare cuts to the quick. "The matter of the Queen Slayer shall be mine. Press the men harder. They must be ready for anything."

"As you wish." March wishes she sat closer to Jonathan, so she could hold his hand instead of Mary Anne. She wishes they could return to the hedge maze and spend the day together as they could in the Hollow. She wishes she could run Mary Anne through in her sleep and be done with her, with all of this.

"I should heed the counsel of my advisor," says Mary Anne, breaking the silence. "As long as I have Jonathan and March with me and the Gryphon in the city, I am sure my safety will not be in question. I trust Jonathan with my life."

"Fine," says the Duchess. "But after the croquet game. Weiss, select two dozen of the prominent merchants and smiths from Stonehaven, who are not loyal to Lysander and Uriah if possible, and invite them. Let us see how Mary Anne fairs amongst a hundred citizens before making herself vulnerable to tens of thousands." He nods and strides from the room, his confidence returned. "I must prepare as well. But before we conclude, Patricia and William, what news do you have?"

"Nothing of note," says Bill. "The hanging cells should be completed by season's end, so the builders can return to their farms for harvest."

"We made some reinforcements to the castle walls, should the necessity arise," says Pat.

"Very well." The Duchess stands and wrings her fingers as she leaves the chamber.

The Gryphon follows her but walks the opposite way, his longcoat dragging the floor behind him.

March gathers her swords and buckles them back on her hip. She gestures for Pat and Bill to wait for her, but before she can make her way to the end of the table, she overhears Mary Anne's whisper.

"Jonathan, would you mind terribly waiting outside? I would like to have a word with March." He nods and slips from the room.

"Will you two wait outside as well?" March asks Pat and Bill. She would rather forego the pointless conversation with Mary Anne and get on with her day, but there are requests to make of them before Pat and Bill disappear into the city. They slip from the room, leaving the door ajar slightly.

Once alone, March endures the long awkward wait while Mary Anne slowly makes her way around the table, gripping the top of every chair, as if she walks along a cliff's edge.

"Yes?" asks March, with six seats remaining.

Mary Anne stops, surprised. "I wanted to apologize for my words during our last session. I did not know what I was saying."

"Yes, you did."

"I only spoke out of the information I have," Mary Anne proceeds cautiously. "I only meant when I am queen—"

"If you become queen, you will have the power to command us all. You can try to take back your words all you want. Your eyes spoke the truth."

"I am sorry," Mary Anne says, confident yet tinged with anger, and takes her hands off the chair tops. "If we could resume—"

"No. As I told you then, those words are not meant for my eyes. If you are meant to be queen, then rise to the occasion. Prove your worth."

"I need your help."

"And you will have it. In the way I see fit. Not as you command. *Not yet*," March says with venom in her tone. "After you." She holds her arm to the door.

Mary Anne swirls her response in her mouth like a cow chewing its cud, swallows it, then leaves the room. March looks at her extended hand and realizes she still wears the blasted ring Mary Anne gifted her. She will remove it when she returns to the maze with Jonathan, and perhaps bury it or smash it.

In the hallway, she catches a glimpse of Jonathan rounding a distant corner with Mary Anne. Pat and Bill lean against the opposite wall, arms crossed, yawning.

"The palanquin. I need you to reinforce it. Steel bars. Iron grating."

"That would be quite a weight to carry," says Bill.

"We could construct a new one," says Pat. Both her and Bill's eyes widen with excitement. "On wheels, but still pulled and maneuvered by guards."

"When can I expect it?"

They approach March, the tips of their boots almost touching hers. "Two days," they whisper together.

"Two days? Rather quick for all that metal work, not to mention what is left on the hanging cells."

"You shall have it in two days," says Bill.

"The only reason the cells take as long is because we merely supervise the workers," says Pat. "If it were by our hands alone, it would be finished much quicker. But we have other duties to attend."

Before March leaves them, a familiar scent, their scent, sparks a memory. Nights ago, when Cheshire met her on the rooftops of the Quadrangle. He smelt of black powder and something else. Pat and Bill have the same mixture drifting off them. March leans in and sniffs Pat's neck, and then Bill's.

"You smell of black powder."

"I should say so," says Bill. "It was all over the pit of the hanging cells. Still lingers in the air." They should be furious at Cheshire for destroying their work and forcing them to rebuild what he destroyed, but it is difficult to decipher their expressions.

March sniffs again and whispers. "What is the other scent upon you?"

They look at each other without expression, having an unseen conversation through thought, much better than she and Jonathan can. Not a muscle on their faces move—only their eyes, ticking side to side and up and down.

"Oil," Pat whispers carefully, more question than answer.

"Was there oil at the hanging cells?"

"Not any significant amount," says Pat. "But we work through the night. Oil lanterns burn longer than braziers. Let us continue without break."

There is no way to uncover Cheshire's plot fully, but the more she knows, the better equipped she will be to respond, either to the city or to Cheshire's rescue. He used the black powder to destroy the hanging cells.

His next target could involve oil, copious amounts of oil from the strength of its scent on him.

"Where are they stored in the city?" she asks.

"Depends, there are small—"

"No." March interrupts Bill. "Where is the largest store? Together."

"The armories of the city's outer wall," says Pat. "There are four. The western end, the eastern end, and two smaller nearest the gatehouse of the Great Gates."

"This evening, after the soldiers leave for their homes, and you are done with your work, I need you to take me and Jonathan there."

The thoughts twist and turn in March's head throughout the day, so much so that she turns the training over to the messenger and the guard from the gate. She walks through the soldiers as they train, distracted, half-watching their movements, half-watching the sun's arch chip away at the day. She sends the two soldiers home without additional guidance and waits in the empty bailey.

After the last glimpse of orange sky disappears, Jonathan joins March, two hooded cloaks draped over his arms and a bottle of rum and a turkey leg with its charred skin hanging off in his hands. He knows how to care for her, knows what she needs and when she needs it. There is no Time for dinner tonight, so he brought it to her. March rips into the turkey leg. Its hot juices explode in her mouth as she pulls muscle from bone. Before she swallows, she takes a hearty swig from the bottle and lets the spiced rum mix with the spices of the meat and swirls it around her mouth.

"I needed this," she says. "The only thing to make this better would be—"

"Potato?" Jonathan pulls half of one from his pocket, roasted and seasoned. He holds it out for March to bite into so she does not have to debate if she will relinquish the drink or the turkey leg.

Her teeth click as she bites through the hot, flaky morsel, and she allows her lips to brush against his fingers to savor his touch as much as the taste. "You really are the perfect man," she says, chewing.

A short low whistle from the gates draws their attention. Pat and Bill wait at the small door between the two lumbering gate men, who groan after the sound. March and Jonathan_don their cloaks, pull their hoods over their heads, and follow Pat and Bill down into the city, snaking through the stairways of the Crest, cutting through the alleyways of Stonehaven, and crossing the Long Bridge over the Boroughs.

"A city on fire," says Jonathan.

"It just might be," says March.

They go through a small wooden door, past twelve soldiers, and up a narrow zigzag of stairs until they reach the top of the outer wall. From here, the view beyond Mirus bathed in the night is even more breathtaking. Pat and Bill are mindful and kind enough to linger for a moment to allow Jonathan and March Time to take it in.

They split up to quicken the search. Jonathan accompanies Bill to the western armory, and March follows Pat to the eastern. The outer wall curves for miles, with pairs of soldiers manning twenty-four-pound cannons, some double and quadruple barreled, archers stationed in between at the parapets, and huge iron vats rolled into the inside of the wide walkway. Soldiers nod at March to acknowledge her as they pass—a feeling to which she will never grow accustomed.

After a long stretch, they near the end of the wall and descend a broad stone staircase to a wide, single wooden door with four iron locks on it. At Pat's request, each of the four soldiers stationed outside the door produce a key and unlock it for them. Four deep clanks free the old iron shackles. They enter the chamber and wait for their eyes to adjust to the darkness. Slivers of moonlight cut through thin windows high in the wall like flaming silver arrows. Rows, stacks of rows, of dark wood barrels, large and small, almost as dark as the iron rings around them, line the long walls.

"Are you sure Cheshire has been here?" asks Pat.

"Do you doubt him?" asks March.

"Not at all." Pat peeks behind the barrels of the outer wall. "He is quite skilled with locks."

"Quite skilled with many things," says March. "Which makes him a greater threat."

After what must be an hour of searching, all they know for sure is the inventory is short twelve small barrels of black powder. Enough to cause a sizable explosion, but not the size that destroyed the hanging cells. Soon thereafter, Jonathan and Bill arrive and inform them there are thirteen barrels unaccounted for at the western armory.

"Other than the missing barrels, everything looks as it should," says Bill.

"Which means it is not," Jonathan and March say together. They walk the length of the room, searching for any last sign, any evidence, of Cheshire's tampering, but find nothing.

Nothing. A chill washes over March's body. Though Cheshire may be rash at times, most times, all the time, he is always methodical. *Could it be?* Her mind drifts to the rooftops of the Quadrangle once more, to Cheshire's arms. She inspects the large barrels stacked in the middle of the chamber, pulls the dagger from her boot, and jabs a barrel just below the second ring. She pulls it free and expects a gush of oil to seep onto the dirt covered stones. *Nothing.*

Jonathan picks up one of the small barrels of powder and by its weight knows it is empty as well. They check every barrel. Every single one, the entire armory, is empty. Cheshire has ferried away every drop of oil and grain of black powder. March assumes the same of the other armories as well.

The explosion of the hanging cells was a singular incident, a single structure, which damaged several surrounding blocks and killed a handful of soldiers and townspeople. Cheshire threw the city into chaos with twenty-five barrels of black power strategically placed. And March and

Jonathan bore the fallout of his action. Whatever Cheshire has planned next is larger, so much larger. He spoke of destroying the city, and March and Jonathan ignorantly thought it hyperbole, but now it truly is within his power, and they find themselves completely at his unpredictable mercy.

CHAPTER 27

GRYPHON

The old, worn planks of the harbor piers clack beneath the Gryphon's heavy boots. The sound of lapping water on the posts beneath, the slight jostle of loose boards, the spray, all seem so familiar and yet so foreign—like a dream. A dream he had for almost a thousand years while he wasted away in the dark of the oubliette until he gave up any hope of freedom and gave in to the bottle.

Of all the places the Gryphon patrols through the city searching for Cheshire, the harbor brings him the most solace. This place has its own unique sounds and smells. The brine, the gulls, the low rumble of creaking masts, the freshly caught fish, the pull of the tide on the rocky shore. The rest of the city is cobblestone and dirt. The harbor's winding pathways, long piers, twisting stairs, and every structure are constructed of wood, weathered and discolored by centuries of the salty wind and water.

Inside the city, walls of every shade, huge in height and material, stare back at him. However, in the harbor, he can stare out and get lost in the glistening sea, a sea of smooth, colored glass, twinkling as it spans to the horizon, or what little horizon can be seen. The bay of Mirus is vast and could be mistaken for open ocean, but for the south, almost out of sight, the land curves in on both sides like a closing pincer forming a narrow strait.

Except for the additions made by Patricia and William, the city remains largely unchanged. Through the pipes, gears, and new structures, the Gryphon appreciates the old, worn wood, the old ways, the old world. Fishmongers shout, customers haggle, and the taverns and rigging of ships in port keep the harbor alive with the faint sounds of shanties.

A hooded vagrant stumbles past him. Liquor drips from his beard and leaks from the small cask under his arm. He leaves a trail of his drink on the planks behind him. A sharp, stiff mixture of noxious, odorous, stenches stab into the Gryphon's nose like a hot poker fresh from a hearth. It is not the sour, biting smell of urine but the unnatural, potent aroma of liquor. The drunkard stumbles and sloshes up several sets of wooden stairs, leaking everywhere, and relieves himself behind a storehouse, still holding his cask.

The sweet, intoxicating smell of whatever drink this man carries latches on to him. A cold sweat forms on the Gryphon's brow. His heart races, his mouth dries, his cock pushes against his trousers, and his fingertips begin to itch. He has been sober for mere weeks but a slave to the bottle for near a millennium.

He hurries to the giant lift that takes cargo up to Stonehaven. "Up. Now," he commands the operator.

A thin man in a leather skull cap obeys and pulls on a lever almost as tall as he is, releasing the counterweight.

The lift rises, half full of crates of fish packed in salt. He leans over one crate and inhales to drive the lingering scent of liquor from his nose. The gears tick and clunk. The lift knocks against the side of the wooden shaft. He cannot tell if it's the lift or his legs that shake, but his armor rattles either way. While on his patrols, he makes the conscious decision to stay clear of the taverns and the brothel, leaving their inspection to his soldiers for fear of this exact occurrence.

The Gryphon has endured three prisons in his lifetime. The oubliette was by far the easiest of the three. While a sentence of its own, the drink was also an escape from the true prison he finds himself in—Mirus. Though he walks the streets again, freedom is an illusion. Not just for him but for all who dwell within the city, if not all of Wonderland. This prison he cannot escape, but not because of shackles or chains or cages, but because of a promise. And because of this, the temptation of the drink, his second prison, a prison of numbing isolation, becomes too great.

He serves the crown. The Gryphon will see a queen on the throne again, protect Mirus, deal with Cheshire, and some day keep his promise. He must. It is all he has left.

CHAPTER 28

MARY ANNE

Mary Anne looks down from the balcony of the Long Hall to a nearly empty room. She remembers the crowd the first time the Duchess brought her here. Hundreds of townspeople packed both sides of the room, waiting for answers, talking over one another like Parliament discussing any minutia. Today, one hundred people at most mill about, all on the left side of the room, all from Stonehaven.

The Duchess holds tight to the banister to keep her hands from fidgeting. Small curls of hair fall out of the back of her normally pristine snood. She waits for any townsperson to take the dais, but none do. They wait to see what the Duchess says, but she remains silent most of the afternoon.

Mary Anne has never seen her so affected. The Duchess still retains her air of grandeur, but her neck and face twitch. She twists the ruby ring on her finger. She inhales after realizing she has held her breath.

She worries not of what to say but rather the lack of townspeople in attendance. Lysander and Uriah's numbers grow while theirs dwindle.

"Is there a request amongst you?" Mary Anne asks in the Duchess's stead. "Please, step forward. Let us hear you."

Finally, a young boy, no more than twelve, dressed in overalls and a large linen shirt, steps forward onto the dais, his stray hat crumpled in his hands. "Please, ma'am. My mother has been missing for some days. She ain't returned when she went to work in the harbor. I've been tending to myself and younger sister, but we're worried, you see."

"Say no more," says Mary Anne. "I shall see the guards supply you with enough groceries for a month. Also," she motions a guard forward, "describe your mother in detail to this gentleman. We shall find her."

"Thank you, ma'am," the boy says with a quivering bottom lip. He steps from the dais and follows the guard out of the hall. The boy's bravery sparks others.

Another man steps forward and asks about the disturbance at the Forge.

"We have deployed more soldiers to the area and will stand vigilant day and night to make sure such a brawl does not happen again," says Mary Anne with a confident nod.

"It's not the fight what's the problem." His eyes meet Mary Anne's. Dried paths of tears cut through the dirt on his cheeks. "People are going missing. It's not just soldiers anymore. It's people. Wives, sons, the butcher for the gods' sakes. Everyone is turning on each other. Aren't you supposed to be doing something about it?"

Mary Anne looks to the Duchess for an answer.

"Not her," says the man. He points to Mary Anne. "You. Many of us remember the time of the Queens and wish to return to them. But more and more people are losing faith. Dinah would never have let this happen. We need a queen, not a Duchess or some young girl playing at princess. People are dying, nothing is being done."

"I... I am sorry."

"We don't need your apologies." The man's neck grows redder, veins bulging. "We need action. We need a ruler, a true ruler."

Another man of slimmer build steps up on the dais with him. "Who are the guards in the city there to protect? They patrol all night hunting the Queen Slayer while you all sleep peacefully in your large beds. We sleep when we can, with barred doors and windows, but we're the ones suffering from him. Not you lot."

He steps down from the dais. "Maybe it is time for a change." The other man follows him from the Long Hall, and not long after, the rest of the townspeople do as well.

What do I do? I shall be stuck here forever. I shall never return home. If the entirety of the city turns to Lysander and Uriah, Mary Anne will never be able to be queen, nor be able to return home. The word *impossible* creeps into her mind again after all of these weeks.

"Well done," says the Duchess.

"Well done?" asks Mary Anne. "I said nothing. I did nothing. I could do nothing."

"You helped a young man and his family." The Duchess sighs and turns to Mary Anne for the first time since they entered the hall. "As queen, you cannot save or help everyone. Many will pose questions you will want to answer and make promises to, but you are wise enough to know what you do not know and not answer. You do what you can. Being a queen is not easy."

Mary Anne's heart sinks. So much work. So much disappointment. Feeling so powerless at every turn takes a toll on her. She can see the fatigue in the Duchess's eyes, heavy like Mary Anne's.

As they walk back to the main part of the keep, Mary Anne asks, "What troubles you, madam? I mean no disrespect, but I cannot notice the difference in your demeanor."

"Perceptive, you are," the Duchess says. "I have recurring nightmares. A face staring at me in the darkness. I can see it in every shadow, behind me, in every reflection, and when I close my eyelids. I end up not sleeping much at all and read by candlelight. The light saves us. Without it, who knows what the monsters will do?"

Monsters. Mary Anne knows she means Cheshire, the Queen Slayer, and knows those shadows are no hallucinations. Cheshire is in the castle, watching her, tormenting her. But for what purpose? She has seen him be murderous, but to be cruel is far different and far more troublesome.

"Pat and Bill have informed me the alterations to the palanquin are finished," says Mary Anne. "Perhaps, if I were to go out and be among the people. If they saw me as much as Lysander and Uriah—"

"Mary Anne, do you think this the best time?" the Duchess interrupts. "Look down. The balance no longer favors us. We are losing the people. It is not safe for you out there."

"If I lose the people, I lose my way home," says Mary Anne. "I cannot sit here while Lysander and Uriah overrun our city. I have faced men who would see me fail before. Though these events have different, more dire consequences, I am learning not to fear them."

A hint of a smile raises the Duchess's plump cheek.

"Surely with the adjustments, Jonathan, the Gryphon, and the soldiers, I would be safe."

"We know where Lysander and Uriah are during the day," says Jonathan's soothing voice from the open door behind them. Mary Anne did not know he joined them on the balcony. "They gather at the Fireside Quadrangle with their supporters. If this is what Mary Anne wishes, we could take Mary Anne to another part of the city. Use the soldiers to divert pathways, block roads, to keep them from her."

"I understand you are her advisor, Master Carter," says the Duchess, "but I cannot allow it. Will not allow it. We not only contend with Lysander, Uriah, and their followers, the cultists are another matter."

"We must try," says Mary Anne. "If I am ever to return home, we must try."

"I am sorry, Mary Anne." The Duchess walks from the balcony leaving Mary Anne and Jonathan alone. "I leave her in your hands, Master Carter."

If only those words were true.

This time, Mary Anne glares down at the empty hall. Her lip quivers, not out of sadness but anger. "She is wrong," she tells Jonathan. "I can do this. I must do it."

"She is right to worry," says Jonathan, who steps shoulder to shoulder with her at the railing of the balcony. "But you are not glass, you are not a prisoner. It is your life to live or to lose. Which do you choose?"

His scent, herbal and musky, calms her nerves. Heat radiates off his body. Out of the corner of her eye, she can see the bulge, the curve of his chest muscle in his half-open linen shirt. Every heartbeat in her chest screams to reach out and touch him, or at least to put her hand on his. They rest on the balcony a finger-width apart.

"The brawl and deaths at the Forge—the disappearances are yet too fresh," says Jonathan, using logic to dispel Mary Anne's lust unknowingly. "It was unexpected to say the least, but not to be expected given what we face. Everything in its time. I promised to keep you safe, and I agree with the Duchess. The risk of your injury or capture runs too high. I promised to protect you, and I will. You will see the people soon enough, and you will win them over." She chose him as her advisor, and thus far he has not led her astray, so she will not protest. And for some reason, his smile captures Mary Anne. If she must wait to see the people, there is no better company to keep. The longer they remain in the castle, the longer she has Jonathan to herself.

During the following days, the Duchess meets with Mary Anne more frequently during her lessons with the Chamberlain, three times a day, oft not saying anything, only lingering and pacing slowly, watching over Mary Anne as a concerned mother would. This afternoon, the Duchess circles around the colonnade of the courtyard while Chamberlain Weiss informs her of all the dignitaries from the great, the old, cities of Wonderland who have arrived by sea. Much like the Duchess, whose mind seems off in distant thought, Mary Anne cannot concentrate.

Her lessons, wherever they may be—the Chamberlains study, a courtyard, the dining hall, or the garden—become increasingly awkward. The Duchess asked Jonathan to join her lessons, as her advisor, which Mary Anne adores, but the Duchess also requires March to be at the evening lessons after she trains the soldiers. They do not involve themselves with the lessons. Their presence is for protection, not participation. Jonathan speaks up sometimes to correct the Chamberlain. Jonathan finds great amusement in this, while the Chamberlain picks at his white gloves incessantly, which is why Jonathan keeps his distance. The Duchess slips away during their banter.

Mostly, Jonathan and March keep to themselves, oftentimes with Jonathan sitting on the grass or in a corner of the Chamberlain's study, his back against the wall, his arm draped over March as she leans against him. She sometimes wears a beautiful black oval pendant with a silver border on a chain around her neck. It hangs low between her breasts, and Jonathan circles the black gem with his fingers as he whispers and smiles into her ear lovingly. Mary Anne has seen March's brutality and vulgarity. This sickly, sweet, soft demeanor she puts forth when she is with Jonathan cannot be real. It is a guise to keep Jonathan entertained, to keep him all for her. Thomas's wife did the same. She was beautiful of face and gentle of spirit, from what Mary Anne could see through the windows of their adjoining brownstones and their limited interactions, but Mary Anne was the one he pleasured, not her.

The thought of Jonathan touching March makes Mary Anne's skin crawl. March wears a linen shirt, one of his no doubt, with billowing sleeves and tied with twine at her navel. Most of her breasts and body are visual for all to see. Jonathan adjusts the shirt's unfinished hem too close to her nipples. Mary Anne will never admit the impressions in her palms from her fingernails, the thumping of her heart in her throat and between her legs, and her breaths as jealously, but when she wears the ring and feels him every night and every morning, she cannot help but want his hands upon her body, his manhood inside of her instead of March.

"Pardon me." The doorman surprises everyone, breaking all from their thoughts. "There are visitors at the gates."

"And what of it?" the Chamberlain sneers. "The castle has dozens of visitors every day. Why now have you decided to disrupt my lesson?"

The doorman rolls his eyes. "Believe me, I would rather not be here at all. But these two ask for Mary Anne by name. And the small one, the young one, the boy, is quite persistent to see the 'lady from the engine'."

Emilia and Alden.

Mary Anne's heart leaps and she runs for the gate as fast as her legs will carry her, dress in hand. The clack of her heels grows faster at the thought of Alden's and Emilia's smiling faces shining brightly.

Dormy runs past her in the opposite direction. The smile on her face cannot hide the determination in her eyes. Something is afoot, and she looks for Jonathan and March.

Mary Anne will find out about it, eventually, but there are more pressing matters. When Mary Anne reaches the gate, she expects to see them waiting for her, but only the two large gate keepers and a handful of the Castle Guard mill about.

"Where are they?" she asks.

"They're waiting outside the gate," a guard says, his voice ringing in his helmet. "We cannot let anyone in just because they ask."

"Well, I am..." Mary Anne chooses her words wisely. "I command you to let them in."

The guards nod and open the small wooden door in the massive gate. He beckons someone unseen with his hand, and immediately Alden's hands grasp the side of the door, as they did on the train. He peeks in, eyes curious as ever. Once he sees Mary Anne, he runs through the door. A guard offers a hand to Emilia to help guide her through.

Mary Anne kneels, her dress puffing out with the air beneath it, and hugs Alden. She stands and hugs Emilia as well, catching her off guard at first, but Emilia returns the warm, motherly embrace, something Mary Anne has not felt and been in dire need of for so long.

Mary Anne finally lets go, though she does not want to. "What brings you here?"

"I wish I could say something more exciting," says Emilia, "but just replenishing our stores of medicines. The apothecary in Rookridge was destroyed, so we thought why not go on an adventure and come to Mirus to stock up on what we need? Imagine our surprise when we hear talk in the market of a girl with brown hair and eyes in the castle. Once Alden heard this, there was no stopping him. He pulled me halfway up the city, certain it was you."

"And I was right," says Alden proudly.

"I know this may sound odd, but I have missed you." Mary Anne does not go into any more detail about how Emilia reminds her of her own mother—her looks, her gestures, her smile—but she is sure Emilia knows.

"We missed you too," Alden shouts. He turns to look at the large gate men. "Are they giants? I've never seen a giant before."

"Shhhh." Emilia covers Alden's mouth and laughs nervously. "Forgive us. What do I call you? What do I address you as?"

"Mary Anne, always, and nothing more."

"But from what I've heard—"

"It does not matter. Please." Mary Anne takes Emilia's free hand in hers.

Emilia nods and holds Alden close, who says her name muffled through Emilia's fingers and points behind Mary Anne.

Jonathan and March walk to the gate at a brisk pace, swords on their hips. Dormy follows but breaks off and climbs the stairs back to the top of the outer wall. Jonathan tips his hat, and the spark of recognition shines in his eyes.

"Briarwell," he says.

"Yes, sir," says Emilia with a slight curtsy. "Nice to see you again."

"Likewise," says Jonathan. "However, we must be off." He looks to Mary Anne. "Our mutual friend has information, so we must go see what he has to tell us."

"Please be careful," Mary Anne pleads.

He nods, and he and March disappear through the gate, its circular iron handle clinging like prison shackles. She does not know why such a morbid comparison comes to her mind first. Perhaps it is the danger Jonathan faces with Lysander and Uriah. Or perhaps it is because the mutual friend he speaks of, no friend to Mary Anne, is Cheshire. The Queen Slayer. The one responsible for so much death and destruction in the city. Or perhaps they can move freely, while Mary Anne must remain in the castle.

"How long are you in town for?" She shakes the thought from her head to come back to the here and now.

"Until the engine comes again to take us back north. We plan to stay in a small inn with quite a lot of plants in the southern part of Stonehaven."

"I will not hear of it. You two will stay here." Mary Anne smiles wide to hide any concern about the troubles of the city. She does not need to trouble them with her own problems, but she can keep them safe. "If you will allow it?"

"Stay in a castle?" Alden pulls from Emilia. "That one?" He points at the top of the highest tower.

"Yes." Mary Anne laughs. "Unless you know of another castle."

Alden shakes his head wildly, wide eyed.

"Are you sure we are allowed?" asks Emilia.

"How much exactly did you hear in the market?" Mary Anne grins, proud for once to say genuinely she will be Queen of Wonderland and thankful for the opportunity to share time with Alden and Emilia once more, a chance she never thought she would have again.

CHAPTER 29

JONATHAN

T he sheer amount of perfume in the air overpowers Jonathan's senses, stabs at his eyes, and prickles his lungs. More potent than the incense in the Garden. But no matter its strength, it cannot veil the truth—the scent of death. The familiar medley of blood and human excrement, once it finds its way through the perfume, hits Jonathan's jaw like a backhand from the Gryphon. It does not matter how many times over the centuries this particular medley has wafted up his nose; he is never prepared. At least there is no scorched flesh this time.

Dormy told them she saw Cheshire's cloak waving through the highest window of this house through her scope. Cheshire wants them to see something here, but from their first impression, Jonathan fears what it might be.

"Crude, but effective." March sniffs the air. "Valerian root. Sage. Mint. Cheshire could easily gather these from the market." She sniffs again. "Something else. Hemlock, from the Crooked Market. He has been busy."

The beautiful home they stand at the threshold of appears pristine, no sign of struggle or stains, though it seems the neatest looters have set upon it. Clear shapes in dust on shelves, tables, and walls show where valuables once occupied. But the horror, the source of the stench, hides somewhere deeper within the home. Jonathan spits to get the odor out of his mouth.

"How many?" he asks March, who shuts and bars the door behind them.

"Three bodies at least." Her fingers dance at the hilt of her sword, but instead she pulls two daggers from her hips and flips them to lay the blades along her forearms.

The unassuming, thin, tri-level home sits abandoned. But there are no empty homes in Mirus—there are too many people for a house this large to be empty. A suit of armor sitting on a table near the door gives Jonathan his answer. The home belongs, belonged rather, to one of the turncoat soldiers. They stole away so quickly after the revolt that no one had Time to pack except the clothes on their back and their swords. Though there would be little need. Lysander and Uriah could refit them all ten times over and promise them the return of their homes once the city falls.

"Hello, my loves." Cheshire hangs upside down from the second floor above the staircase. His eyes are blood-shot, heavy with exhaustion.

"What is all this?" Jonathan asks.

"What was asked." He smiles at March, then frowns to make it appear he smiles upside down, but he cannot keep his composure and lets slip a dark chuckle. "Come along." He reaches up and pulls himself out of sight.

Jonathan looks at March, trusting her always, but curious as to what exactly she asked for.

"I do not appreciate dawdling. I am a busy man, after all," his voice calls from above.

The stairs clunk and groan as they walk up and make the turn to the second floor. Three doors line the hallway and another staircase hooks around the far corner. Nothing should surprise Jonathan, but Cheshire is not himself. He could see it in his eyes, his beautiful lavender eyes clouded with hatred.

Jonathan has seen enough atrocities in his long lifetime that nothing should shock him again. It is not the palpable mystery of the unknown before them that turns his skin to goose flesh, nor the intensifying stench in the air. It is Cheshire's disembodied hum, some song, drifting through the air like smoke from Death's own pipe.

March and Jonathan peek into the first bedchamber. Another suit of armor lies scattered around the floor, bed overturned, and scratch marks dug into the wooden floorboards. The prisoner's ankles, wrists, elbows, knees, and finally his neck, twist at odd directions at the joints. The dead man lies face up, if he in fact had a face. Shriveled muscles, exposed teeth, and bare eyeballs dry in the musty air of the house. The man's beard-covered face drapes over the side of a small table, dried and withered, with leather twine sewn through its ears and temples, like a discarded mask.

"I tried to gather information to hasten your departure from Mirus," says Cheshire, his voice drifting down from the second stairway. "This fellow had little to say. Do not mistake me, he said quite a lot. He said he would tell me anything as long as I released him. Which means I could not trust a word out of his mouth. Fortunately, I had other uses for him. Hurry along now."

Jonathan and March walk by the second bedchamber without stopping. A man in a long coat hangs from the rafters by a length of thick rope from the docks. Below him, a short stool flipped upside down was all the man had to stand on to keep himself alive. This man, like the other, is faceless, with dried blood from his neck to the tips of his boots. The remains of his face and beard sit by the stool like a wadded piece of parchment.

"He had one of those rusty blades on him," says Cheshire. "It was not his, or so he says. He won it in a drunken card game. Either he told the truth, or he lied—devout to the end. I did try, March."

The third door hangs from its hinges. A rotund man lays prostrate on the floor. A butcher from Stonehaven. He always had the same jovial smile at dawn and dusk—gone now, peeled from his face. Jonathan recognizes the tattoos on the man's arm, since there is little else left to identify him. Large wooden splinters—no, not splinters, shards of wood with narrowed tips the length of March's daggers—stick out from beneath all ten of the man's fingernails.

"Of all the questionable things I have done in my thousand years of life, flaying someone's face off is among the most curious. Not difficult to think about. The blade follows the hairline—best to keep the ears—then down below the jaw, and circle low on the neck. So many veins and sinews under the skin like worms through the soil. Pulling the skin free from the muscle takes care. Did you know, a healthy portion of fat needs to stay beneath the skin in order to keep the follicles from ripping free, to keep the beards intact and shapely?"

"Enough of this morbid gallery." Jonathan climbs the stairs, March at his heels, and finds Cheshire crouched at the top landing, hood pulled over his head, casting his eyes in deeper shadow than the already dark hall.

"Two more rooms to go," says Cheshire.

"Must we slaughter people everywhere we go?" Jonathan asks.

"It is what we do," says March from behind.

"It is what we are good at. And we enjoy it." Cheshire springs backward and flips toward the first of two doors on the upper level.

"Just because you are good at something or enjoy it does not mean it must happen in every city we travel to," says Jonathan.

"You brought us here, need I remind you," says March.

Jonathan knows he cannot protest. It is his fault they are here, his fault the people of Rookridge are dead, his fault the magistrate and company in Briarwell are dead, and his fault Cheshire found his way into Mirus. The body count is not by his hands, but he does feel the responsibility for them all.

Cheshire opens the door and enters the first chamber. "You did not care for the dozens of murdered soldiers before this day. You did not care for the burning city when we pulled each other off in the weaver's storeroom. Why now?"

Jonathan and March follow him in, expecting an escalation of the inhumane torment, but instead discover a young man, smooth faced, eyes rolled back in his head and mouth agape, but without a mark on his face or body.

Cheshire squats next to the body and taps on the young man's forehead with a single finger. "Fear is a powerful force. I had no use for him but saw his conspirators. The two lackeys of Lysander and Uriah who followed us here. If I could get my hands on them. I had so many questions to ask him, but he heard everything I did to those on the floor beneath him. The thought of what I would do to him was too much to bear."

"These are not soldiers," says Jonathan. "These are people. Innocent people."

"Everyone is a person, and innocence is so subjective." Cheshire removes his hood for the first time. The deep circles under his eyes a darker shade of purple than his hair.

"What have these people done to deserve this treatment?" asks Jonathan.

"You haven't been listening to me. When I say I will see this city punished, I mean everyone. I do not care what uniform they wear or their allegiance. All politics and theatrics. Everything burns—the rich, the poor, the working class, wood, stone, gold, even iron. I proved so much already. So much panic, and I have done so little." Cheshire grins. "Just wait for what comes next... I will see this wicked city dashed from the earth."

March leans against the door frame. "All villains believe they are the heroes of their own stories."

"Darling." Cheshire approaches March, silent as the grave, his cloak trailing behind him like some dark phantasm. He stands toe to toe with her. "When have I said I was anything to the contrary? I am Wonderland's reckoning." He licks her on the lips and swoops back toward Jonathan. "Does this make you love me any less?"

"Of course not, you silly ass." Jonathan kisses Cheshire on the forehead and holds him close. "We are all villains in our own right."

Cheshire scoffs and pushes away. "As much as I would like to fuck you both here and now, and you do not know how badly I want to, but one more room awaits." He darts past them and pushes the last door at the end of the hallway open with this foot.

Inside, a man well into his years, hair and beard gray with speckles of cornflower, kneels in the middle of the floor, hands bound behind his back, gagged, and blindfolded. He barely has the energy to scream as they approach. All he can manage is a stammered moan. Tired tears and snot run down his face, into the cloth gag and into his mouth.

Perhaps it is the state of the old man before them, but this chamber appears grim, darker, like a dungeon, even though none of the previous chambers were any different except for the level of disrepair.

"This is our lovely host for whom you can thank for all you have seen," says Cheshire. "Unlike the gentleman in the previous room, he has heard every muffled scream, every death. Luckily for him, my need for faces ran out before I got to his room."

Jonathan looks to March, trying to comprehend what in all of Wonder Cheshire's plan could be.

She shrugs her pinched eyebrows to say, *Simple. Disguises.*

Cheshire steps behind the man, pulls the gag to his neck, and rips the blindfold from his face. "As I promised, speak and I will release you."

Terrified, panting, the man looks to Jonathan and then March for mercy. "Please. Please, help me," he begs Jonathan, staring into his eyes. The man would sob if he had the water in him, but from the look on his face, Cheshire has left him without for days. "Save me. Please." He catches a glimpse of Cheshire and recoils, whimpering. "Queen Slayer."

Cheshire laughs softly through his inhales, then widens his grin unnaturally, forcing his cheeks higher. The man cowers and clenches his eyes, as if Cheshire would steal his immortal soul.

"Speak, and perhaps your words can buy your freedom," March says briskly.

Jonathan kneels in front of the man. "Please. Tell us something." His tone, a sharp contrast to Cheshire and March, calms the man, however slightly.

"I boarded soldiers in my home." The man's dry lips crack and turn a deep crimson as he speaks. "That's all I did."

Cheshire puts his foot on the back of the man's head, grips his hair with his toes, and jerks his head backward. "Be more specific."

"They fled the city with the Red Knight weeks ago. They all did."

March sheaths her daggers and settles back against the wall an arm's length away from the door, hand on the hilt of the sword at her hip.

"Quite a number fled that night," says Jonathan. "All loyal to Lysander and Uriah." The old man nods. "Where did they go?"

"They scattered," the old man continues. "But... but they camp at the outer perimeter of the Queenwood. Some have spread out to the Warrens."

"Almost two thousand by our count," says March. "Quite a number to go unseen, let alone supply."

The old man's nerves subside further, his thoughts clear and voice confident though still weak. "Farmsteads near the Queenwood are paid handsomely to care for the soldiers, house them in their barns."

Cheshire laughs, circling around them. "The amount of people who hate this city astounds and amuses me. It truly brings joy to my heart."

"Even so," says Jonathan. "The amount they would consume. There would be a notable disruption in the market."

"No," the man says. "The farmers send everything to the markets in Stonehaven as they always do to not draw attention. Certain townspeople are called upon to make purchases and ship them back out of the city."

"Damn it all," says March. "The rallies Lysander and Uriah hold in the Quadrangle are not just to incite the crowd. You use it to pass information between each other without detection."

The old man nods again.

"And all they wait for is word from Lysander and Uriah," says Jonathan.

"Word from the Lords, yes." The old man's humor improves. "The soldiers can rally in a day and storm the capital. Please. I've told you what I know. I won't aid them anymore. You have my word. I... I'll leave the city at once. Take the house. Take it all. Let me leave. Let me live."

"You have indeed been helpful." Jonathan unties the cloth gag and drops it to the piss-stained floor and then takes a dagger from March's thigh.

Her eyes never raise from the floor. She remains stoic, contemplative, arms crossed, leaning against the wall.

The man winces when he sees the blade. Jonathan raises his hands. A meager show of mercy after all this man must have endured, his torment more psychological than physical. He kneels behind the man and saws through the coarse rope. When the last fibers pop, the man falls to the ground, hands in front of his face, knees to his chest, awaiting a strike or death blow from Jonathan or Cheshire.

"You have nothing to fear from him"—he gestures with his head to Cheshire—"or me. Take the little life you have left and run. Now."

The man remains still, eyes darting to Jonathan and Cheshire to search the lie in their faces. Once convinced, or perhaps when he realizes they could change their minds, he scrambles to his feet, knees buckling like a fawn, and lunges for the door.

Jonathan spoke a half truth. The man had nothing more to fear from Cheshire or himself. But Jonathan knew the moment he saw a captive remained alive, there was no chance he would leave with his life.

In the blink of an eye, March unsheathes the sword at her hip and holds her arm out straight to the side along the wall. The cross-guard rests against one side of the door frame while the end of the blade lies against the other. Her eyes remain trained on the floor.

Only concerned about his escape, the man does not see the thin blade across his path. His weight betrays him. He stumbles forward, and his throat finds the blade. Had March swung, he would have been decapitated completely. The blade cuts through flesh and muscle but catches on the man's spine. He releases a horrible, gargled rasp as he drowns. Blood splatters to the floor like spilled paint, heavy and thick. He collapses, convulses, and realizes the betrayal seconds before his light finally leaves him.

March swipes her sword through the air and flings the excess blood from it, adding to the splatter, before wiping the blade on the dead man's trousers.

"I would say this was a success. Hooray us." Cheshire's sardonic, dark glee worries Jonathan—more than usual. "Tea?"

Jonathan knows Cheshire's request is to distract him. He gives it thought for the briefest of moments, but there is no way to enjoy tea here. In the hedge maze. Not here.

"Information or not"—Jonathan tosses the dagger back to March— "do you realize your abductions have caused a civil uprising?"

Cheshire perches in the doorway, back against one side of the frame, his feet propping him up on the other. "If the people in this city wish to tear themselves apart, then all the better. Less work for me. And it saves them from what is yet to come."

"What is yet to come? Why will you not just tell us?"

"Because it would ruin the surprise. And I have worked so hard on it. It is also better you not know."

"Your work makes ours all the more difficult," says Jonathan, rising to his feet.

"Then stop," says Cheshire, without even a hint of the smile which brightened his face moments ago. The room has darkened to a shade of gray, if it is even possible. "But I know you will not. Therefore, I will not ask, and I expect the same respect in return."

"Of course," says Jonathan. "But to appease the townspeople, can you at least show us the bodies of the women you abducted, so we might return them to their families?"

Cheshire's face twists. "Mind still so far into the future, you miss the details of the present. These are the sum total of those I have taken. Did you see a woman, any woman among them? You did not, because I did not abduct any."

One of the many truths about Cheshire Jonathan depends on is his brutal honesty. Despite all else he does, Cheshire will never lie. If he wishes to hide something, he simply chooses to remain silent on the matter. Which means Lysander and Uriah play a more complex game and further manipulate the people of Mirus. The Twins feign innocence while they abduct townspeople, more than likely all women, and use their disappearances to fan the flames of rebellion, using the fear of Cheshire, fear of the Queen Slayer, and the Duchess's silence, as their kindling. The end game is clear—Lysander and Uriah want the throne. Now the players are falling into place, knowing where the traitorous soldiers lie in wait.

Jonathan knows he misses details, but he sees the larger picture, like a grand landscape painted on canvas. Lysander and Uriah will wait for Cheshire to attack the city again and use it to their advantage. If the Duchess does nothing again, especially after the incident with the hanging cells, and now the abducted, they will have justification to march into the city and demand the castle from her, and with it Mary Anne. And the townspeople will rally to them. If this comes to pass, then all they have worked for will be for naught. And it all hinges on the capricious whims of Cheshire, the match that will burn the city down.

CHAPTER 30

MARY ANNE

Mary Anne's heartbeat pulses through the hot water of her bath. She gasps—a final release as Jonathan finishes with March this morning, finishes with her. She rocks the back of her head against the curve of the porcelain tub and circles her hips slowly in the water, not wanting the sensation to end, caressing the ring on her finger as if it were her own nipple, breeding its own stipulation, waiting to see if Jonathan will have another go with March as he has done for the past several mornings. But there is nothing more. Just the lingering ache.

She is about to pull the ring from her finger when Grace's familiar knock on the bathroom door instead of the bedchamber, much more frantic than usual, jars Mary Anne from her peace. Grace busts into the room without warning or permission, hands trembling, and shoves a rolled parchment closed with a purple seal toward Mary Anne.

"Can this not wait?"

Grace shakes her head, breathing quickly through her nose, and pushes the scroll farther, insisting Mary Anne take it.

Something is wrong. Grace, as long as Mary Anne has known her, always stands on ceremony, whether or not Mary Anne wishes her to.

Mary Anne wipes the beads of condensation from her face and stands in the tub, arms outstretched to her sides for the water to flow off of her, waiting for her robe. But Grace grabs Mary Anne's hand and puts the edge of the scroll into her palm, then grabs a towel from a wooden peg on the wall and begins to dry Mary Anne's hair from behind her.

Even though the air is not cool, her body covers with chills now out of the protection of the bath's warmth. Is it the air? Or is it fear of what she holds in her hand? What has Grace acting so peculiar?

She breaks the seal and reads. *The time has come*, she reads. *Meet me at the croquet field immediately, ready for your match. Everyone else has already arrived. Time to put your queenliness to the test.*

The mere suggestion Mary Anne could be ready instantly is utter insanity. Her hair, make-up, her wardrobe—to leave now would be impossible. Even if she ran from the room in only her robe, she would still have to make her way through the castle and then around the hedge maze to get to the field. *Impossible*. She steps out of the tub and almost slips on the damp stones as she returns to the bedchamber, Grace in tow. *No. Nothing is impossible*. She clings to Jonathan's words. She and Grace have a monumental task to accomplish in minutes, but it must be done. There is no choice.

It takes the better half of an hour, but Mary Anne walks the last stretch of grass between hedge and castle wall toward the croquet field at a brisk pace. The heavy white and gold gown she wears was not intended for quick maneuvers. The material scratches at her skin and pulls down on her shoulders. When she reaches the corner of the hedge wall, she lowers the front of her skirt back to the ground, tugs at her lace-lined collar, and makes sure the snood holding her hair stays firmly attached. What she first thought as opulent and regal has become burdensome and irritating.

On the other side of the field, dozens of the most prominent citizens in Mirus, as well as Lysander and Uriah, wait for her, wait for her to fail. Now even more so since she has kept them waiting. She can hear their chatter, their mutters, their impatience. She blows out all of her breath, shakes her hands to gather her nerves, and breathes in a full clean breath —a ritual she abided by before she entered every consortium meeting in London.

The white and gold of her gown catches the morning light when she steps from the shadows of the hedge, gleaming, a beacon drawing everyone's gaze to her. The crowd falls silent. Someone clears their throat and sucks on their teeth. She walks across the field at a casual pace, though she should walk to the thundering of her heart. Besides those from the Crest, dignitaries from the major cities of Wonderland are in attendance.

From what Mary Anne can recall from Chamberlain Weiss's lessons, those dressed in the golds and purples, long gowns and furs, chains, and jewels adorning their necks have journeyed across Wonderland from the gilded city of Adamas. The light blues, beiges, and ambers signify the city of Clava in the Winds. Their fabrics, out of all those in attendance, appear the heaviest. She believes she saw the city in the distance when she rode with the Duchess to Mirus. Those dressed in simpler, yet still elegant gowns and tunics, all pale greens and ombre browns, with golden filigree and decorative rope embellishments hail from Ilex to the south. Lesser in number are the dignitaries from Clypeus, who stand out with different shades of gray garments flecked with silver, and what look like pieces of armor, breastplates, shoulder pieces, and gauntlets altered to become a part of their fashion.

At the center of them all, Lysander and Uriah bask in the attention. Their long white tunics pierce through the decadent rainbow of the other dignitaries. Both of their sleeves are a rich violet with golden embroidery around the cuffs, and chests bare for all to see.

Mary Anne expects their stares to rip her in half, but they both nod with a trace of a smile in the corner of their mouths. Peppered among the crowd, the Gryphon stands head and shoulders above everyone, as does Weiss, and hidden off to the side, Jonathan. His smile fills her with the strength she needs. His posture says he must keep his distance. He is here for support but cannot intervene. This is Mary Anne's test.

The Duchess steps forward out of the crowd and leads everyone in a collective bow. Lysander and Uriah lower their heads instead. She floats across the grass and meets Mary Anne in the middle of the field, out of earshot of the crowd, and pretends to kiss her on the cheek to whisper, "Remember what you have learned." She pulls away, winks, then turns to address the crowd with speaking arms. "Ladies and gentleman, may I present to you, Mary Anne Elizabeth."

The crowd responds with a mix of soft applause, light gasps, a few grumbles, and even more side-glances to each other.

She needs time to gather her thoughts. Instead of responding, she lifts the front of her skirt once more and glides across the field to join the others, leaving them waiting once more.

The people spread away from Lysander and Uriah, whether it be to gain a better look at Mary Anne or to not show their allegiance. Bronwyn March, however, stands her ground between the two brothers. She pets her raised collar of peacock feathers as if it were alive.

Mary Anne sets her dress upon the grass and glances at Jonathan. He nods, the only affirmation she needs.

"I am not sure what has warranted this unenthusiastic reception." She lifts her nose high into the air.

A portly gentleman with gold chains hanging around his neck and from the pockets on his gorged stomach clears his throat. "Unenthusiastic is a harsh term," he says with a nasal sneer.

Bronwyn raises an eyebrow. "Tired would be a better description, since we have been made to wait out here for quite some time. The Duchess's invitation to croquet stated it would be an early-morning game, so we were here promptly at the time specified, and you... were not."

This woman. Mary Anne knows this woman—or rather the type, regardless of sex. She knows this game. She knows this game far better than croquet, though the stakes could not be higher. The path home hinges on her next words.

Mary Anne inhales sharply through her nose. "The queen's game does not begin until the queen arrives. Is it not still morning? I arrived precisely on time. The fault falls to all of you who showed up early and thought I would appear at your arrival." Her heart races in her ears like a sputtering motorcar. "Would you rather I leave you here while I return to my chambers and finish my bath, have my hair and makeup retouched, as well as have my royal dresser prepare me once more, before coming back out to meet you here again? I guarantee you all, I will still arrive precisely on time. Hopefully then I will receive a warmer and more respectful reception."

"You are not queen yet," Lysander says in a low growl.

A noblewoman amongst the crowd starts a robust round of applause, drowning out his words, to which everyone else joins in—all except Lysander and Uriah. Even the portly man's tired expression turns to exuberance as the beads of sweat stream down his face. The entire crowd's demeanor changed simply by Mary Anne's words. No magic, only words. They know how to play the game as well, better than Lysander and Uriah.

"Let us begin," says Mary Anne with a cheeky smile. She claps twice. She has no clue why but does so anyway to give a clear indication she is in control.

Guards, in their polished armor and white tabards, distribute mallets to Lysander, Uriah, Bronwyn, and Mary Anne. Another places the spiked balls on the field, then they all scatter to take their positions, nice as the wickets, arms behind their backs, feet apart, and as the starting and finishing stakes. Servants, hidden from view until now, set down stools at the edge of the field, each as different as the dignitaries who sit upon them. They whisper to each other, confused and curious.

Mary Anne strikes the first ball through the closest guard's legs and sets the game into motion. The crowd applauds softly on the backs of their hands. As they play, Lysander, Uriah, and Bronwyn dictate the conversation, talking of shoes, the lands they own, ships, and where the finer jewels can be found, loud enough for the noble men and women to hear.

Bronwyn picks up on Mary Anne's silence. "Oh, you must not feel included, having no experience with these matters."

"No," says Mary Anne. "I am bored. I thought speaking with the wealthiest woman in Mirus, and two sons of Mirus, would prove more exciting, but if you would rather continue to speak on such trivial matters, I will allow you to waste my time this once."

The Duchess rubs her cheeks with one hand to cover her smile.

"Then let the conversation shift to you." Uriah approaches Mary Anne—too close for her liking. The sharp edges of his inner chest muscles through his open tunic, less than two feet away from her face, are almost as pronounced as Jonathan's. "Where do you hail from? Why are you here? I think you are far more interesting than any jewel or spit of land."

"England. Far from here. So far, you will never be able to experience its beauty."

"England." Lysander sloshes the word around his mouth as if it were rancid fish.

"What did you do in your world?" asks Bronwyn. "Surely something magnificent to believe you are worthy of the throne?"

"Worth does not come from deeds." Mary Anne does not believe her own words. "But if you must know, I headed a consortium. Industry, we call it. A fleet of over one hundred ships at my command, which I sent around the world, my world, to collect goods, riches, or anything else I saw fit." A lie, but one they will never uncover. Mary Anne can spin whatever tale she likes, as long as she can back up her claims.

"Intriguing." Bronwyn's tone brightens. "A woman of business, as we call it. I can respect that."

"I must admit, you seem different from when we last saw you in the Long Hall." Uriah strikes his ball.

"I had only just arrived in a strange world, and you wished me to be myself? You took it upon yourself to announce me before I was prepared, as if you knew best." She should not have said the last part, but it is too late to take back, too late to apologize. Something shifts in Lysander and Uriah, but their smiles remain.

"Who are you to say we do not?" Lysander strikes his ball. "After all, our ancestors, our blood, once ruled this entire kingdom."

"Queendom," says Mary Anne. "What is past is Wonderland's prologue. These are different times and a brave new world. I will see Wonderland returned to its prosperity and splendor, under my rule."

"Have you been in the throne room yet?" Uriah whispers, circling around Mary Anne as she takes her next turn. "I dare say you have not seen it. My brother and I have. We will see it again."

"I am sure you will. I will be certain to send word of my coronation."

Whatever Uriah says in response, she cannot hear. Something moves across her breast, inside her gown. At first, she thought it some insect from the hedge found its way inside while she passed, but the sensation is most different. It is a hand squeezing her breast, and then teeth and a tongue on her other. She looks down at her left hand in horror. The ring. In the rush this morning, she forgot to take it off after the bath, as she has done every other morning.

It should be Jonathan and March, but he stands at the edge of the field, arms crossed, with an innocent, unknowing smile. Mary Anne never thought it a possibility. She thought she would first feel a blade if she ever forgot to remove the ring. March is with someone else at this moment, ravaging her body. The ring tightens no matter how hard Mary Anne tugs at her finger. As long as the sensations continue, the ring will not budge.

Its true purpose. She worries she will lose the digit before the ring slides off.

The clack of Lysander's shot brings Mary Anne back to the conversation. "Will you or will you not?"

The tongue slides down Mary Anne's torso to between her legs, hands to her thighs, and her own jaw stretches, taking whoever March is with into her mouth. She cannot speak, cannot respond. She can only breath out of her nose. Panic sets in, but she cannot show it. Her heartbeat pounds against the inside of her face, ready to shatter her veneer to pieces. All Mary Anne can do is take her next turn, controlling the mallet as best she can with the overstimulation of her body.

"If you do not wish to visit Adamas," says Lysander, "simply decline the invitation. Keep in mind, the wealthiest city in the kingdom would not take your dismissal lightly. Just as the citizens of Mirus begin to shake the bars of the cages they are in, waiting for their silent jailor to notice them."

Mary Anne is at the mercy of March's infidelity. Her thighs shake and spasm beneath her gown. Finally, her mouth is hers to control again. "I appreciate the invitation." Her voice trembles. "Once crowned, I will visit your fine city, and the rest. But I must start my work in Mirus first."

The crowd applauds. Mary Anne splits in three different directions all at once, unable to process any of them. The pleasure her body feels, Lysander and Uriah's conversation, and the audience voyeurs to it all, as well as Jonathan, who she cannot bring herself to look at.

"Perhaps we have acted too rash," says Uriah. "What would Mirus gain, or all of Wonderland, if we remain at odds? Surely, a middle ground can be reached."

The stranger's mouth and hands return to her breasts, biting, licking, groping. She can feel an entire face rub against them. Easy to ignore until his manhood rubs back and forth against the twitching muscles between her thighs. It is only a matter of time. Mary Anne must leave now.

"Together," Uriah continues, "Wonderland could unite under the old house and the new. The rightful blood of the line of Kings and the might of Wonderland's Queen united. In more ways than one. A queen requires a king, or two, after all." He leans close to her ear. "I am sure the queen's bed can hold three. My brother and I can train you in the way of things the Duchess cannot."

"I must leave you," she says. "The game is over." The audience mutters, the Duchess looks concerned, as does Jonathan, and Lysander, Uriah, and Bronwyn lose their patience.

Jonathan drops his arms and raises his brows, aware something is wrong.

"Unacceptable," says Bronwyn. "We have waited for this opportunity to speak with you, acquaint ourselves with you, and now you try to leave."

It happens. March holds her breath, cutting off Mary Anne's, and welcomes the stranger into her, slowly. The muscles of Mary Anne's neck tense. She had just grown accustomed to Jonathan, his ways, his movements, his size, but this man, whoever he may be, pushes deeper, stretches her wider.

"What do you wish to hide?" asks Bronwyn.

"Nothing. Thank you for your attendance this morning. We shall reconvene another time."

"You seem affected by something." Bronwyn looks to the dignitaries to elicit the same questions.

The stranger's hand presses down on her lower abdomen. Thrust after thrust pushes Mary Anne to the brink of collapsing on the field. A pressure builds in Mary Anne's stomach. She wants to scream out in pain and in ecstasy and fears she will piss herself here and now before she ever reaches her climax. If they would stop for a moment, if they could release their hold on one another, Mary Anne might be able to pry the ring off her finger, but March and this man are relentless.

"The game is not over," says Uriah.

Mary Anne holds out the mallet, outstretched like a sword, and screams. "Guards, move!" It is all she can do but hopes they understand her meaning. All ten guards run to a straight line directly in front of her ball, one behind the other, the toes of their boots pressed against the heels of the man in front of him, except for the last guard who is the finishing stake. Mary Anne swings with a newfound strength and knocks the ball through all of their legs. It skids over the cross, knocking against boot after boot until it smacks against the last guard in line.

"It is now."

She drops her mallet, picks up her skirt, and walks off the field without looking back, hoping Jonathan does not follow. As soon as she turns the corner of the hedge maze, she runs as fast as her trembling legs will carry her. Bursts of intense pleasure as the stranger pushes deep, deeper than Mary Anne thought possible, send her to her knees, gasping. She has to fight against it, no matter how her body feels. She gets to her feet and runs again as the intensity swells between her thighs.

Tears stream down her face, a horrible mixture of pleasure, embarrassment, and shame. She can hear Jonathan's voice call after her. She cannot allow him to see her in such a state. No explanation could hide the ecstasy on her face.

She will not make it to her room, let alone the back entrance of the castle, next to the kitchen where all the cooks will see her. The hedge maze is the smartest recourse, her only recourse. She passes through the green arches of the maze and rounds the first corner to conceal herself should Jonathan glance in to search for her. His voice passes, headed toward the castle.

Her legs give out one last time. She falls to her knees, and her fingers grip at the bush with all her might as she releases the long, low moan kept at bay, which jumps with every thrust. Mary Anne holds on and waits, enduring, yet enjoying, the waves of pleasure, climaxing again and again. There are moments in between she could pull the ring from her finger, but waits until after the third time, until her body cannot take the spasms. Finally, after the third, she wrenches it free, and her body experiences a free fall, feeling everything and then nothing all at once, until her own senses awaken again. She tries to lick her parched lips, but both they and her tongue are dry as an arid stone.

What has she done? How will she ever recover? Will she break Jonathan's heart and tell him of March's betrayal? How will she ever face any of them again? She clasps her hands over her face and sobs, silently, so no one will discover her.

Mary Anne waits until the sun is directly above her to pick herself up again. She wipes the dried tears from her face and stretches the corners of her burning eyes. The bottom of her pristine white gown is now tarnished with brown dirt and grass stains. Her legs still tremble from the experience, but she makes her way back into the castle and up to her room, encountering no one. The longest walk she has ever taken. She needs to bathe again, soak in scalding water and wash the experience from existence.

The Duchess sits on her bed, leaning on one arm, waiting once Mary Anne opens her bedchamber door. Grace stands by the foot of the bed, hands clasped over her mouth.

Mary Anne pulls in her bottom lip to keep it from trembling, unable to tell the Duchess's thoughts from her expression. She thinks back to her mother's face, the last time she saw her, when she confronted Mary Anne about her affair with Thomas, full of absolute disappointment.

"I ruined everything, haven't I?" Mary Anne asks.

The Duchess huffs. "In a single instance, you spurned Uriah and Lysander's proposal, who will no doubt hasten their attempt to retake the throne, utterly confounded Bronwyn March, ran off without so much as a word, and demonstrated to the dignitaries from Mirus and beyond that you are not to be trifled with or challenged. My girl, it was a truly extraordinary sight to behold."

PART III

THE CREST

CHAPTER 31

JONATHAN

Jonathan needs the hum, the drone, some noise to calm his nerves. This morning, he sits on an angled roof of an apartment building enjoying a simple cup of Lavender tea one street above the Forge. The rhythmic low and high-pitched clangs and bangs of steel and iron soothe his mind while March attends to the soldiers. For four days after the incident, the Forge slept. Cold, silent, empty—a tradition of the smiths' if one happens to pass while at the anvil. The customary Time would be sunup to sundown on a single day. But no one wanted to set foot anywhere near the Forge. It takes up a major part of the thoroughfare, and townspeople went out of their way to avoid it.

The townspeople reacted with fear after the explosion of the hanging cells. Rightfully so. There were several deaths and bodies to deal with, mostly soldiers and injured townspeople. But the brawl at the Forge was an unfamiliar and jarring sight for most Mirusians. It is one thing to watch a dead body be carried by, but it is quite another entirely to watch a man bludgeon another's skull in with a smith's hammer. Jonathan waivers somewhere between indifference and numbness, but guilt always festers when the innocent are the ones to suffer.

Lysander and Uriah took advantage of Cheshire's actions for their own devices, and it worked like a charm. Below on the streets, those who pass no longer wave or greet each other. They do not know what side of the line, the scales, or their own neighbors stand. Jonathan sat here rather than the Row, which should resound with chatter and bargaining, but even such a bustling place has been reduced to whispers and hushed deals. All while the dignitaries and nobles drink and enjoy their revels in the Crest feeling safe, feeling invincible, while in the city, Lysander and Uriah believe they are winning. And they are correct.

This morning, the smiths began to work again, keeping Time as they swing their hammers and beat their anvils. Jonathan takes his timepiece from his pocket and holds it to his ear, comparing the two beautiful, mechanical symphonies.

A pebble clacks against the shingles next to Jonathan, then another. He shuffles down to the edge of the eaves and discovers the pink-haired pansy ready with another pebble in hand. She gestures east with her head, toward the Garden, which sits not far from the Forge, and flits away into the alleyways.

Jonathan finishes his tea and secures his cup and saucer in the small leather holster hanging from his belt. He climbs down the gutters and windows and follows four streets higher into Stonehaven, thirty-six stairs, into the storehouse district, and finally the Garden. He keeps his fingertips at his nostrils hoping the lavender will overpower, or at least decrease, the overwhelming incense in the air.

The old man with the large nose Jonathan saw the day at the Forge saunters down the front steps from the Garden, a swagger of contentment in his spindly legs. They took care of him well. He passes in his own world, eyes glazed over with satisfaction.

By the Time Jonathan enters the main doors, the pansy has already discarded her corset and wool skirt leaving only the sheer petal dress she must have worn underneath.

Jonathan unbuckles his belt and hands it, his sword, and teacup and saucer, to the flower at the weapons closet in the Garden. She winks at him and swivels her hips as she walks to place his blade at the back table.

The pink-haired pansy greets him at the closet. "What brings you here, sir?"

"A silly question."

"But you followed me," she says with a slight whimper in her voice, moving uncomfortably close to him. "Don't I look like her?" She places her hands on the half door of the closet and turns her back to Jonathan, her dress leaving nothing to the imagination. "You cannot deny I don't look like her from behind. Grab my hair, and fuck me here and now. Imagine I'm her. Or we can go someplace more private. That's more your style. Bend me over and fuck me as you fuck her." She looks back over her shoulder. "Just once." She pushes her backside toward Jonathan, who backs away to the other side of the hall.

The pansy looks down to his crotch. "Damn it. Not even a little aroused?" Her tone drops back to normal. "Fine. Worth a shot."

"I am sure you are quite convincing with other men," says Jonathan. "Now why did you call me?"

She sighs, defeated. "Two of the men you said to look out for, they're upstairs now being entertained by my sisters."

Jonathan follows again, up the spiral stairs to the top floor. Sixty-four stairs. Behind the door to the cushioned room, he can hear the rough, sporadic, and almost humorous moans and shouts from Lysander and Uriah's lackeys, Walter and Horace, or whatever their names are. The ones who met him weeks, almost months ago, in the Rookwood.

"Are they finished?" Jonathan mouths to the pansy.

"Give me a moment." She cracks the door and slips in, closing it behind her.

"Here we are then, the third one's returned," says the unmistakable nasal voice of Walter.

"Come over here and give us another tug," says Horace, his partner with the milky eye.

"Now, boys," says the pink-haired pansy. "I've brought someone else to join us." Her voice returns to the fake whimper. "You were too much for the three of us. They are shy, but would you like them to come in and join us?"

"Fuck, yes," Walter and Horace shout together.

Jonathan takes his cue and opens the door. The two men kneel on the edge of the cushioned pit, trousers down around their boots, shirts open, hands tied behind their back with strips of linen. The blue and yellow pansies lounge in the pit and continue to stroke and tease them even when Jonathan closes and locks the door.

"Fuck me," says Horace.

"Thank you, but no," says Jonathan. "This is not my shift."

"Oh, piss off," Walter says to the blue pansy. He pulls away and falls to his side, trying to unbind his hands, but ends up with his hairy bare ass to the ceiling.

Horace, on the other hand, gets to his feet and waddles to Jonathan. "What you think you're going to do to us here? Kill us?"

"The thought crossed my mind."

"Nah, people will notice," says Horace. "We have friends in high places if you couldn't tell before."

"If we could only lure them here," says the blue pansy.

Jonathan removes his jacket, cracks his neck, and approaches the men slowly.

"We'll scream," says Walter, finally getting to his knees again.

"I'm sure you will." Jonathan looks to the pansies. "Ladies, would you mind?"

The trio of pansies take their cue and begin moaning, panting, and screaming at the top of their lungs while they sit on the opposite side of the pit.

"Wait, wait," Horace stutters, "just wait."

Jonathan grabs Horace by the throat, squeezing the last word out of him. He drags him to the other side of the room, grabs Walter, and throws them both down into the pit. Jonathan kneels and presses down on their throats.

"There has been a conversation brewing between us for some time."

The men hack, wheeze, and drool as they choke. "I offer a simple game. I ask you a question, shake or nod your head to answer. If I do not believe you, I push down harder, eventually snapping your necks. If I believe you, I relieve the pressure and you can answer and gain a chance to fill your lungs again. Understand?"

They shake their heads, their lips turning a shade of plum similar to some of the fabric swags overhead.

"I know the answer to this one already, so consider this a test. After you fled the Rookwood, you went directly to Lysander and Uriah, correct?"

They nod vigorously.

"Wonderful. You understand the rules." Jonathan releases his grip slightly. "Now, do you know the next step of Lysander and Uriah's plan?"

They shake their heads, and at the slightest increase of pressure, they nod again.

Horace rasps out, "What's the point? You will kill us no matter what we say."

"I would very much like to release you both, but you are making it quite difficult. And I would hate to sully these fine women's bedchamber."

Walter and Horace stretch and flex their necks, trying to inhale.

"What comes next?" asks Jonathan. "I know Lysander and Uriah's endgame, but what is their next move?"

"They—" Walter tries to say.

"Fuck off," says Horace. "Shut your fucking gob."

"I'm not dying here, like this," says Walter. "The soldiers... the soldiers outside the city are preparing. They just wait for the signal."

"What signal?"

"Your purple-haired friend," says Horace. "Whatever happens next, whatever he destroys, that's the signal for the soldiers to move on the city."

Cheshire is the key. Whatever complex plan Cheshire concocts, Jonathan must stop him, or at least delay him somehow.

"How long will it take the soldiers to arrive?"

There is no Time for them to answer. It is already too late. The pansies fall silent. The city bells toll signaling an emergency, a crisis in the city. *Cheshire.*

"You could keep questioning us," says Horace.

"Or you could go be the hero you think you are and find your chum before he makes things worse," says Walter. "But I guess it's too late for that."

Jonathan releases his hands for enough Time for them to gasp for a full chest of air, and for him to squarely crack them both in the jaw, knocking them unconscious.

"Keep them bound until I figure out what to do with them," Jonathan tells the pansies. "Can you do that here?"

"For what you're paying us," says the yellow pansy, "sure. It's off to the basement with them. We can keep them in an opium dream for days. And the girls down there are less particular. They'll make sure these two are well occupied."

Jonathan tips his hat and runs from the Garden. The soldiers race toward the east, the harbor. In the flurry, he can see a streak of pink hair, March, among the silver helmets. The rest of the bells ring throughout the city now, tolling the countdown to the invasion of Mirus.

CHAPTER 32

CHESHIRE

The Time is nigh. The gentle waterfall of Cheshire's hidden grotto splashes down, patters, and massages Cheshire's muscles. His arms, shoulders, legs, his entire damned body nears exhaustion after carrying barrels back and forth, up and down thousands of stairs for days. Even while he rests on the cold cobbles in the catacombs or the misty spray of the river, he can feel every sore fiber of his muscles ache with each movement. His only regret? The pain it takes him to pleasure himself, but he manages.

The stolen soldier's armor he reclaimed from beneath the weaver's shop hangs over rocks near the cave's entrance. He sighs. Cheshire thought through seventy-eight scenarios, and this is the one he chose. Not the wisest, not the safest, but the most efficient.

Stretching from the tops of rocks tied around fat roots, and spread out as far as it can, the wax-covered canvas hangs bloated, filled with dozens upon dozens of barrels of oil. Each barrel Cheshire brought here to empty, then return to the armory with no one the wiser, until March and Jonathan became involved. Fortunately, by then, he'd emptied every cask.

Almost all of them. He kept a few barrels of oil and several of black powder for what comes after today. If there is indeed a day after today.

Half here, in the swollen bladder, and the other half he carried, dripped, spilt, and slashed through the harbor disguised as disheveled drunkards. He walked every wooden deck, pathway, and pier, splashed every wall, and pretended to relieve himself in corners to spill more oil. He even made it on a few ships whose guards were preoccupied by drink or women.

The masks played their part perfectly for as long as they lasted. Skin dries and shrivels after three days. The Gryphon even collided with him once and could not escape fast enough. Not due to his appearance but because Cheshire made sure he reeked of rum to cover the scent of the oil, and to keep the former drunkard at a distance.

He takes a smooth, sharp stone and slices the bladder at its lowest point over the river like the entails of a pig. The oil trickles out in thick globs and catches the ginger current. Its pearlescent shimmer flows around the bend and out to the open bay and the harbor, where merchant ships and those of dignitaries from the other corners of the country dock. The canvas shrinks and sags as it empties. Cheshire waits until the last drop of oil falls and washes away, leaving the water as clear as if he were never there.

Now, the risk. The next part of his plan he cannot complete from afar. If he were to ignite the oil here, the evidence could be traced back to his grotto, and his secret door into and out of the city would be uncovered, a secret too precious to reveal, as well as the third part of his plan.

He lies on the rocks of the shore to dry his body, then dresses, making sure to wrap his sash and cloak around his waist before donning the stolen soldier's armor again. The armor scrapes as he stands, as if the creaking came from his own bones. Cheshire pulls the canvas down, rolls it into a large bundle, places his hand on the rock door, and stashes the canvas inside. Once the door rumbles shut behind him, he makes his way up the winding stairs and through the long corridors toward the harbor.

Traveling would be easier without the weight of the armor, but he needs Time, Time for the oil to disperse into the bay, into the lapping waves of the shore and the bottom of every hull in port.

The closest door to the harbor is below a stone stairway three streets behind the brothel. Cheshire, out of breath, leans the side of his face against the door and listens for the next patrol soldier to pass. At this Time of day, the Gryphon should be close to the Row, so at least his archers will not be near. Cheshire's body wants to give in to fatigue, and his eyes flutter shut for a moment, or an hour—he cannot tell. His body jerks awake, heart racing, armor scratching, and he listens, waits again until the clatter and squeak of improperly cared for armor. Once he Times the soldier's pass, he slips out, seals the stone door, and follows just as the next soldier in line rounds the corner, without ever knowing.

Cheshire's breath, his heartbeats and swallows, resound in the iron helmet. It suffocates him. The armor pinches and rubs at his body. He fears tripping over the clunky boots but walks as confidently as any other soldier. He must in order not to raise suspicion. The path the soldiers follow leads away from the harbor, but since the soldier behind Cheshire can only see him, he turns and leads a new path back to his destination. The soldier may question, but from what Cheshire has witnessed, they follow out of habit like ants without thought until something disrupts them.

There are two ways to enter Mirus from the harbor, both on the eastern side of Stonehaven—the long, zig-zagging, ornate oak stairways against the mountainside which lead from the harbor floor to the street just above the Row. No matter what level of the harbor, whether they be the small dwellings at the top as well as the lookout posts, the four levels of storehouses, or the lower two which make up the seaside market, anyone who wishes to enter the city must first descend to the bottom of the harbor before they can take the stairs into Stonehaven. The architects who designed the city long ago made sure there are no direct routes, whether by land or sea, to any of the vital areas of Mirus, especially the castle. The only other way to travel is the large platform lift used to carry cargo and visitors too important to dare walk the stairs all the way to the top of Mirus. A miraculous invention from Pat and Bill. A shame it will burn with the rest of the harbor.

Cheshire gradually quickens his pace, putting slightly more distance between him and the soldier following him. He turns a corner with just enough Time to slip away and descends the stairs to the harbor. Even if the soldier saw him, it would not matter at this point. He has come too far.

He passes travelers, fishermen, and those merely going to market. As before, no one pays him any attention. He would set the fire at the highest level, but the dwellings and outposts are the smallest tier, easily extinguishable. On his way down, he grabs two lanterns, one hanging from the side of a storehouse, the other posted at a crossway in the middle of the fish market. A thick glass bottle wrapped in iron bands keeps the candle secure. The candle itself floats on a wide cork in water, in case some foolish person knocks a lantern from their hooks. The small amount of water would extinguish the flame on the off chance it catches the boards or fish oils on fire.

This would be the case if the candles did not have intricately carved designs from the skilled hands of the candle maker's apprentice in the Crooked Market. Cheshire makes it all the way down to the docks. He positions himself next to the large gears that power the lift, their ropes wider than his waist with the slight shimmer of oil between their coarse fibers. He holds a lantern in each hand, swinging them gently back and forth.

A fishwife behind a table of trout notices. Her eyes squint, unsure if something is amiss or if a soldier tries to occupy his boredom. Another soldier farther down a pier cocks his head to the side. A man somewhere to his left calls to him, tells him to wait, or asks Cheshire what he is doing, or to stop. It is all unclear and muffled in the helmet. Cheshire could not hear him over his own heartbeat either way.

Before the man can say a word, Cheshire lobs a lantern as hard as he can into the open water between two ships. It sinks below the surface. Cheshire slows his breath and waits. Seconds later, the lantern bobs up to the surface, glass full of water and oil, and bursts into flames, coursing over the surface faster than a raging torrent from a broken dam, from which there is no escape. Fire spreads out over the bay as if the water were dry kindling.

Soldiers push through the panicked townspeople to get to Cheshire. He swirls the lantern in hand, brings it up over his head, and smashes it at his feet. The glass within the iron bands shatters, and the flames catch the oil soaked into the boards, as well as the ropes to the lifts. The fire spreads quickly, scattering the soldiers. Within seconds, the fire crawls to the second level, then the third. The wet ropes of ships, who have sat in the harbor for weeks and even days, become serpents of fire, traveling all the way up the rigging and masts. Black smoke bellows and obscures the harbor from view.

Cheshire stands and watches. Soldiers rush to help. They foolishly try to put out the fire. Even if they bring their wagons with their alchemic orbs, there is no way to stop what has begun. The wagons cannot descend into the harbor unless by the lifts, which are currently ablaze, and their ropes snap. Throw their orbs all they like, the distance is too great, and the harbor too expansive. Water will give them no relief either. They have no choice but to let it burn. The harbor is lost, as Cheshire willed it to be. No one else will enter Mirus from here, and no one will leave. This is just the beginning. And now, he waits.

CHAPTER 33

MARCH

Over the weeks, every soldier's and guard's form and skill improves considerably, even to the point of March allowing them to wear their armor again, as opposed to bare skin. Their aim becomes truer, their intent clear, and their footwork a marked improvement, albeit still clunky. She wonders how long this standoff between Lysander and Uriah will last. Within only a few weeks, the soldiers and guards unify into a legitimate army. What could she do with a year?

March trains against the messenger and the guard from the gate personally while the fourth company spar in their groups. She gives as much time to them as possible to improve more than their skills, to improve their instinct in battle, even more so than the other companies. These two have proven themselves to be leaders of men and formidable fighters in their own right. She faces them two-on-one, in every match, not just for their benefit but hers as well. When she faces Lysander and Uriah, it will not be one-on-one.

While the messenger lunges, he asks March, "If I may ask, madam—"

"Do not refer to me as madam," says March, parrying his attack and side stepping the guard as he slashes at her back. "Madam is what you would call my mother."

"Forgive me," says the messenger. "March." It fumbles uncomfortably from his mouth. "We have seen you fight. You have bested every soldier in this army, in Mirus, and all of Wonderland from the tales sung about you. Have you not given thought to facing Lysander and Uriah yourself?"

"I think about it all the time." She ducks and counters. "But this war is far more complicated and will not be determined by who has the better fighter. If you know your history, the days of wars fought and won by contest champions ended long ago. As of now, they have done nothing to prove themselves an enemy, at least to the townspeople of Mirus, besides having a difference of opinion. To a growing number, they are heroes, legends, the right heirs to the throne." March hides her own concern about the Twins' skills and, in a furious spin, slices at the men's shins, then their necks, which they block as trained. "We fight a political battle rather than one of steel. It is the same reason they have not tried to take the castle or kill the Duchess. The majority of townspeople, we hope, still favor the Duchess, and the idea of a queen on the throne. If they remove the Duchess by force, they have the city to contend with, and vice versa."

With a quick flip of her body, she parries the messenger's strike. The cropped leather jacket she wears rises as she spins to reveal more of her under breast. The messenger averts his eyes to preserve her modesty.

She laughs and kicks him in the jaw, knocking him to the ground. "You would be dead." She points the tip of her blade at his throat.

"What was I supposed to do?" the messenger asks.

"Live. If you think honor will save you, I have just proven you wrong. The honorable are always the first to die." March blocks a slash from the guard to her side. "He does not hesitate or look away. He continues to fight. Why is that?"

The guard continues an impressive, skillful barrage. "Do you wish me to answer honestly?"

"If you give me bullshit, I will slice your throat here and now."

"When we first crossed paths at the gate, I thought you nothing more than a bawd. I heard the stories of your master skill but also your beauty and your reputation talked about in the corner of taverns. I never thought I would stand face to face with you, and I couldn't resist. I wanted to see your breasts, perhaps fuck you if given the chance."

"And now?"

"That was when I thought your body was your greatest worth. Now I see it is your leadership and skill."

"And why do you fight so hard?"

"To win your respect. And your forgiveness. I do not look away because you are not some delicate flower. I keep my eyes on you because I do not see you as lesser any longer. You are my commander, and I know you will kill me regardless of what part of your body shows. But don't mistake my words, I still want to fuck you, now more than ever."

March chuckles and knocks the sword from the guard's hand and sweeps his leg. He falls next to the messenger.

"I appreciate your honesty," says March, helping them both to their feet.

"I do respect you," says the messenger. "I hold you in the highest regard. To the likes of the Triumvirate."

"Stop speaking. If I thought you did not respect me, I would not have selected you to train against me personally, to lead in my stead when I am pulled away to other duties. Now pick up your blades and reset."

They scarcely have time to collect their swords from the ground when the city bells toll their low, ominous notes, reverberating through the air and stones—a warning. *Cheshire.* March looks up as if to pluck the bells' notes from the air to discover the location, the origin. More bells toll across the city. Once the chain starts, finding the source becomes difficult, but not impossible. She searches for the first toll in the grim choir ringing through Mirus. Low. Echoing before it ever reached her ears. Muffled. No, not muffled. Blocked. She turns, following the notes to the castle, beyond the castle, below the castle.

The harbor. Cheshire is burning the harbor.

"Men of Mirus," she commands, "to the harbor. Soldiers, gather the fire wagons, divide, and take the four stairways to the east. Castle Guard, to arms, secure the castle and prepare for anything." Cheshire will not attack the castle. Not yet anyway. Either way, precaution must be taken for the machinations of Lysander and Uriah, for they will surely take advantage of the chaos.

The soldiers gather their swords and shields, the large gate men lift the lock bars and open the gates, the Castle Guard takes defensive positions, and the fourth company file out with a unifying pounding of the stones.

As expected, hundreds of other soldiers join them as they filter down through the stairways of the Crest into Stonehaven and surge toward the harbor. However, the defenses against invading forces from the sea will be the harbor's downfall. The lift and two wide wooden stairways are all that connect the port of Mirus to Stonehaven. Soldiers bottleneck at the stairs, fighting against the flow of townspeople trying to escape the inferno. There are no ways to get the fire wagons lowered, with the lift already in flames, ropes snapped, and parts of its shaft collapsed in on itself.

Black smoke bellows from the shops, dwellings, and storehouses. It crawls up the steep cliff face, pools and swirls at the pointed overhang where the castle gardens and croquet fields are.

March climbs the nearest structure, a grain storehouse, to gain a better vantage point. It is far worse than she imagined. The hells have broken open. Every structure, every pier, every ship in the harbor, and the water itself burns like the sulfur lakes. Ships collapse in on themselves. Masts burn in an instant, and rigging collapses, dragging some ships beneath the fiery waves.

Jonathan's whistle draws her attention from below. "What do you need?"

"A faster way down would be lovely."

He draws his sword and runs to the wooden shaft of the lift, studies the crashed lift platform at the bottom and the way the sides of the shaft connect—not single planks but full wooden pallets. He swings his sword and knocks one side free, intact. It falls to the bottom of the shaft, and its corners wedge it between the walls, creating an angled platform above the first. Jonathan knocks the other two walls free, and they, too, create a precarious, jagged pathway below. He holds out his hands for March.

March drops to the ground just as the fire wagons arrive. "Concentrate on the stairways and their supports. Shatter as many orbs as you can to keep the fire from spreading up to the people and to Stonehaven."

"What of the citizens?" asks a soldier. "The glass."

"Must I think of everything?" March snarls. "Soldiers, position yourself at every platform and in the middle of every flight of stairs. Create a tunnel. Hold your shields above your heads. Those of you with the best aim, aim for the shields."

"Come, darling," says Jonathan. "Our way down deteriorates quickly." He grabs March securely around the waist, and she around his neck. After a few quick breaths, he grabs the back of March's head and leaps into the shaft. The first drop must be twenty feet at least. Jonathan grunts as he lands on the angled platform but rolls to avoid the impact, shielding March from the first fall. He stops their descent with his feet against the remaining standing walls. He grunts and hisses in pain.

"Talk to me," says March.

"Fine, as always," he says through a pained grimace. The platform below them groans, its edges cut into the wooden walls, and slides down at least two feet with a hard *thunk*. "I fear we must part ways here, my dear."

"For the moment."

March slides from Jonathan and through the narrow space to the next platform below. Jonathan pushes off with his legs and slips through an opposite sliver to balance the weight. As soon as they land on the next platform, the previous above them cracks and snaps.

"Remind you of anything?" asks March.

"The mine collapse on the outskirts of Rutrum," says Jonathan. "The lichen there made for wonderful tea. Worth it."

"Of course it was," says March.

They both drop through the next opening just as the first platform crashes down into the second, which thankfully holds. They do not test their luck to drop to the third platform, and then the remains of the lift platform, covered in fish. The supports framing the shaft burn through, and the entire structure falls like a flaming house of cards. Jonathan and March dive out of the way. Jonathan scrambles to her and wraps his body around hers to shield her from the fiery debris. While the dust settles from the collapse, he helps her stand.

She checks on the crowded stairways still intact. Hundreds of soldiers have made their way down with orbs in hand trying to put out what flames they can, though it will do little good. They too are stunned at the sight of the burning sea. Water ablaze with the fires of the hells, consuming all.

"The harbor is lost!" she shouts to the soldiers. Loud snaps of support timbers from every level count down to the harbor's destruction. "Rescue the townspeople. Search for survivors. Clear them before this entire side of Mirus is reclaimed by the sea."

The Gryphon has made it down to the docks as well, but he did not come for the fire. He came for the arsonist—for Cheshire. His large person stands two heads above everyone, eagle eyes sharp, searching every corner.

Jonathan helps March to her feet. "He is here," he tells her. "I must find him."

"Go," she says simply. Neither of them can afford to lose Cheshire, no matter his actions. She watches Jonathan run off into the crowd of townspeople who try to save their livelihoods, searching the visor of every soldier. The townspeople grab and pile baskets, blankets, and crates onto their backs. Soldiers must knock some from their grasp once they catch fire.

"Is this another part of the glorious plan of the Duchess?" Lysander's voice scrapes at March's back like a rusted rake.

"Please, tell us," says Uriah. "When will this queen of yours save the people? It seems she has only brought destruction to Mirus since her arrival."

They stand defiant. Lysander with his broadsword drawn, held to his side, its tip inches from the dirt. Disrespectful. Uriah rests his glaive across his shoulders, one wrist draped casually over its hardwood pole, his other hand playfully swirling the dirt with his whip.

She does not draw her swords but stands against them. Flecks of ash and cinder float between them. They did not orchestrate this, but they prepared. Her mother's manor is not far from the harbor. They would have been amongst the first to know and had the foresight to know March would be here. They share the same thought in their steely silver eyes. They do not care for the harbor or its people. Their gaze is set on March, waiting for the answer to their question, and the proposition they made earlier. They would rather fuck her than fight her.

CHAPTER 34

JONATHAN

Somewhere in this inferno, amidst the roaring hellscape, Jonathan knows in his gut Cheshire hides himself within soldier's armor—the only way he can be here to witness the destruction, as he did before at the hanging cells. Jonathan cannot stop every soldier he passes to look them in the eyes, to search for the unique lavender hue possessed only by Cheshire, but he can join the soldiers, help them save as many townspeople as he can, and look into their visors when possible.

The explosion of the hanging cells damaged several city blocks and killed many, but at least the attack was contained. Here, the townspeople in the harbor had no warning, no chance, no clue the armories were emptied of their oil reserves. Cheshire found a way to douse the entirety of the harbor, nearly a quarter of Mirus.

The flames travel with the speed of dragon's breath, wild and relentless. They defy the laws of nature as if they were alive—climbing, swimming, swinging, and would laugh if they could at the townspeople's futile attempt to stop their wrath.

Jonathan joins the nearest group of soldiers, Cheshire not among them. They usher a parade of women from the third level, wrapped in shawls for their modesty. They stripped out of their skirts, bottoms soaked with oil from walking across the tangle of plank walkways. These few are the fortunate ones.

In the bay, five sailors run from their ship, skin scorched beyond recognition, hair and most of their clothing burned away. They leap into the burning sea, hoping for relief, but only pain and death consumes them. Only two resurface. They scream, then gasp for breath, mouths now wet with oil. The flames follow the air and oil into their lungs, burning them instantly.

As Jonathan runs to each new area to aid where he can, he searches the faces of the soldiers. Every color eye meets his except Cheshire's. He wastes time helping the townspeople, but after Rookridge, he cannot turn a blind eye. Cheshire is his priority, but he will save who he can.

Every pathway and stairway burns. Cheshire made sure escape was not an option. Jonathan finds a hanging barrel of uncontaminated drinking water. He smashes the end with his fist and douses himself from head to toe until soaked. The water will do little to extinguish the fire but may act as a barrier from the oil.

Jonathan uses brute force to smash through stalls and storefronts, places Cheshire would not have been able to walk freely, in order to reach trapped townspeople. Most walls are reclaimed painted wood from ships. He smashes through them shoulder first and finds three women, huddled around a fourth on the ground, the left half of her face gone, scorched to the bone, teeth exposed, eye popped and receded into its socket. She gasps quick breaths, only inhales until she stops completely.

Insensitive as it sounds, Jonathan speaks the truth. "Leave her," he tells them. "Nothing more can be done."

The women shake their heads, wailing. He does not give them a choice. He picks two up at once in one arm and throws them over his shoulder. The other two women fight, scratch, claw, and curse, unwilling to leave the dead woman.

"The tavern!" a voice shouts from outside. "The tavern!"

337

Jonathan leaves the two women mourning their friend, kicks through a door, and jumps to the lower level just as the tavern's storehouse of spirits ignites and explodes. The tavern, along with the shacks next door and the three women, are gone, their voices silenced, as if they never existed. The force of the explosion knocks Jonathan off his feet and sends him skidding across an area of rocks between walkways. He sets the two women he saved down and pushes them gently toward the stairways out of the harbor. His ears ring. His head pounds. He squints hard to try and suppress them both, to find some comfort in the darkness behind his eyelids, but shades of crimson and orange fight back, antagonize him, let him know there is no time.

Where are you?

Ropes securing supports snap, timbers and posts crack and split. Signs the harbor's reign over the bay nears its end. He can see townspeople call and scream for aid, but the roar of the inferno, the constant, crushing, unyielding thunder overpowers their voices and beats against Jonathan's eardrums once the ringing stops.

At the highest level, the small dwellings and watch towers crumble and create a cascade of fire, charred posts, and beams. Soldiers, focused on rescuing survivors from beneath collapsed walls and awnings, remain unaware of the rain of fire from above. Jonathan grabs at the collars and arms of soldiers and townspeople, no matter if they fight back, and pulls them with him. There were seven. He saved two. Soldiers meant to be saviors scream beneath the fallen debris. It would have been a mercy if they were crushed under the weight of the rubble, but they survived by the strength of their armor, the armor which will now cook them alive from the heat. Still no sign of Cheshire.

Until now, Jonathan ignored himself, but the searing heat from all around him becomes painfully clear on his skin. The water from before dried before it could be of any use. Nevertheless, he persists in his search across the harbor and counts and weighs the numbers on the scales in his mind, those he saves against those he cannot reach in time, or for whom he is already too late—the difference staggering.

The sixth and the fifth levels of the harbor buckle, crack, and lurch forward, ready to fall at any moment. His eyes dart everywhere for one last fleeting attempt to find Cheshire, but there are hundreds of soldiers in the harbor now. A crowd of hundreds more townspeople gather on the rocks and sand at the foot of the stairways, safe from the fire thanks to the soldiers' efforts.

Even if Cheshire was among them, his height works to his advantage, allowing him to conceal himself within the crowd, especially if he wears Mirusian armor. Townspeople may brush or bump against him without ever knowing it was him. There is a high probability Jonathan passed him as well. The only reason Jonathan saw him during the aftermath of the hanging cells was because Cheshire wanted him to, but now he does not need Jonathan to lure the Gryphon as before, so there was no need to make his presence known.

The Gryphon.

The likelihood of finding Cheshire now nears the impossible, but nothing is impossible. Jonathan believes this. He searches the crowd again, not for Cheshire, but for the Gryphon, whose height will always betray him, who stands at least a head and half taller than any other man in Mirus. However, his imposing figure does not seem to be anywhere among the crowd of survivors.

The Gryphon would not have retreated, yet he does not help with the evacuation. It stands to reason his attention focuses elsewhere, on the reason he descended to the harbor in the first place—to hunt for Cheshire.

Damn it.

Jonathan feels a fool. He should have thought to seek out the Gryphon or follow him from the start. There are few places left unmarred, fewer still where the Gryphon could maneuver let alone stand.

The search begins anew, while the hourglass of the harbor reaches its final grains. Jonathan must hurry before the harbor meets its inevitable end, and to assure Cheshire does not meet his own at the hands of the Gryphon.

CHAPTER 35

MARY ANNE

Painting after painting flies by on both sides of Mary Anne as she tries to keep pace with the Duchess through the castle corridors. Mary Anne assumed for someone her age, she would not move with such speed, but it is all Mary Anne can do not to lose her from sight. The Chamberlain follows behind them, panting and rubbing at his temple.

He delivered the news to Mary Anne and the Duchess while they were in the middle of dinner. "The harbor is ablaze," is all he said.

The Duchess waits for her and the Chamberlain in the tower lift around the final bend. "Hurry."

As soon as the Chamberlain whips into the lift and closes the gate, securing all three passengers in, the Duchess throws the lever. Gears grind beneath them, and they fly into the dark tower above. The pinch of the Duchess's brow, the slight twitch in her bottom eyelid, the growing pressed scowl, sends Mary Anne's stomach into a tumble more than the lift. The cage rattles at the speed, and Mary Anne fears it will shake itself apart and they shall all fall to their deaths, since this technology has no business existing here.

Everyone loses their balance when the lift lurches and clanks to a stop at the top of the tower. The Chamberlain flings the gate and door open, and the trio runs around the conical turret to the backside of the balcony. Far below, beyond the lush, verdant castle gardens and hedge maze, a wall of black smoke as wide as the city and as tall as the Pinnacles of Wonderland overtakes the sky.

Mary Anne thought the column of smoke from the hanging cells ominous. But this hellfire blots out the heavens on the entire horizon. Embers float through the air like dark elemental fairies and snuff out in the darkness.

"Is this an attack from Lysander and Uriah?" asks Mary Anne.

"Do not be a fool. They do not want to rule over a city of ashes and ruin." The Duchess's face twists and quivers. "You know precisely who has done this."

"Cheshire," Mary Anne attempts to say under her breath.

The Duchess's crazed eyes burrow into Mary Anne. "An awfully familiar way to refer to the Queen Slayer." She studies Mary Anne's face, her ticks, her winces. "You have seen him. Spoken with him." Mary Anne tries not to think of any memory with Cheshire, but it is no use. The Duchess reads all as if their misadventures were scribed on Mary Anne's face. "He has been in the castle." She loses the color in her cheeks and stares back out at the harbor. "First the hanging cells, then the harbor. He is trying to cripple our city. And you foolishly invite him into my home."

"Never. I have never done such a thing."

"You play a deadly game. The Queen Slayer wants to destroy the queendom we have built for his own selfish ends. He has killed queens before, and we," she points to herself and the Chamberlain, "we had to tend to their broken, bloody, and mangled bodies. Do not trust him. Do not believe you are safe from his wrath, because you are not. He will kill you as easily and quickly as the other queens of Wonderland. Mark me."

The Duchess's words unleash a primal, unearthly fear within Mary Anne she has not felt since her encounter with the Ace in the Rookwood.

The fear of death, the fear of losing her mortal soul, once again made real. But Jonathan would never allow Cheshire to harm her. Never. She does not trust Cheshire in the least, but she trusts Jonathan unconditionally. He protected her then, he protects her now, and he will protect her against Cheshire should the time come.

"Madam," the Chamberlain whispers to the Duchess, "you must hide yourself if he is near."

Curious. Should he not be more worried about Mary Anne, who would be queen, instead of the Duchess? The Duchess's face betrays her. More than anger clouds her eyes. Fear, no, terror pours over her face like sweat. What does she have to fear?

"Not yet." The Duchess settles her nerves and regains her composure.

The trio descend in the lift once more but stop and exit halfway down the tower. Around one of the curved walls of the main shaft, beyond the marble stairs, dozens of copper pipes—a tangle of metal—protrude from the wall, ceiling, and floor. At the center of the Gordian knot, a silver, petal-edged phonograph horn, or at least this is the only comparison Mary Anne can make.

The Duchess stands before it and speaks. "Citizens of Mirus. Do not lose heart. This attack on our home, our people, our freedom, will not go unanswered. We shall respond. Mirus shall endure. We shall not falter. Be strong." She steps away and looks out the closest curved window facing the city.

"What does that do?" Mary Anne asks.

The Chamberlain clears his throat. "This marvel contraption takes the Duchess's voice and distributes it throughout all of Stonehaven and the Crest in seconds, through all of these tubes."

"And now what?"

"Now we wait," says the Duchess.

"Is that all?" asks Mary Anne. The Duchess does not respond. "The people need more than encouragement."

"My dear, the soldiers are already out in the city handling the blaze."

"They do not need soldiers, they need you. They need more than a disembodied voice and hollow words."

The Duchess sucks at her cheek and continues to gaze into the city.

"Or has fear of the Queen Slayer crippled more than the city?" asks Mary Anne. "Has it crippled you as well? Is this why you never venture outside of the castle walls?"

The Duchess turns to Mary Anne, jaw askew. "If I did not venture outside of these walls, you would surely be dead by now somewhere on the road between Briarwell to Mirus. I found you before Lysander and Uriah. Imagine what would have become of you if they found you on the open road."

"That may be so, but this does not excuse your cowardice now."

The Duchess turns back to the window, ignoring Mary Anne's words. "We will have another gathering in the Long Hall soon to see what needs the people have."

"No. It is too little." Mary Anne races back to the lift and throws the lever without closing the gate. As the chains overhead scrape against each other, she wonders what came over her. Was she tired of feeling out of control? Helpless? Something needs to be done, and if the Duchess will not, cannot, then she will. The people are scared and need reassurance. And once this catastrophe passes, she must have a word with Jonathan about Cheshire. His actions endanger her return home. She cannot win over the people if they are in a constant state of fear, and if the Duchess will not do more, Mary Anne will—she must.

CHAPTER 36

MARCH

The collapsing timbers should have her focus. The heat of the fire so near should cause her dry eyes to blink. The screams and wails from all around her should draw her eyes, but they stab with the sharpness of her strongest blade at the unwavering, arrogant eyes of Lysander and Uriah.

"This is not the time." March stands, arms crossed, ready to draw her blades. She can out draw them easily but knows better than to antagonize them, especially in public. Some of their own followers have made their way down the stairs to watch the performance. There is enough fuel on the fire, a foul wind blows, and she will not be able to escape a brawl this day.

"This is precisely the time," Lysander roars, more for the panicked crowd to hear than March. "Look at what your inactions have wrought. The destruction of our city falls on the heads of those who oppose the line of kings. Our divine birthright."

"You cast your lot to the wrong side," says Uriah, eyes licking at March's body. "It is too late for the Duchess, the charlatan queen, and all those who align with them."

"If this is your city, should you not help save it?" March shifts her weight and widens her stance.

"The harbor is a lost cause," growls Lysander. "There is no saving it."

"But it need not be too late for you," says Uriah. "We stand by our offer if you honor our arrangement."

The fire reaches the uppermost level. The supports of the dwellings highest against the cliff collapse onto the storehouses. Soon they will buckle and fall onto the fishmongers and other stores. The wharfs, the piers, the dozens of ships in the harbor, large and small, already sink into the burning sea. The harbor is lost. No amount of orbs or water can save it. Cheshire made sure of it. Truth be told, March could not care less. She would rather see Lysander and Uriah burn with the rest of the screaming townsfolk, unable to escape the inferno.

Lysander's bare chest heaves through his open tunic. He shrugs his shoulder and adjusts the single pauldron he wears. Uriah mirrors his brother, stretching his neck against the pauldron he wears on the opposite shoulder. They wait for the moment for March to move first.

Sweat runs down March's brow, her torso, and the small of her back. She cannot hear her heartbeat over the chaos but feels it in her palms and the soft bit of flesh where her collar bones meet.

"It does not need to be this way," says Uriah, taking a step toward March. "This can all end in a much more pleasurable manner for all of us."

"Our ideas of pleasure differ greatly." March finally unsheathes the swords from her hips. Their ting against the metal locket of her scabbards sends a welcome and needed shiver up her arms and down her spine. "I will lie with my men tonight. And you spineless boys will lie in the crags with the discarded bodies and slaughtered animal remains."

She plays to their lust, breathing hard, flexing the muscles of her stomach, which Lysander cannot take his eyes from. She shifts her hips, and Uriah's eyes travel down between her legs. Neither Lysander nor Uriah make eye contact with her, as if she were not a threat to them anymore. Regardless of their lecherous nature, they pose a substantial threat whether they meet her eyes or not.

Lysander's smile grows. "You draw against us. You will be fucked one way or another this night. We promise you that."

There it is. In this match, she could face them and hold her own, but they would not be trying. They want to bed her, not kill her. Worse, if they managed to knock her unconscious, she doubts they would wait until they took her back to her mother's manor. They would fuck her unconscious body here for the pride of the achievement, for all to see, welcoming the audience.

March laughs to cover the uneasy feeling growing in the pit of her stomach. She swallows, blows a sweat-drenched tendril of hair from her eye, never allowing the smirk to slip from her face. March waits and plays for time, but her wiles will only entertain Lysander and Uriah for so long. She does not wait for Jonathan though. He handles matters on the far side of the harbor. Her strategy relies on the foolish dedication of others, who thankfully do not fail her.

While hundreds of Mirusian soldiers rescue townspeople and try to salvage what they can from the harbor markets and homes, the messenger and the guard from the gates run to her sides, shields up, swords drawn, faces smeared with ash.

"Lay down your weapons," the messenger commands Lysander and Uriah. "Do not take a step farther."

"You advance," says the guard, "and your actions will be taken as an act of sedition. Audrianna March commands the armies of Mirus. You know this to be true. Move against her, you move against the city itself and all its forces."

Uriah and Lysander share an untroubled glance. "How quaint," says Lysander.

"We outnumber you here," says the messenger.

"Do you now?" asks Uriah, smugly.

The messenger whispers to March. "Your efforts, your leadership, are needed elsewhere. We will hold these disrespectful ruffians at bay."

You won't.

"Go," says the guard. "The men and the people need you. This is what you trained us for, is it not?"

It is.

"You move and you're dead," says the guard. He and the messenger step in front of March to block her from the Twins. They step forward, poised skillfully, as she taught them. Their posture—perfect. The angle of their blades—sharp. Their footwork—calculated.

Lysander sucks at one of his teeth.

Uriah inhales deeply and sighs. "I say we move and you're dead." With the speed of lighting itself and the crack of thunder, Uriah swings his whip and slices open the messenger's cheek to the bone and teeth. "Any other remarks you would like to make? Please, share."

The guard and messenger charge out of blind fearlessness. Uriah twirls his glaive from behind his shoulders, dances circles through the ash, and blocks every strike from the guard, with ease. At the same time, he swings his whip low, back and forth, building up its speed, its lethal strength. Uriah snaps at the guard's face, but he luckily deflects off of his blade at the last second, saving his eye.

The messenger, with true form, strikes at Lysander repeatedly, but to no avail. The clangs of steel begin a beautiful, albeit short, elegy. Lysander moves slowly but gracefully for such a brutish man, using the flat side of his uncommonly wide broadsword to shield each strike, covering his arms and back, even shoving it into the ground to block low strikes at his legs.

March studies every gesture, no matter how slight, of both Lysander and Uriah while they fight. Lysander refrains from using his sword, but while he steps to block, he maneuvers the geography of the fight without his opponent realizing. Uriah uses his glaive defensively and offensively at the same time. When he does swing, the force behind his strike twists his body. The muscles on the sides of his abdomen squeeze almost to the point of bursting for him to control the blade. Though his body and lips show strain, he swings with the effort of a thresher.

March has faced several men who wield double swords and, while troublesome, they all fell to her skill. However, watching Uriah's dance, spinning his glaive around his neck, his waist, around his back while he ducks to counter, all while keeping his whip poised to strike, sends the slightest shiver of doubt, along with a flood of fury, down her spine.

Uriah finds his target and then looks away before striking—a sign of pure arrogance but undeniable skill—and still manages to avoid the next attack, almost as if he can read his opponent's mind and movements.

No. Not precognition. Manipulation.

Uriah uses both the crack of his whip and spin of his glaive. He uses his speed, dexterity, even the flourish of his long silver hair to position his opponents where he wants them to be, just as Lysander does—both masters of controlling their opponents.

Uriah shoots the blunt end of his glaive into the dirt to catch the messenger's next step. Once off balance, Uriah holds the top of his glaive, leaps up, and perches both feet on the staff like some monkey, then kicks the staff out from under him, sweeping the messenger off his feet and spinning him in the air.

March sees herself and Cheshire in Uriah.

Lysander, more beast than man, and solid as a Rookwood oak, stands his ground and takes the brunt of every blow from the guard. He starts to use his vambrace to deflect any attack, followed by a swift punch or backhand.

March sees herself and Jonathan in Lysander.

When the guard recoils from an attack, Lysander swings his broadsword overhead, swooshing the air as if summoning a storm, and swings with the force of a hurricane. The low notes reverberate through the turbulent air, as if someone plunked at the lowest note of an organ. The blow knocks the guard off his feet, denting his breast plate severely.

He and his armor crunch to the ground ten feet from where he once stood.

The Twins toy with the messenger and the guard, who do their best to hold their own. If March had to calculate, Lysander and Uriah use roughly a quarter of the effort of which they are capable. She analyzes every shoulder movement, every step, side glance, twist of a forearm, and looks for any tells, searing them into her mind.

Uriah glares at March, his lust now clouded with frustration. He sees her skill, her moves in the men they fight. Lysander huffs, annoyed at the waste of time.

The guard and the messenger look up at March, wondering why she has not left the battle to help the others. They take her presence as a sign of confidence, of encouragement. How wrong they are. They rise to their feet again, and with one last valiant nod to their commander, face the Twins.

Uriah rolls his eyes and cracks his whip. It wraps around the neck of the messenger. The shock forces the blade from the messenger's hand. Uriah swings his arm overhead and, with a second crack, slams the messenger into the guard. At the same moment, Lysander ducks under the whip, and with a single blow cleaves through all four of their knees just above their greaves.

The guard howls in pain when the full weight of his body collapses on his stumps. He cups the bottoms of both knees with his hands in a futile attempt to stop the bleeding. Blood pumps and spirts through his fingers. The color of his skin drains with every second.

The messenger writhes on the ash and dirt and tries to scream but the leather whip holds his breath captive, lips turning the color of a predawn sky. Uriah steps on the messenger's chest, grabs the thinner end of the whip in hand, and pulls. With a horrible final rattle, the whip slices through the messenger's neck clear to his spine. He chokes for only a second before Lysander presses his boot on the exposed bone, snapping it, claiming his life.

Lysander grabs the guard by the back of his gorget and flips him over, shoulders on the ground, ass in the air, and sits on him as if he were a tree stump or rock. The seeping blood from his wounds pours down into his face, choking and eventually drowning him. His eyes, full of sadness and betrayal, filling with blood, look to March, wondering why she did nothing before his life leaves them.

While Uriah inspects the end of his whip and Lysander stretches his neck, March backs away and disappears into the crowd. She pulls the hood of her cropped jacket over her head to conceal her pink hair and squirms through the masses escaping to the stairs. In their bloodlust, Lysander and Uriah lose sight of her.

It is a shame to lose two soldiers she can trust, but the messenger and guard served the purpose for which she chose them. The honorable and the brave are always the first to die. They fought valiantly, ferociously, remembered every detail of her training, but stood no chance against the skill of the Twins. March knew this before they stepped forward. The Twins are an impeccable example of speed and strength, and like Jonathan, March, and Cheshire together, the Twins' movements fill in the gaps left by the other. March could face one brother, kill him possibly if faced in single combat. But facing their forces combined, even with Jonathan and Cheshire at her side, she is unsure of the outcome of the battle. A sour song indeed.

CHAPTER 37

CHESHIRE

Cheshire walks through the harbor and watches the panic ensue. Townspeople run for their lives with what meager possessions they can carry in their arms. The flames snake and writhe up post and plank until every structure on all seven levels and all twenty piers burn in brilliant yellows, oranges, and reds. A work of art.

March and Jonathan run past him without taking notice. She barks orders at the soldiers to clear each building and search for survivors and the injured. She does not call for the dead. The fire will tend to their bodies. Jonathan runs to help without order or fear—ever the hero. Soldiers stampede by, thinking he is one of their own, while Cheshire stands like a rock in a raging river. These soldiers have their bows slung over their shoulders. The only swords unsheathed are to cut through locked doors or clear fallen timbers and walls.

A crushing weight slaps down on the nape of Cheshire's neck. At first he believes it a piece of falling timber, but the unmistakable sensation of fingers, the Gryphon's fingers, tighten on him. His feet leave the earth. This moment of weightlessness does not have the same serenity as before. With one arm, the Gryphon hurls Cheshire through the wall of a fishmonger's shop. The armor limits Cheshire's movement. He tries to spin, to rebound with his feet against the wall, but cannot right himself in the air with the added weight. His back cracks against a wooden beam, knocking the air from him, and his helmet flies off in some direction he cannot tell. He gasps and chokes at the same time, stuck somewhere in the painful middle of living and dying.

As soon as he hits the ground, the Gryphon stands above him, not allowing Cheshire a chance to recover. He grabs Cheshire by the collar of his breastplate, lifts him off the floor, and slams him back with the force of a full punch. The floorboards creak and strain. Cheshire can taste the blood in his mouth and the sharp tingle from the back of his head against the boards.

The Gryphon lifts him again and punches Cheshire into the floor twice more. Cheshire has no choice but to endure the punishment until he can regain his breath. The fourth time, Cheshire manages to wrap his legs and arms around the Gryphon's arm, to at least lessen the recoil. However, the Gryphon raises his hand over head even higher, carrying Cheshire's full weight, and smashes him down again. It is not Cheshire that breaks first, but the floorboards. They shatter, and he and the Gryphon tumble down the supports, the sloped stone rocks of the cliff, and splash into a shallow pool of seawater.

Cheshire manages to get to his feet and hugs one of the support beams, sucking in and coughing out as much sea water as air. He smiles at the Gryphon with bloody teeth. The Gryphon charges faster than his size should allow, but Cheshire readies himself. Though slowed by the armor, and now his injuries, Cheshire manages to slip around the post as the Gryphon's large gauntlet punches a sizable chunk from it. Cheshire positions himself near another post, waits, and hopes to topple the entire stack of buildings down on the Gryphon as he did to the Ace with the train platform in Rookridge. But the Gryphon takes one look at Cheshire's position, then up above at the groaning structures, and walks toward him. The water ripples away from him, as if his own power resonates from him.

"Not going to bite?" Cheshire asks, wincing from the pain in his side. "Worth a shot?"

"What the fuck have you done?" The Gryphon wipes the long hairs from his face. "Do you realize what you have done to this city?"

"Yes."

"I warned you. Now look at you, battered. Soon to be broken. It is over, Cheshire."

"You did warn me, and hunted me, and had your men shoot at me, and tried to split me in two yourself, yet here I stand. Battered, yes. Broken, unforeseeable. But there is one victor here. *Me.*" While he has the Gryphon's ear, Cheshire peels his armor off and drops it in the water, until he is left only in his trousers, vest, sash, and cloak. "I wanted you alone, and here we are. You could have avoided all of this. All I wanted was a civil conversation. Information about my mother. Without me punching you or you punching me. Is this so much to ask?"

"You want to have a civil conversation now, after you have crippled our city?"

"Not mine." Cheshire hides the pain and stalks a circle around the Gryphon, displacing as little water as possible and keeping as many beams between them as he can. "Turn a blind eye to my actions. It would not be the first time."

The Gryphon lunges, arm outstretched, toward Cheshire's neck, but without the armor, Cheshire proves harder to catch.

"How dare you say such a thing to me?" The Gryphon lunges again and misses, and a third time, and a fourth.

"What?" asks Cheshire. "Will you make good on your threat and kill me? Have yet another death on your hands?"

The timbers creak above the Gryphon's head. He reaches up with one arm, catching and supporting the large beam overhead meant to bury him. "Did you think you were the only one who knew how to play this game? I thought more of you, boy." With his free hand, he unsheathes his sword and hurls it at Cheshire.

The massive blade spins through the air. Cheshire ducks, barely missing it. The sword cleaves through the two supporting pillars behind Cheshire.

Planks, posts, counters, and closets come crashing down directly over Cheshire's head. Instinct takes over and he leaps out of the way of the collapsing structures. A large beam catches the end of his wet cloak.

The Gryphon releases his weighted load and grasps Cheshire by the neck, slams him to the ground, and holds him in the vile mixture of seawater, oil, and fish remnants from the mongers above. It laps over his ears, creeps up his to his eyes, and depending on the tide from the debris, covers his mouth and nose.

"I am not responsible for your mother's death," the Gryphon shouts, like a distant flood crushing through a forest, louder than the fire raging above.

"You are responsible." Cheshire says, spitting out salt water. "Until two weeks ago, I thought her imprisoned. Kept from me purposefully. I searched the entire country for her for a thousand years, on a lie, a lie told by the Duchess. But I knew, I knew she was within these walls. I should never have left, but the Ace finally chased me from the city once and for all. I thought I would find her when I returned, but instead I found you. And you are the one who told me she is dead. You were meant to protect her. And you failed. You *failed*."

The Gryphon presses down on Cheshire's chest and head to make sure the water stops his rant. "I tried. I tried to protect her. For a thousand years I have thought about my failure. That is why I so eagerly turned to the bottle. The choice between wine or water was simple. Only one dulled the thoughts churning in my head of my greatest failure." His grasp loosens, and Cheshire raises his face above the water to gasp for air. "It is over. For both of us."

"No."

"What more do you want, you impudent child?"

"Since you have lost your pride and your honor, I want the only thing you have left of worth. I want answers."

"Damn you, boy." The Gryphon lowers Cheshire back under the water. "I gave them to you. I told you everything I know.

Cheshire's lungs burn, feel as though they are about to burst, but he still manages to scream out. "Lies!" Cheshire beats against the Gryphon's face and claws at his exposed neck to free himself.

"You were in your tenth year the last I saw you. Now, a thousand years later, here you are before me again. No matter what I say, no matter the answers I give you, you will not relent."

Cheshire stops fighting the Gryphon and pushes with his elbows to raise his face out of the water. "Never." Cheshire grins, eyes wide, burning with saltwater, tears, and hatred. "I am the single pulled thread in Wonderland's tapestry, and I will see it all unraveled."

The Gryphon huffs and pushes Cheshire back under the water with all of his weight. "I foolishly thought a warning would be enough. I believed you expelled whatever grievance you had after the hanging cells. I am sorry I failed you again. But I will not allow you to destroy any more of this city."

Fire, as hot as the inferno above, explodes in Cheshire's chest. His throat fights for air. His body wants to breathe, needs to breathe. Cheshire claws at the Gryphon's eyes. He will not die like this. Not by his hands. Not in this way. There is so much left undone. Darkness encroaches on the edges of his eyes. They blur, and his sight becomes as small as if he peered through a keyhole. He cannot fight his body anymore. He opens his mouth and takes a breath, filling his lungs with the horrid seawater warmed by fires. But the sight he sees before succumbing completely to the darkness is Jonathan running and pulling at the Gryphon's shoulder. Then all is black.

CHAPTER 38

MARCH

The streets empty the farther March walks through Stonehaven. Iron locks catch, and wooden shutters slam shut. Women and men cling to their sons and daughters and run for their homes. They are safe from the fire. What they fear is Cheshire and where he will strike next. As March snakes through the zig-zagging stairways of Stonehaven, the silence of the streets melts away, overcome by shouts and chants ahead of her. She crosses into the Crest, where shutters clack shut and lock bars behind doors clunk into place. An ominous cacophony of voices swells between her and the castle. Townspeople clog the staircase two street levels below the castle.

March climbs the outside of a jeweler's establishment in the middle of the Crest, from portico to window, sign to planter, and finally to tiled roof. She hangs from the iron weathervane along the spine of the roof to get a better vantage. Hundreds, no, thousands of townspeople surround the castle wall. While Lysander and Uriah went to the harbor to stir descent, they unleashed their followers upon the castle to attack on two fronts.

A familiar light, high whistle catches her ear. Four rooftops to her right, Jonathan sits with his forearms resting on his knees and a large, tied bundle next to him. His smirk and shrug bring a smile to March. She walks along the spines on the rooftops and leaps over the thin spaces between structures until she meets him.

"Not the rendezvous I intended for this evening," says Jonathan. "But I needed to see your face."

She kisses his cheek. "Cheshire has outdone himself this time. And we must deal with the aftermath. Do you know where he is?"

Jonathan glances down to the bundle next to him.

March recognizes the fabric. The unique ombre of Cheshire's long, hooded cloak. She untwists the top, and Cheshire's unconscious form flops out. The peaceful look upon his face, coupled with the red marks which will be bruises on the morrow, twists March's stomach. She would think he merely slumbered if not for the contorted position of his body.

"Fucking hells." March runs her fingers through his tangled hair. "What the fuck happened?"

"The Gryphon," says Jonathan. "He would have killed him had I not intervened. This is the only way I could get him safely out of the harbor. Had I known we would face a wall of Lysander and Uriah's minions, I would have found some other place to wait this riot out."

"There is no other place," says March. "From this point on, the streets will be unsafe for anyone loyal to the castle. Lysander and Uriah will make sure of it. We need to get into the castle or leave Mirus immediately."

"You know I cannot. All of my elixir is inside the castle, except for what I have in my flask." He pats his jacket under his heart.

"Damn it all." March wishes Jonathan would have chosen the latter but knows he cannot leave. And they would not make it back to the Hollow in time to get more. "The castle, then. But not through the gates. They will not open for us."

"Then we go over." Jonathan wraps Cheshire in his cloak again, twists the opening around his wrist, and carefully places it over his shoulder.

Together, he and March drop down the side of the building and walk through the Crest until they reach the stairway closest to Dormy's cart.

The townspeople obstruct their path and spill out into the street. The crowd buzzes, the hiss of fire crackling as it follows a line of black powder to a waiting powder keg. Even those farthest from the castle breathe heavy through their noses and clench their jaws and fists.

"I dislike this plan," says March. "We have to reach Dormy first. There are too many people to push through. The smallest thing can agitate the entire mob."

"Then make sure they do not," says Jonathan. An apology mixes with his words. "Your hands are quicker than their tongues."

She nods and positions herself behind Jonathan, keeping Cheshire between them.

Jonathan, ever the gentleman, says, "Excuse us, pardon us," as he leads them through the crowd.

March keeps her left hand on Cheshire and her right poised by the daggers on her thigh. There is no room for swords in this viper's den. Despite Jonathan's cordial and gentle demeanor, the townspeople they push through scowl, sneer, and whisper curses at them.

They have not crossed the first street when a large man in heavy overalls reaches out for Jonathan as he passes.

"Who the fuck do you think, you—"

He does not finish his sentence. March unsheathes the long dagger at her thigh and punches it deep into the man's armpit, stabbing his heart. He is dead before he knows it. His arm drops, and the sheer number of townspeople around him keeps him upright. March wipes his blood on the leg of another man she passes. If only Lysander and Uriah were among the crowd. She could end them with a flick of her wrist before they breathed their last.

The spaces between people shrink to nothing. March can hear her own breath in her ears. The heat around them pulses as the crowd undulates and shifts. Her heartbeat throbs in her fingertips and her eyes.

At the base of the second staircase, two men reach out for her. One grabs her shoulder, the other her hip. She does not give them a chance to speak. She grabs another dagger, spins, and quickly stabs both men through the underside of his jaw. They swallow, and blood trickles down her blades.

When she turns forward again, six people separate her from Jonathan and Cheshire while others squeeze and press against her. And at the worst time, the bundle moves. Cheshire stirs. If he regains consciousness now, his panic and rage will explode, endangering them all. March does not have the brute strength of Jonathan to push through the crowd. She does, however, have steel. March flips her daggers in hand, blade down, and stabs men and women between their ribs, their necks, and armpits to clear the way to Jonathan. She steps over those who fall in front of her. Those townspeople who are quick enough to catch sight of her strikes soon fall to her steel as well. But the crowd cannot ignore the spurts of blood or the wake of bodies following her.

A woman questions the moving sack on Jonathan's back. March punctures her lung. She gasps instead of asking further questions. March reaches Jonathan just as Cheshire's wincing face presses against the fabric. She thanks him for a clear target, sheaths one of her daggers, and pushes him in his jaw with all of her strength. His body falls limp once more, and she grabs onto his cloak as Jonathan steps out of the Crest and wades through the boiling sea of people surrounding the castle. Jonathan finds new difficulty maneuvering through the townspeople. The sea turns to stone.

Dormy stands atop her contraption, waving at Jonathan and March. Clever girl knew they would need a way back into the castle. She whistles with her thumb and forefinger in her mouth, but nothing can be heard over the raucous crowd. Two Castle Guards stand ready at the wheel for Dormy to lower the rope. March pushes against Jonathan's back, forcing themselves through the people, ignoring their groans and cries of pain. They are feet from the castle wall, just under Dormy.

"It's them," a nasal voice says from within the crowd. "They're from the castle. They're trying to get back in."

March searches the crowd and finds the familiar milky eye of one of Lysander and Uriah's men staring back, his partner by his side.

The crowd's focus and anger turn. Hundreds of eyes fall on March instantly. Dozens of hands reach for them, for her. She can feel fingers grasp at her coat, her arms, the exposed skin of her torso, her hair, her swords. This violation is more than she can bear. She stabs the closest six to her, those who have their hands on her. She plunges her daggers through their eye sockets, the fleshy part below their necks, and their mouths, for those foolish enough to keep them open.

"They are killing us," says the man with the large nose. "Killing us!"

More hands reach out, fingers stretched and claws at the ready, inches from her face. She will kill them all.

Jonathan swings his free arm behind them and swats away their arms. He turns, putting Cheshire between his back and the wall, and wraps his arm around March, shielding her.

"It's them," more and more voices say. "It's them. Capture them. Take them."

Jonathan looks up then hugs March as tight as he can, hiding her face and his. Dormy and several guards throw down glass jars and bottles into the crowd. Most are filled with preserves, but many hold Dormy's supply of spare nails. Archer's fire shots to burst the jars of nails over the crowd. They hit their marks and rain down shrapnel. The jars shatter on foreheads and arms. Shards and splinters of glass spray into the crowd. Townspeople bleed from their eyes, faces, and arms. They push away from Jonathan and March, giving themselves room to breathe.

"Now!" Dormy cries.

March spins, throws her hands over Jonathan's neck, and holds on. He wraps the rope of Dormy's bucket around his free arm. March clenches her eyes and feels her feet leave the earth. She can feel fingers scrape and claw at her legs and boots. Her and Jonathan's bodies smack and drag against the wall as they are hoisted up.

At the top of the wall, five guards man Dormy's wheel to compensate for March, Jonathan, and Cheshire's combined weight. Two more guards, along with Dormy, pull them onto the wall. She grabs Jonathan's face with both hands. His eyes bounce back and forth erratically. She digs in his inner jacket pocket, pulls out his flask, and holds it to his lips. She makes sure he drinks all he needs before returning the flask to his jacket. His eyes and breath slow.

"Thank you." March grabs Dormy by the back of her neck and kisses the top of her head. Dormy's doe eyes well up with tears.

"Thank you, all," Jonathan tells the Castle Guard.

"What more can we do?" one guard asks.

"Get word to the soldiers still outside the castle walls," says March. "Tell them to wait, tell them to hide. We will get to them soon."

Once the soldiers disperse along the wall, March feels her neck and jaw tremble. They have lost to Lysander and Uriah more than once this day. They need to get away as fast as possible, before Cheshire wakes again, so she and Jonathan can properly fall apart from the experience. They have all lost in more ways than one.

CHAPTER 39

MARY ANNE

O nce the lift clangs against the stones of the ground floor, Mary Anne bolts through the castle to the main entrance. The doorman holds it open for her the moment he catches a glimpse of her at the end of the hallway. Outside in the courtyard, she can hear the chants and screams of a mob on the other side of the castle walls. The Castle Guard yell back over drawn arrows. Townspeople pound against the tall wooden gates. The two large gatemen lower iron crossbars, as thick as the trees of the Queenwood, into place.

"Do not fear," says a voice from behind her. Pat and Bill appear as out of a whisper. "They will not breach the wall or the gates," Pat continues.

"Can you be sure?"

"Of course," says Bill. "They are our design."

"Should we not let them in to hear what they have to say?"

Pat nods toward the eastern staircase. "Best you hear them from the top of the wall before you consider letting them through the gate."

Mary Anne takes her dress in hand and runs to the stairs, then to the top of the wall. Even out of breath and with her heart pounding in her ears, she can hear the people chanting, "Off with her head!" Men and women pack the entire road surrounding the castle. Whether they mean her or the Duchess is unclear, but hundreds, if not thousands, of townspeople shout and curse at the castle. She makes her way around the curve of the wall and stands to the right of the main gates.

"People of Mirus," Mary Anne says with an outstretched hand, as if the people would quiet for her. "People of Mirus. I hear you. I see you." But she goes unseen and unheard by the masses. What can she say not to sound like the Duchess? What will they listen to? She takes a nearby torch and waves it back and forth overhead. The nearby guards grab more torches and follow suit. The movement catches the eyes of the mob below, and their chants dwindle. "People of Mirus," she begins again. "I hear you. I see you. I will not hide from you. Many of you do not know who I am, but I will soon be your queen. But you need not wait until then for my deeds to begin. I will see the culprit in this attack brought to justice. I do not fear the Queen Slayer, nor will I hide from him. Mirus will be protected under my rule. I promise you. Now return to your homes for the night. Please."

"No," a voice shouts from the crowd.

"You are powerless," another gruff voice shouts.

"Lysander and Uriah would never allow this to happen," a third calls out.

She wants to curse them for their cruelty, but she cannot deny the truth in their words. If she could reach the Fourth Tenet, she could have the power to stop this madness, to stop the likes of Lysander and Uriah. True power.

Then the chant begins again, unorganized at first, but then the words turn deadly crisp. "Death to the whore queen," they repeat. "Death to the otherworld whore." Townspeople throw glass bottles and torches of their own at the top of the wall. Archers draw their bows against their faces.

"No," Mary Anne commands. "Death will only stoke the fire. The only recourse is to allow it to burn out. At least for tonight." She descends the stairs with their chants still echoing and the disdain in their eyes burned into her mind. They meant her as well as the Duchess. The mob wants her dead. Her legs shake uncontrollably.

Businessmen in London want her ostracized from the consortium. They wish she would lose everything and be able to buy her family's business from her. They look upon her as lesser, but never with murder in their eyes. This sensation twists Mary Anne's stomach. She can taste putrid bile in the back of her throat and feel the tingle below her jaw build and gag her.

Across the courtyard, Jonathan drops from a rope near Dormy's wagon, followed by March.

"Jonathan," she whispers. She runs to him. His gaze. His smile will comfort her. She needs him. Mary Anne catches up to them as they ascend the stairs to the keep. "Jonathan," she says louder, stopping him.

He carries a large bundle slung over his shoulder with what appears to be a body crumpled inside. A tuft of purple hair pokes out of one of the holes.

"Is that?" she asks, but already knows the answer. "Why have you brought him back here? Do you know what he has done?"

"Yes," says Jonathan, "which is precisely why I had to bring him here, away from them." He gestures to the wall with his head.

They can speak more of Cheshire and this horrible decision once they are alone. "Jonathan, I must speak with you at once."

"I am afraid I cannot at this moment," he says, out of breath. "I will call upon you in the morning." He quickens his steps toward the keep.

Jonathan has never turned her down. The thought stabs at her already fragile gut. "No. It is of the utmost importance. I need you." She chases after him, reaching out for him.

Just as Jonathan crosses through the door, March pulls a dagger from her thigh and slams Mary Anne against the inlaid stone columns on the outside of the door. She presses the point of the dagger against Mary Anne's throat. Her wild eyes vibrate. She means to use the dagger if Mary Anne says another word.

Jonathan reappears in the doorway. "March," he says. "I am sorry, Mary Anne." He turns, runs up the rest of the stairs, and disappears into the castle with March at his heels.

The doorman peeks through the crack of the door hinge.

"He left me," she says to herself. *He left me.* Her lips shake. Mary Anne cannot be alone tonight. She will only feel safe in Jonathan's company. Her legs will only stop shaking in his presence. She can follow him to his camp in the hedge maze. Jonathan would not refuse her if she arrived. But she must first know how to reach it.

She runs down the stairs to Pat and Bill, who stand in the middle of the courtyard and stare at the gate. "Do you know where Jonathan has made camp?" she asks before reaching them.

Pat and Bill look at each other instead of answering Mary Anne's question.

"Do you know?" she asks again.

"Yes," they reply together.

"Can you take me there?"

"Yes," they say after a lengthy pause.

Mary Anne waits for them to lead the way, but they do not move. "Why are you being so obtuse?"

"We are merely answering your questions," says Pat.

"Ask the correct questions," says Bill. "Or do not ask a question at all."

"Fine," says Mary Anne, annoyed and biting. "Take me to where Jonathan and March have made camp in the hedge maze."

"Follow us," says Pat. She slings her hammer over her shoulder and leads the way through the castle.

As they walk, the weight of responsibility becomes tangible and bears down on Mary Anne's shoulders. The chants of the townspeople fill the silence and keep time with the sound of Pat and Bill's boots clunking through the corridors.

They exit the back of the castle, and Pat and Bill stop shy of the first arch of the hedge maze.

Pat sets her hammer down again. It thuds and its head presses into the grass. "Three rights, two lefts, fourth right, seventh left, right, right," says Pat. "It will lead to a dead end. Walk until you cannot go any farther, then turn around and take the second right that appears."

"Do not deviate from the path," says Bill. "Or you will find yourself lost. The maze is larger on the inside than it is on the outside."

"Preposterous," says Mary Anne. "Nothing can be larger on the inside than its perimeter."

"Do not deviate from the path," Bill repeats.

Pat pulls up her hammer. "If you make a mistake, you will end up in a completely different part of the maze."

"Can I not just backtrack my steps?"

"No," says Pat. "That is not the way the maze works. Even the path we have given you is not a straight path."

"If you were to take the straightest path," says Bill, "if such a thing existed, it would take you roughly three days to reach the center."

"With the path we have given you," Pat continues, "you will jump to completely different parts of the maze to bypass miles."

"All of this just to see Jonathan."

"It is what you wanted, is it not?" asks Pat.

"Can you two lead me through to the center?"

"No," says Bill. "We must assess the damage to the harbor. See how much still stands."

"Is it wise to leave the castle?"

"Not for you," says Pat. "But then again, no one notices us." Pat and Bill nod and disappear around the corner of the castle.

Mary Anne stares into the entrance of the hedge maze. Her dress flaps in a cold rush of air. She second guesses herself. It would be easier to return to her bedchamber, lock the door, and try to sleep, despite the thoughts running through her head. Or she could walk a little farther and find Jonathan, sit with him, and listen to his soothing voice as they share tea and calm her nerves. She will always choose the latter.

The directions are as Pat said, and Mary Anne learns again how impossibilities do not matter in Wonderland. Though the constellations are not of her world, she knows enough to guild herself by the heavens, but after every turn, the stars in the sky shift. One moment she faces north, and the next, west, without rhyme or reason. She has also seen the perimeter of the hedge maze, looked down upon it from the tower balcony, walked its length on her way to the croquet field. However, somehow, she knows she has walked a farther distance after every turn than the full length of the maze. She should be able to see the castle tower over the hedges, but when she reaches the dead end, she struggles to find its lofty towers.

Mary Anne, as instructed, walks to the dead end of the path, so close her breath pushes the small oval leaves of the hedge in front of her. She turns and discovers a new pathway where there was none before—second to the right—and pulsing, warm candle light beckoning her.

"Jonathan," she whispers, relieved to be at the end of her journey. She walks softly, avoiding small twigs on the ground. But when Mary Anne peeks around the corner, her heart stops for a moment, then thunders throughout her entire body. Of all the scenes she could have imagined, has imagined, Mary Anne could never prepare herself for the sight before her.

CHAPTER 40

JONATHAN

The harbor and docks are decimated—all but smoldering, charred kindling which look like jagged rocks on the shore, similar to the Wrecks. If there were any full structures secured to the cliffs, be them stores, storehouses, or dwellings, no evidence remains. The smoke from the inferno faded with the setting sun. Thin wisps catch the light of the full moon in the distance but have no sway over the stars beyond. The moonlight casts a gentle ring on the towering walls of the hedge maze. A ring of protection Jonathan would like to believe. Protection from the riots currently happening outside the castle gates.

March paces slowly outside the perimeter of their makeshift camp at the center of the maze. Doubt weighs down her steps. The light of their four lanterns cast her arcing shadow on the greenery. Jonathan sits with his back against the fountain at the northwest corner of the lawn. And near him, Cheshire lies on the grass unconscious, his cloak and vest folded neatly on the edge of the fountain, waiting for him. Jonathan laid him there gently after smuggling him through the chaos of the city and through the castle. If he had knowledge of how Cheshire sneaks around, the task would not have proven so difficult.

One thing is certain, Cheshire remains safe here, away from the Duchess and the Gryphon. Though they are a stone's throw from the keep, to look upon from the outside the maze appears less than ten acres at most. Thanks to the ancient Arcana of Wonderland, the center of the maze sits miles away in its own expansive bubble where distance warps and has its own rules. Had Jonathan not arrived when he did, he fears he and March would have spent this night mourning instead of waiting. The way Cheshire lies on the short grass, Jonathan would think he slumbers in some deep, peaceful dream. But the scratches and fresh bruises across his body tell the true story.

A rebellion rages outside the walls of the castle, townspeople turn to Lysander and Uriah, and Mary Anne, distraught, may be in need of council, but his place is here with March and Cheshire. Jonathan sips from his flask and allows the cold, tart liquid to dull the thoughts of the outside world.

After hours of sitting, waiting, Cheshire gasps and releases rough coughs to catch his breath. He scrambles to his hands and knees ready to fight, more animal than man, muscles taught, eyes wild, hair a mess, unaware he has lost hours.

"Welcome back," says Jonathan.

Cheshire's eyes dart around the lawn erratically to gain his bearings. His breathing slows, but his body remains tense. March approaches from behind, her steps silent. Cheshire shifts from his knees to his feet, hands still feeling the ground. His fingers spread. His back shifts. He is about to bolt.

A part of Jonathan wants to let him leave. He will disappear into the night, as he has countless times over their relationship, and return to whatever dark place he spends his days. But it is not safe to allow him to leave—not him, not them, not anyone else in the city after what he has done. Catching him, however, is another matter entirely.

Cheshire leaps to his feet, turns for the arch to escape the lawn, but a twinge of pain topples him. He grunts, grabs at his side, and falls face first into the grass and lies motionless.

Jonathan has never seen Cheshire look so helpless. After centuries of battling and lauding the Ace, he would never have thought the Gryphon would be the one to best him. Then again, decades span the Time between Cheshire's visits. With the constant grin Cheshire wears, Jonathan never considered the injuries, the trauma he endures while on his own. If Cheshire had not worn the stolen Mirusian soldier armor, his wounds would be considerably worse.

Cheshire finally rolls to his back, wincing and cursing at the night. Jonathan takes advantage of the brief window and carefully straddles his legs and grabs his wrists, pinning Cheshire to the ground with a firm hand without strain as he does with March in the mornings. The fight has not left Cheshire's eyes. They burn wild and fierce. He writhes beneath Jonathan, twisting and turning, gnashing his teeth, but Jonathan's full weight keeps him firmly subdued.

There is a multitude of questions, reprimands, and curses Jonathan could vomit, but words will not reach Cheshire.

"Let me go," Cheshire cries, spit flying from his lips. "Release me, damn you. Now. Fuck you. Fuck you all. Let me go. I need to leave." His tears block his words. He stretches and contorts his body, screaming like some haunted netherworld wraith, unable to control the pain and sorrow. It is the only expression he can manage. If Cheshire truly wanted to be free, nothing Jonathan could do would stop him. Cheshire needs someone to exhaust his energy, his rage, with. Jonathan and March will take it.

Jonathan's eyes meet March's—her face twisted on the verge of tears —and see the same thoughts reflected in them. What has this place done to him? Both their hearts ache. Their beautiful Cheshire, a creature of both light and dark, at war with himself, tempest raging within his mind, heart shattered by something he will not share.

March kneels at Cheshire's head and places her hands softly at his temples and keeps them there no matter how wildly he thrashes. She hums a simple tune, an old tune. Jonathan recognizes it. It is the eerie tune Cheshire sang in the house with his prisoner, or rather the song how it should be heard. The melody is light but melancholy on March's lips. Each note reaches through the air and falls on Cheshire like tear drops.

The moon travels a quarter of its arch across the sky before Cheshire tires. His escape attempts become meager pushes and pulls, panting in between. Whatever pain he felt initially has gone. He may suffer a whole new set of sore muscles on the morrow.

Eventually, the Cheshire Jonathan and March know and love returns. The darkness in his eyes fades to reveal the tears in his beautiful lavender eyes. They catch the flames from the lanterns and become shimmering amethyst pools as the tears cascade down the sides of his face.

Jonathan releases his grip, stretching and regaining feeling in his cramped hands, and sits back on his heels and Cheshire's legs. An hour passes before Cheshire sits up and rests his forehead against Jonathan's chest. His fingers wiggle behind him, calling March. She moves closer, pulls her hair behind her ears, and lays her head upon his shoulder. The curses that festered in her mind while she paced, unable to say them aloud, have washed away. There is no point in looking back. The path before them is set, and they must move forward together, always together. The most pressing question—what to do with Cheshire?

Jonathan wonders what would have happened if he never ran after Cheshire all those weeks ago in the Hollow, when he stampeded through after the Ace. Cheshire would have escaped. Mary Anne, as much as Jonathan does not want to think it, might have perished by the Ace's hand. And Jonathan and March would continue to spend their days in each other's arms, sparring, and drinking tea until Cheshire returned, whether it be a day or a decade later, as if nothing out of the ordinary happened. A dream.

Cheshire stirs for the first time in an eternity and kisses Jonathan's chest, then his neck, then his chin. The simple act lets Jonathan relax for the first time since the afternoon. The muscles in the back of his neck resist and spasm at first. His temples thunder with his heartbeat. For the moment, they need not worry.

Jonathan pulls back to look into Cheshire's eyes and asks, "Are you certain?"

Cheshire replies with a hard kiss on his lips. Jonathan can taste the salt of dried tears, the bitter soot, and the iron tang of blood. Cheshire presses harder, unrelenting, sharing Jonathan's breath. His fingers find the collar of Jonathan's linen shirt, rip it in half, and push it and his longcoat off his shoulders, catching at his elbows. Without breaking their lips, Cheshire pushes Jonathan back, off of his legs to the grass, and straddles his thighs. He winces from his injuries but pushes beyond them. He needs this. They all do.

March unties Cheshire's sash and unlaces the leather twine holding his trousers together. Cheshire reaches down and unties the panel over his crotch and part of the right leg of his short trousers, its crude seam splitting all the way to the end. March pulls the remaining scraps of fabric from around Cheshire's waist and sits next to the closest lantern to mend them.

Cheshire rips at the laces and buckles of Jonathan's trousers until he pulls him free. Jonathan grips Cheshire's firm buttocks and falls back onto the grass, taking Cheshire with him. Their moans intermingle as they grind their bodies together. Jonathan runs his hand through the back of Cheshire's matted tangle of hair, twisting it between his fingers, pulling back. Their kiss breaks for the first time, and they lock eyes as their hips continue to swivel and press.

The warm lantern light frames Cheshire's half grin, and the stars beyond wash the day's events away into oblivion. Cheshire flips and lies contrary to Jonathan on the grass. They take each other into their waiting mouths without hesitation, creating an infinite circle of flesh and desire. Their tastes, their lengths, satiate their hunger. Cheshire plays with Jonathan's tip while Jonathan takes as much of Cheshire in as his body will allow. He reaches down, grabs the back of Cheshire's head again, and thrusts deeper. Both men moan and grunt, clawing at each other's skin. Cheshire pushes Jonathan's trousers and boots off without looking.

Their lust is palpable, throbbing. When Cheshire becomes too frenzied, Jonathan pulls away, not ready to end the first leg of their marathon. He pushes Cheshire to his back, straddles his hips, and lowers himself on to his waiting body, welcoming his entire length. Jonathan's thighs shake. Cheshire rubs the muscles of Jonathan's torso and pinches his nipples as he bucks up and down. Some primal force of nature shoots through Jonathan's body with every long thrust.

Cheshire beckons for March with ravenous eyes. She unbuckles her long leather skirt, drops it to the grass, slips her jacket off, then takes off her hooded top. Jonathan has no choice but to stroke his aching length at the sight of her walking toward them in only her tall boots, the candlelight catching every scrumptious curve and muscle. He drips onto Cheshire and rubs his cock along the hard, cobblestone muscles of his stomach.

March lowers herself to her knees over Cheshire's face. His full waiting grin disappears between her smooth thighs. She gasps as his tongue plunges and lashes at her most sensitive spot, at the same rhythm as he thrusts into Jonathan. They hold on to each other's shoulders, bring each other close, and kiss, wonderfully helpless at the mercy of Cheshire's passion and vigor. One of his hands strokes Jonathan while the other massages and twists at March's nipple.

She bites Jonathan's lip, hips grinding back and forth across Cheshire's face faster and faster until she shudders, holds her breath, and climaxes, giving Cheshire her love. Jonathan can see the tip of his tongue furiously lapping at March, suspending her in this moment of ecstasy. Once she catches her breath, Jonathan raises her to her feet and brings her to his mouth to taste her as well. She chuckles and twitches as

Jonathan rolls his lips over his teeth to pull and tease her. Unable to bear the sensation any longer, March walks away with trembling legs to her stash of rum hidden in dark wooden crates at the edge of their camp.

Cheshire's face glistens. His hips thrust rough and deep. Jonathan reaches his own climax, filling the deep wells between Cheshire's muscles, howling until he has nothing left to give. For now, he dismounts and raises Cheshire to his feet, stroking and kissing him to completion. The most wondrous sight for Jonathan is watching March and Cheshire orgasm. Cheshire puts his hands behind his head and roars into the night air as he covers Jonathan in his warmth. He squats down and kisses Jonathan tenderly. The look in his eyes still hungry.

Jonathan turns and rests his elbows on the edge of the stone fountain. Cheshire's tongue travels from Jonathan's ass and up the lines of his back muscles until he reaches his shoulders, biting them, and slides into Jonathan once more. He pulls out to the tip and plunges deep every time, rocking Jonathan back and forth. Jonathan does not know how his strength has returned but will not deny him anything. As long as Cheshire remains with them, their little world is right, even if the world outside burns.

CHAPTER 41

MARCH

March holds the bottle to the side as she drinks, rum trickling down out the sides of her lips. The bottle clinks when she sets it down on the stone edge of the fountain. She wipes her mouth with her forearm and lies back on the grass, propped up on her elbows to watch the artistry and passion of her two men, washed in the cold night, the white rippling reflections of the fountain, and the warm, pulsing lantern light. Whether it be the curve of Cheshire's ass, the clench of it as he thrusts, the deep shadows of the muscles on Jonathan's back, the way Cheshire rolls his body, or the way Jonathan arches his body to howl at the night sky, they warm her body better than any liquor could.

Jonathan kneels on the grass, his hands grip the smooth, curved edge of the fountain, his head craned to the side by Cheshire's hand. The rough clap of skin with each thrust forces the air from Jonathan and punctuates the melody of kisses, moans, and laughter. They carry on louder and louder. Nothing else matters here but them. A lantern lies on the grass on the opposite side of them, granting her a spectacular view of Cheshire's full length disappearing into and reappearing from Jonathan, glistening, pulsing. Jonathan's own swings back and forth with every thrust.

Magnificent. She cannot resist the urge. One hand slides down between her thighs and massages her sensitivity.

They carry on until they take notice and crawl to her. Watching them for the next hour would have pleased her enough, but she welcomes them. Jonathan and Cheshire each hook one of her legs over their shoulders, slide their faces down her thighs, and plunge into her, sharing her, lapping, kissing, sucking. Jonathan's tongue is firm, forceful, rough, yet gentle. Cheshire's is wild, reckless, feral, pinching her between tongue and lip. She grabs a fist full of their hair—purple tufts poke out from her right fingers, teal from her left—and pulls them, presses them tight against her. Her thighs shake violently, beautifully. Her stomach tumbles. The only reprieve is when Jonathan and Cheshire share a kiss, licking at each other's tongue, savoring her taste.

March presses her feet onto their backs and raises her backside off the grass. Jonathan knows her mind and guides his tongue down and back, teasing her ass. She screams out to the heavens, circling her hips against their faces. The harder she presses, the harder they press, the further they push.

Cheshire crawls up her body to her breasts, covering them with gentle kisses, dragging his teeth and wet cheeks upon them, swirling his tongue wildly while he pinches the other. Meanwhile, Jonathan takes Cheshire into his mouth, wetting him, preparing him for March, then guides him inside. March inhales sharply, always ready but never prepared for Cheshire. He reaches into her in ways Jonathan cannot. Cheshire grinds, thrusts, pulses with increasing speed and force, never leaving her breast. March wraps her legs around him and holds on. It is all she can do, all she wants to do.

At the center of the hedge maze, they may as well be in the Hollow, surrounded by miles of dense forest. There is no need to bridle their passion from prying ears. Here they can scream into the night as loud as their bodies will allow, and still no one will hear them.

Jonathan's loving smile beams down on her like the goddess moon, brilliant and full. He strokes himself, catching his breath, enjoying the time he has with them both. He kneels next to them, watching his two loves until he can bear it no longer. He takes his place behind Cheshire, grabs his waist with his left hand, his right shoulder with his other hand, and with a single slow roll of his hips, unites them all again in an intoxicating union. Cheshire raises up, roaring in pleasure, a thin thread of saliva connecting March's nipple to his bottom lip. He swells within her with each thrust from Jonathan. Cheshire's muscles tighten, his veins prominent on his neck, chest, forearms, and below his navel. Jonathan's brute force becomes Cheshire's movements and March's pleasure. She pulls from Cheshire, stands in front of him, presses his face in the warmth between her legs, and relishes the vibrations with his every beautiful moan. He grabs her thighs, ravenous, and devours her, almost buckling her knees. She leans over Cheshire's back to watch Jonathan's length slide in and out over and over again, and brushes Jonathan's sweat-covered cheek with her thumb, which he takes into his mouth, and begins to suck on it. A simple gesture, but enough to send a new shiver up her body.

Jonathan kisses the pinched muscles of Cheshire's shoulders, leaves him, and stands behind March, pushing his glistening length between her thighs, rubbing against her sensitivity and meeting Cheshire's mouth in front of her. His mighty arms wrap around March—her waist and her chest—and hold her so tight she feels she forgets all else and lets Jonathan rock her body like the undulating waves upon a shore. Both of her men run heavy hands up and down the silhouette of her body. Cheshire pulls her boots off finally and casts them aside. He looks up at her, mouth full with Jonathan from behind her legs, nose tickling her, a look of pure bliss on his face. She grabs the side of his face and guides him to his feet. He kisses his way up her body, stopping at her breasts again. He pays close attention to both, leaving one wet and chilled by the night air as he attends the other. All the while, his cunning fingers tickle and massage both her and Jonathan.

She can feel the sweat upon her back—hers and Jonathan's. Cheshire's shoulder and arms sparkle like morning dew. She brings Cheshire's lips to hers for a kiss and to taste both him and Jonathan. March reaches behind to grab Jonathan's firm backside and forward to cup Cheshire's as well, as both of her men grind against her, the heat of their bodies sealing her in a cocoon of lust. She wants more.

As they stand, March willing, hungrily, welcomes and guides Cheshire inside her from the front, her breath pushed from her. Then, with a sweet kiss on the back of her neck from Jonathan, welcomes Jonathan in from behind, wet from Cheshire's lips. All three scream to the heavens in utter pleasure and harmony. Time, already irrelevant in Wonderland, slows even further to make this perfect moment, this perfect union, last forever.

She raises her left knee, and they hook their arms under to support it. Such a small shift changes the dynamic, increases their tempo, their ferocity, and the explosion of sensations within her. The sharp, excruciating pleasure causes spasms through every muscle of her body. She gasps, her stomach quakes, her legs shake uncontrollably. She guides their hands down to her other leg, and they support it as well, lifting her from the earth. The sensation of weightlessness intensifies the vibration in every part of her. She leans her head back on Jonathan's shoulder, turning her head to kiss him, his tongue forceful and wild. Cheshire's mouth stretches to take in as much of her breast as possible, his tongue lashing at her nipple. Both Cheshire and Jonathan unleash a low, animalistic growl she can feel through her entire body.

When they move in tandem with every long pulse, the lust, the pleasure, the love, is almost unbearable. But when they move contrary to each other, March loses all faculty. Their voices grow louder to form a divine choir of ecstasy. She cannot move. She cannot breathe. It is

Jonathan's breath that sustains her. It feels as if her heart stops beating, but their rhythm keeps her tethered to the mortal realm, though her mind spins through the heavens. They are no longer separate. They live, breathe, think, feel, thirst, hunger, exist as one perfect being, forever entangled, soul, mind, and body.

She nears the threshold of what her body can endure. Cheshire and Jonathan sense this and push themselves harder, faster to reach her climb. Sweat pours from their bodies, mixing with one another. At her climax, March moans louder and louder into Jonathan's mouth until she throws her head back and wails into eternity, panting, whimpering, with each additional thrust. Though her body quakes, she can feel nothing but the glorious rapture within her.

Jonathan follows soon after, his massive arms shaking, warmth filling her, then Cheshire, clenching down on her nipple as he pushes deep and fills her as well. None want to leave this moment. They roar into her body, moving faster and faster until they must return March to the ground, until they must all return to the earth from the spiritual ecstasy. Their strength spent and their thighs barely able to support their own weight, they collapse to their knees, both men leaning in against March, holding each other up, catching their breath, kissing her gently on her neck. March's body hums even after they have left her. She could fall asleep at this moment, between them, to the beat of their collective heartbeats.

Safe. March repeats in her head. *Safe.* While Cheshire jaunts to corners of the country unknown, she feels safe with Jonathan. But when all three are together, nothing else matters, nothing else exists. Jonathan is safe. Cheshire is safe. *I am safe.* They fill her and feed her spirit. Despite her past, this is why she loves them both so dearly. They wanted nothing from her, as other men did, so she gave it freely. *Safe.*

CHAPTER 42

CHESHIRE

His fingers slide down between March's legs to play with his, March's, and Jonathan's wet lust. Waves of intense damp heat pulse like a smith's furnace and radiate from all of their lower parts. While with them, nothing else exists—no pain, no memory, no mission. Only instinct—the instinct to be with them.

Cheshire kisses March tenderly on her bottom lip, dry from panting, then kisses Jonathan over her shoulder, lips the same brittle texture, then jumps up, leans over the edge of the fountain, and submerges his head into the cool water. It should boil from the heat of his body. The cold dark water whispers and bubbles in his ears, tempting him to remain. There is comfort here in the dull and muffled quiet. Cheshire often gives thought to how he will meet his end once his list of tasks is complete—the Duchess dead, Mirus destroyed, Jonathan and March safe. He imagines walking into the sea's embrace and never returning. Whatever it is, it will be no one else's decision but his own.

March's hands caress his waist and trace the muscles of his back, chasing the thought from his mind. He slowly rises, returning to the world above, and watches the water stream down from his hair, nose, and cheeks, splashing below. Jonathan steps into the fountain, kneels in the water, and places his hands on Cheshire's cheeks. March lays her head upon his back.

"Know you are loved," Jonathan tells Cheshire. "From this day to our last. No matter how many more centuries we must endure, we will endure them together." He places the softest kiss upon Cheshire's lips, the softest he has ever given.

Why? Jonathan did not need to say anything. None. Cheshire tries to lower his face to the water's surface, hoping the drops running down his face will mask his tears, but Jonathan holds him firm.

Flashes of fractured thoughts flood his mind. His mother's face. Jonathan's laugh. March's coy side glance. Dormy asleep at the helm of her wagon. Their trio perched on the rigging of a ship, sailing far from Wonderland. And finally, an image of Cheshire himself older, much older than he is now, as if Time started again, smiling, content, having lived a full life. But none of this is possible. None. Their Time together is to forget all else—to feel, not think.

Cheshire returns Jonathan's kiss, long and passionate, because he wants it and hopes it will hush Jonathan's silver tongue. He places his hands on Jonathan's hips and guides him to his feet. Water drips from Jonathan, still swollen, sensitive, and throbbing. Cheshire kisses Jonathan's head as tenderly as Jonathan kissed his lips, then takes him fully into his mouth. Jonathan's slow, soft inhale and his hands cupping the back of Cheshire's head are all Cheshire needs to cleanse the thoughts from his head.

March reaches around Cheshire and grazes her fingertips along his length. Her other hand slides down his ass, and with one finger, causes his body to tremble. He arches his back, pushing his ass out for March to do with as she pleases, and her massaging fingers do not hold back. Cheshire grabs hold of Jonathan's thighs, smooth marble pillars unto themselves, as Jonathan rocks back and forth, his smile comforting. March replaces her fingers with her tongue, as talented as her hands are with a sword, and Cheshire's eyes roll back. Cheshire succumbs completely. His hands slip from Jonathan's legs. The only reason he remains up is Jonathan's gentle control over him.

Eventually, March pulls away, leaving a chilly breeze in her wake, and rummages through a satchel near a lantern. Jonathan jumps from the fountain, kicking up water everywhere, and picks up Cheshire around his waist. They laugh heartily for the first Time in ages. They try to wrestle one another to the ground, but their wet bodies allow neither Jonathan with his strength or Cheshire with his speed an advantage. The exhilarating, slippery, fumbling sensation drives their lust as high as the Spires of Wonderland.

Cheshire slips from Jonathan's arms, pushes him playfully, forcefully, to his chest, and straddles his thighs, placing his length perfectly between Jonathan's buttocks. However, Jonathan twists between Cheshire's legs, overpowers him, and reverses their positions easily. While March remains occupied, they continue their battle, building up their desire, until their game changes. Instead of pinning the other to the ground, they slide into the other to see how many thrusts they can achieve before they flip again.

They end on their knees, Jonathan behind Cheshire, his bulging arms wrapped around Cheshire's slender body, one around his neck, the other his waist. Cheshire holds on to Jonathan's thighs and savors every long stroke, feeling his love within him. Their bodies rock back and forth like the night tide lapping against a beach. Jonathan breathes heavily directly into Cheshire's ear. Cheshire squeezes Jonathan's thighs, a signal to stop so he can take over. He pushes back against Jonathan as hard as he can, over and over again, building to his release, throbbing, ready to burst.

Jonathan stops him. Cheshire does not want to, but Jonathan whispers in his ear, "Wait," and guides his gaze to March.

She walks toward them, the lantern light framing the fearsome symmetry of her figure. Around her waist she wears a harness of brown leather held together by iron rings, and a phallus attached to its front, swaying back and forth as she approaches. When Jonathan mentioned this in the weaver's shop, it piqued Cheshire's curiosity, but to see it, on March no less, reveals a new sensation of excitement Cheshire has never felt before. She stands in front of him, and he marvels at what appears to be a replica of Jonathan's cock. He would know it anywhere—firm, yet soft to the touch, the texture of wax, almost mimicking actual flesh except for its tepid temperature. More questions to ask later.

March lays Cheshire on his back. He does not resist. She grabs hold of his ankles and holds them in the air. Jonathan moves to her, wets the phallus with his own mouth, and guilds her, merges her with Cheshire.

This divine sight before him confuses his mind, feeling Jonathan, seeing March. Jonathan kneels next to Cheshire's head and cradles it with a firm hand. He welcomes Jonathan into his mouth without hesitation. This sensation, this undiscovered, wondrous experience, to have Jonathan and March at the same time in a completely new way is almost more than he can bear. His body tells his eyes to shut and give in to the overstimulation, the overindulgence of every one of his senses, but his mind will not allow it. This view is better than the grandeur of any mountain top in Wonderland.

The magnificence of March. Her stomach muscles flex and relax as her body rolls with each thrust, and her firm breasts heave with each breath, dripping with sweat. Her pink hair clings to her sparkling, wet skin. The snarl of a smile resides on her face, the final crown jewel of the masterpiece she is. Then there is the monument of Jonathan towering over him. His massive arm cradling Cheshire's head as if the gods themselves, if they cared, reached down from the heavens. The light catches every muscle of his torso. A ladder to his breathtaking smile and dazzling eyes peeking over his massive chest. They thrust contrary to each other, as he and Jonathan do with March. Not fair, but oh so welcome.

Cheshire wraps one arm around Jonathan's flexed thighs and clings to them as if they were a post in the ocean saving him from March's undertow. His other hand reaches up to March's breast and squeezes and massages with a trembling hand. His thumb circles her nipple. Her snarl turns to a smile of gritted teeth, and her rhythm intensifies.

He holds out as long as he can, but he no longer possesses any remnant of control. His legs shake in March's grasp. Jonathan's cock muffles his moans and screams. With his free hand, Jonathan points Cheshire skyward and strokes as he climaxes and rains down upon them all.

Jonathan and March slow their pace, but Cheshire mumbles, "No." They continue until they push him past his euphoric peak twice more, body jerking, arms and legs quivering, and he finally gasps for air and falls limp on the grass, random muscles twitching.

Close to the edge already, Jonathan kneels behind March and unbuckles her harness. Together, they climax once more while they stare into Cheshire's eyes.

Perfection.

March helps Cheshire to his feet, and they all wash in the fountain, still unable to keep from caressing and kissing each other. All three collapse to the grass where Jonathan and March wrap their arms and legs around Cheshire, both to be close and to assure he does not disappear during the night.

A knot grows in his throat. Cheshire does not know why he speaks, but he feels compelled. Perhaps the exhaustion from his work in the city or this Time with March and Jonathan have dulled his wits. Perhaps it was the movement of pure vulnerability between them all. Or perhaps the weight of the mask Cheshire wears just tires him.

"The Duchess killed my mother. I know she did," he says. A stillness falls over their trio. "I thought for so long she had my mother prisoner somewhere. I searched the city as a child and could not find her. Then I searched the entire country one hundred times over." He chokes on his words. "It was not until I returned to Mirus I found out she was dead. I will kill the Duchess, but not before I destroy everything she loves, this vile city, and all who forgot about my mother. This is my purpose. My fate."

Jonathan and March tighten their hold on Cheshire. His tears flow, stomach spasming.

March rests her head on his shoulder. "No one can hear us here."

The dam cracks, then breaks within Cheshire, and the flood rages. He wails into the night, held by Jonathan and March. He cannot recall the last time his tears were not silent. Why do they have this effect, this power over him? March rocks them all back and forth gently while Jonathan strokes Cheshire's hair. They say nothing more. They do not need to. Jonathan pushes into Cheshire once more, March takes him in as well, uniting them together for the night.

"Please stay with us tonight," says March. Not a command, but a soft, sincere plea.

"Before we ever close our eyes, we already miss you," whispers Jonathan, "mourn your absence before the dawn ever crests."

"Never think you are separate from us." March leans her head upon Cheshire's. "When you leave, you take a piece of us with you, and that hollow space does not fill again until your return."

"You are the air we breathe," says Jonathan. "And we wait, bated, for you to appear again. We cannot go on without you."

Cheshire fights against his heavy eyelids. Any pain he felt before was erased by Jonathan and March, their healing touch mending his broken body and spirit. Before he fades off, he turns to March, wide awake, and Jonathan, who has never taken his eyes away from Cheshire's. They wait for him to fall asleep first. March kisses his cheek, Jonathan his forehead. He wants to tell them he loves them but fears if he speaks the words aloud, it will herald their undoing, and so he remains silent. Cheshire has said more this night than in the thousand years they have known each other. But while his eyes shift out of focus, before he descends into the realm of his dreams and nightmares, he cannot help himself, and whispers, "I love you."

He stays in their company, their embrace, their own reality, for three days, shutting out the rest of the world, as they wish they could have done from the start. They do not speak of the events of the harbor, Mirus, or Mary Anne. For them, nothing exists outside of the four towering verdant hedge walls. At first, Cheshire thinks Jonathan and March stay with him to keep him from destroying some other part of the city, or to keep him safe from the Gryphon, but the twinkles, the reflections of himself in their eyes tell the truth. They see his pain, feel his pain, and know their presence, their touch, will heal him, mend the cracks of his mind and heart.

Dormy occasionally visits and delivers food and teas from Jonathan's room. The Duchess, Weiss, the Gryphon, and Mary Anne are probably all furious, out of their wits dealing with the aftermath and whatever else takes place outside the castle walls currently. This deep in the maze, none of them can hear it. They can stay lost here, but eventually, someone will come calling, and it will all start again. It was peaceful while it lasted, but Cheshire must attend to his business, and Jonathan to Mary Anne, and March to the soldiers.

Cheshire opens his eyes to the gray world before dawn on the third day. The moon in all of her glory, almost full, a sliver on the left side of her face sits in shadow, watching over Cheshire. He has not looked up to meet her gaze in weeks. Even in the pale light of the encroaching day, she looks after him.

He slips from his lovers' embrace, half awake, walks to the far corner of the lawn, and takes a much-needed piss. He stands, cock hard as ever, like every morning. He puts his hands behind his head and enjoys the relief the release brings. A shiver runs down to his toes and back up to his shoulders. It is not long before March steps beside him on his right and takes him in hand while he continues to relieve himself. Jonathan joins on his left side and takes hold as well. They both gently massage the curve of his ass until he finishes. They shake his cock and together begin to stroke him with decided purpose. Cheshire's body gave into their will the moment they touched him. Jonathan grabs hold of Cheshire's hands to keep them in place behind his head. Cheshire turns from side to side, welcoming the warm kisses from March, then Jonathan, back and forth, their tongues soft yet forceful. Still sensitive from the night before, and sooner than he thought, his toes curl and legs shake as he pants. They all look down to watch the beautiful display Cheshire rains down upon the lawn, hips and ass circling in Jonathan and March's hands. He knows their intention—to keep him here longer. As much as his body and heart yearn to stay, his work is not complete.

Before departing, he kisses them both again, holding their faces tenderly, longingly. He gathers his clothes in a bundle under this arm and walks to the eastern arch of the lawn. He winces at the sore muscles running down the middle of his back, the back of his legs, his neck, and his entire right arm. Cheshire felt nothing during his Time with Jonathan and March, but as he walks away, the pain returns. *Fitting.*

He waits until he rounds the bend of the hedge wall before he grits his teeth at the pain and limps through turn after turn until he reaches another smaller courtyard with an unassuming circular slab of stone at its center. Seven other identical slabs sleep undisturbed, scattered through the maze. A braided, embossed carving follows the perimeter of the slab with larger oval lengths every foot or so. It takes Cheshire a few tries to find the correct one, but with a single push, sections of the slab lower and *thunk* into place to create a spiral staircase down to the catacombs of the castle.

With his injuries, the walk through the castle and return to the city take longer than Cheshire appreciates. The soft rumble of a bustling Mirus Cheshire could hear in the catacombs disappears. It is as if the townspeople tread softer, fear muffles their voices, and hopelessness sucks the air from the city.

He has made Mirus, the untouchable city, bleed, burn, fear. The slight noise above the city's inevitable death rattle, heralding its end. Cheshire peeks out of hidden doors and portholes, enjoying the fruits of his labors. On every street and in every alley, townspeople whisper obscenities to their neighbors, call out for help, pray to the gods for salvation, and some pack crates and boxes preparing to leave the city. Some brave townspeople even plot to overtake the castle.

Cheshire makes his way back down to the Crooked Market, through the broken storm drain. He leaves his hood down. In the middle of the day, the vendors sleep or labor above in Stonehaven. With what little shops are open, few patrons frequent the Market for fear of being spotted in broad daylight. The soldiers have abandoned the Boroughs to protect the castle. He did not think he needed to return here, but there is unfinished business he needs to attend.

At the candlemaker's shop, the old man sleeps in the backroom, and the apprentice sleeps on a small stray mat under the workshop table. Cheshire walks to the back cautiously and taps the boy gently on the shoulder not to startle him. The apprentice yawns a hearty yawn for one so small and wipes the sleep from his eyes. He smiles and sits up when he finally realizes Cheshire has returned to see him.

Cheshire points to himself, to the boy, then to the gates of Mirus. "I told you to leave." He raises his hands and then points to the ground twice. "Why are you still here?"

The apprentice makes circles in the air with his forefinger, then throws his hands up. "Where am I supposed to go?"

He assumed this young boy would be as resourceful as he was at his age, but the apprentice has probably never left the Boroughs, and the thought of leaving the city would be terrifying to him. It was for Cheshire the first time he stepped foot outside the Great Gates of Mirus—the last time he stepped outside the Great Gates of Mirus.

Cheshire pulls a scrap piece of parchment from around a candle and a small chunk of coal from the fires under the cold vats of waxes. He traces his hand on the parchment and draws a crude square around it. He holds it up with one hand like a sign, a tavern's sign, and with the other hand points to the boy's chest, his eyes, then taps the paper. "Look for this sign."

The boy raises a hand, palm open like the sketch, with a curious look on his face "A hand?"

Cheshire makes several dots in a line on the dirt floor and emphasizes the last dot, then points to the parchment again. "Last Hand."

The apprentice looks away, nervous at the prospect of leaving. Cheshire shifts to put himself in front of the apprentice and looks him in the eye, and without words or gestures lets him know he will be safe there.

The apprentice makes a half circle on his wrist asking when he should leave.

Cheshire points down and touches his shoulder. "Now, please." He watches the apprentice pack a small worn rucksack with a large piece of dry bread, a nectarine, two thin normal candles and a striking stone, and the compass Cheshire gave him. Cheshire holds up a finger, points to his temple, then one of the candles on the shelf. "Remember to take the candle." He taps his temple, his lips, points at the boy, then gestures over his shoulder. "Remember what I told you last time."

The boy smiles a crooked smile and selects the most exquisitely carved candle from the shelf and places it in his sack as well, and with one last nod to Cheshire, says both "Thank you" and "goodbye," then disappears into the Market on his way to the eastern stairs out of the Boroughs.

Cheshire leaves the old man slumbering, pockets a few more candles for good measure, and makes his way back up to Stonehaven. He hopes the boy does not turn back, for his own good, and for Cheshire's plan to work. He did not intend to come to this city to save anyone. There are thousands more who will die by Cheshire's hands before he is done. He may be a murderer, but he is no monster.

On his way back to the castle, coincidentally, ironically, two streets away from the Row, Cheshire catches a glimpse of a familiar face caught in the rushing tow of the mob—Ogden. As long as Cheshire has known her, Ogden never leaves the Last Hand. Others employed at the tavern handle the daily errands into the marketplace. She curses and slaps at whoever shoves her or even comes too close.

The owners of the home across the street from where Cheshire stands left moments ago, pulling a small cart with their personal effects. Cheshire dresses quickly, pulls his hood far over his head, and darts into the crowd. He slips through faceless bodies, following Ogden's particularly coarse voice. The spaces between bodies fill with more bodies, making it difficult to navigate. He could take down his hood, terrify them, scatter them, in order to find her. But then again, in their frenzied state, they could easily descend upon him. He pushes through until his arm hooks on to hers. She swats at his head repeatedly as he guides her out of the mob. Cheshire kicks open the narrow wooden door of the abandoned home and pulls Ogden in before dropping the meager lock.

"What is the meaning of this?" Ogden spits in her palms and raises her fists. "I'll fucking kill you, you twat."

"Calm down." Cheshire pulls down his hood, and his face is quickly greeted with a brisk slap across his left cheek. The taste of blood creeps into his mouth again.

"Someone needed to slap the shit out of you." Ogden shakes her hand. "Glad it was me."

"I have suffered my fair share of lumps and bruises these past few days."

"I'm glad I can add to the count. Hopefully knock some sense into you."

"Why are you in the city?" asks Cheshire. "Especially now."

"Because I've been looking for you, you little shit. Been here every day for the past week, looking for any sign of you. 'The Queen Slayer is destroying the city' is all I hear in my tavern now. Mostly what I hear. I came to tell you something. Something else I heard, which I know you need to know, from some blokes from outside of Mirus. But first let me make one thing clear. I tolerate your presence in my tavern. Don't confuse that with caring for you."

"You do on some level, otherwise you would have turned me in for the bounty years ago. You could have turned me in when I was a child, but you have not. All it would have taken is signaling to a guard I was there at any point, and I would never have returned."

The annoyance in Ogden's face drops for a moment as a memory passes behind her eyes. "It hurts to see you. It hurts me so deep to see you. But I would rather see you and remember my Silvie than ignore the hole in my heart. I see her in your eyes. It's only been a few years, but it feels like I lost her this morning."

Cheshire stays silent. In actuality, like everything else, Sylvie died over a millennium ago, before Time stopped. He must have been in his twelfth year. To him, outside of Time, it is a distant memory. To Ogden, however, she sees Cheshire's face and still believes she lost Sylvie seven years ago. Her grief frozen in Time with her.

"What did you want to tell me?" he asks, to avoid the memory himself.

"I noticed several soldiers who used to frequent my establishment suddenly stopped. I take it they were defectors. Had not seen hide nor hair of them for weeks. Until a few days ago. A few came in, hoods up and all the theatrics, but I could tell who they were by what they ordered and how they carried on once they had a few drinks in them."

"This is an enthralling tale. Does it have a point?"

"Let me finish. Fucking brat. They paid with Adamas gold coins. And when they thought the usual drunken revels and debauchery drowned out their conversation, one let it slip that they found a way into the castle. They've already tried it."

"And this matters to me how?"

"I've known you since you were up to my waist. Don't think I don't know what your mind is planning. I'm a mother. I was a mother. I know your game." She sniffs the air, and her rough demeanor returns. "There. I said my piece. Don't be stupid. As much as the sight of you puts a dagger through my chest... I've never turned away a stray."

"That's what got you into the mess."

"Don't I know it." She lifts the lock bar, never expecting a thank you to come from Cheshire.

"Regret it?"

Silence.

"It would be best if you left the city immediately and did not return," Cheshire warns.

Ogden holds her cloak tight around her neck and braves the frantic crowd without so much as a glance back.

When Cheshire returns to the catacombs, a foreboding chill runs the length of his sore spine and neck. Lysander and Uriah's soldiers lie in wait outside of the city. Entrance to Mirus by water is no longer an option. Cheshire has seen to it. The Long Bridge would be a poor choice of attack, funneling their numbers. The only other way into the city Cheshire knows of is the passage concealed in the river below. He runs, pushing past the pain in his body, through twists and turns down one corridor and then another, his bare feet flapping against the stones. Is it possible the hidden door opens to any who touches it? Surely he would have noticed someone, anyone, trespassing during his days of ferrying the casks of oil and powder there.

Cheshire descends deeper and deeper into the dark tunnels, down the final staircase, until his feet squish into the damp earth. No sign or scent of anyone else but him. He tests the door, ready for an assault of some sort waiting on the other side, knowing he poses little threat in his current condition. The stone wall is the only adversary waiting when the door opens. Even on the banks of the river, nothing seems disturbed by any hand or foot other than his own.

The rumble of the stone door seals Cheshire into his artificial moonless night again, grateful his secret remains solely his. However, he cannot ignore this new information. If some other way into the castle exists, he will find it. He is so close and will let nothing stop him.

CHAPTER 43

MARY ANNE

O ver the past three days, Mary Anne could not have felt more alone. The Duchess sits in her room to mourn, to hide, hopefully to come up with some solution to this predicament. The only time Mary Anne sees Chamberlain Weiss is when he paces through the halls. He picks so hard at his hands; red splotches of various shades of dried blood stain his white gloves. Her lessons stop. It seems the world stops. Grace's silent company provides little comfort. Pat and Bill, Mary Anne assumes, assess the damage at the harbor. From what whispers she hears from the servants, the Gryphon stays outside of the wall to watch over the soldiers who could not return to the castle after the fire.

It is by God's grace Emilia and Alden arrived when they did, otherwise they could have been harmed. She shows them the kitchen. The oldest cook, with green hair and long gray roots, welcomes them in her heavy, almost cockney, dialect. Mary Anne tours them through the castle and courtyards. The amazement on both their faces is enough to soothe Mary Anne's anxiety, which has been constant. She wishes she could stay with them the entire day, but these past events wear on them as well. They keep to the quarters that are just outside one of the interior courtyards to allow Alden room to run and play while Emilia reads.

Mary Anne misses her mother, misses her home greatly. She stands on her balcony and looks down at the hedge maze—the entire hedge maze. She can see the center, but it appears so small, too small to make sense. Mary Anne should be able to see Jonathan, but whatever strange enchantment—Arcana—surrounding the maze does not allow it.

Jonathan and March have isolated themselves at the center of the hedge maze since they returned to the castle with Cheshire, though unbeknownst to them, Mary Anne pays them visits regularly during the day and night. Often, she wants to burst in to interrupt their torrid affair and chastise them for abandoning her in her time of need. Other times she wants to fall at Jonathan's side and weep, lay her head on his lap, and ask what she should do, knowing after the events of the harbor her journey home has extended significantly, if not indefinitely.

She cannot bring herself to do either. All three, Jonathan, the unfaithful March, and the devil—the Queen Slayer, Cheshire—lounge together with barely a scrap of clothing between them. They laugh, they lay together, cuddle and converse while the clouds drift overhead. Jonathan kisses Cheshire as tenderly as he kisses March.

They have sex with each other in every combination, in positions Mary Anne could never imagine, throughout the entire day, like the world around them does not fall apart. It does not help her anxious heart, but to watch them here in this secret place, to know that this is probably the life they live in the Hollow, both satiates her lust and angers her.

Both men share March, just as March shares Jonathan with Cheshire, and Cheshire with Jonathan. Separating Jonathan from the others will not be an easy task. This arrangement, however unique and troublesome, intrigues Mary Anne's imagination and her body. Even when March finds herself between both men, in any position, Mary Anne would have thought it tawdry or obscene. However, Mary Anne sees power in March. Jonathan and Cheshire treat her like a woman, no, like a queen, no, a *goddess*, pleasing her, pleasuring her, worshiping her. Mary Anne craves this. March's freedom. This power. A power that should be reserved solely for the queen. There are many things Mary Anne still does not, cannot comprehend, the dynamic of their relationship toward the top of her list, but above all, how can Jonathan—so pure, so gallant—associate himself, give himself, to such heathens? She cannot deny the curiosity of what the experience would feel like and the temptation to wear the ring again, but she does not want Cheshire. Jonathan is her prize to claim.

On the fourth day, Mary Anne meets the Duchess on the balcony of the Long Hall. Her makeup and hair is pristine, but no amount of makeup can truly cover days of crying and stress. The Duchess leans on the banister, head hung low, and looks out at the empty hall.

"We are losing," says the Duchess. "Never have I seen this hall empty when open to the people. Not even Lysander, Uriah, and their brood came. Their absence, the townspeople's absence, speaks louder than any proclamation they could make. The scales have shifted. They have the people. I have a gathering with the delegates from the other cities of Wonderland, whose ships lie charred in what remains of the harbor. I have much to answer for." The Duchess looks at Mary Anne for the first time. "I am truly sorry, Mary Anne. There was more I could have done—"

"There is still more to be done," Mary Anne interrupts. "You said we are losing. We have not lost. Not yet. I refuse to resign myself, my fate, to this world. It is possible to win the people back. Nothing is impossible."

"I appreciate your youth, and your mettle." The Duchess smiles and exhales to expel her doubt. "Fortunately for us, Lysander and Uriah have all but gone quiet these past days. They have not even been seen publicly."

"And in their absences, they plot."

"Wise woman," says the Duchess. "Come along. Let us continue this conversation somewhere else. Lead the way."

Mary Anne, so used to following behind the Duchess, takes pause to think of where she would want to go, to lead. "The castle wall. I cannot save anyone inside the castle but myself. I need to see the people."

They exit through the back of the Long Hall and make their way to the western stairs of the castle wall, holding their thoughts until the city is in sight. The Castle Guard atop the wall stand at attention but blink weary eyes. Mary Anne expected the mob to remain below the castle wall, but the road to the castle, like the Long Hall, has an uneasy emptiness about it. She would rather the crowd remain. This way, she knows what to expect.

The Duchess waits for Mary Anne to speak.

"The air feels different," says Mary Anne. "Electric."

The Duchess returns a quizzical look.

"Forgive me," says Mary Anne. "I mean, it feels charged, like an uneasy tension coursing through the air and on your skin."

"I understand, I think," says the Duchess. "But at my age, I feel it in my bones. It is the sensation before an impending storm arrives. And a storm is coming."

"It is already here, is it not?"

"No, my dear," says the Duchess. "You have been privy to attacks, marauders, arsonists, and anarchists, but you have not experienced war. When I mean a storm is coming, know that I mean war will come to Mirus like the shadow of a winter's night."

"Lysander and Uriah want the city for themselves. They want the throne. They would not lay siege to the city, would they?"

"You speak more truth in your words than you know. They want the city. Though they rally the people to their side, they care nothing for them. They want the title, the power, that comes from occupying Mirus. They would rule over a graveyard if it meant they sat on the throne. And anything they destroy, they can afford to rebuild."

Mary Anne looks down at the city, imagines it in flames, the death, the blood. Before arriving in Wonderland, she had little experience with either of the latter, not even in her own imagination. However, after

Rookridge and Briarwell, she can imagine the dead multiplied a thousandfold.

"But they can never truly have the power," says Mary Anne. "A queen must sit upon the throne. I must sit upon the throne. Then there would be no question. I would have the power, and they could do nothing about it. Dinah, the first Queen of Wonderland, decided the last war. I will decide the next."

The Duchess smiles and nods proudly. "The queen is all powerful. She does what she wishes and takes what she desires. Even her own Queendom. Or something simpler."

"If you will excuse me." Mary Anne curtsies, lifts her dress, and walks down the stairs until she reaches the courtyard, then runs the rest of the way to the throne room doors. Her heartbeat increases the closer she gets. Now she understands the breadth of the journey, and how stupid, selfish, and proud she has been. A moment of selflessness, to admit she is as worthless as the Third Tenet demands, would take a moment in time. What did she have to fear? The men in England no longer hold sway over her or her decisions. A simple admission and she could, she will, become queen.

In secret, over the weeks in Mirus, she has come here, to the throne room doors of her own accord and pushed against them, tested them to see if they would budge a fraction. Nothing.

She stands before the large stone doors, chest heaving, fists clenched, steadfast. "I admit..." she whispers to herself. "I acknowledge I am worthless. I must be nothing to save Mirus. I am nothing. I. Am. Nothing." She places her hands against one door and pushes. Nothing. She even feels the sense as though it pushes back. "I am nothing." She pushes again. "I am worthless." Nothing. "Is this not what you want to hear?" Her whispers become shouts. "Do you not want me to say I am nothing? I have thought I was fucking nothing, useless, worthless, my entire life. What more do you want from me?" She wants to beat her fists against the door again but knows nothing will come of it except more blood spilt.

Her voice echoes against the stone—her only answer. What else is there? What is she missing? There are surely answers in the damned book the Chamberlain has not covered. She must know. The want is no longer a need, it is desire.

Mary Anne races to her room, out of breath, heart feeling like it will burst from her chest. She closes the door, latch clicking, and walks toward the Book of Queens sitting on her bed. Through her window, the sun's rays shine on its dark binding, quiet and serene, as if it does not know it possesses her future within, her life, or her death. Somewhere in the ruins on these pages, she will find the truth, and the means.

She picks it up with newfound determination and runs her hand across the cover as if it were Jonathan's back. She will pull the Chamberlain from his study, demand he translate every page word for word, find March to make sure the translation is correct. The answers are in her hand, in her head, in her heart. She will be queen, she will save Mirus, and she will return home.

A knot grows in her throat, a sense of pride in herself unfamiliar to her, but she welcomes the sensation. She catches her breath, composes herself, and walks for the door, but before she can reach for the handle, a knock comes from the other side, startling her.

"Jonathan," she whispers, ready to see his bright beautiful eyes, his smile, every part of his body.

However, when she opens the door, her heart drops. It is not Jonathan's smile which greets her, but an unfamiliar grin on a unfortunately familiar, dark, and vindictive face—that of the Red Knight.

CHAPTER 44

MARCH

March sits on the grass, back against the fountain in the hedge maze, and pulls up her boots. She leans her head back on the seat of the fountain, already missing Cheshire. He left them less than half an hour ago, but she, like Jonathan, worries when they will see him next, and if it will be alive or dead. On the grass next to her lay several small scrolls with updates from beyond the maze, delivered by Dormy in baskets of food. She waited until this morning to read them all. March dared not break the bliss of the past three days. They found a shard of home in this shattered world and enjoyed it for all it was worth while it lasted.

Jonathan laces his trousers and slowly straddles March's legs, sitting on his heels. His linen shirt hangs open, framing his chest. March traces the muscles of his stomach with her fingertips.

"Are you ready to rejoin the outside world once more?" he asks.

March looks down at the scrolls. According to Dormy, Lysander and Uriah have mostly stayed in Bronwyn's manor. Slight disagreements happen on the streets, but no more assemblies, brawls, or bloodshed. She wishes these are signs of fortune but knows they are a portent of the storm. They had their fun, but to ignore them any longer would be unwise. There may already be consequences waiting for them.

She wraps her arms around Jonathan, beneath his shirt, feeling his warm chest against her cheek, squeezes his hard back, kisses his chest, then slaps his ass for him to stand.

He chuckles and helps March to her feet with one last tender kiss as they come together.

"Every step away," she says before he can, lips gently pressed together.

"Is a step back to you," he finishes.

"I will see you at dusk." March nods, grabs two belts with two swords sheathed in each, flings them over her shoulder, and heads out of the center of the courtyard while Jonathan prepares a quick cup of tea. She cannot hide the smile he brings to her face.

She enjoys the early morning tune of the rub of her leather belts against her leather jacket, the clacks of her wooden scabbards and clicks of their iron tips. But absent are the twitters of the robins and greenfinches that frequent the garden. March follows the quickest path out of the maze. She pauses before stepping through each archway. There is almost the slightest sound of an exhale, as if the magic of the maze breathes as it sends her from corner to corner until allowing her to exit through the maze's front archway.

The morning sours quickly. The Duchess, March's mother, a half dozen unfamiliar soldiers, and representatives from houses from Adamas, Clava, and Rutrum, block the stairs to the back entrance of the castle near the kitchen. Her mother returns the same glare of sharpened steel. The Duchess's pressed lips fidget, stress and sleeplessness clear in her eyes.

March could turn back, run, return to Jonathan. The Duchess would be the only one among them who knew the proper way to the center of the maze. If kind, she could lead them on a snark chase, and March and Jonathan could have two days to plan at best. Cheshire may even still be within earshot, should she choose to call out. She could also easily dispatch these unknown soldiers with ease, slice her mother's throat, and not raise a sweat. However, this play, this strategy, intrigues March, and she wants to see where it will lead.

"What is the meaning of this?" asks March, unable to be bothered.

The Duchess steps forward. "I am sorry, my dear. With tensions high, I have little choice in the matter."

March looks past the Duchess to her mother—hair pulled tight into a high bun with strings of small pearls woven in, a collar of furs and feathers so high on her neck she strains to look over them.

"What have you done?" asks March.

"What have *I* done?" Bronwyn asks, hurt, holding a handkerchief to her bosom for effect. "What have *you* done?"

"A great many things." March chuckles. "Of which do you ask?"

"Murder," Bronwyn whispers sinisterly, lips pressed forward, almost hissing like the snake she is.

"Thousands of times over," March says proudly. "What of it?"

"I noticed something when you came to see me those weeks ago." Bronwyn approaches, swaying back and forth like a pompous peacock. "I should have known from your complete disregard for life. I should have seen it, sensed it all those years ago. But how could I believe my daughter capable of such a vile, wicked, unforgivable deed?"

"Of which do you speak," says March. "There are many."

"The murder of your father, Casek March."

The entire group on the lawn falls silent, awaiting an answer, eyes squinted with predetermined judgment.

"He was the most noble of us all. The most generous," Bronwyn continues. The dignitaries in the gallery nod their heads. "But the truth was undeniable—the look of disdain, the look of hatred, of malice on your face when I spoke of him upon your visit."

"Surely there are more pressing matters at hand." March looks to the

Duchess. "Perhaps the uprising outside the castle." She glares at her mother. "Or inside."

"Do you deny it!" shouts Bronwyn. "Did you slaughter your father?"

March should feel something, anything, but decided long ago—the night she killed him—she would not waste another modicum of energy thinking of her father. "Of course I did," she says numbly. "And you know why."

"You see." Her mother feigns shock, but the triumphant tone in her voice remains. "She admits the deed. She willfully killed her father, her own flesh and blood. One of the greatest of sins against the gods—patricide." Her mother's theatrics continue with crocodile tears, marching back and forth among the dignitaries, as if they needed more convincing. They are already in her pocket. "She took my love from me, left me a widow, and took one of the greatest souls from all of us."

Bronwyn quickly approaches March again, heated, raises her hand to strike, and swings for March's face.

March catches her mother's wrist and squeezes, making sure the small bones scrape against one another. "Strike me," says March, "and I will strike you down here and now before your arm returns to your side."

The eyes reveal all, even for the briefest of moments. Where there should be fear or terror, anger and disgust boil behind her mother's dull eyes. She gasps, pulls away, and resumes the ruse. "You foul creature, whom I bore in my womb and raised at my breast. Your father gave you everything. How could you?" She charges the Duchess and stops when they are toe to toe. "And this is who you placed in charge of our city's defenses. Someone who cares nothing for the people of Mirus. Who killed its greatest benefactor? A... woman who abandoned this city long ago to live a life of depravity. We are to trust her with the security of our city? The safety of our soldiers?"

The truth would fall on deaf ears in this crowd if March were to expose her mother and father for the people, the monsters, they truly are. Her mother must have known for years, or at least speculated March killed her father, and chose to say nothing.

It was the night after he gave her to Lysander and Uriah. She escaped, returned to his study, drugged him with crushed nightshade in his tea, and bled him out slowly, painfully, to watch the life leave his eyes. In truth, her mother benefited from his death. His entire fortune, connections, and weapons trade empire fell to her. Some of which who profited the most stand behind her now, increasing the drama of the charade.

"We demand she be arrested at once," Bronwyn commands. "And plan a swift execution."

The Duchess turns, her full gown spinning and furling like a cape. "You asked for an audience with your daughter. You asked for justice."

"I demand it, and I will have it," says Bronwyn.

"You will," says the Duchess, calm and in control, "with a trial."

"She confessed," shouts Bronwyn. "The verdict has been given."

The Duchess steps toward Bronwyn, cautious but confident. "It is true the city has come to depend on you and your wealth, and you therefore have sway. But the law belongs to the crown and the castle. And since you are neither—"

"Neither are you," says Bronwyn.

"Yet, no matter how high your ivory manor sits in the Crest, my head sits, sleeps, and eats, higher than yours, here in the castle." She turns her head back to March. "I am sorry, my dear. Until we can rectify this matter, you will need to be taken into custody."

The Duchess and March's mother bicker back and forth over her life. The request, outlandish as it is, makes sense and plays into Lysander and Uriah's plan. Whether or not the Twins admit it, the soldiers March trained, though dead now, put up a decent fight against them. Lysander and Uriah view March as a threat, perhaps have always viewed her as a threat, as they should, and her mother was one of their contingencies. They cannot bed her, will not kill her, are fearful to face her in battle, so the fourth and most strategic choice—remove the queen from the board before they strike. Mary Anne tries to claim the title, but on the battlefield, all know March is the most powerful piece to claim.

A soldier steps forward, a soldier unfamiliar to her, and holds his hand outstretched. "Your swords."

She slides the leather belts from her shoulder down to her hand, grips them tight, then turns and flings them over the hedge maze wall. "I would rather they touch dirt than your hands. The third option would be your throat."

The soldier swallows audibly and steps back with the others.

March huffs, irritated, "Lead on," she says, waving her hand. "The quicker we can conclude this bit of theatre, the sooner I no longer have to look upon Bronwyn's face." She approaches the soldiers; two put her hands behind her back in manacles, and all six of them escort her from the garden. Before she crosses the threshold into the castle, she looks over her shoulder and sees Jonathan standing at the mouth of the hedge maze, fire in his eyes. Even from this distance, the raise of her eyebrow and confident twinkle in her eye tell him to stay. They will find each other.

Three soldiers flank her on both sides as they lead her away. All of their faces, from what she can see through the opening of their helms, are unfamiliar. She adjusts her wrists in the manacles to hear the links scrape against each other—old iron. Approximately just under a foot's length of chain, made for men with wider frames. It would be a simple matter, under the right circumstance, to lower and step back from them. The hallways are wide enough for all three rows to stand shoulder to shoulder, but not wide enough to draw swords. If she so chooses, escape could be possible, not fully knowing the skill of the men who surround her.

In the distance, several corridors away, the slight scuffs of dozens of boots, the shushing and whispered cursing of inexperienced trespassers, pique her curiosity and concern, but her gut tells her to leave the matter to Jonathan.

The soldiers do not head toward the front doors of the keep. They have no intention of leaving the castle. Besides, Pat and Bill have not finished reconstructing the hanging cells. They lead her deeper into the lower levels of the castle. But to where? There are too many questions that need answers, and if she were to escape now, they would be lost to them. She will play their prisoner for now, but when the need arises, she will become their executioner.

CHAPTER 45

CHESHIRE

C heshire limps his way through the lower hallways of the castle. The Castle Guard patrols are almost nonexistent. He should finish his work. He is so close. But his Time with Jonathan and March has stirred his emotions, which take him to his mother's room, or rather the hallway where his mother's room once was.

As he rounds the corner, he pauses. The hairs on the back of his neck bristle and his heart thunders, adding to the swell of emotions in his chest. The Gryphon sits across the hall from his mother's once-door, slumped, his back against the wall, arms on his knees, head held low, hair covering his face, and a bottle in his hand. A telltale sign of resignation, of defeat.

The soft, quick and slow pats of Cheshire's feet do not rouse the Gryphon.

"Have you returned to the bottle after so little Time?" asks Cheshire. "Or is this all a ruse? There are no places for soldiers to lurk nearby. Or shall we have our final confrontation here so you can finish me yourself?"

The Gryphon huffs. "Shut up and sit down." He uses his bottle to point at the wall across from him. What little liquid remains at its bottom sloshes.

"You have no right to be here."

"Shut up. Sit down," says the Gryphon in the same calm voice he used when he left Cheshire in the weaver's shop. "You want to talk. Let's talk."

The Gryphon does not raise his face, but Cheshire can see the shame in his eyes, and in the way his fingers fiddle with the lip of the bottle. Cheshire moves slowly, steps turning silent until he reaches his mother's door and sits down. He grunts from the twinge of pain in his lower back.

"You outsmarted me. Outmaneuvered me," says the Gryphon with a lasting, contemplative sigh. "Impressive. You are a lucky one. I am not sure how many lives you have left."

"Quite a few, I imagine."

The Gryphon finishes the remnants of the bottle and sets it down on the floor beside him. "Carter pulled me from you."

"I remember. Before I blacked out."

"As Jonathan took you from the water, from the scents on you, I understood how you managed it all. I must have seen you disguised at least a dozen times, because you knew how to exploit my weakness. I underestimated you. Thought you still remained the capricious, rambunctious youth I remembered. I did not account for the level of your cunning."

Cheshire reaches out with his leg, grabs the neck of the bottle with his toes, and pulls it to him. He sniffs the rim. Not liquor, but something sweet. Vital information. The Gryphon has his bearings and wits about him.

After a length of Time and silence, the Gryphon asks, "What is the last memory you have of your mother?"

The question shocks Cheshire. A shiver runs from his neck to his ass. He did not believe the Gryphon would be straight to the point.

"'Remember our game?'" says Cheshire. His mother's last words play over in his head every day since she spoke them "'Run. Hide. They are coming. Let no one find you.' Her voice was weak. It trembled. 'I love you. Go. Far from this place. Outlive Wonderland. Now run, my heart. Go.'" He remembers the last look his mother gave him, the color all but drained from her face from the sickness. The beautiful twinkle that shone in her eyes dulled, nearly extinguished. During the last year of her life, she was too weak to even accompany Cheshire into the catacombs. "No one remembers her."

"Toward the end," the Gryphon begins slowly, cautiously, "the illness that plagued her took its toll. She grew weaker by the day. Her coughing fits became more severe to the point she struggled to catch her breath. She told you to go off and play often so you would not see her in such a state. She saved every ounce of strength for when you were by her side."

Cheshire tries to keep his lips from quivering. The tempest of emotions stops instantly, leaving a hollowness in his chest. Tears well in his eyes, distorting his vision, and run down his face every time he blinks. No one speaks of his mother. Ever. Only of her murder.

"I spent the next two days hidden... in the castle, snatching food from the kitchen in the night like a rodent." Cheshire chooses not to divulge the secrets to the castle's catacombs to the Gryphon. "I could hear the screams, the clatter, the crashes. The silence. Two days later, I returned to my mother's room to find it in shambles. The down feathers of her bed strewn across the floor. The bed itself where she laid was destroyed, in pieces across the room, finials snapped. Drapes that veiled the beautiful garden on the other side laid shredded as if by a wild beast and barely clung to their silver poles bent at crooked angles."

"I am sorry," says the Gryphon.

"You should have protected her against the Duchess. It was her who poisoned my mother, made her sick, destroyed her, destroyed me."

"What proof do you have of this?" asks the Gryphon.

"My memories."

"The memories of a ten-year-old boy—"

"Are still true." The words fall from Cheshire's mouth like the tears from his eyes. "Everything I have endured is seared into my mind, like etched metal or carved stone. I have more memories of sleeping on corpses than beds in order to avoid capture. I have more memories of the Ace trying to take my head than warm meals in my stomach. And this is all before I... all this is in the first nine years outside the castle. I remember everything. The perfume my mother wore. The cadence of her speech. The way her kisses feel on my forehead." Cheshire leans forward, closing the gap between him and the Gryphon. "The Duchess killed my mother. What proof do you have to the contrary?"

"That morning, the morning I returned, the morning you ran into me in the hallway, there was an assault on the castle, if you remember. It was Lysander and Uriah's last effort to reclaim the keep. I reached your mother's chamber before the invaders and escaped with her and a few others to keep them from their foul, desecrating hands. I carried her myself, cradled her in my arms. They destroyed her chamber and every other chamber on their way to the throne room."

Cheshire's lips shake uncontrollably. "Not true."

"Your mother died the next day in the infirmary. The sickness took her. She stopped breathing. I saw her body with my own eyes. Inspected her body. Poison leaves traces, blackens the tongue, among other signs. Your mother's body was pristine. She died from her illness. I have no reason to lie to you. We lost a great number that morning. Take your rage out on the city, destroy it if you must, but know the truth. She would want you to know the truth."

Cheshire hears the Gryphon but does not believe him, cannot believe him. Wonderland is the lie, and the Duchess its chief architect. Cheshire commands every emotion and muscle in his body to still.

"If what you say is true, then answer me this," Cheshire says with grim severity. "Why, then, do I bear the title of Queen Slayer for the murder of my own mother?"

The Gryphon's face twists, and he lowers his head farther.

"The Duchess did not accuse Lysander or Uriah. Nowhere on the lips

411

of anyone in the city was her illness mentioned. She wove a tale of an assassin, a Queen Slayer. She blamed a ten-year-old boy. The queen's own son."

The Gryphon finally lifts his head and speaks through the fallen hairs in front of his face, like prison bars. "A child no one knew existed."

Cheshire tries to slap the Gryphon across the face, but he catches his wrist. "It makes no difference. You knew, and you still said nothing."

"I tried." The Gryphon rises to his feet, a vice hold on Cheshire's wrist. "I said the Duchess did not kill your mother. I did not say she was innocent. There are games and schemes far beyond your understanding."

"You could have left. You could have done something. What of the hero of Wonderland?"

"The last one standing." The Gryphon collects himself. "I did something. I stayed. I watched. With the entire Queendom at stake, I could not afford to act reckless. And when I did finally decide to speak up, I found myself in the oubliette. The one act I could do was take your mother out of this place."

They sit in silence for an eternity, or a second, until Cheshire finally decides to listen. "You said you buried her in the Wrecks."

"Yes. I wanted her to be free of this place. Free of these walls. If Lysander and Uriah succeeded, I feared they would desecrate her body if they found her in the crypt. I buried her myself underneath a lonely, dead yew tree, high on one of the sea stacks. There is a stone marker as a headstone with an x carved into it. If you want your irrefutable proof, journey there. You will find her grave just as I have described."

"You say this to get me out of the city."

"I say this because your mother, Queen Dinah, was the only true and honest ruler this land has ever known, and she deserved so much better than a pauper's grave. It was the only way to ensure her body, her memory, was not defiled."

Cheshire approaches the Gryphon, leans his forehead against his chest plate, sobbing. "You said her name. I have not heard it aloud in such a long Time, nor have I spoken it, for fear it will shatter me into a thousand pieces, and I shall never recover. I miss her. I miss her terribly."

The Gryphon rests his hand on the top of Cheshire's head.

"I will do what you say." Cheshire sniffs. "I will go to the Wrecks and find her grave. But I know in my heart, with the love I bear my mother, the Duchess is responsible. I will destroy everything she has built and then kill her."

"You know I cannot allow you to do such a thing," says the Gryphon. "I will fight you at every turn, thwart every attempt."

"You have been so successful thus far."

"Do you really believe I wanted you dead? Do you not think I told my archers to take you alive? I would not kill you. But as I've said before, if I need to break you or imprison you to stop you, I will. I am oath and honor bound to protect Wonderland, and currently she is Wonderland."

It is for this reason Cheshire knows the Duchess is to blame. "Loyal to her, until a new queen is crowned?"

"Correct."

"And once a new queen is crowned, you shall be loyal to her over the Duchess, correct?"

"Correct."

"If the queen ordered you to strike her down, you would?"

"Without hesitation."

Suddenly, helping Mary Anne achieve her goal to become queen becomes more of a priority. Cheshire will continue his own plans and destroy what he must. His third target is already planned and placed, and he does not plan on stopping it. When he has his chance to throttle the Duchess, he will take it. But should the Gryphon prove too much of a nuisance, Mary Anne will serve as a nice contingency.

Cheshire's ears twitch. The sounds of dozens of footsteps, boots running through the castle corridors, catch his attention. Dozens, possibly hundreds. He and the Gryphon both look in the same direction. His keen hunting skills have heard them as well.

"Is this a trap?" Cheshire asks again. His muscles tighten, ready to run.

"No," says the Gryphon. "Something is wrong. Listen closer. What do you not hear?"

Cheshire crouches lower to the ground, the pads of his fingers pressed to the stones. "There are no scrapes of iron, nor the distinctive clink or clatter of armor. These are not soldiers or Castle Guard."

Far in the distance, servants shriek and scream.

The Gryphon grabs the hilt of his sword and lowers himself like a lion stalking his prey, staring beyond the hallway. "The castle has been besieged."

Whatever words the Gryphon continues to say are lost. Cheshire bolts down the hallway, heart pounding, and into a hidden passageway concealed behind a tapestry. The quickest way to find Jonathan and March. He recalls Ogden's words. 'They found a way into the castle.' He was so consumed with the thought of anyone finding the secret entrance by the river that he did not truly heed her warning, and he never gave thought to which 'they' Ogden spoke of. But it is too late to question. They have arrived in force.

CHAPTER 46

JONATHAN

Jonathan's hand grips the pummel of his sword and shakes so furiously the blade rattles against the locket of its scabbard. He cannot move, not yet. The right side of his upper lip ticks the seconds, waiting for the slow procession of the soldiers, the gentry, March's mother, and then finally the Duchess to enter the castle.

Once all out of sight, Jonathan runs for the small kitchen door, next to the entrance the rest took. The cooks gasp as he dashes and spins between them. He knocks several trays from their hands, unable to avoid the collisions. He apologizes. At least he thinks he does. Words cannot form. Images flash and distort in his mind—March's eyes, the shackles around her wrists, Jonathan's bloody fist pulling from the hole in a soldier's head, swords clashing, screams, laughs, tea, sex, it all runs together. He cannot stop blinking. He pulls the flask from his coat pocket and drinks a mouthful. Jonathan needs a clear head. The elixir works quickly, even though his jaw and eyes continue to shake from the fury overtaking his body.

Jonathan takes the hallways he knows will put him in front of the group of soldiers and March. He cannot risk confronting them, but he needs to know more. With March's mother involved, this move is Lysander and Uriah's.

He turns a corner, expecting to come face to face with March, but a crowd of people he could not hear, could not see, because of his focus on March, knock him to the ground. Dozens, no, hundreds of boots, sandals, and bare feet fly by him. He shields his face with his arms after the first boot heel contacts his cheek. These are townspeople, not Lysander and Uriah's men. Through the sliver of space between his forearms, he catches a glimpse of an old rusty knife with three missing jewels in the boot of a woman. When he looks up, he can see men and women brandishing their daggers in hand, no longer hiding them. The cult has finally made their move—their timing conspicuous—and they hunt for Mary Anne.

Knowing who these intruders are now, Jonathan has no remorse and gives no quarter. He kicks his legs out, knocking several of the cultists to the ground. Their jaws and teeth break as they hit the hard stones of the castle floors. The pile of bodies temporarily slows the stampede. Jonathan raises to his feet, punching, kicking, and elbowing anyone in close proximity.

The cultists slice at him with their rusty knives. He uses the thick sleeves of his jacket to take their hits, shielding his face once again. His sword will do no good in the hallway's width and against the sheer number of people.

March has already been taken. He must fight against his heart and get to Mary Anne at all costs. He returns to an empty kitchen, already ransacked by the cultists. But thinking their knives are protection enough, they only grab food. Unfortunately for them, they left the two large cleavers imbedded in the long wooden table, the cleavers the length of two grown men's hands, the cleavers that are used to slice through sides of beef and pork in a single swing.

Jonathan pulls them from the cutting boards and slashes his way through the torrent of cultists. He swings wildly with his anger behind each strike. The freshly sharpened cleaver passes through skin and bone with the ease of cutting through parchment. His first chop slices through one cultist's neck and the top of another's head diagonally just above his cheek. His second slices the necks of four cultists in one swipe. He swings both into the air and brings them down, slitting two cultists between neck and shoulder down to their waist.

At the end of a corridor, he catches a fleeting glimpse of the Duchess barricading herself and the others from the garden behind thick oak doors. Down another corridor, the Gryphon slams cultists into walls and flings them into the air. But where is March? Where is Mary Anne?

The fear finally grips the cultists. They realize they are no match and flee in terror. Jonathan looks back briefly at the trail of dismembered bodies and pools of blood creeping across the floor. It pains him. These are not soldiers, however they are not innocent either. He shakes the thought from his head, screams, shouts, and continues to swing the cleavers to clear his path.

Eventually, the hallways empty, the cultists scattered like roaches. He can see some of them run across adjoining hallways, but they steer clear of him. Peculiar. The same cultists run back and forth without method or plan. Which means one of two things. Firstly, they hopefully do not know Mary Anne's location, neither does Jonathan for that matter, otherwise they would all run to the other side of the castle. Secondly, someone brought them here, orchestrated this, not as an attack but as a distraction, which means they do indeed have a leader, and the women in the Garden have lied all this Time.

He sprints toward the wing with Mary Anne's bedchamber, hoping they have not reached it, and have not found her yet. The cultists avoid Jonathan as he approaches and dare not follow him after the first who tries loses his right arm to a cleaver. Finally, Jonathan reaches the long spiral stairs leading to their bedchambers. He counts by threes as he leaps the distance up the thirteen floors, pushing past the burn tearing at his thighs and heat gripping his lungs.

Mary Anne's handmaiden lies face down, half on the stairs and half on the landing, unconscious but breathing. He is too late. Down the hallway, scrapes on the stones and sunlight peeking out of Mary Anne's door signal a scuffle. Jonathan kicks open the door, knocking it from its hinges, unsure of what scene unfolds. Empty. Jonathan's heart drops, but he is still thankful he did not stumble upon a body. The chamber remains undisturbed—no sign of struggle, except Mary Anne's book dropped by the door. Whoever the abductor, they took her by surprise.

"What the fuck is all this business?" asks Cheshire. Jonathan never heard him approach.

"They have her," Jonathan pants. "They took her."

"Took who?" Cheshire asks with deadly severity.

"The cultists, I assume, took Mary Anne. But they have March as well. Soldiers escorted by March's mother, under Lysander and Uriah's influence no doubt, took her into the castle in shackles. I lost them in the swarm."

Silent rage and hurt fill the room like a crushing flood, a wave of heat from the bowels of the hells' pits themselves. Whatever chance Jonathan ever had to reason with him has passed. And now, Jonathan will not say another word. Cheshire will kill all of them for their transgressions, and he will allow it, if not help in the deeds themselves.

Jonathan runs from the chamber and back down the stairs, Cheshire at his heels. Far below, on the ground floor, the cultists surge like ants on a hill. Some unfortunate souls wander up the stairs. Cheshire leaps across the void from floor to floor, a graceful angel of death, and snaps the neck of each cultist, brutally, unforgivingly, before Jonathan can ever reach them with his cleavers.

While Cheshire kicks at the knees of a larger man and wrenches his neck backward, another man charges Cheshire, knife in the air, ready to bring it down on Cheshire's head. Jonathan flips the cleaver in hand and launches it across stairs. It severs the man's arm completely at his shoulder, cuts through his head just above his lips, and embeds into the wall.

The larger man, with a thicker neck, proves more difficult for Cheshire. He allows the man to rise just enough to kick him into the waiting blade. It cuts through half his chest, but Cheshire, unsatisfied, kicks at the man's back repeatedly until he rips in half completely and falls to the ground like two bloody sacks of meat.

Cheshire unleashes a scream unlike any Jonathan has heard before. He is Jonathan's counterpart, his flipped image in a looking glass. Jonathan fights to remain in control every moment of his life, emotionally, mentally. Cheshire, however, avoids the fight all together, or has already slain that part of him.

His scream spooks the crowd below. One man in the crowd whistles with his fingers in his mouth. Everyone but him scatters at his signal, clearing the floor below. Only the man remains. The man with a large nose, a crooked neck, an unkempt mustache, and a coat dragging the ground— the old man Jonathan saw in the Forge and leaving the Garden. Even from three floors up, the smirk on his face, the smirk of victory, tells Jonathan all he needs to know. This man, however unassuming, must be the leader of the cult. He locks eyes with Jonathan and waves, knife in hand.

"Him," Jonathan shouts to Cheshire, pointing down.

"He has March?" Cheshire's eyes latch on to his prey.

The old man shivers, mustache twitches, and runs away like a scared rat.

"No. Mary Anne," Jonathan shouts.

"What of March?" Cheshire screams, defiantly.

"Cheshire!" Jonathan shouts, matching Cheshire's frustration and anger.

Enraged at the answer, Cheshire screams while he runs down the length of the stair's railing, his cloak whipping behind him furiously.

By the time Jonathan joins Cheshire on the bottom floor, the halls are empty, with no way of knowing which of the corridors the cult leader, the old rat, fled into. Cheshire crouches on the ground, more animal than man, shoulders heaving with vengeful breaths.

"We cannot let them leave the city," says Jonathan. "Any of them."

Cheshire slows his breathing. "They won't, they can't," says Cheshire, numb and ominous.

"You cannot be sure. Lysander and Uriah have March. The Cult of the Mother has Mary Anne. With thousands of guards in Mirus, they will surely run, and once they are outside of Mirus, they will be lost to Lysander and Uriah's forces who move on the city, even now."

"They can try, but they will never make it in Time," says Cheshire. "No one will leave the city. Not anymore. I have made sure of it."

CHAPTER 47

THE APPRENTICE

He stands at the gates of Mirus clutching his sack to his chest, even though he could wear it by a strap on his back. His fingers fiddle with the loose leather strings at the sack's bottom corner. His small bare toes tap against the cobblestones of the bridge nervously. The gates appear almost as tall as the cliffside of the Boroughs.

A large, portly soldier near the gate walks over to him and says something, waves his hands in the air, points to the city and to the gate. The boy figures the soldier wants him to move one way or the other.

The apprentice turns back over his shoulder to take one last look at Mirus, his eyes wide with wonder at the mountain he lived at the foot of all his life. He looks down at the Boroughs, gray and plain compared to the rest of the city but beautiful none-the-less. A world in shadow, overlooked by so many, but full of kindness and life. Other than his fellow dwellers in the Boroughs, the generous woman with the pink hair who threw him apples down from the bridge weeks ago, and now the purple-haired boy, the one whose face is on the wanted parchments throughout the city, are the only people from above who showed kindness to him. If this mysterious purple-haired visitor never came to his shop, he probably would have spent the rest of his life in the Boroughs, between the wall and the cliff, in the city's shadow, and thought nothing of it. He would still be there, but the stranger's eyes, though dark, were filled with sincerity and earnestness. With one final exhalation, a release, he turns back toward the gate and points forward, out of Mirus.

The large soldier pinches and rubs his mustache between his nose and upper lip, and then signals to the other soldiers to open the small door beside the large gates. The soldiers pull up the lock bars and usher him through as if he was someone of great importance—at least in his own imagination. Once on the other side, the soldiers slam the door immediately, and the lock bars fall back into place with loud iron clangs.

His mouth drops open in awe at the vision before him. It is a looking-glass image of what the gates hold within. Another long bridge, as long as the one over the Boroughs, stretches out in front of him. Instead of a mountain of stacked and crammed buildings, a lush towering forest rises tall as giants in front of him. Their tops sway in the breeze, a breeze the walls of the city never allowed the people of the Boroughs to experience.

He holds his rucksack tighter to his chest and runs across the bridge. The air smells softer, sweeter outside of the castle. The sun shines brighter. His feet carry him over the large valley below to the other side, to another world, with colors and scents he never knew existed. The other townspeople he passes do not seem to share in his excitement of the moment. Perhaps they are used to this. The boy hopes he never becomes dull to this world.

The cobbles of the bridge stop and give way to a dirt road which stretches even farther into the forest. His heart pounds. Whether it be from excitement or fear, he does not care. He wants to run as fast as he can, feel the grass against his shins, the dried leaves beneath his feet.

But first, before he leaves and explores the wondrous unknown, he must keep his word to the stranger. The railings of the bridge are short but too high for him to look over. However, there are small arched openings in the balustrades, large enough for him to slide his head through to see down. He peeks through the arch farthest from the city. A river rushes far down below, so small it looks like a ribbon he would tie around one of the many decorative candles in the shop. The supports of the bridge are wide, sheer, stone walls which narrow to a fine point at the bottom of the valley.

He sits up, takes the large candle and striking stones from his sack, and lights it. The wick sparks to life with the alchemic twinkle only he and the old candlemaker would notice. He shuffles his back through the arch, this time his head and arm a tighter fit. He holds the candle next to the bridge itself, as instructed, and lets it fall. It shrinks as it falls faster than he thought it would. He wonders what it sounds like, or if it would make a sound at all.

The boy cannot afford to become mesmerized by the sight, remembering the stranger's other instructions. He covered his eyes and shook his head. "Don't watch."

The boy pulls himself back through, steps off the bridge quickly, hops to the grass on the side of the road, and wriggles his toes in the short blades. He runs, as he wanted to, around trees, jumping over logs, and smiling larger than he can recall in his life.

The moment is short-lived. The earth shakes beneath the boy's feet and knocks him to the grass, followed by another rumble within the ground, and another, and another. The boy feels this is the end of the world. He remembers this sensation from once before. Something exploded in Stonehaven, or so they were told, and it shook the whole of the Boroughs. But this sensation, though similar, feels different, feels ever so much larger, and the sensation lasts longer.

Once the rumbling stops, the boy gets to his feet, not sure what to expect—a giant, an army, or some other monster that visits his dreams. A man on a horse headed toward the city rears up, turns around and gallops away. A woman stands, drops her baskets of cabbages to the ground, and covers her mouth with her hands, looking toward the city.

Another man on the road grips the sides of his head, mouth stretched wide open.

Smoke, both light and dark, caught by the winds twists and rises from the valley. Through the quick gaps of smoke, the boy can barely make out the giant gates of Mirus. Soldiers lie on the ground and shout to one another. Disoriented, he leaves the grass and walks closer to the bridge to see what happened—the bridge he laid on and crossed moments ago. But there is no bridge. No sign of the bridge. As if it never existed at all. Gone in an instant. Only the wide chasm of smoke and dust.

The boy crawls, creeps, to the edge of the road on hands and knees, the only one on his side of the valley brave enough to approach. He slowly peeks down into the plumes of smoke and dust. Piles, mounds, of white stones, boulders, brown cobbles, and short lengths of the rails look like nothing more than toys at the bottom of the valley. Such an impressive structure reduced to rubble, which now seems no larger than pebbles at the edge of a brook.

The boy does not know what caused the explosion and collapse, but he knows the responsibility lies with the purple-haired stranger. He did not understand the stranger's request, simple and odd as it was, but did what he was asked... because the stranger was kind to him. From the moment the stranger appeared in the candlemaker's shop, he was kind, no matter what his motive was. There was no way of knowing what would happen when the boy dropped the candle off the bridge, but somewhere deep inside he knew. He could see it in the stranger's eyes. No, not a stranger—a friend. He takes the stranger's goading to leave as another kindness, sparing him from whatever events are to unfold within the city. Now everyone, highborn or low, those who live in the Crest, in the castle, in Stonehaven, are trapped in the city with the purple-haired stranger and at his mercy.

ACKNOWLEDGMENTS

An everlasting thank you to my friends who helped bring this story to life all those years ago. Dakota, Ryan, Ashton, Abigail, Julie, Lani, Karen, Kristie, and Rachel. This world would never have existed without you.

To Matte, Ismael, Seth, Stacey, Jessie, and Travis for continuing the journey with me and breathing new life into it.

And to Luke, Tommi, Brian, Bailey, Marisa, Katie, Ricardo, Jordan, Tari, and Kathy for making it real.

ABOUT THE AUTHOR

BRANDON T BERNARD is an international award winning playwright and has been featured at the Edinburgh Fringe Festival. The works of Lewis Carroll have been his favorite literature since he was a boy, and cultivated his peculiar imagination. He has been a storyteller and artist from an early age, and worked behind the scenes in the film and theatre industry for almost twenty years. It's now time for him to tell his own stories.

tiktok.com/@AuthorBTB

instagram.com/AuthorBrandonTBernard

twitter.com/BrandonTBernard

LOST SOULS
I

BEDLAM RISING
II

MAD WORLD BOOK 3
COMING 2023

For more information and exclusives,
Join the Madness at

www.BrandonTBernard.com

"The fuck is this."

— CHESHIRE

Printed in Great Britain
by Amazon